The Glamorous (Double) Life of Isabel Bookbinder

Holly McQueen

arrow books

Published by Arrow Books in 2008

4 6 8 10 9 7 5 3

Copyright © Holly McQueen 2008

First published in Great Britain in 2008 by
Arrow Books

The Random House Group Limited
20 Vauxhall Bridge Road,
London SW1V 2SA

www.rbooks.co.uk

Addresses for companies within The Random House Group Limited
can be found at www.randomhouse.co.uk/offices.htm

The Random House Group Limited Reg. No. 954009

A CIP catalogue record for this book
is available from the British Library.

ISBN 9780099524632

The Random House Group Limited supports The Forest Stewardship
Council (FSC), the leading international forest certification organisation. All
our titles that are printed on Greenpeace approved FSC certified paper carry
the FSC logo. Our paper procurement policy can be found at
www.rbooks.co.uk/environment

Typeset by SX Comping DTP, Rayleigh, Essex
Printed and bound in Great Britain by
CPI Cox & Wyman, Reading, RG1 8EX

For Josh: TD

Acknowledgements

With very grateful thanks to the wonderful team at Arrow for their boundless talent and enthusiasm, and their profound understanding of the importance of pink cake. Thanks in particular to the brilliant Vanessa Neuling, for editing so expertly and for enduring my rambling emails with charm and patience, and to Kate Elton, Publishing Goddess, for running the whole show with consummate flair, for her infectious sense of excitement, and for getting the jokes.

And very special thanks to Patrick Janson-Smith, Agent-in-a-Million and lunch companion extraordinaire, for everything.

In the Beginning

God, I feel inspired.

I woke up with the dawn, for starters. At least, I thought it would be the dawn, but it turns out that in early January, dawn doesn't start dawning until about half past seven. I'd set the alarm for four, because that sounded a lot like dawn to me, but when it rang it was still so pitch-black outside that I bashed it off and slept a few hours longer.

When I woke up again, there was a glowing winter light coming through the curtain, so I've been admiring that for a bit. Novelists are supposed to do this kind of thing. It's my first day on the job, so I want to make sure I get the basics right.

I must say, it's very pleasant.

I'm not too clear exactly what I'm meant to *do* about admiring the light, though. I mean, it gets a little bit boring after a while, just staring in raptures at a gap beneath the curtain. Do I just lie here? Take some notes? Knock up a sonnet?

On second thoughts, I think the whole admiring-the-glowing-winter-light thing is a bit stressful. You can't be creative when you're all strung out. I'm going to go and make myself a coffee.

I bypass my usual frothy instant cappuccino in favour of strong black stuff made in the stove-top pot. This is another of the basics that I'm determined to get right at the outset. While the pot bubbles away, I contemplate lighting up a cigarette. One of those slim, elegant French ones would be great. I could wrap myself in a cashmere blanket, sip my black coffee, and draw languorously on my cigarette while doing a bit more of that gazing-at-the-dawn stuff.

The only problem is that I don't smoke, so I haven't got any slim, elegant cigarettes lying around. I'd have to pinch one of Russell's horrid shrivelly roll-ups, which isn't quite the same thing. Still, I must think about investing in a cashmere blanket.

Coffee in hand, I go back to my room, dig about in the back of my wardrobe, and assemble an Inspiring Outfit to really get the word-count flowing. I pull on an old pair of Chinese silk pyjamas a couple of sizes too large, a Tie Rack 'pashmina' and a little knitted bobble hat Mum gave me for Christmas.

But when I glance in the mirror, I don't look artsy and creative. I look like Judi Dench doing the decorating. So I change into my Diesel jeans and a black polo-neck jumper instead. Perfectly artsy enough. I pile my hair into a messy chignon, secured with (I'm very pleased with this little touch) a pencil. Then, because the last thing I want to look like is some kind of Booker-winning bluestocking, I add a spritz of Envy and a slick of the Chanel red lipstick I've been saving for just this sort of occasion.

I'm sure I once read that Jackie Collins has her hair blow-dried and a full face of makeup before she writes a word. And everybody knows Barbara Cartland wrote her novels wearing head-to-toe pink. So these details are important if I'm going to be a bestselling Novelist. Perfecting my Look is one of the essentials.

Of course, there are other important parts too. Like the writing, for example. With that in mind, I take a few of those deep-cleansing yoga-style breaths, sit down at my dressing table, and reach for my notebook.

Ah, my notebook. My gorgeous new black leather Smythson notebook.

You know how some women have a Thing about shoes, and some women have a Thing about bags, and some women have a Thing about matching under-wear? Well, I have a Thing about stationery. (Actually, I have a bit of a Thing about shoes and bags too. Never seen the point of matching underwear.)

Every time I pass the Smythson store on Bond Street, I can't resist going in and browsing through all the stuff I'd buy if I could possibly afford it. Dinky address books in jewel colours, and rich chocolate-coloured photo albums, and those cute little pocket pads saying 'Fashion Notes' and 'Husbands and Lovers'.

Mum knows about my stationery Thing, and I think she wanted to make up for my miserable Christmas. So when she and I hit the sales the day after Boxing Day, she concocted some spurious story about a pair of brown boots she'd seen in Russell & Bromley, then dragged me into Smythson as we passed by. The snooty assistants, who know me quite well now, encircled us as we stepped through the doors. I think they'd started suspecting I was some kind of international stationery thief, and I'd finally brought along my accomplice for the big paper heist. But Mum was wonderful. 'My daughter is about to begin writing her debut novel,' she announced to the snootiest and most suspicious assistant of all. 'We would like to buy a suitable notebook. Money is no object.'

Well, then they couldn't do enough to help. We hmm'd and haa'd over an emerald-green one with a pink lining, and a pale blue one with a cream lining, and then the snooty assistant made a suggestion.

'Classic black,' he said, 'looks particularly wonderful with silver lettering. If there's anything personal you'd like to put on the cover . . .?'

Mum and I looked at each other. And we went for the classic black with silver lettering.

'Isabel Bookbinder's Debut Novel,' says my little black notebook, now on my dressing table in front of me. It's perfect.

I inhale the spicy scent of leather, run my hands over the covers, then pick up my pen.

Then I put it down again.

Then I pick it up again.

God, I feel inspired.

I mean, really, really inspired.

Now all I need is a Debut Novel.

*

IN THIS WEEK'S *HIYA!* MAGAZINE, BESTSELLING AUTHOR ISABEL BOOKBINDER SHOWS US AROUND HER STUNNING MANHATTAN APARTMENT, AND TELLS OF HER EXCITEMENT AT THE INTERNATIONAL SUCCESS OF HER DEBUT NOVEL.

There's an aroma of fresh coffee and warming bagels as gorgeous Isabel, 27, welcomes us into her sunny apartment. Casually dressed in Diesel jeans and a simple vest that shows off her gym-honed size-eight figure, the only hints of her new-found fabulous wealth are the huge Tiffany diamond studs in her ears, and the Stephen Webster gold bracelets around her tanned wrists. And the Gina Couture sandals on her pedicured feet. And the subtle caramel-coloured highlights in her glossy, totally frizz-free hair.

It's been a roller coaster ride for Isabel since her debut novel caused a bidding war between major UK publishers on the basis of two paragraphs scribbled on the back of a napkin. ~~The steamy romp through The heartbreaking saga of~~ The novel received a seven-figure advance before it was even written. Once in the shops, it broke all records for a first-time author, hitting the top of the bestseller charts in London and New York. To cap it all, film rights have been sold to top Hollywood producer Mitch McMagnus for yet another seven-figure sum.

We speak to Isabel as she stops off at her brand-new Manhattan home for a well-deserved break after three weeks of non-stop international promotion.

HIYA! So, how has life been for you since all this began?

ISABEL What can I say? I'm living a dream.

HIYA! You certainly are! Your first novel has made you a millionaire overnight.

ISABEL Yes, it is quite good, isn't it?

HIYA! And now it looks like a film is set to go into production any day. Do you have any updates on that?

ISABEL Well, Reese Witherspoon, Lindsey Lohan and Cameron Diaz are keen to star, and I've had some very productive meetings with George Clooney, who's desperate to direct.

HIYA! Ah, yes, George Clooney! We've all seen those paparazzi shots of you two getting out of his private plane!

ISABEL (smiling secretively) We spent a lovely week together at his villa on Lake Como, but I really shouldn't say any more just now . . .

HIYA! So, tell us about your typical day as a bestselling author.

ISABEL No two days are the same. But usually I'll get up late, do a little shopping for a launch-party outfit, then lunch at The Wolseley with my agent. Then it's off to Daniel Galvin for a blow-dry, a live interview with Richard and Judy, then straight off to a glamorous literary bash, quite often at Claridge's. When I'm on a publicity tour, things are much tougher. I race around appearing on all the top TV shows and staying in a different luxury hotel every night. It's hard even to find time for a swim in the hotel pool or an aromatherapy massage.

HIYA! Any time to spend some of your millions?

ISABEL Of course! As well as this place, I've just

bought a riverside penthouse in London, and a sweet little weekend retreat in the Cotswolds, you know, where Kate Moss lives. And whenever I have any time off, I love to go shopping and treat myself, my mum and my friends.

HIYA! It must be very hard to find the time to write. Do you have a new book in the pipeline?

ISABEL Certainly. I have a whole page written already.

HIYA! And can you reveal what it's about?

ISABEL Top secret, I'm afraid, But I can tell you that Brad Pitt's production company is already interested. Brad and I are having lunch at Soho House later today, to discuss it.

HIYA! In that case, we'd better leave you to get ready! Thank you, Isabel, and thank you for your wonderful ~~historical romance~~ ~~epic saga~~ novel. The world was a poorer place without it.

Chapter 1

In this week's newspapers, there were:

> two hundred and twenty column inches on a
> Page Three girl's raunchy romps with a High
> Court judge;
> two hundred and fifty-nine column inches on
> whatever's going on these days in the Middle East;
> three hundred and forty-four column inches on the
> American President's visit to Britain;
> and four hundred and fifteen column inches on the
> latest *Big Brother* winner's Sex Addiction and
> Cocaine Hell.

I should know, because I've just finished measuring them all.

This is not for fun, you understand. This is my job. I work on *Re:View*, a six-page pull-out section that comes with the *Saturday Mercury*. You know the kind of thing: *Re:View* rounds up the news stories of the week, prints snippets from the best columnists, and distils other papers' reviews of new films, TV shows and restaurants. Which means that *I* round up the big news stories of the week, *I* print snippets from the best columnists, and my colleague Barney distils reviews of new films, TV shows and restaurants.

Lately, though, a thrilling 'Column Inches' section has been added to my responsibilities. Every Friday morning, armed with only my trusty wooden ruler, I pick four or five big stories of the week and measure how much space they take up in the entire week's papers. I honestly think it may be the most pointless task in the entire universe.

When I got the job, I had no idea just how tedious working on a national newspaper was going to be. Well, you wouldn't, would you? You think you're going to be part of a crack team in some thrilling, noisy newsroom, arguing the toss over which of the week's world-shattering events to run, sprinting around wearing those little American visor hats and screaming 'Hold the front page' every five minutes.

Or, more accurately, as I was really secretly hoping to work on the gossip pages, you think you're going to be staggering in at noon, hung-over from the previous night's debauchery with assorted boy bands and soap stars, hiding your eyes behind huge designer sunglasses, and sloping off for expense-account sashimi lunches with a 'showbiz source' every five minutes.

In fact, my job on *Re:View* consists of none of those things. There is no crack team; there are no visor hats; there are no designer sunglasses and there are definitely no expense-account sashimi lunches.

Re:View itself is no more than me and Barney, slumped at graffiti-covered desks in the unloveliest corner of an unusually unlovely open-plan office. Toilets to the right of us, toilets to the left of us, and a bank of recycling bins blocking us from the view of all the proper arts and features journalists who also work on this floor.

Though if you want my opinion, calling them 'proper' arts and features journalists is being a bit generous. The *Saturday Mercury*'s features team consists of interchangeable thirty-something men who seem to have fallen into journalism by accident. Either that, or they do really, really want to be journalists – just on *Nuts* or *Loaded* rather than the *Saturday Mercury*. As far as I can tell, they're all named Chaz and Baz (I think there may also be a Jaz). They chuck balls of paper at each other a lot, snigger about the receptionist's cleavage, and go on bungee-jumping weekends to the Brecon Beacons wearing specially printed T-shirts.

The arts team is a more professional outfit, but like Barney and me there are only two of them. Chris Macbeth, the Arts Editor, and his Assistant Editor, Lindy Lyons. You've probably seen Chris on one of his many television appearances. He's the large, red-faced man with slightly too-long hair who's always popping up on *Newsnight Review*. Wears velvet suits and a stripy Oxbridge scarf. I'm not really sure what his job involves, apart from going out for lunch a lot (expense-account sashimi, probably). Lindy does the real work. She covers for Chris, rewrites most of his material, and lies to his wife when he doesn't come back from press trips in time.

If you're wondering why I spend so much time observing what Lindy Lyons does with her day, it's because I have to.

My parents think I *am* her, you see.

Well, obviously they don't think I *am* her. They haven't known me for twenty-seven years for nothing. I mean they think I am the Assistant Arts Editor of the *Saturday Mercury*.

Actually, it's not as hard to pull off as you might think. For starters, it helps that Chris Macbeth has an ego the size of Siberia. Even though Lindy writes loads of his articles, he swoops in and adds a comma here or a semicolon there and claims it for his own. So I can tell my parents, with a totally clear conscience, that every article that *appears* to be by Chris Macbeth has *actually* been written by somebody else. I just don't tell them that it's Lindy, not me.

So that's *how* I pull it off. *Why* is a little bit harder to explain. All you really need to know is that I'm doing it for good reasons. It's not like I enjoy lying to them. It's just better than forcing them to acknowledge the truth. The truth being that, once again, I'm stuck in a low-status, dead-end job, with crappy pay, even crappier prospects, and nothing for my dad to boast to his friends about.

I'm doing everyone a favour, really.

Anyway, now that I've got cracking on my Debut Novel, I won't have to carry on the pretence much longer. Believe me, the very minute I get that phone call confirming my six-figure book deal, I'm writing my letter of resignation. In fact, just to save valuable time, why don't I make a start on that now?

I pull out my Smythson notebook, turn to a fresh page and start drafting the letter. It's easier than I thought, actually, and I'm just getting into it when my phone rings.

It's Mum.

'Just me. Am I interrupting anything?'

Mum thinks I have the most exciting job in the world. Even if I was the *real* Assistant Arts Editor, my life couldn't possibly be as much fun as Mum thinks it is. Lindy Lyons just seems to spend most of her day glued to her computer screen, looking suicidal.

'Not much, Mum.'

But this doesn't satisfy her. 'No famous authors to interview?'

'Joanna Trollope,' I lie, to keep her happy.

'No new films to review?'

I snatch this week's *heat* from my desk drawer and flick to the film reviews page. 'Just the new . . . er . . . Steven Soderbergh.'

'Is it any good?'

'*Sharp and edgy,*' I inform her, '*with a fabulous central performance from Catherine Zeta-Jones. Soderbergh is back to his* Ocean's Eleven *fighting best.*'

'How lovely, darling. Any good launch parties?'

I sigh. Mum is obsessed with launch parties. I mean, I don't know what she imagines they're like. Witty, glamorous celebrities standing around in Claridge's, drinking champagne and eating smoked-salmon blinis and mini strawberry tarts, and having their photos taken for the society pages of *Harper's Bazaar*?

And yes, they probably are just like that, but what's the point of this unnatural obsession with them?

'Only a couple,' I say, flicking through *heat* again for inspiration. 'One for Nigella Lawson's new cookbook and one for Jade Goody's autobiography.'

'Didn't Jade Goody's autobiography come out a year ago?' Mum asks sharply.

Oh God, have I been rumbled? I peer into my magazine again. 'Actually, Mum, this is her *second* autobiography.'

'Second autobiography,' Mum sniffs. 'When I was younger, only proper people wrote their autobiographies – Winston Churchill, Laurence Olivier. Oh, darling, I almost forgot! How's your novel going? When can I read it?'

'Mum! I've barely started.'

'But this morning you said you'd already written three pages.'

Now I think about it, it may have been a mistake to tell her why I was up and about when she phoned at ten past seven this morning. I was so pumped up with the caffeine and the thrill of the new notebook that I may have exaggerated ever so slightly. I mean, I *have* written three pages. It's just that completely strictly speaking, it's not three pages of novel. It's three pages of what my friend Lara, who's a psychologist, calls 'creative visualisation'.

Apparently, conjuring up a picture of where you want to be in the future is a very powerful technique for achieving your ambitions. And the sky's the limit, according to Lara. The bigger the better, in fact. So there's nothing at all weird about visualising a romantic Como rendezvous with George Clooney, or a power lunch with Brad Pitt.

And I will be a honed size eight once I've got my book deal – swear to God. I'm going to the gym at lunchtime today, and everything.

'I think I may need a little bit more than three pages,' I say severely. 'A debut novel is a very serious undertaking, Mum. I mean, I have to think about . . . er . . . plot-lines, and characters, and . . . and a title . . .'

Oh God. Do I really have to think about plot-lines, and characters, and a title? This is going to take me *ages*.

'I actually think,' I add, 'that I may have a little bit of writer's block.'

'Writer's block!' Mum sounds impressed. 'I must tell your dad.'

'No! Don't tell Dad!' He'll just think it's another of my excuses.

'You know, Iz-Wiz, if you're finding it hard to get going, you could always work on something you've already written.'

'I haven't got anything I've already written.'

'Yes, you have, darling. I found some of your old school exercise books when I was putting the Christmas lights away. You used to write some lovely stories!'

'Mum, I'm writing a *proper novel*, not lovely stories.'

'Well, I always liked them,' she huffs. 'And it'd save you no end of time.'

'It's a novel, Mum, not a two-in-one shampoo and conditioner.'

'No. Of course. You know best.'

'You've been very helpful, really. But I need to be getting on.'

'Sorry, Iz-Wiz. I just need a quick word about the seating plan for Sunday.'

This Sunday, my older brother, Marley, is getting married to his Swiss girlfriend, Daria. Mum has phoned, texted, emailed and, once, faxed me about arrangements at least three times a day for the last month. Me – not Marley, not Daria. Me.

'Matthew and Annie are awfully difficult to place, bless them,' she's saying now. 'They do rather *alienate* people . . .'

What she means is that my other brother, Matthew, and his girlfriend, Annie, are both so extremely attractive that anyone in their orbit can do nothing but drool, speechless, in awe and admiration. It's something of a conversation killer.

'. . . so we thought we'd probably have to put you and your Russell on a table with them, if you don't mind, darling.'

'No, it's fine, Mum. I don't mind where I sit.'

'Thank you, darling. I knew you'd be nice and easy. And we're really looking forward to meeting your Russell.'

I change the subject. 'Who else is sitting with us, then?'

'Well, Lara, of course, so it'll have to be an odd-numbered table. Unless she's found herself a boyfriend yet?'

'Not yet, Mum.'

'Poor thing. Anyway, you'll have Barbara and Ron, of course – I knew you'd want to sit with them – and Malcolm and Vanessa Deverill . . .'

Suddenly, involuntarily, I feel a spasm in my gut. Because I know what's coming next.

'. . . and Gina Deverill too, of course. I thought it would be nice for the two of you to catch up.'

Well. That all depends on your definition of 'nice'. If 'nice' means an experience comparable to walking barefoot over red-hot needles to a soundtrack of Daniel Bedingfield while hooded youths pelt you with sharp bits of brick, then fine, it would be nice for the two of us to catch up. But I don't say that to Mum.

'Right,' is all I say. 'I see.'

'Now, I know she's not always been your favourite person . . .'

I make a very rapid mental list of all the reasons why Gina Deverill is not my favourite person:

1 I have known her all my life, and all my life she has been prettier, taller, thinner, smarter, and more frizz-free than me.

2 During our fifteen years at the same school, and three years at the same university, not once did I get

a higher grade than Gina, run a faster 100 metres than Gina, play more solos in the orchestra than Gina, throw a cooler birthday party than Gina or go out with a fitter boy than Gina.

3 My dad, whose oldest friend is Gina's father, Malcolm, thinks that Gina is the bee's knees and I am the dog's dinner.

4 When we were six, Gina stole my then best friend, Nadine, and got Nadine's mum to uninvite me from Nadine's roller-skating party, which meant that I was the only one in the class who . . .

Look, there are about a hundred and one very good reasons why Gina Deverill isn't my favourite person. It's not my fault if, under pressure, I can only remember the rubbish ones.

'She's bringing her new boyfriend,' Mum is continuing, 'which I thought would be nice. I mean, as you'll have your Russell with you.'

That's done it. That's really done it.

I've got a new reason why Gina Deverill was not, is not, and never, ever will be my favourite person.

5 Because she will come to my brother's wedding with a drop-dead gorgeous, Paul Smith-wearing Alpha male, very possibly a multimillionaire.

And I will be there with Russell.

Chapter 2

The aroma of something yeasty and delicious-smelling announces the arrival of my fellow *Re:View*-er, Barney. Barney is tousle-haired and shaped just like a rugby ball, and he's about as resilient as one too. In the whole time I've known him, I don't think I've ever seen him come into work without a smile on his face, even though he hates the job nearly as much as I do. This is his first day in after the holidays and his Christmas break has made him even more ball-shaped than ever, but he still looks cuddly rather than fat.

He sits down at his desk opposite, gives me a little wave, and starts taking the yeasty and delicious-smelling item out of a Paul bakery bag.

'Mum, I really do need to go now. I'll see you on Sunday. Lots of love!' I replace the phone in its cradle with a little more force than necessary.

'Iz,' says Barney, shoving a chunk of pastry across the desk to me, 'you have to taste this.'

'What is it?'

'Brioche.'

'I don't like brioche.'

'You'll like this brioche.'

I chew off part of the chunk. Barney's right. When

it comes to food, Barney's always right. His knowledge is encyclopaedic, his taste impeccable. He's only wasting his talents working on *Re:View* in the hope that somebody sees the light and offers him his own restaurant column.

'Lovely.'

'Told you. Anyway, Happy New Year, Iz. How was your Christmas?'

'Horrendous. You?'

'Awful. Grandma forgot to put the bacon in with the Brussels, and the roast potatoes didn't crisp up.'

'Awful,' I agree, because I know these things matter to Barney.

'What went wrong for you?' He pulls a face. 'Did your mum stock the house to the rafters with Quality Street and Ferrero Rocher?'

I can't tell him I actually like Quality Street and Ferrero Rocher. 'Worse than that.'

Appalled, he puts down his brioche. '*How*?'

'Just the usual festive Bookbinder Christmas. Mum in the kitchen panicking about the bread sauce and Dad in the living room disapproving.'

'Disapproving about the bread sauce?'

'Amongst other things.'

Barney probably thinks I mean the chipolatas, the chestnut stuffing and the brandy butter. But actually, Dad's net of disapproval is cast much wider than that.

'My brothers weren't at home this year,' I add. 'Normally they take some of the flack.'

'But I thought you said your dad was pleased with

19

you at the moment because he thinks you've got a really great job instead of the crap job you've really got. Instead of the crap jobs *we've* really got,' he corrects himself loyally.

I sigh. 'Dad's only pleased when he's got something to be displeased about.'

Barney frowns. 'But that means . . . he's *never* pleased.'

'Exactly.'

'But, Iz, you're *Assistant Arts Editor of a national newspaper*!'

'Not good enough,' I say. I don't point out that I'm not, in actual fact, anything of the sort. 'He started up while we were decorating the tree on Christmas Eve: *what* are my career plans for the new year; *how* am I going to build a portfolio if Chris Macbeth keeps stealing my by-lines; *when* am I going to apply for an editor's job . . .'

'As if you haven't achieved enough,' huffs Barney.

'Anyway, I'm not going to let him bother me any more. I'm taking direct action. I'm going to *prove myself*.'

'Brilliant!' Barney thumps his desk with one hand and opens a second Paul bakery bag with the other. 'You'll show him, Iz. What's the plan?'

'I'm writing a novel.'

'Oh,' says Barney. 'Ah.'

'As a matter of fact, I've already started.' I wave my Smythson notebook at him, but back-to-front, so that he doesn't see the silver lettering. 'Well, I've started visualising how things will be when I've written it, which is actually the best place to start. It's very motivating.'

'Yeeees . . .' Barney is looking a bit doubtful. 'Iz, didn't you once tell me you *always* start writing a novel at New Year?'

'I don't think so.'

'You did! Not long after I first met you it was Pancake Day, and you came round to mine for pancakes . . .'

'And very tasty they were too,' I say, hoping food-talk will distract him. 'Was that *aged* maple syrup?'

'. . . and we talked about giving things up for Lent, and New Year resolutions, and said I always give up fried breakfasts for Lent, and you said your New Year resolution is always to start writing your novel.'

'I may have said something like that,' I admit. 'But things are very different this time.'

'Different how?'

'Well,' I say, 'I've got a really posh notebook.'

Barney almost chokes on a chunk of brioche.

'And!' I say hastily. 'And . . . I don't know how much longer I can keep convincing my dad I've got this really great job, so I have to do *something*.'

Barney is still looking dubious.

'And I'm not getting any younger, so if I don't do it soon, I'll be too old to wear anything nice to my launch party. And I'll look rotten on *Richard and Judy*. And Richard and Judy aren't getting any younger either. They could be retired in a couple of years' time, and then whose show will I go on to promote it?'

Barney says nothing.

'And,' I say, placing a hand on my heart, 'I just really, *really* want to write this novel, Barney. I have a passion for it.' Foodie types are always big on passion. Gordon and Jamie practically never shut up about it. 'It's all just . . . simmering inside me. The plot-lines, the characters, the title . . .'

Barney looks a bit more impressed. 'What's the title?'

'That's top secret, I'm afraid, Barn.' I cast a couple of glances over my shoulder. 'I just can't risk somebody stealing my ideas.'

'You actually seem really serious about this,' says Barney. 'Well, good for you, Iz. I only hope you'll remember me when you're rich and famous.'

'You can be my personal chef!' I say. 'Magazines will do those "What's in My Basket" features with me, and I'll say my glowing skin and honed size-eight figure are all down to you!' Though knowing Barney's penchant for patisserie, it'll be more like a hefty size eighteen. 'You can create lovely salads and everything,' I say, already trying to steer him in the right direction. 'You'll have your own cookbook deal before you know it.'

Barney's mouth falls open. 'God, Iz, you have to get on with this! Have you thought about any literary agents?'

'I have, as a matter of fact.'

22

Well, I've thought a lot about how great it will be when I can just drop the phrase 'my agent' into general conversation. As in, 'I was having breakfast at The Wolseley with my agent the other day . . .' Or, 'Wear Stella McCartney for my launch party tomorrow night? But Alice Temperley are interested too – I'll have to check with my agent . . .'

I haven't actually thought much beyond that, but it's at the top of my to-do list now, thanks to Barney.

I open my notebook again and turn to the to-do list I started on the bus this morning. 'Get top literary agent', I write, in between 'Work on Look – hire personal shopper?' and 'Go to gym much more often'.

'I don't believe it,' Barney suddenly says.

'What?' I cup my hand protectively around my writing, like you do at school when somebody's trying to copy your work. But Barney hasn't seen what I'm writing. He's staring over my shoulder, out beyond the recycling bins.

'This is *weird*. Kinky Chris is in before Lindy.'

Kinky Chris is Barney's name for Chris Macbeth. It started when Barney shared a lift with him one hot day last summer and noted the overpowering scent of Johnson's baby oil. He also swears he noticed red marks on Chris's wrist that could only have come from handcuffs, even though I pointed out they could easily have been from a badly fitting watch. I go along with Barney's little theory for fun, but I've never thought Chris looks particularly deviant. Although his wife, Caroline Macbeth, is the Home Secretary, so I suppose that backs Barney's theory up a bit.

I glance round the bins and see Chris rifling through Lindy's desk. He's purple in the face, which matches today's velvet jacket, and looking unusually stressed. And Barney's right – it *is* weird that Chris is in before Lindy. Come to think of it, it's weird that Barney and me were in before Lindy. She's so dedicated to the office, I wasn't even sure if she was going home for Christmas.

'He's waving over here!' Barney is slumping down in his seat, trying to hide behind the recycling bins. 'Look away, Iz! God only knows what he wants to do to you.'

'Hey!' Chris calls.

Despite the fact he's nominally (very, very nominally) our boss, it's the first word Chris Macbeth has ever addressed to me. I don't count the time he said, 'Anything but a fucking Frappucino,' when I offered to get him a coffee last August.

'Hey! You there. Brown-haired girlie. Whats-your-name.'

Seven words. Nine, really, if what's-your-name is hyphenated.

While Barney continues cowering, I circumnavigate the recycling bins to see what he wants. 'Yes, Mr Macbeth? Can I help?'

'I don't know yet, do I?' he snaps. Up this close, you can see the broken capillaries around his nose, and the crater-like pores on his forehead. He's better-looking on TV. 'That's why I called you over. You're a friend of Lindy's, aren't you?'

I hesitate. 'We . . . go for coffee. Sometimes.'

'That'll do.' He brandishes the papers in his hand. 'Has she ever told you how her fucking filing system works?'

'We're not that close,' I say.

'Jesus Christ Almighty.' He flings the papers back onto her desk and runs his hands through his slightly too-long hair. Several strands come loose and settle on his velvet shoulders. 'I haven't got time for this today. Fucking Lindy.'

'Is she all right?' I ask. 'I mean, shouldn't she be in by now?'

'Of course she fucking should. She's taking sick leave.'

'Sick leave?' I echo. '*Lindy*? It must be really serious.'

'Death, I gather.'

I clutch the back of Lindy's chair. 'Oh God.'

Chris's face mottles a little more. 'Not *hers*, girlie.'

'Oh God,' I repeat, with relief this time.

'Close member of the family. Might be her mum or something.'

'But that's awful! I'd better phone her . . .'

'You do that.' Chris picks up Lindy's phone and shoves it at me. 'Give her a call, send your condolences, and then ask her where she filed the "New Year, New Reads" piece, there's a good girlie.'

'"New Year, New Reads",' I repeat. 'Right.'

'And you'd better sit here this morning and answer Lindy's calls.' Chris is already pulling on the overcoat he keeps on an old-fashioned hat rack inside his own office. 'I'm out all morning at . . . er . . . Tate Modern,' he calls out to me, 'but someone has to be here to man this fucking ship.'

I can feel a little bubble of excitement rising beneath my ribcage. *Chris Macbeth wants me to do Lindy's job.* All right, it's only for a morning. And despite Chris trying to make it sound like night patrol in Fallujah, all I'm really doing is answering the phone. But think of the stories about my amazing job I'll be able to tell at Marley's wedding! And they'll all be totally true this time.

Chris swings his Oxbridge-y scarf around his thick neck, stuffs a pack of cigarettes into his case, and pushes past me towards the lifts.

'I'll be back after lunch. My mobile number's in Lindy's Rolodex if there's an emergency.'

I can tell by the tone of his voice that only an emergency in the order of fire, flood or terrorist attack would qualify.

'No problem, Mr Macbeth. I'll leave you in peace.'

I watch him stride away, already clamped to his mobile, then sit down in Lindy's ergonomic desk chair.

Chapter 3

Naturally, my first call is to Barney.

'Look where I'm sitting!'

I see him peer out from behind the larger of the recycling bins.

'What are you doing at Lindy's desk?'

'Doing her job!'

'Oh my God, you've been promoted? *Isabel!*'

Now I wish I'd been more downbeat. 'Well, all right, I'm just answering her calls for the morning. Chris has gone to Tate Modern.'

Barney snorts. 'Yeah, right. A bondage parlour in Bexleyheath, more like.'

'Barney, even if he's as deviant as you say, I hardly think he'd indulge his fantasies in office hours. He's a very busy man,' I add primly.

Barney rolls his eyes.

'I'd better go,' I trill. 'Lots of important phone calls to answer!'

The minute I put the phone down, it rings again.

'*Saturday Mercury*, Assistant Arts Editor speaking, how may I help you?'

Barney just sniggers into the receiver.

I pull a face at him and hang up again. I don't think

he's taking me at all seriously. I mean, sitting here now in Lindy's chair, I feel super-efficient and organised. Just like Lindy, in fact, only perkier. If I do an even more efficient job than Lindy, who knows where this could lead?

I'm just wondering if I should nip to the shops this evening and buy some black-rimmed glasses and a sensible twinset when the phone starts ringing in Chris Macbeth's office.

This takes me a bit by surprise, as I thought people only ever phoned Lindy. It's a hot and sweaty few moments of trying to divert the call across to Lindy's phone – star star nine? Star nine nine? Hash nine hash? – until I give up and dash into Chris's office to get it in there.

'*Saturday Mercury*, Assistant Arts Editor speaking, how may I help you?'

'What? Who?'

'Lindy!'

'Have they given my job away *already*?' Lindy's voice sounds blotchy, as though she's been crying all morning and is just about to start up again.

'Oh God, Lindy, no. Not at all. It's just Iz here.'

'Oh, Isabel.' She sounds relieved. 'I thought you were someone important.'

'I'm so sorry, Lindy. I hear you've had some bad news about your mother.'

'My mother *is* bad news.' Lindy sounds furious now, not blotchy any more. 'I mean, I've never taken a day off in my *life*, but Mummy threw one of her wobblies. I mean, anyone would think it was *her* funeral I was trying to get out of.'

'And it *isn't* her funeral you're trying to get out of?'

'No! Bloody Great-Grandma's.'

'Oh!' I say. 'That's good.'

'What?'

'Chris said it was your mum's funeral. I'm so glad it isn't, Lindy. I mean, a great-granny's sad, and all that, but it's much better than losing your mum, isn't it?'

'Is it?' Lindy snaps. 'Anyway, what are you doing answering Chris's phone?'

'He asked me to sit in this morning. He's gone to Tate Modern.'

'Tate Modern?' she screeches. 'What on earth for?'

I may be the wrong person to ask. 'Art?'

There's a clattering noise on the end of the line. 'I haven't got anything in my BlackBerry about Tate Modern. Oh God. I bet he's—' She stops abruptly. 'Well, you're going to have to help me instead.'

'That's what I'm here for!'

I think I hear a snort from her end, but it could just be background noise from the churchyard. 'Look, Chris is meant to have sent his Millicent Petersen piece over to the subs this morning, and I just *know* he's forgotten to do it. It's all lined up for this weekend's paper, so it has to be subedited, like, *now*.'

'Right,' I say. 'Sure. Er – who's Millicent Petersen?'

'Oh, for God's sake, Isabel – she's only won every

29

literary award going. Don't you read *anything* apart from Danielle Steel? Look, can you just grab a sub and see if they've got it?'

'Hang on.'

I whiz across the office to where the subeditors sit, at the only desks that vie with Barney's and mine for crapness. They're positioned right next to the air-con/heating unit, so they freeze in the summer and roast in the winter.

'Hey, Barry,' I hail the chief subeditor, Barry Goldstein, who's mopping his feverish brow with a damp Starbucks' napkin and drinking an Iced Chai Tea Latte. 'I'm doing Lindy's job . . .'

'Great promotion, Iz!'

'Thanks . . . have you got Chris's Millicent Petersen piece ready for subbing?'

Barry shakes his head, blinking back sweat. 'Nope. Not seen it yet, sorry.'

I dash back to pick up the phone in Chris's office again. 'Nope,' I tell Lindy. 'They haven't seen it yet, sorry.'

'I knew it,' Lindy snaps. 'You're going to have to get into Chris's computer and email this piece to Barry. His password is HEM1NGWAY, with a figure one for the I, OK?'

'Right.' I prop the phone between my neck and my ear and use both hands to type it into the computer's password box. Multi-tasking! 'Done. What's the file name?'

'It'll be in "Features: January". Probably a document called "Millicent Petersen". And you have to send it *right now*, Iz. No faffing.'

'I won't faff!' I start scrolling through the January documents. 'Oh, by the way, Lindy, Chris seems a bit cross with you about something.'

'What? Oh God, what?'

'It's no big deal. He couldn't find something called "New Year, New Reads", that's all.'

'Oh, no.'

I think it may be some kind of a big deal after all.

'New Year Reads. Fucking New Year Reads.'

Now I *know* it's a big deal. Lindy never swears. Proximity to Chris Macbeth seems actually to have made her allergic to swearing.

'How could I forget this?'

'Calm down,' I say. 'I'm sure we can solve it.'

'We can't fucking solve it!' I can almost hear Lindy turning white. 'The piece is due next weekend.'

'That's fine. It won't even need to be ready until Wednesday or Thursday. You've loads of time.'

'But I have to interview Joe Madison for the article. And eleven today is the *only* time he can do.'

'Can't you just give this Joe a quick call and do the interview over the phone?'

'The fucking funeral *starts* at eleven!' Lindy barks. 'Are you suggesting I conduct a phone interview from the graveside?'

'No, no,' I say hastily, before she decides that might actually be a good idea. 'Look, Lindy, why don't you let me do the interview for you?'

'*You?*'

'Yes, Lindy, me. Just tell me what you want me to ask and I'll do it.'

There's a silence. Then she says, 'My interview questions are on my computer.'

'Fine. I'll print them out and take them with me.'

'*No.* Just call him, Isabel. Say . . . say there's been an emergency, and I can't leave the office. Just get his answers down on paper and leave it at that. I can file the piece next week, after I've made it sound acceptable.'

'Thanks, Lindy.'

She misses my tone. 'Eleven o'clock *sharp*, Isabel.'

'Yes, I know. I'll call him at eleven sharp. Who is he, anyway, this Joe Madison bloke?'

Lindy emits a moan. 'Christ Almighty, Isabel, do you live under a rock? He's only one of *the* most influential literary agents in London.'

I almost drop the phone. '*Literary agent?*'

'Yes, and he's got all kinds of new authors he wants to push, which is why he's so keen to do this interview. His phone number's in my Rolodex. A for Agents, subsection M. The Madison/Salisbury-Kent Agency.'

'Madison . . .' I start flipping through the Rolodex, '. . . Salisbury-Kent . . .'

I can hardly believe this. Lara's creative visualisation works after all. On the *very day* I start my debut novel, up comes the chance for a face-to-face meeting with a top literary agent!

And I do mean face-to-face. I know I've promised

Lindy I'll just call, but that was before I found out who Joe Madison actually is.

Got it! Lindy's Rolodex lists the phone number and – hurrah! – the address. It's somewhere in Soho. If I get a taxi, I can still make it there in time for eleven.

'And don't forget to make sure the Millicent Petersen article gets to the subs!' Lindy howls, rightly suspecting that I'd completely forgotten about it. '*Please*, Isabel. It's already overdue. Oh, and for God's sake, forget Chris's password right away. Chris hates anyone snooping around on his computer.'

'I won't snoop!'

'You'd better not. Seriously, Isabel. Hang on a moment.'

I hear background noises: some organ music, some weeping, then some spiteful-sounding hissing.

Lindy comes back on the line. 'I have to go. I'll call you later.'

'Enjoy!' I say, before I remember it's a funeral.

Lindy hangs up.

I really need to get a move on now. It's already twenty-five to eleven. I click back into 'Features: January' and open a document called 'Millicent Petersen2ndJan'.

From the first paragraph, it's the kind of article Chris Macbeth specialises in: pompous, overblown guff about some prize-winning writer nobody (apart from my dad) ever reads.

In fact, thinking of Dad, I remember that I have heard of Millicent Petersen before. She featured heavily on the reading list that Dad prescribed me one summer. Which was the summer I spent secretly devouring *Flowers in the Attic* and contraband Jilly Cooper instead. I did *start* a Millicent Petersen, but it all seemed to be about Barren Wombs, and the Myth of Motherhood, and the Limits of Patriarchy. The book jackets featured oppressed-looking women clutching dishcloths, while the Jilly Coopers had close-ups of Rupert Campbell-Black's jodhpur-clad bottom. There was really no contest.

Anyway, Chris Macbeth's four thousand words extolling Millicent Petersen's use of imagery will make Dad's Saturday morning.

I enter Chris's inbox, scan down to find an email from Barry Goldsmith that I can reply to, then attach the article and send it off to Barry.

Then something else catches my eye. I don't believe this.

The subject box says 'Re: SEXY KNICKERS'. And it's from Millicent Petersen.

I know I said I wouldn't snoop. I know I did. And I didn't intend to snoop. I'm not a snooper. But this isn't really snooping. I mean, this could be a follow-up from Millicent about the article. What if it's some important knicker-related fact that needs to be changed in the piece I've just sent to Barry? I have a duty to the newspaper.

Plus I really, really want to tell Barney.

I click on the email and start to read. Eight seconds later, I pick up the phone.

'Oh God. Barney, you were right. You were right about Kinky Chris! The handcuffs . . . the baby oil . . . And him with a cabinet minister for a wife, and everything!'

Barney's face shoots around the recycling bin. '*What?*'

'I'm forwarding something to you now, OK?'

I tap in the first few letters of Barney's email address and AutoComplete brings up the rest of it. I press send.

'I'm running late. We'll discuss later.'

'But, Iz—'

'Got to dash!'

I shout across to the subs' area while I wait for the lift, 'Barry, I've just sent you Chris's Millicent Petersen piece!'

'Yeah, just come through, thanks, Iz. Is it *all* of this?' Barry asks, just as the lift arrives.

'I know, it's long. But it's due in tomorrow,' I say, pressing the doors shut. 'So once it's subbed, it needs to go straight off.'

'OK . . .' Barry pushes his steamy glasses up his nose. 'You're the boss, Iz.'

Today really is my lucky day, because I catch a free cab within ten yards of the office doors. We speed away towards Soho.

Isabel Bookbinder
Re:View
The Eighth Floor
Behind Recycling Bins
London

The Editor-in-Chief
The *Saturday Mercury*
The Twelfth Floor
Saturday Mercury Towers
London

3 January

Dear Editor-in-Chief,

It is with great regret that I must inform you of my immediate resignation from your Venerable Publication.

You may have read of my brand-new six-figure debut book deal in this morning's papers; I believe the story was covered by *The Times*, the *Daily Mail* and the *Guardian*. Further coverage is likely to appear in the *Mail on Sunday* and the *Observer*, so if you'd like a feature-length interview I'd advise you to get in quick. Obviously it would give me great pleasure to give my first big interview to the *Saturday Mercury*, where I have been so ~~happy appreciated~~ long. Just put in a request with my publicists and I'll see what I can do.

Please don't feel obliged to spring for a big leaving present – £50 of gift vouchers will do perfectly well, thank you. If you could make these Topshop or Space NK rather than the Marks & Spencer's ones you gave to Melanie Skipper in Human Resources, I'd be extremely grateful.

In addition

36

Chapter 4

I knew my luck wouldn't last long.

Thanks to a snarl-up in Holborn, it's already ten past eleven by the time I finally pull up outside the Madison/Salisbury-Kent Agency.

I take a few calming breaths as I wait for my change, and look up at the building. It's a beautiful old stone townhouse a few minutes' walk from Soho Square. There are bay trees in terracotta pots lining the wall behind shiny black railings, and a polished silver plaque listing the building's inhabitants by the glass front door.

I walk up the steps and press the buzzer next to the intercom.

'*Saturday Mercury* for Joe Madison.'

The door clicks open, I go through, and it clicks shut again.

I'm immediately surrounded by expensive, padded silence. There are thick cream rugs on the oak floor and pale leather sofas surrounding a glass and chrome coffee table. The reception desk, at the far end of the room, is glass and chrome too. There's a brand-new iMac on top of it and a very neat and pretty brown-haired girl behind it.

She smiles at me. 'Hi, I'm Sandy. You must be Lindy.'

'Actually, I'm Isabel. Lindy couldn't make it. There was an emergency at the paper.' I must make Lindy look good. After all, I wouldn't even be here if it weren't for her. 'A really, really vital emergency.'

'Oh dear!' Sandy looks dismayed. 'What happened?'

I'm stumped for a moment. 'Er . . . there was a big last-minute scoop. They had to . . . to hold the front page, and everything!'

'For an *arts* story?'

'Yes. Earth-shattering news about . . . er . . . Millicent Petersen . . .'

Her eyebrows shoot up. 'I would've thought Millicent Petersen would be far too dull for front-page news.'

'You'd be surprised. Anyway, Lindy sent me instead,' I add. 'I'm sorry I'm late.'

'Well, Joe did have to carry on with his schedule as planned, I'm afraid.'

'Oh.' I think I'm going to cry.

'But he should be able to squeeze you in at about eleven forty-five, if you're OK to wait.'

'Brilliant! I mean, yes, that should work.'

Sandy taps a couple of computer keys. She has a lovely frizz-free ponytail and a gorgeous little Ann Louise Roswald swing jacket.

Forget the glasses and twinset. *This* is the kind of perky assistant I want to be.

Now she looks up from her screen. 'It seems I might

be able to get you a few moments with Myles instead, if you'd prefer. He's out this minute, but he'll be back any time.'

'Myles?'

'Myles Salisbury-Kent. Our other agent,' she says, but not at all snottily. 'If you like, you can grab Myles as soon as he gets back and then have your scheduled interview with Joe at eleven forty-five.'

Honestly, you wait ages for a top literary agent, and then two of them show up at once.

'God, that would be amazing . . .'

'Then take a seat.' Sandy ushers me towards one of the leather sofas. She's wearing a knee-length pleated skirt beneath the swingy jacket, and sensible-but-sexy high-heeled Pied a Terre loafers.

I think I'm getting a little bit of a crush on her.

'Can I get you a coffee?' she asks. 'Water? Something to eat?'

'Yes, lovely, thank you.'

She looks a bit surprised. I wonder if I shouldn't have accepted the lot. But she disappears through a door behind her desk and starts making coffee-preparing noises. I fall back into the squishy leather and look around.

The wall opposite is filled with framed photos. There's a large one in the centre of two men dressed in tuxedos and chinking champagne glasses. One of the men is incredibly good-looking – stocky and dark, with a tan and a wicked, white smile. The other is tall, freckled and violently ginger. Despite this, and despite the scowl dappling his forehead, there's something strangely attractive about him too. The pair of them are giving off the untouchable aura of the rich, famous and well-connected. They must be a couple of the Madison/Salisbury-Kent clients. I think I've seen the ginger one on the society pages in the *Tatler*s I read at the leg-waxer's.

There are lots of smaller photographs arranged all around the centre. These feature other really, *really* famous writers – ones I've seen on *Richard and Judy*, and everything. God, this is all going to be great material for Marley's wedding. There's that chubby man who writes those bestselling Chinese spy novels. And there's Katriona de Montfort! She looks exactly like she does in all the magazines, dripping in amazing jewellery and staring intensely into the camera with her tiny black eyes.

Mum is going to *die* when she hears about this.

I'm just scanning the wall in the hope of finding Joanna Trollope when Sandy emerges from the kitchenette with a tray.

'So,' I say, nonchalantly, 'Katriona de Montfort is one of Joe Madison's clients?'

'She's one of Myles's, actually.' She nods at the large photo of the two tuxedo'd men.

'*That's* Madison/Salisbury-Kent?' I stare at the photo. 'I thought they were authors.'

'Nope. That's Joe,' she points at the devastatingly handsome dark one, 'and that's Myles.' She means the strangely attractive ginger one.

I didn't know literary agents looked like that. God, I wish Lindy had *warned* me. I'd have made the cab stop off at Boots for lip gloss and a hairbrush.

'Surely you knew Katriona was one of ours,' says Sandy, putting the tray down on the coffee table and nodding at the wall behind me. 'Doesn't *that* give it away?'

I glance around and take notice of all the framed posters on the wall. With one or two exceptions, every single one of them is for Katriona de Montfort's Captain Kidd series.

'Ah,' I say. 'Wonderful books.'

Actually, I must be the only person left on the planet who's neither read a single Captain Kidd book nor seen a single Captain Kidd film. If people divide into a Harry Potter camp and a Captain Kidd camp, then I'm firmly in the former.

'Of course. Wonderful,' says Sandy, with a little smile that makes me suspect she's secretly in the Harry Potter camp too. 'I hope this is all right for you,' she adds, indicating the tray.

There's a chilled blue bottle of Ty Nant water, a tiny cup of rich espresso with hot milk on the side, and a plate of those posh oblong continental biscuits with the slab of chocolate on the top. It's the closest thing to expense-account sashimi I've ever had.

'Fantastic.'

'I'm sure you've got some work you need to be getting on with while you wait. I won't disturb.'

Oh God. Work. In all the excitement, I'd almost

forgotten that I actually have to have something to show Joe Madison. He's not going to be very impressed by a Novelist without a Novel.

This is going to have to be really nippy.

'Out of interest,' I ask Sandy, who's tapping at her keyboard again, 'what's the average length of book that Joe takes on?'

She blinks at me.

'I mean, how much do writers give him to look at, you know, before he signs them up?'

'He usually likes about two or three to start with.'

'Paragraphs?'

She blinks again. 'Chapters.'

'Oh,' I say. 'Oh. I see.'

I slump back in my seat, stunned for a moment. How am I going to knock out two or three chapters in the next half-hour? Come to think of it, how am I going to knock out two or three *chapters* in the next half-*month*? I'm still at the creative visualisation stage, for goodness' sake.

'I mean, sometimes it's less.' Sandy is peering at me like a visitor to the zoo. 'The new author Joe's meeting right now, for example. He signed her on the strength of just a few pages. But then,' she adds, as I plunge into my bag and haul out my Smythson notebook and biro, 'she's a really big hope for the future, so . . .'

'Yes, yes, fine, thanks so much . . .' I really can't be wasting another moment, not now I know there's two or three chapters to be written. I turn to a fresh new page.

Suddenly there's a buzz from the front door. Great. Just when I was about to really get going, it's already too late. Now I'll have to meet this Myles Salisbury-Kent without anything to show for myself . . .

But it isn't Myles Salisbury-Kent at all. It's Katriona de Montfort.

She comes stalking into reception on teetering heels, pulling off her Hermès scarf as though it's trying to throttle her. There are sapphire chandeliers trembling in her earlobes, and yet more big blue stones on her tiny hands. She's even smaller in the flesh than in the photos, but she's instantly recognisable.

'Where is he, Sandy?' Her voice is shrill, and surprisingly loud. 'Is he sorting it? Is he back yet?'

'Hello, Katriona. I'm afraid Myles is still out. Why don't you wait in his office?'

'I don't want to wait in Myles's office.' She stamps her expensively shod foot. 'Myles's office is freezing and miserable.'

'He likes it,' says Sandy. 'It reminds him of Eton.'

'Well, it reminds me of having the gas cut off. I'll wait out here. And get me a coffee.'

'Of course,' says Sandy. 'You wait where you like. I'll just ask this nice journalist if she'd like another espresso while I'm at it.'

'Journalist?' gasps Katriona, staring at me for the first time. 'God, Sandy, what does she know? What has she heard? Get her the fuck out of here!'

I'm shocked. I mean, children's authors aren't supposed to swear.

43

'Don't worry about me!' I say. 'I'm not a proper journalist. All I do is measure column inches. If I wanted to sell a story about you, I wouldn't even know where to begin.'

'*Sandy!*'

'I can't throw her out, Katriona. She's here to interview Joe,' Sandy says. 'But I thought I should let you know. You know, before you said *anything you didn't mean to.*'

'So she's nobody?' Katriona eyes me through narrow slits.

'Oh, a *total* nobody!' I agree.

'All right,' Katriona snaps. 'Forget about that coffee, Sandy. I need a camomile tea. You know my nerves are on the edge as it is.'

I wish I knew what all the stress was about. It certainly seems to be affecting Katriona. She can't normally be like this.

She slumps on the other sofa like a Victorian with the vapours and takes off the jacket that I think – I *think* – is actual Chanel. Well, multimillionaire novelists don't wear Zara knock-offs, do they?

I feel that I should say something. I mean, there's obviously an atmosphere. And I'm never very good at awkward silences.

'I'm a big fan.'

She emits an audible sigh.

'No, really! I admire all your work,' I say, desperate to distinguish myself from the ordinary crazed fan. 'Not just the Captain Kidd books.'

Hang on. Has she actually written anything but the Captain Kidd books? I scan the wall behind me, hoping that there's some evidence of other novels there.

Captain Kidd and the Haunted Compass.
Captain Kidd and the Brave New World.
Captain Kidd and the Mystery Mutiny.

'Not just the Captain Kidd books,' I repeat, feeling the sweat pooling in the small of my back, 'for their wit, their jokes, their *joie de vivre* . . . but also the Captain Kidd books for their wisdom, their warmth, their . . . their message of hope.'

Katriona de Montfort picks up *Grazia* from the coffee table, flips through to the beauty pages, and starts reading.

I can't believe how rude she is. I mean, has she risen so high that she forgets to be polite to people who spend their hard-earned money on her books? Not that I've ever bought one. But she's not to know that.

'Right,' I say. 'Sorry to have bothered you. I just thought that a rich, famous writer like you might give a few words of encouragement to a young novelist, but obviously . . .'

Katriona de Montfort puts down *Grazia*. 'You're a novelist?' Her black eyes are fixed on me now. 'Who are you? Have I heard of you?'

'I'm Isabel Bookbinder. You . . . er . . . won't have heard of me.'

'So, tell me the names of your books.'

'Book.'

'What?'

'I mean, it's not plural yet.' I don't add that it isn't even into plural *words* yet. 'I'm just starting out, as a matter of fact. I'm sort of a . . . a novelist-in-training!'

'Oh!' she says. 'You're an *unpublished* writer.'

Nobody's ever made it sound so impressive. 'Yes.'

She leans closer. 'So what kind of thing are you writing at the moment?'

Rather weakly, I wave my Smythson notebook at her.

'But what is it? A children's book?'

'No, no!' I don't want her to think I'm just one of those people who are jumping on the bandwagon because children's books are suddenly big news. 'Quite the opposite, in fact. It's sort of a . . . a . . .'

'Yes?'

'A bonkbuster!'

She blinks. 'A bonkbuster?'

'Yes, a bonkbuster!'

This is actually a fantastic idea. I don't know why I didn't think of it before. I mean, I actually wrote a bonkbuster – a very short one – while I was still at school. We had this exam assignment to write a novella in the style of our favourite author, so of course I picked Jilly Cooper.

God, I sweated blood and tears over that bonkbuster. *Showjumpers*, I called it, and it was a real labour of love. There was a feisty titian-haired heroine, if I remember rightly, called Laetitia Lovelock, and a dashing rake called Barrington Bosworth-Bounder, and oodles and oodles of gravity-defying sex. Well, gravity-defying snogs. I was only fourteen when I wrote it.

I wonder if *Showjumpers* is one of the things Mum found with my old school exercise books. Not that I'm really thinking of turning some old schoolwork into my debut novel. I mean, that would just be ridiculous. But the *title* was great. Using the title wouldn't be ridiculous.

Katriona is wrinkling her button nose, looking doubtful. 'I thought bonkbusters were terribly old-fashioned these days.'

Not if I have anything to do with it. 'Well, I'm on a mission to . . . er . . . bring back the bonkbuster.'

'Bring back the bonkbuster?' Katriona blinks.

'Yes! With a . . . a huge, nationwide publicity campaign! You could have handsome men in hunting jackets handing out complimentary riding crops at bookshops!' I must be on some kind of a roll this morning. I mean, how fantastic is this? 'And ladies in tartan taffeta ballgowns offering mini bottles of champagne to commuters on the trains . . .'

Katriona covers her mouth with her hand. I think she's hiding a smile.

'But it wouldn't just be a great publicity campaign,' I say defensively. 'The book's a cracker too.'

'Oh, really?'

'Well, there's a feisty heroine. And a dashing rake, called Barrington Bosworth-Bounder. *And* oodles and oodles of gravity-defying sex. I mean, isn't that the kind of thing people like to read?'

'On the beach, maybe.'

'And planes! Oooh, you could give the riding crops away to people at the airport too! Unless they're classified as offensive weapons . . .'

'Well, it sounds as though you've really thought this through.' Katriona pats my hand. 'It's lovely to see a debut novelist with so many . . . quite extraordinary ideas.'

'Thank you!'

'I tell you what, Isabel, why don't you give me your phone number, and perhaps we can chat a little more some time?'

Now she's got my attention. 'Are you *sure*?'

'Of course!' Her grip on my hand tightens. 'You're quite right – someone in my position *should* make time to offer a few words of encouragement to a . . . a . . . what did you call it? A writer-in-training?'

'Novelist-in-training.'

She lets go of my hand and scrabbles in her handbag for a moment, then passes me a small leather diary – Smythson, yay! – and points at an empty page. 'Jot your number down here, sweetie.'

My hand is actually shaking a bit as I scribble down my mobile number. I mean, I know I was secretly hoping for Great Things from my first ever visit to a top literary agent, but this is just insane!

I mustn't get too excited, though. Probably she's just trying to find a polite way to fob me off. I mean, as if Katriona de Montfort – *Katriona de Montfort*, for heaven's sake – is going to call me.

'We must speak soon,' she's saying now. 'Things are rather fraught at the moment, but . . .'

Proving, as if I couldn't already tell, that things are fraught, the door to the reception is flung open and in comes Myles Salisbury-Kent. He's wearing the same scowl as in the big photo on the wall opposite, and he's just as violently ginger and freckled. But in person he's not so much *strangely* attractive as . . . well . . .

Mmmmmmmm.

The photo doesn't show how tall and well-built he is, in a bracing-country-walks-and-fancy-a-round-of-golf sort of way. And the other thing I missed in the photo is that the fire of his hair and skin is almost completely quenched by a startling pair of ice-blue eyes. He's dressed in that way that only the very rich and very posh can actually pull off, which is to say, in green jumbo cords, a khaki crew-neck sweater whose elbows have seen better days, and a tweedy jacket with a moth-hole in each lapel. Anybody else would look like an idiot, but Myles Salisbury-Kent looks extremely sexy.

He also looks like he's about to murder someone. Although, God help me, I find that extremely sexy as well.

'Katriona!' he barks, sounding even posher than he looks. It's the kind of voice that has ordered people around on battlefields and rugby pitches for a good couple of centuries. 'What the fuck are you doing here? I *said* I'd call you.'

'I couldn't sit around and wait!' Katriona runs to him. 'How did it go? Did you speak to Her?'

Sandy emerges from the kitchenette. 'Myles, you have a visitor.'

'What? Who?' Myles's piercing gaze shoots in my general direction, but I suspect he's the kind of man who only notices stunning leggy model-types.

'Isabel is here from the *Saturday Mercury*. She's been waiting nearly half an hour.'

It's nice of Sandy to be indignant on my behalf, but I really, really don't want to upset a top literary agent.

'Honestly, it's fine . . .' I begin.

'Then she can wait another half-hour!' snaps Myles, who's posh enough to disregard pesky things like manners. 'Katriona and I have things to discuss. Can't she speak to Joe?'

'Joe is in with his new author. He's taking longer than I thought.'

Myles lets out a bark of laughter. 'With Gina Deverill? Don't blame the man.'

What? *What?* I'm not sure I can possibly have heard that right.

'Excuse me, did . . . did you just say . . . ?'

Myles Salisbury-Kent's mobile rings.

'Is it *Her*?' Katriona hisses.

Myles glances at the caller display and nods grimly.

Katriona lets out a little moan.

'Oh, for Christ's sake, Kat, pull yourself together,' Myles snaps, sounding more like the captain of the First XV than ever. He looks like it too as he man-handles Katriona towards his office. 'Not a single call, Sandy,' he shouts over his shoulder. 'And get rid of this bloody journalist, will you?' His door slams shut.

'I'm *so* sorry.' Sandy is looking mortified. 'God, he can be an arrogant git . . .'

I've got bigger concerns than Myles Salisbury-Kent's rudeness. 'Sandy, did I just hear that right? Is *Gina Deverill* in Joe Madison's office?'

Sandy nods. 'Do you know her?'

'Yes, but she's . . . she's one of Joe's *new authors*?'

Sandy nods again, then, hearing a noise, glances down the corridor behind her. A door has opened. There are voices approaching.

'Oh, this'll be them now. You can say hello to your friend!'

Over my dead body.

'I think I need a breath of fresh air!' I head for the exit. 'I'll be back to speak to Joe in . . .' How long will it take for Gina to leave? '. . . about five minutes.'

'But, Isabel . . .'

But I'm already out of the door. I nip down the alley at the side of the building and wait. It's only a couple of minutes until I see Gina Deverill pass by on the main street, clicking her way on high-heeled boots towards Soho Square.

Chapter 5

By the time I finish hiding from Gina Deverill and get back inside, Joe has vanished into his office.

'I *am* sorry,' I tell Sandy. 'I just needed some air. I suddenly came over all funny.'

'Joe often has that effect on women. But normally he's actually made it into the room with them first.'

I give a little laugh and sit back down on the sofa.

Sandy stares at me. 'I'm afraid he's on an important call to New York now. You're going to carry on waiting?'

'I suppose I am,' I say miserably.

'Well, he's got a lunch at twelve-thirty. I'm sure he can give you a few minutes in the taxi over there if you'd like.'

I nod. 'Sandy, this phone call to New York Mr Madison is making – does it have anything to do with Gina Deverill?'

'I'm afraid I can't tell you about that kind of thing, Isabel.'

'Of course, of course. Client confidentiality and all that.'

Sandy nods.

'Which means she *is* a client?'

Sandy just gives me a smile, and busies herself with her in-tray.

I didn't mishear, then. Gina is one of Joe's new authors.

Dad is going to *kill* me. It was bad enough for him when Gina wiped the floor with me in all the subjects he taught us at school. It was even worse when she got a first-class degree and I got a lower second. It was almost unendurable when Gina got her first paying job at a glossy magazine while I was still making the tea on a local freesheet.

Now she's gone and got a top literary agent ahead of me, I don't think I'm going to survive it. God, I'm glad I avoided her just now. I bet she's like the cat who got the cream. Whereas I'm now far too shaken to make any progress on the damn novel while I wait. I pick up Katriona de Montfort's discarded *Grazia* and bury myself in Jennifer Aniston's Six Top Tips for Glowing Skin instead.

It's so riveting and informative that I barely notice Joe Madison coming back out of his office until he leans down and taps me on the knee.

'Isabel Bookbinder? I'm Joe. Sandy tells me you've been waiting a long time for me.'

Only all my life.

But I don't say that. I just mumble a bit and shake his hand.

The photo didn't do him any justice. In person, he's sort of ridiculously good-looking. High, arrogant cheekbones and bright sapphire eyes. Flawless, in fact, except for the deep chicken-pox scar just above one eyebrow, which only makes him more attractive still. He's wearing a black Paul Smith suit with an open-necked white shirt that shows off just a very tiny bit of lightly tanned chest.

I think I see what Sandy meant about coming over all funny.

He smiles at me, and holds the reception door open. 'Hop in a taxi with me, and I'll make sure I give you everything you need.'

Now I feel more than just a bit funny.

'Great . . . good . . . fantastic . . .'

''Bye, Isabel,' says Sandy. 'Sorry about all the delays. It was nice meeting you.'

Outside, Joe hails a taxi, opens the door, and holds out a hand to help me in.

'Comfortable?' he asks, having settled in himself, and requested the driver to take us to Sloane Square. 'I do apologise for all the madness this morning. We're only just back after Christmas, so there's a lot of catch-up to do. Nice Christmas yourself?' he adds, conversationally, as we lurch around a corner and I slide across the seat into him.

'Lovely, thank you.'

'Go anywhere fun?'

'Shepton Mallet.'

'A good, English countryside Christmas. I was skiing in Aspen with a big gaggle of pals.' He pulls a face. 'Much better to be at home with your nearest and dearest. All cosy.'

Even in my dazed state – his knee is pressing *right against mine* – I recognise a charm offensive when I hear one. And I've got a job to do. Lindy needs her article, and I'm nothing if not professional.

'So, your new authors for the New Year,' I ask. 'Is Gina Deverill one of them?'

'As a matter of fact she is.' Joe rakes his hair backwards and gives me a dazzling smile. 'I'm surprised you've heard of her, Isabel. The ink is barely dry on her book deal.'

'Gina already *has* a book deal?'

'The auction went right up to the wire. Now we're just haggling over the finer points of the contract.'

I open my mouth, but this time no words come out. This is even worse than I thought. All right, Gina has a brand-new literary agent, but I didn't expect she'd already have the brand-new book deal to match.

Just when I thought I was making real progress, what with picking a title and everything. I mean, Gina must actually have completed a *whole novel*. Whereas I'm still several bonks short of a whole bonkbuster. I haven't got a single bonk, in fact.

'What . . . what kind of debut novel is it?'

'Oh, it's fabulous.' Joe waves his hands expansively. 'High-minded, thought-provoking, award-winning stuff.'

I brighten. 'You mean, it won't sell any copies?'

Joe laughs. 'God, no. No, this one has real mainstream appeal. It's got major international bestseller written all over it.'

'Oh. Right.'

'Gina Deverill is Very Promising. One to Watch.' Joe leans a little closer. 'Isabel? Aren't you going to make any notes?'

'I won't forget this, believe me.'

'Well, which other authors are you featuring?' He pulls back to his side of the seat and pouts ever so slightly. 'Lindy promised we'd get at least six mentions in the piece.'

Bugger Lindy's piece. All I can think of is Gina's book deal.

'I know what Chris told you. But I think the – er – thrust of the article has changed somewhat. We're actually hoping for a sort of Top Tips for New Novelists instead.'

'Top Tips?'

I pull my Smythson out and flip it open.

'Like, how to start your debut novel. What kind of plot-line. What characters. What title. That kind of thing.'

Joe's blue eyes widen slightly. 'My Top Tip would be get a plot-line and characters before you even start.'

'And a title?'

'I think that can generally wait. Look, Isabel—'

'And how would you recommend approaching an agent? Some people seem to think sending two or three chapters is about right, but I think many of our readers would prefer a speedier approach.'

Now it's his turn to fall silent.

'And I'm sure the question everybody wants answered

is: just how important is it to find your own Look?'

'Look?'

'Look. Image. Persona, if you will. Is it the kind of thing a personal shopper could help with? Do you have one you'd recommend?'

Joe puts a hand on mine. 'Isabel, are you all right?'

'I'm fine. All I need is your Top Tips, and I'll be on my way.'

'You've had quite a stressful morning, haven't you? All the waiting around.'

'Well, meeting Katriona de Montfort was certainly an experience.'

'Ah! You met *Katriona*!' His face clears, like a little boy who suddenly understands his maths homework. 'No wonder you're feeling a bit out of sorts.'

Our taxi pulls up outside Oriel on Sloane Square and Joe gets out his wallet.

'Keep this,' he says, handing the driver a twenty-pound note, 'and take this lady wherever she wants to go.'

'Oh, no, I'll just hop on the tube . . .'

He pushes me back into my seat. 'Take the taxi, Isabel. And can you take the afternoon off work at all?'

'I don't think so. Chris—'

'Tell you what, I'll call Chris – he's an old pal – and tell him to give you the afternoon off.'

Now I think of it, I am feeling the stress and strain of everything that's happened this morning.

'That's really nice of you, Joe.'

57

He's already stepping out of the taxi, pausing only to take something else from his wallet. 'My direct line is on here,' he says, handing me a business card. 'Can you get Lindy to give me a call for a proper chat about this "Top Tips" piece?'

'Oh, absolutely.'

I pocket the card, which has instantly become the most precious thing I own. I may not have a whole bonkbuster yet, but I've got a direct line to a top literary agent. Plus I've got all that invaluable advice about plot-lines and characters. And even though he said a title can generally wait, it can't *hurt* that I've already got a title, can it?

As the taxi pulls away, I turn back to watch Joe going into Oriel.

But he isn't going into Oriel. He's standing outside, staring after me.

'SIX OF THE BEST' WITH YOUR FAVOURITE STARS

This week, Isabel Bookbinder's Top Tips on How to
Become a Celebrity Novelist

1. Get the Basics Right
Feeling like a Novelist is all-important. Gaze at things a
lot: the winter dawn is always a good place to start, but
other possibilities are spring dew, summer twilight
and/or autumn mist. Switch to plain black coffee, and
consider taking up smoking. For those who can afford it,
a cashmere blanket is an invaluable accessory.
Spending just a short time getting all this right at the
outset will save you many hours in the long run.

2. Get a Really Good Notebook
Don't waste time or money shopping around for a
bargain. Treat yourself to something special, possibly
leather-bound. Get a kind friend or a relative to buy it, if
possible. You can pay them back out of your enormous
advance later.

3. Perfect Your Look
The most important tool a celebrity Novelist has at their
disposal. Whether it's wall-to-wall pink and Pekinese,
like Barbara Cartland, or a big white beard like Ernest
Hemingway (I would strongly advise against this), you
need to work hard at the image you want to project. A
good personal shopper may be able to help, if you can
pluck up the courage to make an appointment. Avoid

overaccessorising at all costs. Remember: for the committed Novelist, less is always more.

4. Establish a Serious Fitness Regime

Being a Novelist can involve an awful lot of sitting around at a desk/champagne launch parties/nibbling on canapés, etc., so you'll need to make sure you fight those lumps and bumps. Nobody ever gave a book deal to a wobble-bum. Why not invest in a personal trainer, or some swanky new home gym equipment? You have to speculate to accumulate.

5. Get a Top Literary Agent

Keep your eyes and ears open, and a Top Literary Agent might just fall into your lap. Obviously it's best to make real headway on the Serious Fitness Regime first, just in case your literary agent turns out to be devastatingly good-looking. If Top Literary Agents aren't falling into your lap, you'll probably have to send out a sample of your work. This should be two or three chapters, though if you've followed Top Tips 1 to 4 religiously, you may well find you can get away with two or three paragraphs instead.

6. Think Up Plot-line and Characters

Though a title can generally wait.

Next week, Patsy Kensit's 'Six of the Best' on How to Marry a Rock Star

Chapter 6

Joe Madison is a liar!

Well, all right, that might be a bit strong. I don't want to accidentally libel him or anything. Though if that meant we'd meet again in the electric atmosphere of a courtroom, sharp one-liners zinging back and forth like with Katharine Hepburn and Spencer Tracy (I could wear fantastic wide-leg trousers), then maybe I *should* just go right ahead and libel him.

The point is that Gina Deverill hasn't actually written a *whole* novel at all. Not yet. I've spent ages trawling Google, and there's only one teeny, tiny mention of Gina. It's on some specialist trade website for the publishing industry, in an article dated just before Christmas.

> Currently creating a lot of heat on both sides of the Atlantic is newcomer Gina Deverill's novel, *Wave/ Lengths*. In a maverick move typical of the Madison/ Salisbury-Kent Agency, Joe Madison snapped up Ms Deverill's debut last week, despite the fact that only the opening chapters are complete. Mr Madison will no doubt be hoping that publishers share his optimism about the project when an auction is held in January.

Ha!

This is such promising news that I've even managed to completely shake off any feelings of bitterness about the excited tone of this article. I mean, 'creating a lot of heat on both sides of the Atlantic'. It's just flimflam, right? Just a bit of padding to make the story sound better. Gina isn't *really* going to have a bestseller in America. It's pure speculation. Creative visualisation run mad.

And what kind of a stupid name is *Wave/Lengths*? Is it a novel about swimming? Hairdressing? The heart-breaking struggle of one woman to achieve the perfect perm?

Anyway, the really important point is that Gina isn't very far ahead of me. All right, she's got the high-flying agent. And all right, there's a big book auction about to go ahead. But only a couple of weeks ago, all *Gina had written* was a few crappy opening chapters! I mean, *I've* practically done that!

Well, all right. But I've sat down and had a really long, hard think about it. And I've been thinking, for example, that maybe Mum's idea about saving time isn't so silly after all.

I mean, Joe Madison did seem pretty adamant that I'd be needing actual *chapters* before I can proceed to the next stage. Well, *Showjumpers* had chapters. OK, it had three little stars dividing up each section. But that's almost the same thing. Changing three little stars into the words 'Chapter One' and 'Chapter Two' is the work of an instant, isn't it? And I really could do with saving a bit of time on the actual writing part, because all the other aspects of being a Novelist are really falling into place.

Marley's wedding day approaching has proved a real catalyst for my Look, for example. I've found the most gorgeous silk dress to wear, in a very sophisticated kind of pinky-beige colour – 'putty', the girl in Selfridges kept calling it. Because it's January, and I don't want to freeze, I bought an ivory cashmere-mix shrug, too. I also found a little feathery fascinator for my hair, and some bronze pointy shoes in the sale rack at Kurt Geiger. Well, they were *near* the sale rack at Kurt Geiger.

And it isn't only my Look that's blossoming. Thanks to this special 'Last-Minute Shape-Up Plan' I've followed in the *Brides* magazine I'd bought for Daria, a honed size eight really isn't that far away.

With all these firm foundations already laid, it can't hurt to have a *read* of *Showjumpers*. Just to see if it really could save me any valuable time. Just to see if it could help me catch up with Gina Deverill for a change.

That's all.

You know, thanks to all my careful preparations, I've actually started looking forward to Marley's wedding.

Gina Deverill or no Gina Deverill, I'm going to out-glam everyone else there!

This isn't me being boastful or anything, by the way. My brother is a mathematician. He's marrying another mathematician. Most of their friends are mathematicians. If I *didn't* out-glam everyone else there, I'm not really sure life would be worth living.

The only real problem is that my landlord, Russell, is coming with me.

He isn't *just* my landlord, I should say. He's been my boyfriend for nearly five weeks. And while I quite like the theory of falling in love with my landlord – aren't Catherine Cookson heroines always going gooey over masterful landlords? – it isn't quite so romantic in practice.

Russell isn't terribly masterful, and he's not exactly that kind of landlord. He just owns the flat that I've rented a room in for the last four months. He does something with insurance, I think, or possibly computers. Computer insurance, possibly. He's thirty-ish, or maybe in his late twenties, and he's from . . . Scotland. Or Northern Ireland. Maybe Yorkshire. I find accents quite tricky. Anyway, our relationship isn't about silly little details like jobs, or age, or where people come from. It's about intellectual stimulation, and a deep sense of attraction.

Though, if the truth be told, Russell isn't particularly intellectually stimulating. And I can't honestly say I find him very attractive.

My friend Lara, speaking in her professional capacity, thinks I'm only going out with Russell because I have a 'fragile sense of self-worth'. Actually, there's nothing remotely fragile about my sense of self-worth. My sense of self-worth is tough as old boots. I just didn't want to have to go to Marley's wedding as a single saddo, and have everyone pity me while I dance to 'Agadoo' with a six-year-old bridesmaid.

Well, *that* was a misjudgement. Because Russell has made it quite clear he won't be doing dancing of any kind. Weddings, as he's told me, all the way on the tube from Hammersmith to Paddington, aren't really 'his thing'. I think he's in a bit of a mood.

Now he's stalked off into the station WHSmith to stock up on papers for the journey while I wait by the Krispy Kreme doughnut stand to meet Lara.

As always, she's bang on time, wheeling her overnight case across the noisy concourse towards me.

I give her a hug. 'You look amazing!'

She does, as well. Her hair's in lovely, beachy waves, and she's bundled up in the white cashmere-mix scarf and earmuffs I gave her for Christmas. She always makes sure to wear my presents when I see her. Lara's very good like that.

'No, Iz, *you* look amazing.'

Lara's very good like that too.

'So how weird is this, Iz? Marley getting married.'

Lara has known my entire family since we were both seven. Marley is like an older brother to her. Well, he's as much like an older brother to her as he is to me, if being vague and woolly and barely remembering our names counts.

'And you're certain Matthew will be there?' Lara asks, suddenly staring at the ground and scuffing it with her foot.

This is where Lara really lets herself down. No matter that she's an incredibly successful psychologist who can spot self-esteem issues at thirty paces. She's been hopelessly in love with my younger brother, Matthew, ever since he teased her about her braces on the school bus, and pinged her bra strap through her shirt at the end-of-term disco.

And she thinks *I* have a fragile sense of self-worth.

'Yes, Lara, Matthew will be there. And his *long-term girlfriend*, Annie, will be with him.'

I hate doing it, but this year, I've decided to take a new approach with Lara's Matthew obsession: from now on, it's Cruel to be Kind.

'Oh,' she says. 'Of course. Right.' Beneath her earmuffs, her little pixie face falls.

I don't think I'm going to be very good at the Cruel part. 'Come on, Lars! At least you'll get to *see* him. And maybe you'll meet someone at the wedding!'

'I don't want to meet a mathematician.'

'Not *all* Marley's friends are mathematicians,' I tell her. 'Quite a few of them are analytic number theorists.'

'What's the difference between a mathematician and an analytic number theorist?'

You'd think Lara was trying to tell me some kind of joke, but actually I know that there's an *enormous* difference between mathematicians and analytic number theorists. Marley's friend Henrik spent most of Marley's last birthday party telling me all about it. And he ought to know because he *is* an analytic number theorist. Or a mathematician. I can't actually remember which.

'The point is, Lara, you can't just sit around hoping Matthew will decide to dump Annie and—' I'm interrupted by my mobile phone.

'Shouldn't you get that?' asks Lara, who just wants to avoid the lecture.

I glance down at the screen. 'It's only Lindy Lyons.'

'Your boss? Shouldn't you answer?'

'Lindy Lyons is not my *boss*. Anyway, she isn't meant to disturb me out of working hours. Just because she has no life outside the office. It's about the ninth time she's called me already this weekend.'

'Maybe it's an emergency.'

'Lara, I work on a weekly arts supplement. How much of an emergency can there possibly be?'

'But if it's her ninth call . . .'

'I exaggerated.'

Well, I exaggerated a little bit. It's actually her eighth. I avoided the first call on principle, but once I heard the message she left, I've been avoiding the rest out of nerves. Well, would you return a call to someone who practically burst your eardrum shrieking, 'What the fuck have you *done*, Isabel? Call me *now*!' at the top of their lungs?

She's most likely found out that I went along to Madison/Salisbury-Kent in person, instead of phoning them like she told me to. Well, I'll just buy her an extra large Frappucino tomorrow. She'll calm down about it.

The instant we board the train, Russell takes up residence behind his five Sunday newspapers, and remains there for the rest of the journey.

'It's very passive-aggressive,' Lara hisses at me, somewhere around Swindon.

Lara thinks a lot of things are passive-aggressive. But the fact is that Russell always reads five Sunday newspapers. He's one of those people who like to have a lot of facts at their fingertips. For example, he's always the first one at a party who can say, while passing the nibbles, 'Did you know that the average bowl of peanuts contains twenty-two different strains of E. coli bacteria?' I must remind him not to do it today.

Anyway, I'm glad he's in retreat, because it gives me the chance to update Lara on the Gina situation.

'I can't seriously believe *Gina Deverill* has actually written a novel,' Lara says, once I've finished telling her everything.

'Not just a novel. A bestselling literary sensation.'

'Who says it's going to be a bestselling literary sensation?'

'Her agent. You know, the one I met on Friday.'

Lara sighs. 'Iz, don't you think Gina's agent might just have the teeniest bit of a vested interest in telling journalists her book's going to be a bestselling literary sensation?'

I hadn't thought about it that way.

'Well, he had a very honest face,' I say. 'Big, clear blue eyes. Soft lips . . .'

Lara is giving me a funny look.

'Anyway,' I continue, 'why shouldn't Gina write a bestselling literary sensation? She's outshone me all her life. Why stop now?'

'Just ignore what your dad thinks,' says Lara, gently. 'The only thing Gina outshines you at is being a stuck-up cow. Her book will be rotten. I mean, what kind of a stupid title is *Wave/Lengths*, anyway? And if Gina Deverill can write a bestselling literary meister-werk, so can you.'

'Well, the bestselling bit, anyway,' I agree.

'Exactly. So how's it going, anyway?' She reaches towards my Smythson notebook, which is peeking out of my bag, but I slap her hand away.

'Lara! It's a work in progress!'

'Well, as long as it's a *work*.'

'Of course it's a work,' I say. 'Honestly, Lars, you're as bad as Barney. Neither of you seems to have the slightest faith in me.'

She folds her arms. 'So. How much have you written?'

There's something about the set of Lara's lips that is putting me off telling her my idea about recycling my fourth-form English coursework.

'*Loads*,' I say. 'Absolutely oodles. You know, Lars, that creative visualisation technique of yours is proving really helpful.'

'Iz, you are doing something other than *just* the creative visualisation technique, aren't you?'

'Lara!' I'm hurt she could even ask.

'OK, I'm sorry. It's just that I know you have a tendency to get a little bit . . . carried away.'

'In the past,' I admit, 'that may have been true. But everything's different this time, Lars. And if Gina Deverill thinks I'm just going to sit back and watch *her* on *Richard and Judy*, she's got another thing coming.'

'Iz, it isn't a race.' There's concern etched across Lara's face. 'You don't have to compete with Gina. Your only competition is *you*.'

'Well, in that case,' I say, opening up the *Sunday Times Style* section, 'everything is completely under control.'

I'm just assimilating some really useful information in the *Style* section about what Gwyneth Paltrow's macrobiotic diet consists of (organic blueberries, mostly, with the occasional crazed binge on steamed fish or hot water and lemon) when we pull into Castle Cary station.

Dad is waiting to meet us. Lara goes a bit pale when she sees him. She spends so long thinking of him as my scary dad that she forgets to think of him as her scary former headmaster.

The ride home is typically joyless. Dad is polite enough to Russell, faintly disapproving of Lara's new highlights, and his usual warm and fuzzy self to me.

'How's work?'

'Not bad, Dad, how's yours?'

'Any chance you'll be getting promoted to Arts Editor soon?'

'I doubt it, Dad, what about you?'

'Don't be silly, Isabel, I'm the headmaster. I can't get promoted.'

'Of course, Dad.'

'Marley's being promoted, you know.'

'Yes. You told me all about that at Christmas.'

'Looks like Matthew's in line for a step up the ladder too.'

'That's nice.'

'It'd be nice to see you doing the same, Isabel.'

'Promotion isn't everything,' Russell interrupts.

I can hardly believe I've just heard this. Russell is *standing up* for me? I want to throw myself across the car and kiss him.

All right, so he's not exactly my cup of tea. All right, I only started going out with him to avoid single saddo-dom at Marley's wedding. These faults are mine, and mine alone. Russell is a good, kind person, and I'm truly lucky to have him.

'Long-term training is more important than a quick rung up the ladder,' Russell continues. 'If Isabel really wants to advance in her career, she needs to be investing in some industry-recognised courses, not just frittering away her evenings slumped in front of *24* on the TV or nattering to her friends in Pizza Express.'

Dad meets my eyes in the mirror. 'I didn't know you wasted your evenings in front of the telly, Isabel.'

'Only *24*,' I mutter, wondering if there's any way I can terminate Russell, Jack Bauer-style, with his seatbelt. 'It's critically acclaimed.'

'You told me you regularly go to the Globe.'

'I *do* regularly go to the Globe!'

Regularly . . . occasionally . . . once . . . And I'd have gone back more often if they'd bothered to put a roof on the bloody thing.

'You told me,' Dad continues, 'that you have a season ticket to Tate Modern.'

'Oh, but she *does* have a season ticket to Tate Modern, Mr Bookbinder,' Lara chips in, even though her rigid smile shows how scared she is. 'My mum bought it for Iz for her last birthday.'

'There have been some *wonderful* exhibitions,' I say earnestly. Which is true. Tate Modern does have some wonderful exhibitions. I read about them all the time in the *Metro*.

'I've never seen you go to Tate Modern,' Russell says, undoing all Lara's good work.

By the time we pull into the driveway, Russell and my father have reached a full and satisfactory agreement that I'm:

– a bit of a waster

– who doesn't take anything seriously

– who'll never advance without a lot more application

– especially if I don't stop spending so much time and money at Pizza Express.

I think my father has found the perfect future son-in-law.

I'm so relieved to see Mum come out of the house that I can actually feel tears bubbling up.

'Mum! You look lovely.'

And she does, in a vision-in-fuchsia kind of way. She's wearing the brand-new fuchsia suit I helped her pick in Country Casuals, teamed with the fuchsia hat I advised her against in Phase Eight, and the fuchsia shoes I thought I'd talked her out of in John Lewis. (She's terribly keen on things 'matching', my mum. Many's the time she's warned me against buying a particular pair of plain black trousers 'because they've not put anything with it to match'.)

'Really?' She gives an uncertain little twirl. 'Not too fuchsia?'

'Not too fuchsia at all.'

Mum gives Lara a kiss. 'It's lovely to see you, Lara. How's Mummy and Daddy? And you must be Russell!'

Encouraged by Dad, Russell is trying to slink past her into the house.

'It's wonderful to meet you,' Mum goes on. 'We've heard *everything* about you!'

Russell looks bemused, mostly because my mum has made him sound fascinating and mysterious, but also because we've only been going out for five weeks, and *I* barely know anything about him.

'Nice to meet you too,' he mutters.

'Izzy-Wizzy's throwing you in at the deep end today, isn't she?'

Russell's look of bemusement grows.

'*I'm* Izzy-Wizzy,' I hiss into his ear. I mean, it's hardly rocket science.

'I want you to make yourself at home, Russell,' Mum continues. 'Is there anything you need? Fresh towels? A hot drink?'

'Leave him alone, Moira.' Dad's brought out his top-of-the-range supercilious voice, and polished it up specially for the occasion. 'If he needs anything, I'm sure he's got the wit to ask.'

'I wouldn't bet on it,' I mutter, hauling my case out of the car with no help from Russell, who's followed Dad inside in search of the Sudoku in today's *Observer*.

My mobile is ringing again as Lara and I traipse up the stairs with our cases.

'Bloody Lindy again!'

'Just call her back,' Lara advises. 'I'm sure there's nothing to be scared of, Iz-Wiz. And you have to see her at work tomorrow anyway, so there's nothing to be gained by avoiding her.'

'Who says I'm scared?' I ask indignantly. Honestly, this is the trouble with having a psychologist for a best friend. Not only do they see passive aggression and low self-worth at every turn, but they're constantly overanalysing every little thing you do. *Obviously* I'll have to see Lindy at work tomorrow. And there's no way of avoiding her, even if I *did* want to.

Unless, I suppose, I happened to come down with flu, or something. I mean, then I'd probably have to take most of the week off work. It's actually socially irresponsible to go around spreading germs these days, what with bird flu, and superbugs and everything. And by the time I recovered enough to go back to the office, Lindy would probably have forgotten what I did with Madison/Salisbury-Kent anyway.

I'm not going to *do* that. I'm just saying, it would be a way of avoiding Lindy if I wanted to.

Lara is ploughing into my old room and flinging herself onto my My Little Pony beanbag. 'God, I love the fact that nothing ever changes in here. It's just like being nine again.'

I wonder what her fellow psychologists would make of *that*.

I start unpacking my putty-coloured dress and cashmere-mix cardi, ignoring the cornflower-blue skirt, cornflower-blue jacket, and cornflower-blue shirt Mum has hung, hopefully, on my wardrobe door.

Lara starts rifling through the junk on the desk for more golden nuggets from our childhoods. She discards an ancient stub of Beauty Without Cruelty eyeliner and a Collection 2000 mascara that probably ought to have a 'Hazmat' sign on it, then grabs a dog-eared old paperback.

'Oooh, *Flowers in the Attic*! Remember how cross your dad was when he realised we were all reading this instead of those dreary Millicent Petersens?'

'Oh my God! Lara, I'd completely forgotten to tell you . . .'

I stop myself. I'm not actually sure I should say anything to Lara about Millicent Petersen and Chris Macbeth. It's not that I don't trust her. It's just that I'm kind of wishing I'd never sent those emails to Barney. This is the *Home Secretary*'s husband we're talking about, doing all those inappropriate things with the baby oil. I mean, you only have to read a John Grisham to know what can happen if you find out more than you should about politicians' private lives. I really wouldn't want to get in trouble with MI5 or something.

'Tell me what?' asks Lara. But she's too busy flicking through *Flowers in the Attic* to pay proper attention.

'Oh . . . nothing. I'll tell you another time.'

'Mmm . . . Oh, Iz-Wiz! I remember this!'

She chucks down *Flowers in the Attic*, and snatches up a sheaf of A4 paper from the desk.

'*Showjumpers*,' Lara intones, flopping back down on the My Little Pony beanbag. ' "A Debut Novella by Isabel Bookbinder, 4S." '

I stare at the papers she's holding. They're handwritten in blue fountain-pen ink, and bound with ancient-looking green rope tags. They're also a little bit dusty, from all their years in the attic, which is where I was going to go and hunt them down later.

'What's that doing on my desk?'

' "Laetitia Lovelock had been riding Crispin (her horse) all day, and she was exhausted," ' Lara reads, with relish.

'Lars, stop!' But secretly, I quite want her to carry on.

Lara gives a little wriggle of her shoulders. ' "Her lithe, voluptuous body ached, and she longed to soap her smooth limbs in a hot, sensual bath. The last person she wanted to see striding out of the stables was Barrington Bosworth-Bounder, leader of the Cocklesmore hunt, and breaker of a thousand hearts . . ."'

She's interrupted by a knock on the door, and Mum comes in, carrying a tray.

'Sorry to disturb, girls! I thought you'd want something to eat. I've just done you a few custard creams and some of that posh coffee you always used to like.' She puts the tray down on the bed. There's a small mountain of biscuits and two mugs of that frothy instant cappuccino you make from a sachet.

'Mum,' I give her a penetrating look, 'what was *Showjumpers* doing out on my desk?'

Her eyes go very wide, the way they do when she's pretending she's not interfering. '*Showjumpers*?' she asks, all innocent.

'This, Mrs Bookbinder.' Lara flaps the manuscript at her. 'God, Iz-Wiz, you *have* to read what you made Barrington do to the stable-girl on page four . . .'

I can't help noticing that Mum is turning very pink, and I don't think it's got anything to do with Barrington and the stable-girl.

'You told me all my old schoolwork was up in the attic,' I say.

'Well, darling, as it happens, I've got a little surprise . . .'

Suddenly, the front door bangs shut downstairs, and Matthew's voice booms out, 'Everyone? The party can start! We're here!'

Lara turns an even deeper shade of pink than Mum,

and nips out of my room. I block the door before Mum can scoot away as well.

'Surprise, Mum?'

'Yes, darling?'

This is almost as hard as it used to be getting my pocket money out of Dad. 'You said you had a little surprise. Something to do with *Showjumpers*.'

'Oh, yes!' Mum is picking at her fuchsia nail polish. 'Well, I was going to wait until after the wedding to tell you . . . just in case you got all cross . . .'

'Why would I get all cross?' And to be honest, *when* did I last get all cross with Mum?

'Well!' She puts a hand on her hip. 'Excuse *me* for trying to be sensitive to you, Iz-Wiz! I know writers can be awfully temperamental. Apart from Joanna Trollope, of course. I don't think she's terribly temperamental at all, do you? Oh, but of course, you've interviewed her! *Was* she temperamental at all, did you think . . .?'

She's trying to change the subject. It's something I happen to have an innate talent for spotting.

'Mum. The surprise.'

She sits down on the very edge of the bed. 'Well, the thing was, after I spoke to you on Friday morning, you seemed in a bit of a state about how slowly your novel was coming along.'

'I wasn't in a state!'

'Darling, you were incoherent. Spouting all kinds of nonsense about being a bottle of shampoo or something. I was worried you were pushing yourself too hard. So I thought . . . well, I thought it would be nice to make some real progress. Have something good to tell your father,' she adds, staring at the floor. 'Anyway, I decided to help you out. So I popped down to the library in town, to use their photocopier. I mean, you wouldn't have wanted me sending the original off to a publisher, would you? What if they never sent it back?'

I stare at her. 'You've . . . sent a copy of *Showjumpers* to a publisher?'

'Yes, darling! A big one too. The nice librarian helped me find this wonderful book, with all the names of the publishers and everything. All the writers use it, apparently. Even Joanna Trollope, I'm sure! Now, what was the publisher's name again . . .? Aardvark Something. Something Aardvark . . .?'

'Aadelman Stern?' I grab Mum's hand. 'You sent it to Aadelman Stern?'

'Oh, yes, that's the one!' Mum beams. 'The librarian said they're terribly good. I thought it was best to aim right for the top.'

I open my mouth to speak, but nothing comes out.

Who'd have ever known Mum would have the gumption to do something like this? Dad keeps her on such a tight leash, I wouldn't have thought she'd even be able to think through such a plan, let alone actually get out there and do it.

And *Aadelman Stern*, of all places!

I really wish I'd had the chance to type it up first . . . and turn the snogging into bonking . . . and change the little stars into the word 'Chapter' . . . But it's out there. My debut novel is *out there*. I could be getting the phone call, on Monday morning, that will change my life.

If *only* Mum had told me on Friday, I wouldn't have had those three Krispy Kremes on the train! And I could have got myself an emergency appointment with a personal shopper . . .

'Oh, Iz-Wiz, you *are* cross, aren't you?'

'No! It's . . . brilliant. Scary. But brilliant.'

Mum's mouth falls open. 'You mean you're pleased?'

'Thrilled, Mum!' I put my arms around her. 'You've always believed in me, haven't you?'

'Well, of course I have, darling.'

I give her the tightest squeeze I can without crumpling her suit. 'When the book comes out, I'll dedicate it to you!'

To Mum,
Who always believed in me.

'Oh, Iz-Wiz, I'm so glad you're not cross! I mean, the worst that can happen is a rejection. And every writer has to go through lots of rejection, don't they?'

Well. I'm actually hoping that's all a bit of a myth.

'Though Joanna Trollope probably didn't. Did she give you any tips, Iz-Wiz, when you met her . . . ?'

'God, is that the time?' I get up and pull my putty dress and ivory cardi out of the cupboard. 'I really need to be getting ready.'

Mum's face falls. 'But it doesn't match!'

Chapter 7

An hour later, I'm showered, exfoliated, moisturised, all gussied up in my new putty frock and my cashmere-mix shrug, *and* I've managed to nuke most of the frizz out of my hair with Lara's industrial-strength straighteners.

Lara herself has left her hair all beachy, and she looks tiny and gorgeous in a slate-grey velvet trouser suit and vertiginous heels. Now I come to think of it, it's the same beachy hairstyle, the same slate-grey velvet trouser suit and the same vertiginous heels she wore to Matthew's New Year's Eve party three years ago, when he (infamously) told her she looked very pretty.

But neither of us can get to the mirror to admire our finished looks because of Russell. He's managed to tear himself away from the Sunday papers to come up and get changed, and he's been hogging the wardrobe mirror for a good five minutes.

'How do I look?' he asks us.

'Fine. I mean, great,' I say, which is kind of me, because his blue polyester jacket makes him look a bit like Glenn Hoddle singing 'Diamond Lights' on *Top of the Pops* in 1987. But I'm hoping my generous compliment will result in a tit-for-tat one back.

Russell doesn't oblige.

'So how about me?' I practically sumo-wrestle Russell out of the way to get a glance in the mirror myself.

Russell shrugs. 'Not bad.'

'Not *bad*?'

'Not bad.'

'Well, what does that mean?'

'What does it mean? It means not bad.'

'But . . . does that mean *good*?'

'Well, the opposite of not bad is good, I suppose.'

'You suppose?'

'Yeah.'

'So you're saying I look *good* then?'

'No, I'm saying *not bad*. It's just what it says on the tin, Isabel.'

'Isabel's boyfriend, ladies and gentlemen,' Lara mutters, as she bolts back downstairs to find Matthew again.

As usual, Matthew and his girlfriend, Annie, are taking up a lot of room and making a lot of noise, dashing about yelling that the taxis are here and there's no room for them to park in the driveway.

'Izzy-Wizzy!' they bellow when they see me.

We all exchange hearty, rugby-player hugs, their preferred greeting.

'Iz-Wiz, you look stunning!' Annie declares. Next to her, of course, I don't, but it's nice of her to say so. Like Matthew, Annie is a games teacher, so she doesn't really do fripperies or posh frocks. She's poured her Amazonian frame into a bobbling old sweater dress, dashed a bit of powder across her glowing cheeks, and put up her naturally blond, wavy hair with what looks a lot like a kebab stick. She looks completely fantastic.

Matthew, of course, gets better-looking with each passing lunar cycle. He's just as blond and even taller and healthier than Annie, even though his face is a tiny bit more smashed from rugby.

'And this is my . . . this is Russell,' I tell them, waving forward the much less impressive physical specimen that is Russell.

Like most mortals, Russell is simply staring at them, slack-jawed in wonderment.

Lara, on the other hand, is staring slack-jawed at Matthew with something a lot less pure than wonderment. I'm about to hustle her into one of the waiting taxis when, thank God, Marley and Daria, his wife-to-be, make their big entrance.

Actually, it's not much of a big entrance. All they really do is shuffle down the stairs clutching hands while Marley ho-hums 'The Wedding March' under his breath. But it's probably a big entrance by mathematician standards. Daria is looking pretty in – oh, shit – putty. It's a sweet little tweedy suit, whose effect is only slightly marred by the giant white satin chrysanthemum she has pinned behind her ear. I do wish she'd stretched to some high heels for the day, but at least she's not wearing her Birkenstocks. Marley is wearing what looks like his everyday work suit, with a jaunty red-and-white spotted handkerchief in his top pocket as a nod to the importance of the occasion. Behind their specs, they're both beaming shyly, at us and at each other.

Suddenly I can feel something prickling at the back of my throat. I think I must be thirsty or something.

Once Dad has bullied everyone into standing around outside in the freezing cold so he can take photos and yell at us for not smiling properly, we finally all set off in our fleet of taxis.

And the hotel looks nice, as we approach up the driveway. There's a sort of Winter Wonderland effect on the big semicircle of grass out at the front, which I instantly recognise as Mum's handiwork: fake-snow-dusted pine trees; twig reindeers pulling a sleigh; and the *pièce de résistance* – pottery penguins wearing little fuchsia scarves.

'I wanted Daria's parents to feel welcome,' Mum whispers to me, as we step out of the taxi. 'Does it look Swiss enough?'

'Very Swiss indeed, Mum,' I reassure her.

Inside the hotel conservatory is yet more snow-themed paraphernalia. There are frosted fibreglass snowflakes, a small ice sculpture in the shape of a snowman, and another couple of penguin huddles. In a further attempt to make the Swiss feel at home, the central heating has been deliberately turned off. Lots of my parents' friends are gathering, looking chilly, but excited, and lots of Marley's friends are gathering, looking chilly, but mathematical.

Daria's family must be the Swiss-looking lot gazing in bewilderment at the penguins.

'Can you see Gina?' I whisper to Lara. 'Is she here yet?'

'Oh, for fuck's sake, Isabel, I can't see *anyone* in this crowd,' Lara snaps. 'That's the way it is when you're five foot nothing. I imagine life's a lot easier if you're a six-foot lacrosse-playing Amazonian.'

She totters off on her five-inch heels to help herself to a giant handful of smoked salmon blinis, leaving me alone with Russell. I've just dispatched him to fetch some champagne when a hand grips my elbow.

'Wizzy!'

It's Mum's best friend, Barbara, and her husband, Ron, both head-to-toe in Black Watch tartan. Barbara's suit is tartan. Her handbag is tartan. Even her *tights* are tartan. And Ron is no less committed, in Black Watch trews and a tam-o'-shanter. Mum will be so pleased. I give them both a kiss, then a sudden spontaneous hug when they tell me how wonderful I look.

'Mummy's been telling me how well you're doing,' says Barbara, giving me a little nudge in the ribs.

'Assistant Arts Editor of the *Saturday Mercury*, no less! Lovely to have a job that keeps Daddy happy for a change!' says Ron.

Mercifully, Russell is returning with the champagne.

'*And* Mummy told us you've met Joanna Trollope!' Ron continues. 'Was she as nice as she seems on the telly? We saw her on Gloria Hunniford, and—'

'No, Ron, I'm not talking about Isabel's job on the newspaper!' Barbara says. 'I'm talking about her *novel*. Mummy's been telling us all about it,' she says to me.

Talk about jumping the gun! 'Well, we'll just have to wait and see what the publishers think,' I tell them. 'We mustn't go getting all excited just yet. We don't want to jinx anything.'

'Yes, of course.' Barbara pulls an imaginary zip across her lips, then stands, beaming at me, for a moment. 'Oh, Iz-Wiz, we're ever so proud!' she suddenly squeals. 'Our only goddaughter, a famous author!'

Hang on a moment. I thought we'd agreed we weren't going to jinx anything.

'When will it be in the shops, do you think?' asks Ron. 'We'd like to make sure we get a big order in on Amazon. Do you think it'll be out in time for us to take it to the cottage in Blakeney this Easter?'

'Could you do some signed copies for us, do you think, Iz-Wiz?'

'We'll give you a list of the names we'd like you to write in them.'

'They'll be so thrilled to have a copy personally signed by a celebrity!'

'She might be too busy, though, Barb, off on her book tours, and on the telly and everything.'

I'm suddenly feeling very hot and sweaty. I mean, I know *I've* had book tours and TV in mind, but that's proper, constructive creative visualisation. When Ron and Barbara say it, it just sounds a bit silly and implausible.

'You didn't tell me anything about all this,' Russell suddenly says.

'What?'

'This novel of yours. Last I heard, you'd only just started the thing. And now it's going to be in the shops for Easter?'

I never said that, did I?

Barbara gives Russell a disapproving look. 'Iz-Wiz is very dedicated when she puts her mind to something.'

Russell snorts.

Well, bugger him.

'So if my novel weren't nearly finished, why would I have had a meeting *only the other day*,' I pause, for dramatic effect, 'with a *top literary agent*?'

'A top literary agent!' Barbara squeals.

'Joe Madison of Madison/Salisbury-Kent,' I add airily.

'Never heard of them,' declares Russell.

'They represent Katriona de Montfort,' I snap.

'The *Captain Kidd* woman?' Barbara gasps. 'Oh, *Isabel*.'

'Going to sell millions, Iz-Wiz, just like her?' Ron claps his hands in satisfaction.

'Yes,' I say, with another glare at Russell. 'I imagine I am.'

Barbara lets out another ear-piercing squeal of excitement.

'But, I mean, I don't want anyone to get their expectations up . . .' I begin.

But she wasn't squealing at that. She was squealing at something behind me. 'Malcolm! Vanessa!' she's saying, pushing past me. 'It's been so long!'

It's Gina's parents, Malcolm and Vanessa Deverill. Everybody starts greeting each other in that slightly manic way you do at weddings. Fortunately all the shrieking and the squealing and the flurries of Black Watch tartan give me a moment to glance surreptitiously around for Gina herself.

Thank God. Still no sign of her.

Vanessa, Gina's mother, looks as sweet as ever; the human equivalent of Mole from *The Wind in the Willows*. When I was little, it was a mystery to me how someone as horrible as Gina could have a mum as lovely as Vanessa. But then, when I was really little, I never paid very much attention to Malcolm, Gina's dad. The moment you get to know him – mystery solved. Because if Vanessa is the living embodiment of Mole, Malcolm Deverill is the human incarnation of the chief weasel from the Wild Wood.

'Miss Bookbinder!' Malcolm Deverill greets me now, with an actual, proper punch in the arm. 'How the hell are ya?'

Despite living in Britain for the last forty-five years, his Australian accent never fades in the slightest. He's gone silvery-grey since the last time I saw him, several years ago, but his leathery skin and shifty little eyes are the same as ever.

'I'm fine, Malcolm. Lovely to see you, Vanessa.'

'It's been too long, Isabel.' Vanessa hugs me. 'It's a

shame you and Gina don't see more of each other, now you're both in London.'

'How *is* Gina?' I say. 'And . . . er . . . is she here yet?'

'She'll be here any minute,' says Vanessa. 'They're just parking the car.'

'*They*?' I adopt a gossipy tone, hoping Vanessa will spill the beans on the Alpha Male.

'You'll fancy the pants off him.' Malcolm declares. 'Everyone does.'

'I doubt that.'

Malcolm's eyes narrow. He dislikes insubordination. Well, he's not Dad's oldest friend for nothing. 'What about you, then, Isabel? Got yourself a man yet?'

'Oh, Isabel doesn't have time for *men*,' says Barbara. She's either forgotten about Russell, or, more probably, she's decided he doesn't count. 'This clever girl's only gone and written a novel!'

'I don't believe it,' says Malcolm.

'Well, she has!' snaps Barbara.

'No, I mean, I can hardly believe the coincidence.' Malcolm stares me with those weaselly eyes. 'Gina's done exactly the same thing.'

Barbara and Ron look to Vanessa for confirmation or denial.

'It's true,' says Vanessa, turning more pink than ever. 'Gina's having a novel published.'

'Amazing. Your little Gina!' says Ron, politely. 'How did this all happen?'

'Well, her new boyfriend is some kind of agent . . .' begins Vanessa.

Malcolm bashes me on the arm again. 'When Gina first told us, I thought she said he was an *Asian*!'

We all go very, very quiet for a moment.

'Well, Iz-Wiz has a *top* literary agent,' Ron changes the subject. 'What was his name again, Iz? John Mandison?'

'Yes, yes,' I say, hastily. I should have remembered about Gina being signed with Joe Madison before I blurted out his name to Ron and Barbara earlier. I'm not sure I can pull off the pretence that he's my agent in front of the Deverills. The faster we're off the topic of literary agents, the better. 'Well, did you all have a lovely Christmas . . . ?'

'It wasn't John anything,' Russell interrupts with a belligerent air. 'It was Joe, you said. Joe Madison.'

'I don't believe it,' says Malcolm, again. 'This *is* a coincidence.'

'What's a coincidence?' demands Barbara, brightly.

'Gina has the same agent!' I announce. I think I've swept the wind out of Malcolm's sails, because he shoots me a look of dislike. 'Yes, I saw her at their offices the other day. She and I really will have to have a catch-up about all this some time! Anyway, I'd better be doing the rounds now, chat to some of these Swiss . . .'

'Oh, hang on, Isabel, don't go just yet.' Vanessa suddenly starts waving across the room. 'Look – you can chat to her about it right now!'

We all turn to stare at the icicle-decked entrance doors. Gina is striding in.

WoW! magazine with the *Sunday Sentinel*

YOU ARE WHAT YOU EAT

This week we delve into the eating habits of bestselling Novelist and glamour girl of the London Literati, Isabel Bookbinder.

'Just like my good friend Gwynnie Paltrow, I eat a completely macrobiotic diet. It's how I keep my figure in shape (a honed size eight the last time I checked) while at the same time keeping my energy up for all the many book launches and parties I have to attend.

'I start every day with a cleansing glass of macrobiotic lemon and hot water. If you can't get hold of macrobiotic lemons, I think the unwaxed ones would be a perfectly acceptable substitute. I'm not sure if it's possible to buy macrobiotic water. But I know that ordinary tap water has *microbes*, which is probably pretty much the same thing.

'For breakfast, I gorge myself silly on my first portion of organic blueberries of the day. That's *actual blueberries*, not just cheaty, sneaky blueberries, presented in some sort of delicious muffin format. Just a giant bowl of plain, unadorned blueberries. I mean, can you think of anything more appetising?

'Lunch is often out at a favourite restaurant – The Wolseley, for example – where I ~~enjoy~~ eat plain steamed fish. The waiters are very obliging, and always bring my meal without me even having to order. Even if I'd actually been hoping for a big, juicy hamburger or something.

91

'I go out to so many events that I rarely have the chance to eat a proper dinner, as it's very difficult to guarantee whether the smoked salmon blinis are macrobiotic or not. So I usually slip a handful or two of organic blueberries into my Lulu Guinness clutch bag, and nibble on those if I get a bit peckish. That's the beauty of blueberries – not only are they completely delicious, they're portable too!

'Then some more lovely cleansing hot water and lemon before I go to bed, so I can drop off to sleep feeling incredibly healthy and virtuous. All ready for another hard day's Novelist work tomorrow.'

Isabel wears cream trousers (£300) and black silk Mandarin-style shirt (£240) by Shanghai Tang, and flat pointy pumps (£275) by Emma Hope. Photo by Annie Leibovitz.

NEXT WEEK . . . WHAT DOES ELLE MACPHERSON EAT?

Chapter 8

Gina's Alpha Male boyfriend must be a little way behind, because she's sweeping into the room alone. And talk about a big entrance. She's wearing cream trousers and a black silk Mandarin shirt with flat pointy shoes, thereby showing off her incredible sense of style, her astonishing figure and the fact that she can wear flat shoes with trousers without looking dumpy. A simple black Miu Miu Alice band is holding back her glossy dark hair, and she's tanned enough to get away with no makeup.

With a sinking feeling, I realise she's just nicked the Most Glamorous Guest crown by stealth from right under my nose. In my brand-new putty silk, and my high bronze heels, with my fake tan that is secretly a bit patchy under the armpits and the hair and makeup that I spent over an hour perfecting, I suddenly feel as overdone as Mum's Christmas turkey.

And then I get another very nasty sinking feeling. There's her Alpha Male strutting in behind her, catching her up and slipping a Paul Smith-clad arm lightly around her shoulder. And Alpha Male is none other than Joe Madison.

I think I'm going to be sick.

In fact, *actually* being sick might be a superb potential diversion at this point. If I could aim for Gina's cream suede Emma Hope flats, so much the better. But I've never tried being sick at will. I'll opt for the next best thing: *acting* sick.

'Oh dear, I feel ever so sick.' I clutch Russell by the arm and try to look woozy.

Russell takes a giant pace backwards. 'Woooah. Mind the shoes.'

If I weren't so busy acting sick, I'd point out that his faux-leather loafers could only be improved by throwing up on them.

'Christ,' declares Malcolm. 'You look *terrible*.'

'Do you think it's something you've eaten?' asks Ron, concerned.

'Something she's *drunk*, more like,' bellows Malcolm, snatching my empty glass out of my hand and waggling it in that way people do when they mean someone's a boozer.

But I couldn't care less. Gina and Joe Madison are scanning the crowd, looking for her mum and dad. I need a way to avoid awkward questions until I've had a chance to speak to Joe in private. And explain how all these people have somehow managed to get the idea that he's my literary agent.

'You know, I think it *is* something I've eaten.' I clutch my side. 'Gosh, I hope none of you have had the blinis.'

'There's nothing *but* bloody blinis!' Malcolm barks.

'Get her a chair.' Barbara flaps her hands at Russell.

'No! I don't want to sit down! I need . . . I need fresh air.' I start pushing at the door handle on the French windows behind us.

But it's too late. Gina and Joe have seen us, and they're heading over. You know, even in the midst of my panic, I can't help noticing that Joe looks absolutely gorgeous.

Why didn't I pick a more attractive fake ailment than a dodgy tummy? I should have gone for something feminine and appealing, like . . . a dead faint! Yes! *That* would have been fantastic. I'd have looked delicate and fragile, just like a Victorian lady in a nineteen-inch corset. And if I'd aimed my swoon in Joe's direction, he'd have had to carry me outside to loosen my stays, or whatever it is you do with nineteen-inch corsets. And even though I don't actually have any stays to loosen, it would have given us time for me to explain all about the little misunderstanding.

Plus it would have been awfully nice to see how strong he is.

'Hi, everyone,' says Gina, as they reach us. 'Oh, hello, Isabel.'

Joe's eyes meet mine. '*Isabel?*'

'Oh, of course!' twitters Vanessa. 'You two already know each other!'

Right. It's going to have to be a dead faint after all. I flicker my eyelids, buckle at the knees, and lob myself towards Joe.

'Iz-Wiz!' shrieks Barbara.

Then I feel sharp fingernails clutch my shoulders. Someone is holding me up. 'Oh, fucking hell,' comes Gina's voice. 'What am I supposed to *do* with her?'

Well, this hasn't gone according to plan. I'm about to reverse from my faint and pull myself away from Gina, when somebody else grabs my ankles and hoiks them off the ground.

'I've got her this end,' says Russell.

No! *No!* I was meant to fall into Joe Madison's manly arms and be carried out like the heroine of a Barbara Taylor Bradford novel. Not get propped up at either end by Gina and Russell and be carried out like a sack of potatoes.

'She's too *heavy*!' Gina shrieks, loudly enough for half of Shepton Mallet to hear. 'I can't possibly hold her!'

'I'll take her,' says Joe, in a voice that would make me swoon if I hadn't pretended to already. 'You still got her ankles, mate?'

'Yeah,' puffs Russell. 'But I can't hold on for much longer.'

'She's like a lead *weight*!' announces Gina.

For crying out loud.

I sense a shuffling about at my head end and a much stronger, larger pair of hands grips me confidently instead. This is much more pleasant, for a moment, until the same hands shift to grip beneath my under-arms. Oh, please, God. Don't let my patchy fake tan come off on Joe's palms. Haven't I been humiliated enough?

'Better hold this way,' comes Joe's voice, from above my head. 'Can someone get those doors open?'

I keep my eyes tightly closed as we move off. I don't want to see Gina's appalled face, for one thing. And for another, I'm concentrating on simultaneously sagging in the middle while keeping my stomach muscles flat, just in case Joe should happen to notice. It's not as easy as you'd think. Probably the kind of thing regular Pilates is good for.

As soon as I hear the crunch of gravel, I know we're outside. I open my eyes and make a delicate, fragile sort of murmur.

'Hi, there.' Joe is looking upside down at me. His hair is flopping sexily over his eyes. 'Don't you worry, Isabel, darling. We've got you.'

Darling. Joe Madison just called me darling. Maybe this is going to work out better than I thought.

'Can't we dump her now?' Russell lets go of one ankle so fast that my foot bashes the gravel.

'Ow!'

'Careful, mate!' Joe snaps. 'She's not a sack of potatoes.'

Well, I'm glad somebody's noticed.

'Let's pop her down over here,' says Joe, walking backwards over to the Winter Wonderland on the lawn.

Russell makes a loud 'phew' kind of noise as they hoist me onto the sleigh. 'Thank Christ for that.'

'Don't be a wuss,' laughs Joe. 'She's light as a feather.'

I think I might have just accidentally let out a little moan.

'Isabel? Are you all right?'

'Oh, I'm feeling much better now.' Or I will be, the moment I can get rid of Russell. 'Perhaps, Russell,' I suggest, 'some hot sweet tea would be good.'

'God, yes,' says Russell, who is holding himself up on one of the reindeer as though he's just run the London Marathon.

'For *me*,' I say.

'Good idea.' Joe is taking off his Paul Smith jacket and draping it over my shoulders. It smells of something slightly sharp and citrus – some lovely vetiver scent by Jo Malone, I think – and it's all warm from his own body. 'And have you got someone you want him to fetch, Iz? Friend? Boyfriend?'

Is Joe Madison asking me if I have a boyfriend?

'God, no! I mean . . .'

'I'm her boyfriend,' says Russell. But he doesn't say it territorially. I actually think I can detect a distinct note of weariness. 'I'll get her mum.'

'No, don't get Mum. She'll only worry.'

'Lana, then.'

'*Lara*. No, Russell, Lara has quite enough on her plate. Just the tea will be fine, thank you.'

Russell slopes off towards the conservatory.

Right. I just need a moment to really savour a few things about this situation:

1) I'm alone with Joe Madison!

2) And he just called me darling!
3) And lent me his jacket!
4) And asked if I had a boyfriend! Well, sort of.

So now that the really important things are seared into my memory for ever, I can get on with making sure that Joe realises I haven't told everyone he's my literary agent. Which is basically true, by the way. I mean, all I said to Barbara and Ron was that I'd *had a meeting* with a top literary agent. I never *specifically* said it was *my* agent.

'Gosh,' I say. 'Weddings! You do meet some funny people!'

'I couldn't agree more.' Joe gives me a strange look. 'I mean, what are you even doing here, Isabel?'

Well, there's no need for him to sound so dubious. It's not like I'm stalking him or anything. 'It happens to be my *brother's* wedding,' I say, slightly frostily. 'I really ought to be asking what *you're* doing here.'

'Ahhh. So this Marley bloke is your brother?'

'Yes.'

'Well, no better reason to hit the booze than a family wedding!'

'I have not *hit the booze*,' I say, even more frostily. 'For your information, that was a dead faint.'

'Right,' says Joe, with a smile. 'A dead faint.'

'Anyway,' I say, to get us back on track. 'Weddings. Funny people. I mean, you're just chatting away to someone, and the next thing you know, they've formed the impression that Joe Madison is your literary agent!'

'What?'

'Well, we were just talking about Gina, you know, and how she's about to sign this totally *amazing*, megabucks, international book deal . . .'

He doesn't contradict me. So Gina's book deal is still on, then. Damn.

'. . . and next thing I know, everyone thinks it's *me* we've been talking about. Isn't that ridiculous? As if I'd have gone around making up stories like that!'

Joe just stares at me for a moment. Then he leans in close, and smoothes a bit of hair off my forehead. 'Oh, Isabel. We really do need to get you that hot sweet tea, don't we?'

I've had enough of this. I've no idea why, but Joe seems happiest labouring under the delusion that I'm some kind of lunatic.

'I don't need any hot sweet tea! I'm perfectly fine!' I start clambering down from the sleigh. 'If *anyone* needs hot sweet tea, it's those people in there who just completely misunderstood whose agent you were!'

'Well,' says Joe, 'they do sound a bit confused.'

'Yes! And it wasn't my fault *in the slightest*.'

Joe doesn't say anything. He just folds his arms and looks at me. His lips curl upwards a little bit at the corners. 'You're a very funny girl, Iz-Wiz.'

'Don't call me that!'

'It's sweet.'

'I'm not sweet!' I snap.

'It's a compliment.'

'No, it isn't. How would you like to be called sweet?'

'Well.' He rakes his hair back off his forehead so that he can direct the full force of his blue-eyed gaze on me. 'That would depend on who was doing the calling.'

It's the worst moment in the entire history of the world for my phone to start ringing.

Bloody Lindy Lyons.

'Shouldn't you get that?' asks Joe.

I root vaguely around in my clutch bag. 'Oh, what a shame,' I say, as it stops ringing. 'Still, if it's urgent, they'll call back.'

Joe is looking amused. 'Or you could call them?'

'Oh, no need.' I glance at the call register. 'Nobody important.'

And it isn't. At least, it isn't Lindy Lyons. It's an 01865 number, which I think is the code for . . .

Oh fuck. Oxford.

The only person I know who lives in Oxford is Chris Macbeth. It's his wife's constituency or something.

This means Lindy has told him I abandoned his precious phones and went off to Madison/Salisbury-Kent.

'Isabel? You're looking pale.' Joe steps closer and pulls his jacket around me. His hands linger slightly too long doing up the top button.

It's funny, but suddenly Lindy and Chris don't seem to matter all that much. I mean, so what if they're a bit pissed off? They're not actually going to *fire* me or anything. Like that time when they found out that Barney had actually started going to the restaurant of the week, instead of just distilling reviews of it. They whinged a bit, and threatened to make him pay the money back, but in the end, nothing actually came of it.

'Where's that boyfriend of yours with that tea?'

'You know, he isn't *really* my boyfriend.'

'No?' Joe frowns. 'He said he was.'

'He's just my . . . er . . . my date.'

'Your date?'

'Yes. I feel a bit sorry for him, you know. I thought a fun day at a wedding might be just the sort of thing he needs.'

Joe smiles again, one of the circuit-blowing kind this time. 'Isabel Bookbinder. Quite the philanthropist.'

'Well,' I say. 'I do try.'

'And is this a service you offer to anyone?'

Joe is standing so close to me now that I could stand up on tiptoes and place a kiss on his smooth, soft lips . . . Theoretically, of course.

'Well,' continues Joe, 'I'm not surprised to hear he's not *really* your boyfriend.'

'You're not?'

'No. He doesn't seem . . . your type.'

Suddenly, out of the corner of my eye, I see a tiny, blonde, slate-grey figure popping out of the conservatory doors and pelting towards us.

'Iz!' Lara gasps. 'Are you all right? Barbara told me what happened . . .' She stops dead as she notices Joe. Her mouth drops open slightly. '*Oh!*'

Joe extends a hand. 'Hi. I'm Joe.'

'Hello, *Joe*,' says Lara, in a tone of voice that's meant for me.

'I've been looking after Isabel,' he adds.

'Well,' says Lara, 'isn't Isabel lucky?'

'She does seem a lot better now,' Joe says. 'That's right, isn't it, darling?'

'Oh, yes. Much.'

Lara's eyebrows do a *he just called you darling* dance, but all she actually says is, 'Well, if you're feeling better, Iz-Wiz, the ceremony's starting in five minutes.'

Joe turns to me. 'Would you like me to carry you back in?'

Yes. Oh God, yes.

'Oh, she'll be fine to walk.' Lara starts to pull me back towards the conservatory.

'We've still got five minutes,' I say. 'No hurry.'

'Yes, but Matthew's saving us seats! He'll give them to someone else if we're not there in a minute.'

Having just messed up my chances of being carried by Joe Madison, I don't actually feel all that inclined to help Lara acquire six-and-a-half minutes of proximity to Matthew. But Lara has been in love with Matthew for twelve years, and I've only known Joe Madison for two days.

And it's not like I'm in love with him or anything.

'All right,' I tell Lara. 'Let's go.'

She gives me a grateful look. 'Maybe there'll be room for Joe to sit with us too.'

'Don't you worry about that,' says Joe. 'I'm just

going to get Gina's wrap from the car. It was colder inside than I thought.' He puts a hand on my shoulder, resting his thumb on my collarbone. 'I'm really glad you're feeling better, Iz-Wiz.'

And off he walks, towards his dark green sports car.

Chapter 9

The wedding ceremony is incredibly short and equally sweet.

I wish I could say the same for the receiving line. To the strains of something extremely laboured-sounding on a viola, we all start filing through into the dining room, stopping to shake hands on the way. At least, that's the principle. Naturally, in practice, everything jams up like the M25 on a bank holiday Monday and it's nearly half an hour before I finally reach Mum and Dad themselves.

'Isabel!' Mum gasps. 'Barbara told us you had a hurty tummy.'

'Actually,' I say, in case Joe happens to be anywhere nearby, 'it was a *dead faint*.'

'Darling! Are you all right?'

'I'm fine now, Mum.'

'Oh, of course, she's fine *now*,' scowls Dad. The morning suit he's hired is making him look more headmasterly than ever. Daria's mother is looking positively terrified of him. 'Fine *now*, after I've had the caterers throw out three hundred pounds worth of smoked salmon blinis.'

'I'm really sorry.'

'It's just typical, isn't it, Isabel?' Dad lowers his voice. 'You've always got to be the centre of attention. Even on your brother's wedding day.'

I make sure I give Marley an extra tight hug when I reach him at the end of the line. 'I'm sorry I caused a fuss about the blinis.'

Marley just blinks. 'Er . . .?'

'It doesn't matter,' I say. He looks so happy, I'm not sure he even noticed the blinis before they vanished. 'As long as you're having a wonderful day.'

Nearly everyone else has managed to get to my table before me. Matthew and Annie are pawing each other, while Lara engages them in slightly-too-bright conversation. Russell is doing the Sudoku in today's *Sunday Telegraph*. He's already made inroads on the bread basket and poured himself a large glass of wine.

'Weren't you meant to be getting me a cup of hot sweet tea?' I accuse him.

'Oh, right,' he says, and returns to his newspaper.

Mum has put Ron to the right of me, which is nice, and Malcolm Deverill to the left, which isn't quite so nice. Gina is the other side of Malcolm, with Joe on *her* left. He's already being monopolised by one of Malcolm's rants about immigration, so I catch Gina's eye.

'Sorry about before. I hope you didn't hurt anything, catching me like that.'

Gina shrugs. 'Well, you were very heavy.'

'Right. Thanks.'

'All that fuss,' Gina continues, 'and Joe carting you

out like laundry while everyone was staring.' She flashes her perfect teeth. 'Weren't you *embarrassed*?'

'Oh, not really,' I say, digging into the Gruyère soufflé that's just arrived. 'Joe was *so* nice to me that I really forgot any embarrassment.'

Well, I mean, really. She asked for it.

Gina's eyes glint a bit. 'And is that *your* boyfriend? In the polyester jacket? Doing the Sudoku?'

I'm just about to launch into another strenuous denial of my involvement with Russell, when Malcolm stops haranguing Joe, and turns to me.

'Feeling better now?'

'Yes, thank you, Malcolm.'

'Thought so. Certainly not too crook to guzzle this!' He jabs at my soufflé dish.

'It was a *dead faint*,' I say, for about the millionth time. 'I mean, doesn't anybody listen? 'I need all the energy I can get.'

'So, Isabel, tell us what you're up to these days.' Gina pushes her own, untouched soufflé towards Joe. 'Apart from falling down drunk at weddings, that is.'

I give her my own brand of fake smile. 'I'm a journalist, actually.'

'*And* Isabel is writing a book,' says Malcolm, giving Gina a hefty nudge. 'Joe's her agent, apparently.'

I glance at Joe. He's grinning at me. 'Actually, that's not quite right, Malcolm.' I lower my voice so that Ron can't hear. 'Ron and Barbara got the wrong end of the stick. All I said to them was that I'd *met* Joe Madison. I explained the whole mix-up to Joe earlier.'

'Right.' Malcolm doesn't look terribly convinced, but he at least doesn't actually start interrogating me. 'Why don't you tell Isabel all about *your* book deal, Gina, sweetheart? Give her a bit of encouragement. Some tips, even.'

It's at times like this that I can see why my dad has such a chip on his shoulder about Malcolm. Imagine sharing a boarding-school dormitory with this man. I think it's the kind of thing that, nowadays, the Human Rights Act is there to prevent.

'Isabel already knows that Gina's going to be a big star,' says Joe, sliding an arm around Gina.

I've lost my appetite all of a sudden. It's a good thing our soufflé dishes are being taken away, even though they're being replaced with what looks like . . . yes, it is . . . a giant raclette grill.

Honestly. I appreciate Mum's efforts to welcome the Swiss, but what the hell are we going to get for dessert? Muesli?

'So if Joe isn't your agent,' Gina asks me, as everyone else oohs and aahs over the raclette, 'how *did* you meet him?'

'Isabel came to interview me about new books for her newspaper,' says Joe, tearing into a piece of meat.

Oh God, even the way he eats is sexy. I've really got to get a grip on this. It's turning into one of those all-consuming obsessions.

'Which newspaper?' demands Malcolm, clearly hoping I'll say the *Central Somerset Gazette*.

'The *Saturday Mercury*.'

His face pinches, like he's just sucked a slice of lemon. 'Oh.'

'God, that reminds me!' Joe slams down his raclette fork. 'I can't believe I forgot! Isabel, what's going to happen with your boss?'

'Er . . .'

'There's going to be trouble, isn't there?' He's looking excited.

I can't believe this. He's aware that I'm in trouble with my boss, and he's *pleased* about it?

Joe leans across to Malcolm. 'Isabel's boss is Chris Macbeth.'

Malcolm barks with laughter. 'Crikey!'

Gina is looking annoyed. 'What's so funny?'

'Didn't you read the papers this morning, sweetheart?' Malcolm says. 'The Home Secretary's husband has been caught playing away from home.'

I stare at them. 'What?'

'You know Millicent Petersen?' Joe asks Gina.

'Of course,' she says, swishing her shiny hair, and looking serious. 'I read her at school.'

'She's been having this completely depraved fling with *Mr* Caroline Macbeth. Bondage, baby oil . . . you name it. And of course, they can't resist reliving all the happiest moments over email. *Then* Macbeth's own newspaper runs the emails in the middle of an article about her yesterday!' Joe turns to me. 'Didn't you see it, Isabel?'

'No,' I squeak. 'No, I didn't.'

'Well, it was certainly educational! We learned a lot about all the things the Home Secretary's husband likes to do.'

'God, I hope it brings down that bitch,' Malcolm is saying with satisfaction. 'Her and her "Stop the Sleaze" crap.'

'Let me . . . let me get this straight,' I hear myself say, although my voice sounds very far away. 'The *Saturday Mercury* printed an article about Millicent Petersen which contained . . . *lewd* emails between her and Chris Macbeth?'

'Yup,' Joe says. 'In his *very own* section, would you believe? God only knows how the emails got out. Must be an employee with a grudge.'

'Must be,' I croak.

'They'll root out whoever's responsible,' Malcolm is saying. 'Make them take the heat. Try to deflect attention off the Home Secretary.'

If the phone calls I've been avoiding all weekend mean what I think they mean, the *Saturday Mercury* already knows who's responsible.

'Hey,' Joe calls across the table to Russell, who's still buried in his Sudoku. 'Is that the *Telegraph*? Chuck it over here a second.'

Grudgingly, Russell does so.

'MACBETH'S DUNCE-INANE BLUNDER' says a box down the right-hand side of the front page.

The Home Secretary had no comment last night on the newspaper blunder that led to the exposure of her husband's affair with author Millicent Petersen.

Renowned arts journalist Chris Macbeth was in hiding yesterday after his own newspaper, the *Saturday Mercury*, included the text of explicit emails in an article Macbeth had written about Ms Petersen. Their affair is believed to have started when the pair met at a book launch party several months ago.

News of the affair could not have come at a worse time for Caroline Macbeth, who has just launched a 'Stop the Sleaze' campaign, calling for a return to traditional values. Mrs Macbeth was seen hiding her face in her hands as her car sped away from 10 Downing Street to her Oxford constituency last night.

The source of the leak is not yet known, but government insiders insisted that it was politically motivated, and calculated to cause maximum embarrassment to the Home Secretary.

The *Saturday Mercury* said that a full internal investigation would be launched, and

I can't read any more of this. No, I mean my eyes have actually gone all blurry. All I can see right now is Chris Macbeth's computer screen, as if I were standing right in front of it. I can see myself forwarding the email exchange to Barney. I start typing in his email address, which comes up automatically in the address box on AutoComplete . . .

Except it didn't, did it?

What *actually* came up was an email address that starts off with exactly the same letters as Barney's. An email address I'd just sent the *proper* Millicent Petersen article to. Barry_Goldstein@SatMercury.com

I was in such a rush to get away to Madison/Salisbury-Kent that I didn't even notice I'd sent the emails to the wrong person. And Barry Goldstein, subediting genius that he is, thought it was all part of the same article.

This is why Lindy has been phoning me since yesterday morning.

This is why Chris Macbeth was phoning me from his wife's Oxford constituency.

Or, even more scarily, maybe it was Caroline Macbeth phoning me herself. I mean, I've ruined the poor woman's life. I've ruined the *Home Secretary*'s life.

She's going to set MI5 on me.

'I feel sick.'

'What, *again*?' says Malcolm, grabbing the newspaper and turning to page four with a salacious gleam in his eye. 'Look, you can even read the emails . . .'

'Excuse me, please . . .'

I manage to get up and stagger out towards the bathrooms.

Isabel Bookbinder
Re:View
The Eighth Floor
Behind Recycling Bins
London

The Home Secretary
The House of Commons
The Houses of Parliament
Big Ben
London

5 January

Dear Home Secretary,

Oh God. I'm really, really sorry about this.

Would it help at all if I assured you that it wasn't politically motivated, and wasn't intended to cause you maximum embarrassment? I mean, I've got absolutely nothing against you, or anybody else in your government. I may not have actually voted for you, but then I didn't vote for the other lot either.

If it's any consolation, I think you're much, much prettier than Millicent Petersen, and far too good for your cheating wretch of a husband. My friend Barney always said he was sexually deviant.

Please let me know if there's anything I can do to make this up to you. I suspect there isn't.

Yours apologetically,

Isabel Bookbinder

PS. Please, please, please don't set MI5 on me. Eliminating me will not change the fact that your career is in tatters and your marriage a failure.

PPS. Again, sorry.

Chapter 10

All right. Let's try to be positive about this.

I'm not just going to sit in a corner and howl. I've learned a little trick, you see, from Lara. It's this cognitive behavioural exercise she does with her clients whenever they're stressed about something. Which in Lara's clients' case is practically *all the time*.

What you do is, you start by writing down a list of whatever Absolute Worst-Case Scenarios you think are going to happen. Lara's clients, for example, all have these completely bonkers Absolute Worst-Case Scenarios they've got their knickers in a twist about. Like, they forgot to put a piece of organic fruit in the kids' lunchbox last Tuesday, therefore their children will fail all their A levels and grow up to be crack addicts. Or their husbands never help with the cooking, therefore they married the wrong man and their whole life is a meaningless failure.

Well, I didn't stand a hope in hell of getting to sleep after the day I've had, so I've come downstairs to nibble on some wedding cake while I make my own list of Absolute Worst-Case Scenarios.

1) Instant dismissal by *Saturday Mercury*, followed by scary-sounding internal investigation.
2) Higher-than-average chance of being assassinated by MI5.
3) Unless Dad finds out about all this, and kills me first.

The ideal at this stage of the exercise, by the way, is that you start to realise just how ludicrous your Absolute Worst-Case Scenarios sound and laugh it all off. Though I've been staring at my list for half an hour now. And I'm still not laughing.

But that's all right, because the second stage will sort me out for certain. What you do next is Challenge the Assumptions. Lara's very good at this bit. She gently points out to her clients that their children will *not* take up crack cocaine simply because of a missing tangerine, or that they are *not* a meaningless failure simply because their husband has never bothered to find out where they keep the saucepans. And anyway, their husbands' failure to help with the cooking is actually very passive aggressive, suggesting that if anyone's really a failure in life, he is. So everybody goes away reassured and happy.

Apart from the passive aggressive husbands, I suppose.

Still, if Lara's barmy clients can Challenge their Assumptions, so can I.

So. Let's see. OK, the scary investigation by the *Saturday Mercury*. Well, this is a tricky place to start.

The thing is that, technically speaking, this isn't so much assumption as cold, hard fact. I mean, if I turned up at Lara's offices *with a copy of a national Sunday newspaper* stating that there was going to be a full internal investigation of the email leak, even *she'd* have a hard time proving that the assumption was a bit creaky.

I think I'll leave that one for now. Come back to it when I've had a bit more practice.

Right. This MI5 business. This should be a much easier one to challenge. Because even I know this one is all in my head. Pissed off as Caroline Macbeth probably is, she happens to be a cabinet minister. And everyone knows cabinet ministers are responsible, respectable, law-abiding people. Cabinet ministers just don't go around ordering MI5 to assassinate perfectly harmless civilians. Apart from anything else, they'd never get away with it.

Although I imagine that the beauty of using MI5 is that their work is undetectable.

So if I were to die, suddenly, in a mysterious car accident . . . Or drop down dead in a crowded shopping centre, of seemingly natural causes . . . Or 'fall' out of a ninth-floor window, leaving the coroner to record an open verdict, while a whispering campaign hinted at an unexpected suicide . . .

Of course, no one ever tells you the obvious downside to Challenging your Assumptions: when you actually start thinking them through, they suddenly seem a lot more likely. I think this is another one I'm going to have to come back to. And just make sure I avoid cars, shopping centres, and ninth-floor windows until then.

Right, well, I've really sped through these! Now I've only got the last one to deal with.

Dad.

Actually, the fear of Dad killing me is an Absolute Worst-Case Scenario I've thrashed out with Lara on many an occasion before now, with limited success. Lara can tell me until she's blue in the face that Dad isn't *really* going to kill me, that even losing my third job in as many years won't actually drive him to . . . whatever the Latin word for killing your daughter is. Daughter-slaughter?

But I'm just wondering if, this time, I needn't even bother. I mean, it doesn't matter *how* much Dad rants and raves and bellyaches about the chaos I've caused at the *Saturday Mercury*. Because the minute I tell him about my book deal with Aadelman Stern, that sneer will be wiped off his face!

And I do realise that Aadelman Stern haven't actually offered me a book deal yet. I just have this gut feeling that once they read *Showjumpers*, they'll at least want to meet me. And once they've seen what a great Look I've got, and noticed how seriously I've taken all the diet and exercise, and heard about the complimentary riding crops . . . Well, no one in their right mind would turn all that down, would they?

'Iz?' It's Mum, blinking her way, mole-like, into the kitchen. 'Are you all right?'

'I'm fine. I couldn't sleep.'

She puts a hand to my forehead. 'Maybe you're still suffering from those horrible rancid blinis. You were right, Isabel – *everyone* admitted they tasted funny.'

'I'm OK. Honestly.'

She's putting the kettle on. 'I'll do you a cup of tea and a nice cosy hot-water bottle to take back to bed. I need something to help me sleep myself.'

'It's the excitement of the wedding, Mum.'

She turns to me, beaming. 'It *was* a success, wasn't it, Iz-Wiz? And the food was all right, apart from the blinis?'

'The food was delicious.'

'Because I'd had my last-minute doubts, you know, about serving an all-Swiss menu. Your dad said it was a silly idea.'

I make a mental note only ever to cook Swiss food for Dad from this moment on.

'Everyone loved the food.'

'I *thought* so!' Mum makes a little triumphant fist. 'That nice young man of Gina's made a particular point of complimenting me on the chocolate fondue.'

Something about the combination of Joe Madison and chocolate fondue has made me feel a bit funny. 'I . . . er . . . didn't try the chocolate fondue.'

'Yes, I noticed you weren't at your table for dessert.'

'I was feeling sick again,' I say, which is completely true. I spent most of the latter part of the wedding breakfast locked in one of the toilet stalls with my head against the floor. The rest of the time I spent scurrying around the lobby pinching the hotel guests' leftover Sunday newspapers, just to see how bad the Chris Macbeth story really was.

'What's that you've got there?' Mum suddenly asks, pointing at my notebook. 'Some of your novel?'

I turn the page before she can see my Absolute Worst-Case Scenarios. 'Kind of.'

'You know, Iz-Wiz, I wish you'd told *me* you'd got yourself a top literary agent. I had to hear it from Barbara this afternoon. If I'd known before Friday, I wouldn't have gone and sent your book to that Aardvark man.'

Bloody Barbara. Honestly, that woman's got an overactive imagination.

'Barbara got it all wrong, Mum. I told her I'd *met* a top literary agent, that's all.'

'Oh! Well, that's good. Because to be honest, Iz-Wiz, I'm not even sure you'll need a literary agent. *I* can do a lot of those things for you.'

I stare at her. 'Er . . . Mum, do you know what a literary agent *does*?'

Not that I'm all that sure I know the answer to this question myself. But what I do know is that a large part of their job is standing around in Paul Smith suits looking incredibly sexy. And I'm not sure how good Mum would be at that.

'Of course I do! They sort things out with the publishers, don't they? They make all the phone calls and everything . . .' Mum is suddenly looking anxious again, 'Gosh, Iz-Wiz, I hope that Aardvark man won't mind that I gave him *your* phone number, not your agent's. You know, in the covering letter.'

'Covering letter?'

'Well, you *have* to write a covering letter, Iz-Wiz. That's what the writing manual said. I made a photocopy of that too, so you could see I hadn't written anything silly.' She goes over to her handbag, sitting on the telephone table, where Dad hates her leaving it ('It's a *telephone* table, Moira, not a *hand-bag* repository'), and pulls out a blurry photocopy from her handbag. 'Here you are, darling.'

I look down at the piece of paper. 'Dear Mr Aadelman Stern,' Mum has written, in longhand.

Please find enclosed a copy of my debut novella, *Showjumpers*. Though I am sure you get letters like this all the time, I assure you that you will be making a terrible mistake if you do not consider my work. I was only fourteen when I wrote this excellent piece, described as 'certainly original' by the critics.

'You *made up* reviews?'

'No!' Mum looks shocked at the very suggestion. 'That was a direct quote from Mrs Woodmansterne.'

I carry on reading.

I'm sure you'll want to give me a call and offer me a book deal. I should tell you that although you will find me charming and polite, I am certainly no pushover.

120

'I put that in,' Mum says, reading over my shoulder, 'so they don't think they can swindle you.'

'Yes,' I say. 'That's going to be a big help.'

> My phone number is 07700 900103. Please try not
> to call during the day, as I am very busy at work
> (Assistant Arts Editor of the *Saturday Mercury*).
> Monday and Thursday evenings are also a bad time,
> as I attend a weaving class at my local gym.

'Spinning. *Spinning*, Mum.'

'Iz-Wiz, don't be difficult. I was only trying to avoid you missing his call.'

> In conclusion, I firmly believe that I would be a credit
> to your organisation.
>
> Yours faithfully, Isabel Bookbinder.
>
> PS. You may feel that my novel could do with one
> or two small improvements. I can assure you that I
> will be very easy-going about this, and not find
> myself 'artistically compromised'. I was always very
> accepting of my mother's suggestions for improving
> my homework.

'You see?' Mum is saying. 'I told you I hadn't written anything silly.'

I don't even know where to begin. 'Mum . . .'

'Anyway, I really should be getting back to bed.' Mum stifles a deep yawn. 'I'd like a couple of hours' sleep before I start breakfast.' She kisses me on the top of my head before pottering out of the kitchen. 'Sweet dreams.'

Ha! Some chance.

My best hope is that Aadelman Stern are too busy even to bother reading the covering letter. It's a possibility. One of my duties on *Re:View* was to deal with the letters sent in by readers. And I always took 'deal with' to mean 'chuck straight into the recycling bins without opening'. I can only pray that Aadelman Stern take the same kind of professional approach. Because if they don't, I'm screwed.

I mean, *just* when you've delved painfully into your psyche, Challenging Assumptions left, right and centre, you're suddenly dumped with a whole new raft of Absolute Worst-Case Scenarios to sort through. Like:

1) Aadelman Stern are going to think I'm a total weirdo.
2) Total weirdos don't get book deals.
3) So Dad *is* going to kill me, after all.

But I'm not going to panic. It's not like people at Aadelman Stern are going to run about town telling anyone who'll listen about this total weirdo called Isabel Bookbinder, and her barmy covering letter. And there are oodles more publishers in London, bigger and better ones even than Aadelman Stern. Probably now I've made high-flying contacts like Katriona de Montfort, all I'll really need to do is some selective name-dropping, and I'll be back in the game.

'Yes,' I try out, to my reflection in the kitchen windows, 'I *am* a close personal friend of Katriona's, actually. She's been *extremely* encouraging. In fact, it was Katriona herself who suggested I bring *Showjumpers* to you . . .'

See? Everything's going to be all right. Things are even *better*, in some ways, now that Mum's mucked up my chances with Aadelman Stern. I've got the chance, now, to type the manuscript up, like I wanted, and to change the snogging into bonking, and . . .

Oh. I think I just heard the newspaper arrive.

Probably the whole Caroline Macbeth scandal will have died down a little bit by now. I mean, wasn't there a small earthquake yesterday, somewhere in . . . Bolivia? Or Botswana, perhaps. That should have knocked the story right off the front pages. Or there's always the Middle East. They can usually be relied upon to fill up 'Column Inches', one way or another.

I peer around the kitchen doorway into the hall, to see if I'm right, and there's something on the doormat.

I was right. The newspaper is there. Dad hasn't bullied the delivery boy into doing a massive detour to get to this house first for nothing. But – oh God – even from back here I can see the word 'MACBETH' screaming at me from the headline. I mean, it's appalling, really. Doesn't the press have the slightest nugget of humanitarian concern for all those poor earthquake victims in Bolivia? Or Botswana. Now *that's* a story that has a devastating impact on people's entire lives. Not just salacious dinner-party gossip for a nation that has nothing better to do with its time than go sticky-beaking into other people's business.

Gingerly, I pick up the paper, and fold it out, to see what the developments are today.

> Chris Macbeth, disgraced husband of the Home Secretary, last night blamed the email error that led to the exposure of his affair on a junior employee.

I sit down, suddenly, on the bottom stair.

> Isabel Bookbinder, 31, a clerical assistant on the Saturday Mercury, is believed to have been responsible for the gaffe, which has already seen Caroline Macbeth's many critics tearing into her new 'Stop the Sleaze' initiative.
>
> 'I have no idea how Miss Bookbinder votes,' Chris Macbeth said, from his Oxfordshire home, last night, 'but I am deeply shocked that she has chosen to play dirty politics in this manner. She always seemed a very simple sort to me. Clearly appearances can be deceptive.'
>
> For full story, see pages 4, 5, 6 and 7. For editorial opinion and comment, see pages 22 and 23. For letters, see page 24.

Oh my God. Oh my *GOD*.

My name is in the papers. My role – my stupid,

embarrassing role – in this whole sordid affair, is all over the papers.

But something else about me is all over the papers too. Something far, far worse than the fact I've just become a national laughing stock. It's right there, in black and white, in the second damning paragraph.

My little untruth about being the deputy arts editor has been exposed. I've been outed.

Outed, to Dad, as a *clerical assistant*.

Chapter 11

I just managed to make it to Castle Cary station in time for the 06.43 to Paddington.

Lara's going to kill me for sneaking away from Mum and Dad's without her, but she'll just have to join the queue. Besides, she ought to know that I would never leave her alone with Russell to get the train back to London together unless it was a complete and utter emergency.

And as a woman of science, she ought to understand that doing a dawn flit was actually very logical. I mean, it's basic Darwinism, isn't it? Doesn't each species do whatever it can to survive? Well, I wasn't going to stick around and see what happened to the Isabel Bookbinder species when Dad picked up the newspaper.

Of course, I took the bloody newspaper away with me and abandoned it in the taxi on the way to Castle Cary station, but that isn't going to put an end to the problem. As far as I can see from the wide selection of papers that I picked up at the station shop, the discovery of my name has given fresh life-blood to the whole sorry Chris Macbeth affair. There's a range of editorial opinion, from the *Daily Mail*'s apoplectic

126

conspiracy theories to the *Guardian*'s contention that I must be some kind of care-in-the-community mental deficient, more to be pitied than chastised. The only thing they all agree on is my age: apparently, thirty-one.

It's sad, but I suppose Chris Macbeth has had to take his miserable revenge where he can find it.

I've had some time to think since the paper dropped onto the doormat, and I've decided that this is even more of a disaster than it first seemed. I mean, it isn't *only* Dad who'll read this story. What's going to happen when the people at Aadelman Stern connect the name of the author of the barmy covering letter with the name they're seeing in their newspaper? By tomorrow, no doubt, the entire covering letter *and* selected highlights – the embarrassing snogging bits, probably – from *Showjumpers* will be splashed across the papers. Either that, or I'm going to be the subject of one of those humiliating chain emails that wings its way around the world, so that people on every continent can do the virtual equivalent of pointing and staring and laughing.

Though I suppose if that provides a bit of light relief for those earthquake victims in Bolivia/Botswana, then one good thing has come out of this awful mess.

It's not much consolation, though. I mean, *now* how am I going to get a book deal in time to compete with Gina's? I can come up with a pseudonym, I suppose, but any hope of using *Showjumpers* is down the Swanee. Though perhaps if I changed all the characters' names, and made it about . . . rock-climbing, instead of showjumping, I might get away with just repackaging it. But I'll have to rethink the whole complimentary riding crop thing, which will take *for ever* . . .

Oh, and lest I underestimate the damage for a single instant, let's not forget that Joe Madison will be reading all about this as well. God, please don't let *him* believe I'm thirty-one! And I can only hope he takes one of the papers that paints me as a rather glamorous, Mata Hari kind of figure, and not – please, not – the *Guardian*.

This effing story is going to haunt me everywhere I go. I mean, that old man along the carriage is obviously completely engrossed in the whole thing. He's barely looked up from his *Telegraph* since he got on. I don't think he's turned a page in nearly twenty minutes.

It's a bit odd. Come to think of it, it's also a bit odd that he came and sat so close to me. It's a 6.43 train, for Christ's sake. I don't think I've ever seen a carriage so empty. In fact, we're the only people in it.

Great. Trust me to end up with the dodgy old pervert.

Except he doesn't *look* like a dodgy old pervert. I mean, obviously, you never can tell. But he's really rather smartly turned out, in an old-fashioned gentleman-farmer sort of style. A tweedy suit, a stiff tweed cap, a dark green waxed jacket, and leather brogues that are polished to a regimental shine. He must have been in the army or something.

Oh God. I think I know what's going on here. He's MI5, isn't he?

OK, now this is really scary. For crying out loud, where's a train conductor when you need one? I mean, what's the use of carefully avoiding car journeys and crowded shopping centres if I'm just going to be ruthlessly eliminated on the six forty-three to Paddington?

Right. I just need to stay calm. A bit of my customary sang-froid, and I'll get through this alive. All I have to do is e-a-s-e myself out of my seat, so he doesn't notice, and . . .

Shit. He's seen me. His eyes have darted away from his newspaper.

And they're the cold, blank eyes of a ruthless assassin, let me tell you. That fake gentleman-farmer's garb is fooling no one. MI5 have quite obviously sent one of their very top men. Which, in a way, is sort of a compliment.

I e-a-s-e myself back into my seat. My assassin has started 'reading' his paper again. OK. So it seems as if making a mad dash for it probably isn't going to fool this wily old pro. And he might *look* a bit doddery, but you just know that if I reach for the emergency cord, he'll have crossed the aisle and slashed my throat before I've even stretched my arm out. But he needn't underestimate me just yet. Like a Masai warrior, knowledge of my home terrain is my power. 007 over here won't know that this carriage will fill up with commuters the moment we get to the next station, and his chance will be lost. In the meantime, I'm going to make sure that if he *does* strike before the next stop, he won't get away with it. There's a very good reason why they say the pen is mightier than the sword.

I edge my Smythson notebook from out of the top of my handbag and start writing, as casually as I can. I knock off a letter to the police in no time at all, then start a heart-rending goodbye to Lara . . .

Oh my God, he's getting up. The train is slowing down for the commuters' stop, and he's getting up, and moving towards me.

So this is it. All I ask is that it's swift. Swift and merciless. And totally painless. And non-disfiguring . . .

Oh. He seems to be getting off at Pewsey.

Well, probably he realised I was writing a damning statement that would expose him and his employers. Either that, or he really *was* a gentleman farmer. The really scary thing is that I don't know either way. I'm just going to have to be permanently on my guard from now on.

I loiter at Paddington for an hour or so, waiting for the rush hour to die down, hop onto the Hammersmith and City line, then set off through the freezing streets back towards Russell's flat.

The Russell situation is one I'm going to have to address, I suppose. That is, once I've first addressed the fact that I'm a national laughing stock, and that MI5 are after me. You've got to prioritise. I'll just sit him down, probably with a calming Sudoku nearby, and tell him gently but firmly that things don't seem to be working out between us, and . . .

Hang on a moment. It looks like some kind of protest is going on outside the flat. There are about fifteen or twenty men, and one or two women, jostling for space on the icy pavement. You can tell right away that they're not MI5, because MI5 are trained to be covert, aren't they? They don't gather in great big huddles like this, chowing down on KitKats and passing round cardboard trays of Starbucks coffee cups; pointing those long camera lenses up at the bedroom windows.

'Excuse me, love?' One of the men sees me hovering. 'You don't live around here, do you?'

'Er . . .'

'I'm with the *Daily Mirror*. D'you know an Isabel Bookbinder at all?'

It's the paparazzi. Oh, my God! I've got my very own paparazzi! Under different circumstances, I'd be absolutely thrilled.

'Isabel Bookbinder?'

'Yeah. She's the one that leaked this Caroline Macbeth sex scandal.'

'*Chris* Macbeth sex scandal,' I correct him. I mean, it's the least I can do.

He frowns. 'Yeah, whatever. Anyway, have you ever seen this Isabel Bookbinder around the street? Woman in her early thirties? Might look a bit . . . you know . . . simple.'

'She's *not* in her early thirties! And she isn't—' I stop myself. 'No, I don't know her, I'm afraid.'

'Oh, well, not to worry, love. Maybe this gentleman will be able to help us. 'Scuse me, sir,' he calls out to someone else coming up the street behind us.

'Yeah?'

It's Russell. I'd know that flat, expressionless voice anywhere. He must have been on the train behind me, which means he left Mum and Dad's before breakfast this morning. That's pretty rude. Still, Russell's manners are the least of my concerns right now. I walk away, fast, without turning round to face him. Only when I've gone round the next corner do I stop, and peer around the wall to see what's going on outside the flat.

He's opened up the front door, and he's letting the paparazzi in!

I pull my phone out of my bag and dial Russell's mobile number. 'Tell anyone it's me,' I say, when he answers, 'and you're dead.'

'Isabel?' he says.

I can hear the chorus of, 'Is that her? Is that her?' in stereo, both down the phone and somewhere a little way along the street.

'For God's sake, tell them it's a *different* Isabel,' I hiss.

'It's a different Isabel,' Russell announces to the paparazzi, unconvincingly. 'God, Isabel,' he continues, barely bothering to lower his voice, 'you're in a bit of shit, aren't you? Have you read the papers today?'

'*Yes*, I've read the papers.' The gang of photographers are still trooping through the front door.

'And I know I'm in a bit of shit! So why are you letting the paparazzi in?'

'How do you even know the paparazzi are here?'

'Sixth sense,' I say hastily, before the man from the *Mirror* puts two and two together and starts combing the surrounding streets to find me. 'Just tell them all to go away! This is a gross invasion of privacy! Tell them you'll report them to the Press Complaints Commission.'

'Well, I've *got* to let them in, Isabel.' Russell sounds disapproving. 'It's barely two degrees outside. I have to offer them a cup of tea.'

I have to say, I've absolutely no idea where this new-found milk of human kindness is coming from.

There's a bit of conversation in the background for a moment, then Russell speaks again. 'Quick question, Isabel – the man from the *Sun* wants to know if you'd be interested in doing a Page Three photo shoot with the headline "Office Boob"? They say it'll pay really well, and they'd make it very tasteful.'

'*No*, Russell. Tell him *no*.'

'But he says plenty of over-thirties have done them . . .'

My call waiting is bleeping. Even though I'm strenuously avoiding incoming calls, I check to see who it is: *Mum Mobile*.

'Just get rid of them, Russell.' I switch the calls. 'Mum?' My voice has suddenly gone all wobbly, the way it does when someone's unexpectedly nice to you in the middle of a horrible day. 'Oh, Mum . . .'

'No, Isabel, it's your father.'

'Dad?' But Dad never, *ever* calls me. My heart skips a beat. 'Is everything all right? Is Mum . . . ?'

'No, your mother is *not* all right.' Dad sounds even more clipped than usual. 'Isabel, there are eleven newspaper photographers on my doorstep. They want to know if you live here.'

'Oh my God. They're there too?'

I can hear Mum's voice in the background. 'Did you get hold of her, John? Is she all right?'

'I'm fine, Mum,' I call. 'Tell her I'm fine, Dad. It's all . . . it's all a big misunderstanding.'

'I certainly hope it *is* a big misunderstanding, Isabel. Because I'm extremely interested to hear why the *Telegraph* is calling you a "clerical assistant".'

'It's a mistake,' I croak. 'You know what journalists are like, Dad. Newspapers are always full of factual inaccuracies. They've all managed to get my age completely wrong, for heaven's sake! And the *Guardian* said I'm an imbecile!'

Dad's silence speaks volumes.

'Look, Dad . . .'

'You have excelled yourself this time, Isabel,' he spits. 'Not only have you lied to me, but you have made me a laughing stock as well.'

'No, Dad! *I'm* the laughing-stock! Not you!'

'Isabel, *my friends* are reading these newspaper articles. *My staff* is reading these newspaper articles. *My pupils* are reading these newspaper articles.'

'Oh, yes,' I say miserably, 'I suppose that's true.'

'I have spent months telling people – *boasting* to people – that my daughter is the Assistant Arts Editor of the *Saturday Mercury*.'

This is too much to believe. 'You've boasted?'

He doesn't answer my question. 'What is Malcolm Deverill going to say now, Isabel? Tell me that.'

I should have known it would all come down to Malcolm Deverill in the end.

'Look, Dad, I'd better go . . .'

'Hang on,' he snaps. 'Somebody else wants to talk to you. For pity's sake, Lara,' I hear him say, as he walks away from the phone, 'talk some bloody sense into her.'

'Isabel?' Lara sounds a bit breathless, and extremely stressed. 'Are you all right?'

'I've been better.' My voice has gone very wobbly. 'Things have gone a bit pear-shaped.'

'*Pear-shaped?*' Lara hisses. 'Isabel, there are reporters everywhere. You've pissed off the *Home Secretary*. MI5 might be after you! You could meet a horrible death in a suspicious road accident!'

'Hey! That's *my* Absolute Worst-Case Scenario! It's not allowed to be yours.'

'All right. You're right, Iz. I'm sorry.'

'I need you to Challenge my Assumptions, for God's sake! I mean, what would you say if this was a client of yours talking? You wouldn't start panicking them with . . . with *irrational* fears of suspicious car accidents, would you?'

'It's true,' she says. 'I wouldn't.'

'Good.'

'But . . . I mean, you will be extra specially careful, won't you, Iz? When you're crossing the roads and things?'

'Yes!' I snap. 'I'll be extra specially careful.'

'OK,' she says. 'I didn't mean to panic you. It's just . . .' she lowers her voice further, 'things are a bit stressful around here. Your dad's not happy. He kept yelling at your mum until Matthew stepped in and calmed everything down.' She lets out a little sigh. 'Matthew's being great in general, actually. He's going to drive me to the station later. Do you think I should buy him a little present or something, to say thank you?'

'Lara! I'm having a crisis here! I need you firing on all cylinders, not going all cow-eyes and drippy over my stupid brother! Just for God's sake, get yourself back to London as quick as you can . . .'

From the noise Lara makes, I know there's a problem.

'But, Iz-Wiz, I'm going straight from Paddington to Heathrow, remember? I've got a conference in Edinburgh all week.'

Now I *do* remember. 'But . . . what am I going to do without you? I can't stay at Russell's, Lara, with all these paparazzi around! I need you here! I need your help.'

'Iz, if I could skip it, I would, but . . .'

'Fine.' I know I shouldn't take it out on Lara, but I'm at snapping point here. 'Go to your conference.

Swan around your swanky hotel while I spend the night out on the freezing streets of Hammersmith.'

'Iz, call Barney. You know he'll let you stay.'

'I don't need charity, thank you! Enjoy your drive with Matthew.'

'Isabel, wait . . .'

'I've got to go. Call me when you're back.' I hang up.

This is an Absolute Worst-Case Scenario, unfolding right here before my very eyes. And I'm far too cold and miserable to do any Challenging of bloody Assumptions.

My phone rings again, and with a surge of temper, I snatch it up. 'What?'

'Is that Isabel Bookbinder?' says a woman's voice, a voice I don't recognise.

'No comment!' I snap. 'Just bugger off and leave me alone.'

'I *beg* your pardon?'

Hang on a moment. There's something very familiar about this voice after all.

'I'm extremely busy today, Isabel, and I don't have time for silly games.'

Oh my God. It's Katriona de Montfort.

'You . . . you're calling me.'

'Of course I'm calling you.' She sounds slightly exasperated. 'I said I would, didn't I? You've made *quite* an impression, Isabel.'

Great. She's obviously been reading the papers this morning. Now she'll have me down as a blundering, blithering idiot instead of the glamorous, sophisticated debut novelist she saw me as the other day. Still, maybe she's calling with some advice on how to handle the media. God knows, a woman as famous as Katriona de Montfort must be hounded by journalists all the time.

'It's really nice of you to think of me,' I say miserably. 'And whatever words of wisdom you can share, I'd be ever so grateful. I mean, do I have to speak to the press eventually, or do you think I—'

'The press? What press?'

'Er . . . the ones on my front doorstep?'

There's a confused silence.

'Perhaps you haven't seen the papers yet today?' I add.

'I don't read the papers,' she says sharply. 'Are you trying to tell me that you have spoken to the press about *me*?'

'God, no! This is all about a . . . er . . . small mistake I made at work. I haven't spoken to anyone about you, Miss de Montfort, least of all the—'

'Good,' she interrupts. 'I need to know I'm working with people I can trust.'

Now I'm the one supplying the confused silence.

'Isabel? You would *like* to work for me, wouldn't you?'

'*Work* for you?'

'I phoned you because I thought you'd be interested. But if you're not . . .'

'No! I mean, I'd love to!' I'm not sure I'm hearing

this right. Has Katriona de Montfort really just offered me a job?

'Lovely, Isabel.' She sounds pleased for the first time. 'I'll need to do a proper interview first, of course. How does three o'clock today suit you? I know it's terribly short notice, but we're all busy people, aren't we?'

I don't like to tell her that I, in fact, am not. 'Three is fine.'

'Then three it is. You'll need my address.' She quotes a Kensington address at me, which I repeat back at her request, even though it's seared on my brain the moment she says it. 'Good. I'll see you then. Looking forward to it.'

'Oh, me too . . .'

''Bye, Isabel.' And she hangs up.

To Whom It May Concern

If you are reading this, you will know by now that I have been ~~brutally horribly~~ swiftly and painlessly murdered on the 06.43 to Paddington.

The ruthless killer you are looking for is a man in his mid-to-late sixties. He has thinning grey hair, ruddy cheeks, and an assassin's cold, blank eyes. He is wearing a tweedy suit and a green waxed jacket, sort of like a gentleman farmer. This disguise should fool no one.

I have good reason to suspect that my killer is one of MI5's *very top* men, and is in the pay of the government. Recently I inadvertently exposed a secret that may have motivated a high-up cabinet minister to seek revenge upon me. I will not name the cabinet minister in question, in the hope that in recognition of this small kindness, (s)he will leave my loved ones alone.

If you are making this final statement public, which I believe that you should do, I also wish to state that I alone was responsible for the aforementioned unfortunate email error. My good friend and colleague Barney Fox is innocent of all wrongdoing. And Barry Goldstein is guilty of nothing more than blind idiocy, probably due to the addling of his brain by the extreme temperatures to which his employers have subjected him for twenty years.

In addition, I wish to state that my tragic death could have been avoided if First Great Western bothered to employ full-time conductors on their trains. This, surely, rather than revenge killings of otherwise model citizens, is a matter for Caroline Macbeth, the Home Secretary.

Yours,

Isabel Bookbinder

RIP

Dearest Lara,

I write these final words to you, my oldest friend, because I have some very important last requests that only you can fulfil.

DO NOT LET MUM BURY ME IN THE CORNFLOWER-BLUE SUIT. In fact, DO NOT LET MUM BURY ME IN *ANY* OUTFIT OF HER OWN CHOOSING. Tell her you are quite certain that my choice of burial clothes would be my Seven for All Mankind jeans (the grey ones that make me look *very thin*), my black sparkly halterneck from Pinko, and the Barbara Bui platform sandals I bought (in the sale) last January.

I have never made a will, dearest Lara, but I heretofore bequeath to you my Russell & Bromley handbag (and all its contents), my extensive and almost completely unused Trish McEvoy makeup collection, and of course Mr Bumble, the cuddly bee. Help yourself to anything else you'd like from my wardrobe, if it doesn't drown you.

~~Do not weep for me~~ ~~Move on with your lives and forget me~~ It would be really nice if once a year, perhaps on my birthday, everyone who knew and loved me could gather to spend a day of quiet reflection. If it isn't too much trouble, some sort of foundation in my memory would be nice, for ~~children dogs~~ victims of political killings.

Look after Mum, and

Chapter 12

You know, when I eventually become a bestselling Novelist, I think living in Kensington will suit me just fine.

I've got here for my interview with Katriona de Montfort early enough to have a little wander up and down Kensington Church Street, and I must say that she's picked a nice place to live. There's lots of sweet little boutiques, some great cafés, and the park is only a stone's throw away. And the houses. The *houses*.

I mean, seeing where Katriona lives is somehow making me more inspired to become a bestselling Novelist than ever. I suppose it's just another form of Lara's creative visualisation.

But it's a good sign, surely, that I'm getting back the will to creatively visualise. Let Aadelman Stern do their worst! If I get this job with Katriona, she'll be A Contact *for real*. Maybe she'll even put in a good word for me with her own publishers. She can explain that I'm not actually a total weirdo, and my own book deal could be closer than I think! Now all I need is that pseudonym, and a few days to rework *Showjumpers* into *Rockclimbers* (complimentary crampons?), and something in W8 might not be out of my reach. 'Start checking out Kensington property market' is the very next thing that's going on my to-do list!

God, this will shut Dad up once and for all. I mean, even if he can't handle the fact that my bumper book deal is for a juicy bonkbuster instead of a literary masterpiece, it'll seriously impress him if I invest some of my enormous advance in bricks and mortar. He'll probably be expecting me to go out and blow it all at Kurt Geiger, or something stupid like that. And not only that, but I'll get to live in a giant four-storey house in one of the swankiest streets in London.

I don't see any drawbacks to my plan whatsoever.

Anyway, with the huge advance I'm planning on *Rockclimbers* getting, there'll be plenty left over for a little celebratory spree at Kurt Geiger. Because it's not as if you could live in this area and go around poorly shod. There's probably some kind of Residents' Committee in place to prevent that kind of thing.

In fact, *there's* a nice-looking place, in one of the estate agents' windows. Six bedrooms, which sounds a bit on the large side. But it would mean I'd have a spare room for Lara to stay, once I've forgiven her for abandoning me in my hour of need, and Mum, if Dad would let her. And I suppose I'll need a room for Barney, if he's going to come and be my personal chef. *And* I should probably allocate a whole room for one of those super-organised walk-in wardrobes, because when I'm in a real hurry to get ready for an interview with Richard and Judy or something, knowing exactly where I hang all my Missoni scarves will save valuable minutes. Well, that's five bedrooms accounted for already! Probably five bedrooms is the minimum I'll be needing.

I scan the small print to see what else this house offers. 'Wine cellar' . . . very useful, obviously; I've always had a soft spot for wine . . . 'Large study' . . . again, useful. It's entirely possible, after all, that the main reason I've not yet managed to progress much beyond the creative visualisation stage is my lack of a study. 'Swimming pool' . . . Well, some people might think that's a bit unnecessary, but how am I meant to stay a honed size eight without regular exercise?

All right. How am I going to *become* a honed size eight in the first place, without regular exercise?

And there's a forty-foot living room, which the estate agents have described as 'great for entertaining'. Well, bestselling novelists probably have to do an awful lot of entertaining. Even if you hold your big launch parties at Claridge's, I'm sure you're expected to host the occasional intimate soirée, too. Your personal shopper, for example, would probably feel awfully put out if you didn't invite her round for the occasional meal. And your personal trainer, though you'd have to hope he wouldn't be a tedious old kill-joy about your menu.

And your agent. I wonder what Joe Madison would make of this place, should he pop round for an intimate soirée.

And would he like it enough to stay over?

I push open the estate agent's door and go in.

'Good afternoon, madam. May I help you?'

Normally I'd feel intimidated by this smooth young man, but I've made sure I'm all glossy and groomed for my interview. After no sleep last night, and no shower this morning, the blow-dry at the Aveda Institute was essential. As, I think, were the spray-tan and the manicure. Only the Aroma Body Wrap was an unnecessary luxury, and even that came half-price if you had the Body Polish as well.

Anyway, now I've literally spent all the money I had left in my bank account, it gives me even more incentive to get the job. Is that a great pre-interview technique or what?

'I'd like to enquire about that house in the window,' I say. 'The six-bedroomed one with the wine cellar and the swimming pool.'

'Absolutely, madam.' He reaches for a slim file on a shelf. 'Please, take a seat. My name is Jeremy, by the way.'

We're getting on brilliantly already! 'I'm Isabel.'

'So, Isabel, what were you wanting to know about the property?'

'Well, the forty-foot living room,' I say, 'you've said it's "great for entertaining". I just wanted to get more of an idea what *sort* of entertaining you thought it was great for.'

He blinks. 'Well . . . it's forty foot long. So . . . er . . . big parties?'

'Yes, but *big* parties should probably be held at Claridge's.'

He just carries on blinking at me. I think something is trapped in his eye.

'I was thinking more along the lines of *intimate soirées*,' I continue. 'I'm going to need to host quite a lot of those, you see, and I'm not all that sure if a forty-foot living room will be intimate enough.'

'Well, this house offers the facility for small-scale entertaining too.' Jeremy seems to have got rid of whatever was in his eye. He opens up his file. 'There's a wonderful eat-in kitchen *and* a separate dining room, of course. Beautifully panelled in solid oak. Does that sound like the kind of thing you're looking for?'

'Oh, very much!'

'I can take you round for a viewing if you like.' He's reached for a set of keys on a rack beside his desk. 'It's only a few minutes' walk.'

Damn. I'm due at Katriona de Montfort's in ten minutes. 'I'm afraid I have a meeting. Besides, I'm probably going to need a week or so to work out my finances.'

'Of course. Do you mind me asking if you have property to sell? Your mortgage is all in place?'

'No, no. Nothing to sell. This will be my first house. And I won't need a mortgage.'

His mouth drops open a little bit. 'This would be . . . a *cash* purchase?'

'Well, not cash itself, I shouldn't think. A cheque, most likely.'

He doesn't say anything.

'Oh, don't worry,' I tell him. 'I've got it all in hand.'

'Yes . . . I should warn you, Isabel, that the vendors have just turned down an offer of eight, so you'd probably have to come in a bit higher than that.'

I stare at Jeremy. 'Eight *hundred thousand*?'

He's got that thing in his eye again. 'Er . . . eight *million*.'

'Oh.'

Jesus Christ. That's ridiculous. How was I to know a six-bedroom place in Kensington would cost eight *million*? It's not like I've ever been in any position to take an interest in the housing market before. No wonder they say London's a tough place for first-time buyers.

'Well,' I say, getting up, 'I'll have a think about it. But the more I think about it, I'm not quite sure if this place is *exactly* right for my requirements. I mean, who really needs a forty-foot living room when Claridge's is only a few bus stops away?'

'Of course. Would you like me to take your details so that I can contact you if anything . . . er . . . *less* spacious comes up?'

I'm not going to give him my full name, and then watch him fall about laughing and/or put in a swift phone call to the *Sun*. 'No, thank you. I think, after all, I'm going to wait until my . . . er . . . finances are a bit more certain.'

I swish out of the office, and back onto Kensington Church Street. The January sun is glinting on the plate-glass windows of the Mac boutique, and the whole street looks beautiful. Well, the eight million thing is a small setback, but I'm not going to let it deter me from living here. I'll just have to down-scale my requirements. Like, three bedrooms will be more than enough. I can probably carry on enjoying my wine without the need for an actual cellar. And I suppose I can manage without a swimming pool, just for the time being, if I join a gym instead.

Either that, or my book deal for *Rockclimbers* is just going to have to be seven figures, rather than a measly six.

Knowing the property market as well as I do now, I actually feel a bit giddy looking up at Katriona de Montfort's house.

It's perfectly, pristinely white, like an enormous wedding cake. It has huge, shiny windows, a big, black front door, and little crenellations all around the edges of the roof. It's five storeys tall, and in a street of big, grand houses, it's the biggest and grandest of them all. This is what twenty million book sales can do.

I'm suddenly feeling rather intimidated.

In fact, it's only just occurred to me that I've absolutely no idea what kind of a job Katriona de Montfort is offering. What if she's looking for someone to manage her finances or something? Would I be able to count that many zeros on a bank balance? Or what if *she*'s after a personal chef? I can't cook! The only thing I can cook is Nigella Lawson's Dense Chocolate

Loaf Cake, and I don't see Katriona de Montfort being much of a cake eater.

Just as I'm about to ring the doorbell, the big black front door opens. A stocky, dark-haired girl peers out at me.

'Oh, hello!' I stick out my hand. 'I'm Iz.'

'You Iz?'

'Yes.'

'You Iz who?'

'I am *Iz*.'

'You is . . . is . . .'

Oh. *That* old chestnut.

'I'm Is*abel*,' I say.

'You are a bell?'

I'll start again. 'Hello. I am Isabel Bookbinder.'

She doesn't look like the sort to read a newspaper, certainly not one in English, anyway, so she shouldn't recognise the name.

'Miss de Montfort is expecting me,' I continue. 'May I come in?'

'Miss de Montfort must be very, very careful about strange people.'

'But I'm not strange.'

'You *very* strange.'

'I mean I'm not a strang*er*. I have an appointment with Miss de Montfort. I spoke to her on the phone this morning. I'm here about a job.'

'Job?'

'Yes. I don't know exactly what kind of job, but—'

'Nanny!' she says, and pulls me inside.

Good grief.

I don't want to be a nanny. I'm not sure I even *can* be a nanny. This is exactly the kind of thing I was worried about. I mean, don't you need all kinds of qualifications that you just can't lie about? Professional nannying diplomas? Certificates in first aid? A rapport with small children?

The closest I've come to nannying is sitting through the occasional episode of *Supernanny*. And even then I have to switch it off if the yowling goes above a certain pitch.

I mean, obviously I adore kids. And Katriona's kids are probably absolute darlings, completely unspoiled by growing up in a Kensington town house with a millionaire for a mother. It's just . . . well, don't children take up an awful lot of time and energy? Time and energy I'm going to need for reworking *Showjumpers/Rockclimbers*, and coming up with my pseudonym?

But I'd look after *seven* kids if it meant the chance of getting to know Katriona de Montfort. Which, let's face it, can't be that hard. I mean, Julie Andrews does it in *The Sound of Music*, and she's not got a professional nannying diploma or anything.

'Please, you come in,' the stocky girl says, pulling me into the hall.

Wow. The hall is about the size of Mum and Dad's entire house. And it looks like it's been done up by Donatella Versace, then accessorised with Barbara

Cartland's Christmas decorations. The whole floor is tiled in pale pink marble, and there's a huge Venetian glass chandelier hanging down from the ceiling. The walls are painted in sort of Neapolitan ice-cream swirls, and there's a sweeping staircase carpeted in something white that looks like cashmere, but probably isn't, with a banister that looks like it's been wrought out of solid gold, but probably hasn't.

'Miss de Montfort busy for the being of time,' the girl is saying.

'Oh. I'll just wait, then. You and I can have a little chat. What was your name again?'

'I Selma.'

'Nice to meet you, Selma. Now, can you tell me, do you know if Miss de Montfort will consider somebody *without* formal childcare qualifications?'

'Oh, yes, yes.' Selma nods. 'No training necessary.'

'You're quite sure? I mean, that might be true in . . . I'm sorry, where are you from?'

She rasps some word at me, from the back of her throat. It may have been Slovenia. Equally, it may have been Slovakia. But there was definitely a *Slov* in there somewhere.

'That may be true in *the old country*,' I try out, 'but here in Britain people generally prefer leaving their children in the care of properly trained experts.'

'No. You perfect. I recommend you most highmost to Miss de Montfort.'

'That's really nice of you, Selma!' You know, maybe I have a 'great-with-kids' aura that I've never really known about before. 'Perhaps I should meet the children while I'm waiting?'

I'm sort of hoping that Selma will blow on a ship's whistle and seven sailor-suited moppets will run down the cashmere staircase. But Selma does nothing of the sort.

'You adore child,' she says. 'He . . . he angel delight.'

'I'm quite sure he is,' I say.

'So you no need meet right away.'

This doesn't fill me with confidence. 'But surely Katriona would like me to introduce myself to him, before she decides if I'm suitable?'

'Miss de Montfort not give flying monkey's toss,' says Selma. 'You like coffee?'

'Well, yes . . .'

'You go living room. I bring coffee.'

She opens a door at the side of the hallway, ushers me through, and then scuttles off down the stairs to what I assume must be a basement kitchen.

The living room is incredible. It may not be exactly forty foot long, but it can't be far off. There's more cream cashmere-effect carpeting, and the walls are oak-panelled. All the furniture is cream and gold, and done in that fancy old French style: Louis Someone-or-other. There are a few framed photos on a gilt-legged console table, so I wander over and have a little look. Mostly, they're of Katriona: Katriona looking stunning in a slightly garish hot-pink couture gown at the premiere of one of the Captain Kidd films; Katriona looking stunning in Chanel bouclé and a

Cosmo Jenks hat outside Buckingham Palace; Katriona looking stunning in a halter-neck bikini on a white beach, sipping something fruity through a straw. This last one is the most impressive: it was obviously taken relatively recently, but nevertheless Katriona has the body of a twenty-year-old. It's a little bit daunting. Then there are three photographs of a round-cheeked boy, from baby to toddler. This must be the angel delight.

Suddenly there's a noise behind me. 'Hello.'

I spin round slightly guiltily, which is silly because it's hardly forbidden to look at someone's photographs. The round-cheeked boy from the photos is standing in the living-room doorway. He's probably about five now, or maybe six, and he's wearing a little cowboy costume, complete with holster and toy gun.

'Are you a friend of Mummy's?' he asks.

'Er – not exactly.' I try out my new great-with-kids smile. 'I'm going to be your new nanny!'

He just stares at me, unblinking.

'Well, I *might* be your new nanny,' I correct myself, 'if Mummy isn't particularly bothered about leaving her child in the care of somebody properly qualified.'

He still isn't blinking.

'So! I'm Iz, but my mum calls me Iz-Wiz!' I say, trying out a great-with-kids voice to go with the great-with-kids smile. It makes me sound like Janet Ellis, in the glory days of *Blue Peter*. 'What's your name?'

'Lysander. My mummy calls me Lysander.'

'Right.' This isn't going brilliantly. He doesn't seem

quite so instantly attracted to my great-with-kids thing as you'd hope he might be. 'Er . . . why don't you show me your favourite toys, Lysander? Or maybe we can play a game.'

He shrugs morosely. 'I'm not allowed to play my favourite game in here.'

This has given me an absolutely brilliant idea. Forget Supernanny, and her Guantanamo-style 'naughty step'. I'm going to be Fun Nanny! I'll tear up the childcare rule book, and establish a radical new way of dealing with tricky tots. I mean, surely just letting them do what they want is the sure-fire way to avoid any disruptive yowling? And if it goes really well, I could even get my own TV series out of it. I'd have to make sure they'd crank up the glamour factor, though – I'm not going on primetime TV in those horrible boxy suits and sensible court shoes they put Supernanny in. What if someone like Joe Madison was watching? And, speaking of Joe Madison, maybe he'd be interested in helping me launch the spin-off books: *Banish the Naughty Step With Fun Nanny*; *Toddlers Without Torture the Fun Nanny Way*. I could write them in conjunction with top experts and child psychologists, which would be really good, as it would basically mean they'd do most of the actual writing, and I'd just appear on the cover and the talk shows looking sensational in something tailored by Stella McCartney.

'Well, Lysander, it can be our little secret, OK? I won't tell Mummy.'

'OK!' His chubby face brightens, and he scuttles away up the stairs. There's a thud or two from upstairs, like he's rummaging for something. Then he runs back down, clutching a large jar of Nutella and a toy tea set's plastic knife. 'OK, Wizbit. This is my favourite game.'

I hide a smile. Fun Nanny does not squash a child's enthusiasm. 'No, Lysander, that's your favourite *food*. I asked to play your favourite *game*. Why don't you tell me what your favourite game is?'

A grin is crossing Lysander's face so slowly that it makes him look just a tiny bit . . . well . . . demonic. 'Spreading,' he says.

Before I can cotton on, he's unscrewed the Nutella lid, stuck the plastic knife into the jar, and spread it in a thick, brown smear across the cream carpet.

'Er . . . Lysander . . .' Fun Nanny is always calm and reasonable. 'Are you . . . should you . . . ?'

He spreads the chocolate-nut mixture down one side of an armchair.

'Seriously, Lysander . . .' Fun Nanny may not know all that much about childcare, but she does know that physical restraint of other people's children is generally frowned upon. Plus, Fun Nanny is wearing brand-new cream trousers. Fun Nanny is not an idiot. 'Stop! You'll get in trouble with Mummy!'

'No, I won't,' Lysander announces. '*You* will.'

Right. That does it. Fun Nanny does not allow horrible spoiled six-year-olds to destroy her career prospects. I wait until he turns his back, to spread

Nutella all down the wallpaper, then run at him and snatch the jar from his sticky hands. He lets out a howl and swipes at my legs with the knife. I press my hand against his forehead, keeping him just about far enough away from my trousers to avoid any serious damage.

'Listen, Lysander,' I hiss, 'if you stop spreading the Nutella right now, and tell your Mummy this was *all* your fault, you might just get me as your nanny.'

'I don't want a nanny,' Lysander is turning purple, and trying to use his plastic blade to catapult Nutella towards my trousers. 'I've never had a nanny!'

'Well, I've never been a nanny, so this will be a new experience for both of us. Now all we have to do is get me through this interview, and then I'll let you do whatever you want. You leave me alone, I'll leave you alone. Agreed?'

Lysander stops swiping his knife long enough for me to grab it. He looks like he's considering my proposal.

'*Isabel?*'

Oh God. Katriona de Montfort is standing at the door.

She may not be that fussed about formal childcare qualifications, but she probably isn't after someone who holds her son at arm's length with one hand while brandishing a plastic knife at him with the other.

'Miss de Montfort, I can explain . . .'

'This is *completely* unacceptable!' Above her pink

tracksuit top, Katriona's little face is turning almost as purple as Lysander's.

'I'm so sorry . . .'

'*Selma*,' Katriona spits, turning on Selma, who has just appeared behind her with a coffee tray, 'you *know* Lysander is not allowed in the drawing room. You *know* Lysander is not allowed Nutella.'

'Yes, Miss de Montfort,' Selma begins, 'but is not my fault.'

'Are you saying it is *my* fault, Selma? Are you saying it is *my* fault that I've been working so hard to meet my deadline that I had to miss my daily playtime with Lysander for an emergency Swedish massage?'

'No, Miss de Montfort! But I thought Lysander in nursery! Besides,' Selma shoots me a dirty look, 'why cannot Is-a-bell control him?'

'Why *should* Isabel have to control him?'

I'm feeling really bad about this. I don't want Selma to get in trouble. 'Really, Miss de Montfort, don't blame Selma . . .'

Katriona ignores me. 'Hand me those coffee things, Selma, and go and get Lysander cleaned up. Then you can get on the phone to Harrods and start ordering replacement furniture.'

Selma lowers her head, defeated. She hands over the coffee tray, then starts to chivvy Lysander out of the living room.

' 'Bye, Mummy,' calls Lysander over his shoulder.

' 'Bye, darling,' says Katriona. She's already settling

herself on one of the (clean) sofa cushions, putting the tray down on the nearest occasional table.

'I'm *so* sorry to have kept you waiting, Isabel, but that massage was an absolute necessity. I was too busy this morning for my normal Bikram session, so my shoulders were like *rocks*.'

That's another thing I suppose I'll have to add to my to-do List. 'Start daily Bikram'. I mean, everyone who's anyone does Bikram yoga. Novelists especially. Madonna, for one. I kind of hope it isn't compulsory, though.

'You know, you should try it,' says Katriona. 'It's wonderful for a sluggish metabolism.'

'Er . . . thank you.'

'I'll get Merlin to give you a few beginner's lessons, if you like.'

'Merlin?'

'My yogi.' She picks up the pot on the tray in front of us and starts pouring the coffee. 'I'm sorry you were at the sharp end of Selma's incompetence just now. I assure you, things like that won't usually happen.'

I'm about to make another attempt to defend Selma, when something strikes me. *Won't usually happen.* 'You mean, I've got the job?'

'Well, of *course* you've got the job!' She gives a tinkling laugh. 'I knew the moment I met you that I wanted to hire you.'

'But . . . are you quite sure?' I don't know why I'm trying to talk her out of it, but after Nutella-gate, I'm not sure I want to start out under false pretences.

'I mean, I don't know very much about this kind of work.'

'So, you'll learn *on* the job!' Katriona gives me a wide, white beam. 'I'm sure there are all kinds of influences you can draw on.'

'Well, there's Julie Andrews, I suppose . . .'

'Julie Andrews?'

'Or Supernanny, of course,' I say hastily, 'if you're looking for a more twenty-first century approach.'

'Isabel,' says Katriona, 'why do you think I want to hire you as a nanny?'

'Er . . . *don't* you want to hire me as a nanny?'

'Well, of course I don't.' She sips her coffee. 'I think I can offer you something a little more suited to your talents than *that*.'

'You . . . think I have talents?'

It's time for her brittle laugh again. 'Yes, Isabel, I do. That's why I want you to come and work here. I'm going to be your mentor. And you're going to be my Special Assistant.'

Isabel Bookbinder
Kensington

The Editor-in-Chief
The *Saturday Mercury*
The Twelfth Floor
Saturday Mercury Towers
London

6 January

Dear Sir or Madam,

It is with great regret that I must inform you of my immediate resignation from your Splendid Publication.

It will probably come as no surprise to you that I feel that the end of the road has come for my career at the *Saturday Mercury*. It has been a long and happy relationship, and I very much hope that you will remember my hard work and generally good intentions when the time comes for the internal investigation.

Hopefully, in time, your paper will cease to be a national laughing stock, and circulation will stop plummeting. I, for one, will continue to purchase it every Saturday. I feel it is the very least I can do.

Please pass the contents of my desk to my colleague Barney Fox, apart from the stack of old *heat* magazines, which can be recycled in the bins close by.

Yours truly,

Isabel Bookbinder

PS. You don't need to worry about me; I've got a fantastic new job as Special Assistant to a bestselling Novelist. My new bonkbuster, *Rockclimbers*, should be appearing in all good bookshops within the next few months.

Chapter 13

I've never been a particularly spiritual person, but it's pretty clear that the gods have started to get their act together.

Only yesterday morning, I was jobless, penniless, and basically homeless. And after just one interview, I've got an amazing job, a terrific salary, and a brand-new swanky place to live. Katriona wants me to move in! She's giving me a really gorgeous room on the third floor, with a view of Kensington Gardens and an en-suite bathroom. I don't have any rent to pay, *plus* Katriona's paying me well over double what I was paid at the *Saturday Mercury*. And there was talk – only talk, mind you; I don't want to get overexcited – of some kind of clothing allowance.

'We must have you looking smart,' Katriona said, as she showed me around the rest of the house. (No wine cellar or swimming pool, but there is a private twenty-seater cinema, a fitness centre/yoga studio, and a study taking up the whole of the top floor, that I wasn't allowed to see into. I got the impression I'd never be allowed to see into it, in fact. But I bet it's amazing.) 'You *represent* me now, Isabel.'

I sort of hope that if there *is* a clothing allowance,

Katriona gives me a free hand in how I spend it. I mean, not that I'm knocking it or anything, but I'm not really seeing wall-to-wall bouclé and hot-pink yoga gear as an integral part of my Look.

So, my duties are, basically, to run Katriona's life while she cracks on with meeting this horrible, looming deadline for her latest Captain Kidd book. Plus she's a very busy working mum, as she told me, and everybody knows a working mum needs all the help she can get.

Though I thought the kind of working mothers that need all the help they can get are the ones that get up at the crack of dawn to feed and dress a houseful of screaming under-threes, dash off to work a twelve-hour shift, then stagger home to burn some fish fingers and iron their body weight in laundry. Not the ones who have their own housekeeper/nanny and a live-in personal assistant.

But mine is not to reason why. Anyway, I've always quite fancied being one of those pert, perky personal assistants. I once read an article in *Grazia* about Catherine Zeta-Jones's assistant, and it sounded brilliant. You get to hang around with all these A-list celebrities, and they rely on you to run their lives, and get them into Nobu at the last minute, and Catherine and Michael call you a Treasure. And it's not as if the job requires a super-human brain. Booking appointments, making phone calls, sorting out her diary. Incredibly simple, as Katriona herself pointed out, for anyone with a modicum of sense and basic organisational skills.

But I think I'll be fine anyway.

Besides, Katriona did admit that I'll actually be the very first assistant she's ever had. So it's not like she'll know for certain if I get anything wrong.

And here's the really brilliant bit – in return for being such a Treasure, Katriona's going to help me get my book published! She'd remembered about the bonkbuster and everything, and she asked me all kinds of questions, and then she said she could tell I was going to go a long way.

Katriona de Montfort told *me* I'm going to go a long way.

And she's going to speak to a couple of people at her publishers, Lemper Snyde Brusoff, and tell them all about me. Jennifer Reilly and Gordon Scott, I think their names were. Or it might have been Jennifer Gordon and Scott Reilly.

No, hang on. It was Jennifer Scott and Gordon Reilly.

Either way, if things are progressing this fast, I need to get a move on. I need to ring round the department stores and set up personal shopper appointments. I need to *not eat anything fattening* for the foreseeable future. I need to come up with that pseudonym, as well. Katriona, very nicely, didn't seem at all bothered about employing a national laughing stock, but even she agreed it might be advisable to allay any of Jennifer and Gordon's worries with some suggested pseudonyms. I haven't had the chance, yet, to mention that I'll also be reworking the tainted *Showjumpers* into *Rockclimbers*, but I'll run it by her as soon as I get the chance.

Unfortunately, working on my pseudonym isn't the very top item on my to-do list right now. My immediate task is moving out of Russell's. I didn't dare go back last night, just in case the paparazzi were still there, but I'm starting work at Katriona's tomorrow, and I need more than just the clothes I'm standing up in. So it's time to do the deed. I'll just explain, kindly and without rancour, that I don't see a future for us. Russell can help me carefully pack my boxes, sharing a rueful laugh over the rightful ownership of the Robbie Williams CDs, and then we can sit down and share one last, civilised cup of tea together, before a final platonic hug as he walks me down to my waiting black taxi.

Hmm.

What I've actually decided to do, though, is to wait until he's asleep, then sneak into the flat with Barney, sling everything I own into a dozen black bin liners, and make a quick getaway without a need for an embarrassing scene. I mean, in some ways it's even kinder, and it would certainly avoid any possibility of rancour.

Hanging around waiting for Barney to finish work isn't all that much fun, especially not when I'm spending the time working up the courage to give Mum a call. I eventually do it withholding the number, just in case Dad is at home. But I'm in luck. Mum answers.

'Oh, thank heavens you've phoned, darling!'

'I know, Mum, and I'm so sorry about all those photographers . . .'

'Don't worry about that, Iz-Wiz. Now, can you remember how old you were when you took your Grade Four clarinet?'

'Pardon?'

'It's just that I've got a man from the *Gazette* here,' she lowers her voice, 'and he's been asking for some background on you. They're running a big feature in the paper on Friday, Iz-Wiz.'

'A big feature?'

' "Local Girl in Red-Hot Political Sex Scandal!" Isn't it exciting?'

'Mum! You're giving out my private details to the press?'

'Not the *press*, darling! The *Central Somerset Gazette*! They won't say anything horrid about you! Their nice young reporter is sitting at the kitchen table just now, having a couple of Shrewsbury biscuits.'

It's as if people who like Shrewsbury biscuits couldn't possibly do anything bad. Though I do wonder if there mightn't be some kind of positive correlation.

'Well, tell him good stuff about me, OK? And make sure he gets my age right!'

'Don't you worry, Iz-Wiz. I'll make sure that's his top priority!'

'Anyway, Mum, I don't have much time. I was just calling to tell you not to worry about me. I've got a brand-new job.'

Mum suddenly lets out a horrified gasp. 'Oh, Isabel! Not the topless photo shoot for the *Sun*?'

'*Not* the topless photo shoot for the *Sun*! For God's sake, Mum!'

'Oh, thank God. I'm not sure that would have made a terribly nice angle for the *Gazette*'s story.'

My mother is talking about 'angles'? 'Well, it's a brilliant job, Mum. Much better paid than the *Mercury*, and really fantastic prospects . . .' I stop myself. 'Mum, if I tell you about this, you can't go blabbing about it to the man from the *Gazette*.'

'Oh, but he's only trying to write a good feature, and he's such a sweetie. He looks about sixteen, bless him. His name's Nathan. He's on work experience.'

You'd think they could at least have sent the editor or someone. I mean, how many other Red-Hot Political Sex Scandals are there in the *Central Somerset Gazette* every week?

'Mum, I'm serious. You can't say a word. My new boss is very sensitive about privacy. She's *extremely famous*.'

'Oh God!' Mum gasps. 'It's Joanna Trollope, isn't it?'

'*No*, Mum.' This has taken the wind out of my sails a bit. 'It's Katriona de Montfort.'

'The Captain Kidd woman?'

'Yes! I'm going to be her Special Assistant! And the best part is, she's going to introduce me to all the top agents and publishers, so it shouldn't be long before I get a . . .'

Hang on. Isn't this the point at which she's supposed to be screaming with delight? That's what all the mothers do on *Pop Idol* and things, isn't it? I mean, Noel from Hear'Say's mum practically had her own spin-off show.

'Mum?'

Silence.

'*Mum?*'

'Sorry, darling!' She sounds like she's just picked up the phone again. 'Nathan needed directions to the bathroom.'

'Mum, this is big news. If you're not going to give me your full attention, I'll just call you back later.'

'No, Iz! Don't do that!' There's something odd about the tone of her voice. She's sounded ever so cheerful until now.

'Why not?'

'It's just . . . well, your dad will be around later. And he's saying silly things, Iz-Wiz. He doesn't mean any of them. He's just angry about the photographers churning up the front lawn.'

'What *things*?'

'It's nothing important, Iz-Wiz. I just think it might be better if you phoned only when he's at work. Just for a few days.'

I know what Dad is saying. It's what he's always said when he feels I've let him down. There's a lot of huffing and puffing, and 'no-daughter-of-mine'-ing, and usually quite a lot about never darkening doors. At some stage in the proceedings, Marley and

Matthew's various professional and personal successes are brought up, and dangled in front of my face like the toys somebody else got for Christmas. And if he's really on form, Dad usually enjoys a couple of rounds of DIY *Mastermind*: Specialist Subject, The Disappointments and Disasters of Isabel Bookbinder, From 1992 To The Present. '*To the nearest five, how many times did Isabel Bookbinder fail her driving test?*' '*To the nearest ten, how many jobs has Isabel Bookbinder lost, not including holiday and/or Saturday employment?*' '*To the nearest one, how many sensible, stable, long-term relationships has Isabel Bookbinder entered into?*'

'It's the flowerbeds, Iz-Wiz. He's just upset about the flowerbeds.'

'You said it was the lawn,' I say.

Mum doesn't reply.

'Anyway, Mum, you can contact me on my mobile if you need me. I'm moving out of the flat, but—'

'Moving out? But where are you going to live?'

I've sort of lost the enthusiasm to tell her all about the house in Kensington, and the gorgeous bedroom with the view of the park, and everything. 'Look, I'll call you when I'm settled.'

'All right, darling, as long as you're OK.'

'I'm fine. And sorry again, you know, about the photographers.'

'Oh, Iz-Wiz, don't be silly. Things would have been ever so flat after the wedding otherwise.'

I never thought I'd say this, but paparazzi give up far too easily these days.

I know it's nearly midnight, and it's freezing cold in the middle of January. But come on – this is one of the biggest political scandals of the year. Practically the *decade*. You'd think they could have got themselves thermal sleeping bags and another round of takeaway coffees, and stayed outside Russell's flat a *little* bit longer. But there's no sign of them now. All that's left of their crazed siege is a pile of polystyrene coffee cups, and a multitude of KitKat wrappers whirling mystically in the wind.

There's something quite haunting about it, actually.

'I can't believe I've agreed to help you do this,' Barney says. We're sitting in his Corsa a couple of doors down from the flat, to afford us the best view of Russell's bedroom window. The light has just gone off, so I want to leave it another five minutes or so before we go in. 'Sneaking away from your boyfriend in a covert midnight flit.'

'Barney, many things I do may have to be covert from now on,' I tell him. 'What with these Secret Service assassins hunting me down and all.'

Barney snorts.

'That man on the train *was* MI5!' I snap. 'You didn't see his cold, ruthless eyes.'

'Isabel, MI5 are trained to be discreet. If they *are* going to assassinate you, you'll be the last person to know about it.'

'Thank you, Barney. You've been nearly as reassuring as Lara was.'

'You're going to be fine. Today's headlines are tomorrow's chip paper.' Barney yawns again. 'Or rather, today's headlines are tomorrow's completely ignored "Column Inches" section in *Re:View*.'

We sit watching the flat for a couple more minutes, until it seems likely that Russell is fast asleep, then clamber out of the car. It's so cold on the street that it actually hurts to breathe.

'Right,' I whisper, as we scuttle across the road. 'We need to be quick about this.'

'Quick?' Barney puffs. 'How quick can we be, Iz? You said you had to pack up *everything*.'

I dig in my bag for the roll of black bin liners. 'Sling everything in these, and we'll be in and out in ten minutes.'

His eyes narrow in suspicion. 'Why am I getting the feeling you've done this before?'

Once we're inside the dark, silent flat, Barney heads to my bedroom with the bin bags, while I sit down at the kitchen table to write a nice note to Russell. I mean, I'm not inhuman. I do feel guilty about this. Of all the ways to dump someone, a midnight flit is just about the worst. And after all, Russell hasn't really *done* anything except . . . well, be Russell. It's basically my fault for deciding to get involved with him in the first place.

'Dear Russell,'
'My dearest Russell,'

'My own,'

'Russell, Words cannot convey how truly sorry I am for'

Suddenly, I hear a noise behind me.

'Barney!' I hiss. 'I told you to be quiet . . .'

But it isn't Barney. A peroxide-blonde girl is standing in the kitchen doorway, blinking in the light and rubbing her eyes. She's wearing one of Russell's Gandalf the White T-shirts on top, and, from what I can tell, nothing at all on her bottom.

'Isabel?' she says.

'Yes. And you are . . . ?'

'I'm Lulu. From the *Guardian*.'

I didn't know people called Lulu worked for the *Guardian*. I thought *Guardian* reporters were miserable, hairy-armpitted vegans, not dyed-blonde girls called Lulu who spend the night with their sources. Not girls with smeared black eye makeup who wander around semi-naked in Lord of the Rings T-shirts.

Well, all right. I'll accept the Lord of the Rings T-shirt.

But how outrageous is this? Here I am, leaving a grovelly note to Russell, and he's sleeping with the enemy. And I haven't even dumped him yet!

So this means . . . have *I* been dumped by *Russell*?

Lulu is staring at me. 'You don't *look* thirty-one.'

'I . . . I'm twenty-seven . . . Look, what are you doing in my boyfriend's flat?'

'He's your *boyfriend*? I thought you were just his flatmate.'

'Well, it's a bit of a grey area . . .' I begin, but Lulu interrupts.

'OK, well, sorry about that, yeah?' She doesn't look the slightest bit sorry. In fact, she looks positively excited as she turns and grabs a pad and pen from the worktop. 'But look, why don't you give me your side of the story? *My* newspaper isn't exactly a fan of the Home Secretary, so I guarantee you'll get a favourable hearing . . .'

'Favourable hearing?' I hiss. I'm still hoping not to wake Russell up. 'Your horrible newspaper's told the world I'm some sort of feeble-minded dim-wit! Do you have any idea who might have read that?'

Lulu shrugs. 'All the more reason for you to give me an interview. I mean, you'd look a lot less stupid if we reported that you'd done this deliberately.'

'I will do nothing of the sort,' I tell her. 'Anyway, I didn't do it deliberately. I would never do something like that. Unlike your kind, I put a high price on integrity, honesty, and doing the decent thing in life.'

'Hey, Iz,' whispers Barney, coming into the kitchen with handfuls of bin bags. 'If you want to get out of here without having to dump Russell in person, we'd better leave right now . . .'

He stops, and stares at Lulu.

Lulu raises a pierced eyebrow at me.

'Come along, Barney,' I say with icy grandeur. 'We'll come back for the majority of my stuff when Russell *is* around.'

Barney looks confused. 'But you said to pack absolutely everything . . .'

I stalk towards the door. Lulu stops me just before I pull it open.

'Look,' she says, 'if you change your mind, just give me a call. Here's my direct line.' She scribbles on her pad of paper, rips it off, and shoves it in my coat pocket.

'Hell will freeze over,' I say, 'before I make that call.'

It's a very dramatic exit. Though it's marred a bit, unfortunately, by the fact that Barney and I have to go up and down the stairs four times to pick up all the bin bags, while Lulu smokes a cigarette, and watches us.

'She was quite sexy,' Barney observes, as we drive away with our bootful of bin bags.

'She was a shameless slut!' I say, not even caring that I sound just like Dad. 'And this is a gross invasion of my privacy! I've a good mind to write to my MP about this.'

'Iz, if you're hiding from MI5, do you really want the government to know where you're living?'

I'm still sulking ten minutes later, as we turn into an eerily quiet Kensington Church Street.

'You don't need to help me in with everything.' I'm feeling a bit bad now, about being bad-tempered, and making Barney wait up, *and* making him do all the packing. 'It's late. You head home.'

'Are you kidding?' Barney parks, and gets out into the cold to stare at Katriona's house. 'I'm dying to see inside this place! Now, you said there was a regular fan oven as well as an Aga . . . ?'

The front door suddenly opens, and Selma is standing on the doorstep, illuminated by the dazzling porch light. She's wearing a khaki dressing gown, and scowling. 'I help you?'

'Selma, you shouldn't have waited up for me!' I'm rather touched, though. It's a lovely welcome, in an odd sort of way.

'Miss de Montfort insist,' Selma says, with a shrug. 'She never happy to leave door unlocked when all are a-slumber.'

'Right,' I say. 'Well, thank you anyway.'

'I help you?' she repeats.

'No, really, it's fine. My friend Barney can do it all.'

She shakes her head. 'Miss de Montfort not let strange people in house.'

'Yes, Selma, I know that. But Barney is a friend of mine.'

'Hi, there!' says Barney, in his friendliest voice, as evidence.

Selma shakes her head again. 'I no let in anyone strange. Miss de Montfort must be very, very careful about security.'

I can tell by the set of her shoulders that she isn't going to brook any opposition. 'Fine. Can you help me in with all this stuff, then?'

Selma pads out in her moccasins, and starts moving my bin bags inside.

'Well, good night,' I turn to Barney. 'Thanks so much, Barn.'

Barney puts his chunky arms around me, all of a sudden, and squishes me against him. 'Iz, you'll . . . you'll be all right here, won't you?'

'Barney! This is the best job I've ever had! I told you everything Katriona's going to do, to help with my book deal and everything.'

'Sure. But just . . . well, take care of yourself, won't you?'

'Hey, why don't I ask Katriona if *she*'s looking for a personal chef? How great would it be if you came to work here as well?'

Barney stares up at the house. 'Yeah. Great. I suppose.'

I watch him drive away before Selma starts the process of locking up for the night. There are three mortice locks, a thick steel chain, plus a kind of iron grille that has to be pulled across the inside of the door.

'Well,' I say, 'you were right about Katriona being very careful about security. I'll certainly sleep soundly tonight!'

Selma says nothing, and pads up the stairs to her room, leaving me to carry fifteen heavy bin bags up three long flights all alone.

Isabel Bookbinder
~~The Rainforest~~
Bolivia

The MP for Kensington
The House of Commons
London

Dear Right Honourable Member for Kensington (and Chelsea?),

I am writing to protest in the strongest possible terms about the privacy laws in this country.

After a small political scandal (you may have read about it in the papers, or heard about it at the House of Commons), I am finding myself hounded and harangued by members of the press.

I am extremely concerned about the likely methods that will have been deployed in order to invade my privacy in this manner. You read all kinds of things in John Grisham novels. Possibly I am being tracked by satellite, possibly I am being bugged. I am sure that you know more about this kind of thing than I do. All I ask is that you have a word with Fleet Street's top newspaper editors (the *Guardian*, in particular), and ask them, politely, to desist.

Before you dash off and show this letter to the Secret Service, please note that I am moving to Bolivia tomorrow morning, where I will live ~~in the rainforest?~~ for at least the next three years.

I promise to vote for you (by postal vote from Bolivia, of course) in the next election.

Yours truly,
Isabel Bookbinder

Chapter 14

Who cares about horrible old Lulu from the *Guardian*, anyway? She's had to spend the night with Russell, in his Middle Earth-themed bedroom, huddling beneath a threadbare Mordor duvet cover and being watched by wallfuls of Hobbits.

Whereas I have slumbered in Hobbit-free luxury in Kensington.

My new bedroom is *gorgeous*. It's got glossy, dark wooden floorboards, thick white paper on the walls, and a beautiful iron bedstead, piled high with pillows. It's my dream bedroom, in fact: a bedroom where you wake to the sound of birdsong, fresh as a daisy from a good night's sleep, to do some light stretching by an open window; a bedroom where you only ever wear crisp cotton pyjamas and Brora cashmere bedsocks; a bedroom where Joe Madison, also in crisp cotton pyjamas, might bring you hot croissants fresh from the oven, and feed them to you in delicate, bite-sized pieces, until he can resist temptation no longer, and . . .

Well, some of this will have to wait. Like the stretching, for example. Even after my power shower, I'm far too sore from last night's moving to do anything of the kind. And I might be able to dig out some cashmere bedsocks from somewhere, but I don't think I've ever owned any really crisp cotton pyjamas.

And Joe Madison is Gina Deverill's boyfriend, so there's no point in dreaming about the croissant part.

Anyway, I can tell things are going to go brilliantly with *Rockclimbers* now I'm settled here. Obviously it's much easier to make progress in surroundings like these. It just makes me feel so inspired. Which I might have said before, but I really mean it now. Not that Lara and Barney are completely right, but I can admit that I probably need to be more productive. Well, there'll be no more excuses from now on. This is the start of a New Me. I'll be rising early, exercising regularly, eating healthily, writing *masses* . . . There's a fabulous antique desk in the corner of the room, which is going to make writing a pleasure. And I'm going to look brilliant sitting at it for publicity photographs.

I'm really tempted to go and try out a few possible poses – chin lightly resting in left hand, right hand poised over notebook? – but it's already nine o'clock, and I think I ought to go and find out how Katriona wants me to spend my first morning.

It takes me a while to assemble the perfect Special Assistant outfit, but once I take Sandy from Madison/Salisbury-Kent as my inspiration, it all comes together nicely. I put a grey pencil skirt with a grey sweater, which matches in a way that even Mum would be proud of. Then, just in case it's an outfit that Mum would be a little *too* proud of, I put on some knee-high boots and wrap my skinny Marni belt around my waist. Perfect. I wish I had a snazzy little conference file to carry around, but for now the smartest thing I've got is my Smythson notebook. I grab it from my desk and stride out, pertly and perkily, for my big Special Assistant's entrance.

Now all I have to do is find Katriona. I pop down to the kitchen, but there's no sign of her. Well, I imagine she skips breakfast. But there's no noise from the fitness studio, either. Maybe she's already up in her study, on the top floor. Well, as a dedicated novelist, that's where *I'd* be.

A pyjama-clad Lysander is lurking outside his nursery door as I go past, in possession of a fresh jar of Nutella and a maniacal grin.

'Morning, Lysander,' I say, in a calm, authoritative voice that I hope to God is going to prevent him slinging chocolate spread at me. 'Do you know where your mummy is?'

'No,' says Lysander. 'Why are you dressed up all smart?'

Well, it's nice that he noticed I'd made an effort. On the other hand, I have a nasty feeling this is just his way of getting maximum sadistic enjoyment out of the spreading game. I take a giant step backwards, down three stairs. 'This old outfit? It's really nothing special.'

He pulls a face. 'Becca didn't get all dressed up like that. Becca wore old-jeans-and-T-shirts.'

'Er . . . Becca?'

'Becca wore trainers,' he adds, looking at my boots with scorn. 'Becca was *fun*.'

Becca – whoever she is – is not endearing herself to me. 'Well, good for Becca,' I say, just as Selma sticks her head out of Lysander's nursery door. She's still wearing her khaki dressing gown, and there are thick globules of Nutella in her hair.

'Lysander,' she says. 'I beg you. Please get dressed.'

Lysander's response is simply to barrel his way past her, back into the nursery, with a war-like whoop. Over her shoulder, I can see him start to up-end his Nutella jar over a pile of fresh clothes on his bed. Selma's head droops.

'Hi, Selma!' I say, before she disappears after him. 'How are you this morning?'

She mumbles something vaguely Slavic-sounding. It's got a lot of *zh*s in it.

'Right,' I say sympathetically. 'You know, you and I really must find an evening to have a meal. Chat over a bottle of wine.'

Her eyes widen as though I've suggested popping round to Buckingham Palace for an impromptu tea with the Queen.

'Well, you have a think,' I say. I don't want to overwhelm her. 'Just knock on my door if you decide you fancy it.'

She nods mutely.

'Great! Oh, by the way, Selma, is Katriona in her study already this morning, do you know?'

'You no go in study!' Selma's found her voice. 'Is no

allowed! Is where Miss de Montfort must be *private*.'

'Well, I won't go in if she doesn't like it. I'll just knock on the door.'

'No knock!'

'All right, fine, I won't even knock.' Jesus. What on earth does she imagine Katriona's doing up there – harvesting marijuana plants? Pouring shampoo into the eyes of helpless beagles?

'Miss de Montfort must be . . .'

'. . . very careful about security. I know.'

There's a sudden, gleeful howl from within the nursery, and Selma spins round. 'No, Lysander! Is four-ply cashmere . . .'

With Selma the Gatekeeper safely wresting Nutella jars from Lysander's grasp, I can nip on up the rest of the stairs to Katriona's study. The house is much narrower up here, with just a single doorway leading off the small landing. I knock lightly on it. No answer. I knock a bit louder. When there's still no answer, I give the door handle a try.

Instantly, I hear a flurry of noise from inside the study. There are footsteps, a key turning in a lock, and then the door flies open.

'What the fuck,' snaps Katriona, 'are you doing up here?'

My morning greeting dies on my lips. 'I was just looking for you. So we could start work.'

She steps outside the study, closing the door firmly behind her, and puts her hands on her hips. She's wearing Chanel, and her hair is scraped back from her face in a very tight ponytail, giving her that wind-tunnel look you see on ageing Hollywood stars. 'This is my *private space*, Isabel. My one and only haven from the stresses and strains of my life.'

Great. Three minutes into my first morning, and already I've pissed off my new boss. I bet this didn't happen to Catherine Zeta-Jones's assistant. I bet Catherine Zeta-Jones is more *easy-going*. 'I'm really sorry.'

Her faces softens, as much as her ponytail allows. 'I may not have made myself clear enough on our tour yesterday. But I'm afraid I must insist, Isabel, that I am allowed to work up here totally undisturbed.'

'Of course. I won't do it again. I just thought you might need me to . . . well, you know. Do some assisting.'

'Oh, Isabel, don't worry about that! When I need something doing, I'll let you know.'

This isn't what I was expecting. Not when I was all geared up to be pert and perky. 'But don't you want your diary organising? Some appointments booking? I could try to get you a table at Nobu . . .'

'That won't be necessary. I tell you what, Isabel, why don't you spend some time getting on with your own novel?' She wags a sapphire-laden finger. 'We want you to be all ready to impress Jennifer and Gordon!'

'Oh, yes . . . I mean, I've been up since six as usual, of course . . . just writing and writing and . . . er . . . writing . . .'

'Excellent!' Katriona beams at me. 'Well, off you go and carry on. As long as you're all ready to come with me to my meeting later. And I must say, you're looking nicely turned-out this morning.'

'Thank you.'

'Very *Secretary*.'

Oh God, I should never have worn the knee boots.

'Myles *will* be pleased.' She gives me a wink.

'Is that who our meeting's with?'

'Yes. We have some things to discuss. Plus I thought it'd be nice for you two to get to know each other properly.' She puts a hand on the door handle, but doesn't open it. I think she's waiting for me to go back downstairs first. 'Oh, here's a job for you, Isabel. We'll need a taxi for half-past ten. The number's up on the board in the kitchen.'

'Sure!' I pull out my notebook, to write the details down. 'And where shall I tell them we're going?'

'The Wolseley, of course,' Katriona flaps a hand, to send me away down the stairs. 'Where else?'

NEW ME DAILY TIMETABLE

6 a.m. – Wake up; spring out of bed; drink lemon and hot water

6.05 a.m. – Work on *Rockclimbers* OR do light warm-up stretching

6.30 a.m. – ~~5 mile run~~ ~~3 mile run~~ Jogging in Kensington Gardens

7.45 a.m. – Dry body-brushing; energising face-mask; brisk shower

8 a.m. – Select outfit; apply light makeup; go into battle with hair

~~8.30 a.m.~~

~~8.45 a.m.~~

9 a.m. – Breakfast (blueberries)

9.30 a.m. – Special Assistant duties

11 a.m. – Work on *Rockclimbers* OR morning coffee break

11.15 a.m. – Bikram for Beginners with Merlin

1 p.m. – Lunch break: read improving book OR *heat* magazine

1.15 p.m. – Special Assistant duties

3 p.m. – Ashtanga for Amateurs with Merlin

4.30 p.m. – Work on *Rockclimbers* OR afternoon tea break

4.45 p.m. – Special Assistant duties

6 p.m. – Dry body-brushing; energising face-mask, brisk shower

6.30 p.m. – Select outfit; apply full makeup; go into battle with hair

~~7.30 p.m.~~
~~8 p.m.~~
8.30 p.m. – Taxi to launch party
11 p.m. – Taxi home
11.30 p.m. – Work on *Rockclimbers* OR have a nice early night, to maximise chances of progress tomorrow morning

Chapter 15

As we sweep into The Wolseley, the entire room looks up and stares at us.

OK. Who am I trying to kid? They look up and stare at *her*. I might as well be the coat-stand for all the interest they're taking in me.

Still, I may be arriving anonymously now, but it'll only be a few more months until they're all staring at me too. Probably there'll be a little bit of clamouring for autographs. Which reminds me – I've really got to get cracking on that pseudonym! I need something glam; glam and Euro-chic. Something that hints at an aristocratic but impoverished past.

Isabel de la Fressange.
Isabella de la Fressange.
Issie von Furstenberg.
Ichabel von Hohenlohe-Schillingsfurst.
Isabel Madison.
Isabelle de la Madisone.

'There's Myles!' Katriona stalks to a table in the middle of the huge, ornate room, where Myles is sitting, reading the *Telegraph*.

He's actually a lot less ginger than I remember from his offices the other day, and dressed in that same way, which only he could pull off – that is to say, shabby and unkempt, with a two-day growth of bright orange stubble and a Prada tie slung around an untucked shirt.

'Sorry we're late, darling.' Katriona kisses him on both cheeks and slides into the banquette. 'Isabel needed some help settling in.'

Myles's pale blue eyes flick over me. I think he's only just noticed that I'm not a coat-stand.

'Who?'

'Myles, don't be dim. I told you I needed a Special Assistant.' Katriona pulls me next to her and wraps a matey arm around my shoulders. 'You remember Isabel? Isabel Bookbinder? From your office the other day?'

'*What?*' Myles slams his paper down and stares across at us.

Oh shit. I think I should probably have finalised that pseudonym before this.

Katriona eyeballs him. 'What's your fucking problem?'

'Isabel Bookbinder? *The* Isabel Bookbinder?'

It's not quite the way I've always dreamed of hearing that said.

'Yes, Myles, *the* Isabel Bookbinder. Is that a problem?'

'Oh, no *problem*!' Myles's super-posh voice drips with sarcasm so thickly that I wonder if he's been taking secret lessons from Dad. 'Only that you've hired the idiot who shopped her boss's secrets to the entire national fucking press.' He brandishes the front page of his newspaper. The headline – 'MACBETH FILES FOR DIVORCE AS HUSBAND MOVES OUT' – brings a hot blush to my cheeks.

'Oh, please. It's not as if *I'm* having an affair with the Home Secretary's husband. And look at Isabel! Does she *look* like the kind of person capable of stabbing me in the back?'

Myles's eyes flick over me as if he thinks I'm not capable of anything.

'Anyway, Iz has told me all about that. It was just a terrible accident.'

'A fucking *stupid* one,' spits Myles. 'Jesus, Katriona, what if she has some "terrible accident" while she's working for you? You really want your private life spilled all over the *Daily Mail*?'

'Actually,' I point out, 'the *Daily Mail* refused to print the emails. To avoid offending its readers.'

Myles just stares at me, with those arctic eyes. He'd have made a very good Second World War interrogator.

'Katriona,' he says. '*Seriously.*'

'Myles, stop being a bully! You know I need all the help I can get. So unless *you* want to sit down and meet this fucking Captain Kidd deadline for me,' Katriona hisses, 'I'd appreciate it if you kept your nose out of my decisions.'

Myles says nothing.

'Iz, sweetie, could you pop to the loos and grab me some tissues?' Katriona sniffles.

I know when someone wants to get rid of me. She obviously wants to speak to Myles alone.

It's about a ten-mile hike down to the toilets, which are just as opulent as I hoped they'd be. I pocket Katriona's tissues, then lurk about beside the basins, hoping some celebrity will come in and start snorting cocaine, so I can text my friends about it. No sign of anything like that, though. A couple of glossy women come in after a few minutes, but the most exciting thing they do is apply those gorgeous limited-edition Tom-Ford-for-Gucci lipsticks.

I mean, no offence to The Wolseley or anything – probably it's too early in the morning for sniffing cocaine – but so far about the most thrilling text message I'll be able to send is one to Barney all about the patisserie trolley. Mind you, Barney will be pretty thrilled about that.

I send him a quick text, including as much detail as I can on the full pastry spectrum. When I think long enough has passed for Katriona and Myles's tête-à-tête, I start the ten-mile hike back up the stairs again.

It looks safe enough for me to return to the table. Katriona is busy ordering from a waiter, and Myles is sipping his coffee, looking slightly less murderous. He even pulls my chair out for me to sit down. Well, he kicks it out for me to sit down. But it's an improvement. And probably passes for beautiful manners at Eton.

'Isabella,' he says, 'my apologies. I've been in a rotten mood all morning, and frankly I wasn't a big fan of Kat's last assistant.'

'But . . . Katriona's never had an assistant before.'

'Oh, I didn't mean assistants like you,' Myles says smoothly. '*Staff*, I meant. Like that barking-mad Balkan.'

'You mean Selma.'

'Is that her name?'

'Yes. And she's from Slovenia, not Balka.'

He stares at me.

'And *my* name,' I say, 'is Isa*bel*, not Isabella. But you can call me Iz. If you prefer.'

'I prefer Isabel.'

'Oh. Right.'

'So,' he says, leaning towards me. 'I hear you're a writer too. Kat's just been telling me about this project of yours. *Showjumpers*, yeah?'

I *love* the fact he's just called *Showjumpers* a 'project'. It makes it sound less like my fourth-form homework, and more like the kind of thing you discuss over mimosas and egg-white omelettes at the Chateau Marmont.

'Well, it *used* to be *Showjumpers*,' I say, 'but due to unforeseen circumstances, I'm actually having to rethink it a bit.'

Myles frowns. 'Why?'

'Creative differences,' I say, which is how everybody seems to explain their 'projects' falling apart in *heat* magazine.

191

Myles's frown only deepens. 'Differences with *who*? You're the only one writing it.'

'Well, I'm terribly indecisive . . .'

He shrugs. 'Have it your way. But I thought it sounded extremely promising.'

'You *did*?'

'Yeah.' Because he's so screamingly posh, it comes out like more of a *yarh*. 'Horse-riding cads, sex . . . it's the perfect bonkbuster.'

'So you don't think that, say, *rock-climbing* cads and sex would make a better bonkbuster?'

He snorts. 'Good grief, no. Stick with the showjumping, Isabel, for pity's sake. There's room in the bestseller lists for something like that.'

Right. Forget about the covering letter mess with Aadelman Stern. If Myles Salisbury-Kent, literary agent extraordinaire, says there's room in the best-seller lists for *Showjumpers*, I'm bloody well sticking with *Showjumpers*.

I mean, now I think about it, it's most likely that Mum's envelope will just sit in a pile at Aadelman Stern for months, anyway. By the time they finally dust it off, everyone will have forgotten that Isabel Bookbinder's a national figure of fun, and I'll already have a brand-new book deal behind the safety of my pseudonym.

'What are you two gossiping about?' Katriona asks, as the waiter leaves with the order.

'Isabel was telling me about her bonkbuster,' says Myles, tapping his coffee spoon repeatedly on the table like a man with a bad caffeine habit. 'Rock-climbing, I gather.'

'*Rock-climbing*?' Katriona's little black eyes widen.

'No, no . . .' I say hastily. 'That was a different project! Showjumping, that's what *this* book's about. Showjumping, for sure.'

'Yes, well, showjumping is *much* more the thing,' Katriona says, with her tinkly laugh. 'She's working *so* hard on it. Up at six to write every morning!'

'Well, I do like to knock out a couple of chapters *before* breakfast,' I say.

'Amazing!' sighs Katriona. 'Lucky you, Iz. It must be nearly finished already!'

I think that's a topic best avoided. 'I mean, I'm not one of those writers who just sits around, gazing at the winter dawn,' I continue. 'Books don't write themselves!'

A smile is playing on Myles's thin lips. 'You know, Katriona could do with a touch of your motivation.'

'I've got *writer's block*, you bastard,' Katriona spits. 'Do you think it's *fun* for me?'

'I stand corrected, Kat. I just think it's funny that you're mentoring Isabel, rather than the other way around.'

'Oh, that reminds me . . .' Katriona stops glaring, and fishes inside her handbag of the day, a blue python-skin Balenciaga Lariat, for a little stack of cards. 'These are for you, Isabel. I popped out yesterday afternoon and had my printers do you a nice set of business cards. You'll need them when you go off to meet all the agents and publishers I'm going to line up!'

She takes a thick, ivory card from the top of the stack and hands it to me.

ISABEL BOOKBINDER – N.I.T. W.I.T
SPECIAL ASSISTANT TO KATRIONA DE MONTFORT

'Nitwit?'

Katriona waves a hand. 'My mistake, sweetie. I couldn't remember if you said you were a *Novelist*-in-Training or a *Writer*-in-Training, so I thought it was best to put both. And there wasn't room for the full spelling on the card.'

Myles leans over to read the card, and practically chokes on his coffee.

'Don't worry, Iz,' Katriona says. 'We'll get you some new ones printed as soon as you've used those up.'

I stare down at the cards. There must be a hundred of them.

'Well, I for one will be proud to keep one of the originals,' says Myles, barely hiding a Cheshire cat grin as he slides a card into his beaten-up wallet. 'It's not every day one is presented with the card of a professional nitwit.'

Fortunately, a waiter is arriving, bearing a tray. He puts down a single espresso for Katriona, and an enormous glass of hot chocolate, topped with whipped cream, for me.

'I didn't know what you'd like, Iz, so I picked for you,' Katriona says. 'You're lucky, being so young. You can eat anything you want, without getting any fatter.'

There's something about the tone of her voice that implies she thinks I'm fat already. I stare at my hot chocolate. My face is suddenly burning.

'Leave her alone, Kat,' Myles says. His voice is soft, but it sounds dangerous.

'What are you talking about, Myles?'

'You know what I mean.'

Katriona looks away first. 'Well, let's get down to business.' She reaches into her Lariat bag, pulls out a folded sheet of paper, and hands it to me.

'CONFIDENTIALITY AGREEMENT'.

Oh my God! This is just the kind of thing Catherine Zeta-Jones's Special Assistant had to sign! It's like going through a secret portal into a world of fame and celebrity.

'You don't mind, do you, Iz?' Katriona is watching me. 'I have everyone who works for me sign one of these. Just have a little look over it, and then sign when you feel comfortable. No pressure at all.'

Well, obviously I have to peruse this contract extremely carefully. Dad has always been very strict about not signing anything until you're absolutely certain you're not being swindled.

But it all looks fine to me. Everything sounds suitably legal. I mean, there are three 'notwithstandings' in the first paragraph alone.

'Anyone got a pen?' I ask.

'You're sure you're happy?' asks Myles, as I sign with Katriona's Montblanc.

'Of course she's happy! God, Myles, it's only a little confidentiality agreement. Isabel will be making her own staff sign these one day in the not too distant future!' Katriona polishes off her espresso. 'Get the bill, Myles. We have a lot of hard work to be getting on with, don't we, Iz?'

Brilliant! 'Would you like your diary arranged, or—'

'Hard *shopping* work,' Katriona continues, as if I haven't spoken. 'We've got to get you kitted out for tonight.'

'Tonight?'

'We're going to a launch party, sweetie! At Claridge's! It's a very important opportunity for you to network. A novelist's life isn't *all* about getting up at six to write two chapters before breakfast. There are loads of important people I want you to meet.'

'Besides, Isabel, you can't really think Kat's going to go about the place with an assistant who's anything other than fabulous.' Myles slaps a twenty down on the waiter's silver salver and stands up without waiting for change.

'Come on, Iz.' Katriona is pulling on her coat. 'We'll get a taxi over to Knightsbridge, start off there.'

There are three very good reasons why being Katriona's Special Assistant is the best job in the world.

1) Only one morning into my new job, and I'm already hobnobbing with literary agents at The Wolseley.
2) Only one morning into my new job, and I'm already all lined up with a launch party at Claridge's.
3) Only one morning into my new job, and I'm about to go off to Harvey Nichols to finalise my Look.

I knew the gods had started to smile on me.

Chapter 16

Until you've gone shopping with a multimillionaire, you don't really know what shopping is. It's great!

Well, it's basically great. My only complaint, if I had one at all, is that I'd thought Katriona had said we were going shopping for *me*. And to be completely honest, all we've really done is go shopping for her.

We've already spent at least two hours at Harrods, in the International Designer Room picking out £2,000 worth of 'options' for her to wear tonight. And now she's piling up even more 'options' on the counter at Harvey Nichols like clothing is going out of fashion. Which, if you're being technical about it, it probably is.

Though I'm not sure royal-blue velvet cocktail-wear has ever really been *in* fashion.

Anyway, like I say, I'm not complaining. It might be a little bit boring, but this is what Special Assistants do. I bet Catherine Zeta-Jones's assistant is in Bergdorf Goodman right now, doing just the same thing.

I bet I'm *better* at it than Catherine Zeta-Jones's assistant, though. I mean, I bet Catherine Zeta-Jones's assistant never has to gently steer her boss away from the Lurex trouser suits at Roberto Cavalli.

'So, this launch party,' I say casually, trying to distract Katriona from something tomato red and sparkly. For the evening, she seems to abandon her pastel Chanel and go all out for the biggest, flashiest Italian designers. 'What's it for?'

'Some ghastly American. We won't stay long. Though Gordon and Jennifer might be there, so I must make sure I introduce you to them.'

Gordon and Jennifer? The two über-publishers from Lemper Snyde Brusoff who are going to go ga-ga over *Showjumpers*? I might be meeting *them* tonight?

OK. What the hell are we doing finding Katriona options? *I* need options. Actually, I need more than options. I need a Look, dammit, and I need one *now*!

Katriona slings her Lariat bag at me. 'Hold this, will you, while I go and try a couple of things on?'

Trying 'a couple of things on' at Harrods took over an hour. I don't have time for this!

'Maybe I could go and find a couple of things to try on too . . .' I begin.

Then I see it. Across the other side of the store. Right above the wall-to-wall beige in MaxMara: 'PERSONAL SHOPPING SUITE'.

'Katriona, would you mind terribly if I went off by myself for a bit? If I'm meeting Gordon and Jennifer tonight, I have rather a few things to be getting on with.'

Katriona sticks her head out of the changing room. 'What?'

'Well, I've got some important preparations . . .'

'Fine.' She waves a hand. 'You pop up to the café and grab a coffee. You should be able to find a quiet corner to write in.'

'Write? Oh, right!' I'm already backing away. 'Well, call me on the mobile if there's anything important!'

I hurry across to the desk beneath the Personal Shopping sign, where a girl with a Louise Brooks bob is sitting. She's wearing the most amazing New Romantic-style ruffle blouse, with a mannish blazer. Not the Look I'm aiming for, but a Look none the less.

She glances up and smiles. 'Hi, there. Can I help you?'

'Yes, please. I need to see a personal shopping . . .' What do you call them? Experts? Advisors? Consultants? '. . . guru.' That sounds about right.

She smiles again. 'Well, I'm glad to hear you think we're so well qualified! Have a seat.'

I sit down. Behind her, I can see the changing area, with floor-to-ceiling mirrors, fresh flowers, and little trays with coffee cups and the remains of light lunches. A couple of equally fabulously attired girls are raking through racks of dresses, skirts, and cashmere sweaters.

'So.' The girl pulls a pad of paper towards her. 'Let's start with a chat about the kind of thing you're after. I'm Jemima, by the way. And you are . . . ?'

'Isabel Book—' Just in time. 'Isabel Book,' I say again.

Jemima doesn't even blink. 'Is that Booke with an "e"?'

'Er . . . yes,' I say. 'Why not?'

'So, what kind of work do you do, Isabel?'

'I'm a Novelist.' God, it sounds great.

'Wow!' Clearly Jemima thinks so too. 'Might I have read anything you've written?'

'Well, not yet. But I'm actually hoping to sign a really big book deal any day now.'

This is only a very small exaggeration. And if I hit it off with Jennifer Thingy and Gordon Whatsit tonight, it may not be an exaggeration at all.

'My God! Congratulations!'

'Well,' I say modestly, 'I've been very lucky. Katriona de Montfort is mentoring me.'

'The Captain Kidd woman? But I *love* her! That's *amazing*!' Jemima lowers her voice. 'You're not . . . er . . . thinking of *dressing* like her, though, are you?'

'God, no,' I say hurriedly.

'Excellent, excellent . . .' Jemima makes a few notes on her pad. She's looking genuinely impressed, even a little wistful. 'God, I wish I could do something like that. Write bestselling novels, I mean.'

'But you're already halfway there!'

She blinks at me. 'I've never written anything longer than a shopping list.'

'But you've already got your Look sorted.'

'My what?'

'Your Look. The bob, the lipstick, the whole New Romantics thing. It's really distinctive! Publishers are very impressed by things like that.'

'They are?'

'God, yes. In fact, that's exactly why I need your help. I need to get my Look right, you see. I've got this extremely important launch party to go to . . .' I pause for the suitably awed silence, which Jemima, bless her, provides, '. . . so I need something really glamorous.'

'I get you, I get you.' Jemima snaps her fingers, and starts scribbling furiously on her pad. 'You need something glam, you need something sexy, you need something fresh.'

'Yes!' I want to kiss her. 'That's it exactly!'

'You want a Look that says powerful, but ladylike.'

'Well, not that ladylike,' I say. 'I'm writing a bonkbuster.'

'OK . . .' Jemima taps the side of her nose with her pen. 'So, Isabel, let's think about the kind of clothes you're going to need in general. You say you're off to a party. Does your profession involve a lot of party-going?'

'Oh, absolutely oodles.'

'So we'll need to find you some gorgeous frocks . . .' Jemima writes this down on her pad. 'Lunch dates? Breakfast meetings?'

'All the time. Mostly at the Wolseley. Put that down.'

Jemima doesn't blink an eyelid. 'The Wolseley . . . sure . . . so perhaps you'll be wanting a funky little suit for that kind of thing. Or some great trousers, with a nipped-in jacket and a Stella McCartney T-shirt . . . And will you be doing TV too?'

I nearly forgot about that! 'Oh, yes! Lots and lots of TV.'

'Then you'll want some fabulous jeans . . .' Jemima stares, briefly, into the middle distance. 'Glamorous, but approachable. We'll get you some amazing boots . . . Oh, I know! We've got some fabulous new round-toe knee-highs by Marc Jacobs! You'd look fantastic in those.'

'Jemima,' I breathe. 'I'm so glad I've found you.'

'. . . and then, of course, you'll need something comfortable, for writing in.'

'Oh.'

'I mean, at the end of the day, that's the most important part of your job, isn't it?'

'I suppose so.'

'Well, we've got some amazing cashmere tracksuits. We can start with those.'

Oh, well, *that* sounds all right. Because *obviously* the most important part of this job is the writing part. And just think how much easier the writing part will be if I do it wearing a gorgeous cashmere track-suit, rather than a pair of jeans and a grotty old jumper.

'Right, Isabel. It sounds like I've got a pretty good idea of the kind of thing you're after.' Jemima leafs through a large desk diary. 'A total working wardrobe for a hip young novelist.'

I beam at her.

'So,' she continues, 'how does three weeks tomorrow sound to you?'

'What?'

'The thirtieth. That's the earliest we can possibly squeeze you in, I'm afraid.'

'But the party is *tonight* . . .'

'Oh, I'm really sorry, Isabel.' She looks it too. 'Listen, for tonight, just put on a very simple little black dress and accessorise it up until you feel it expresses your personality.'

'But I don't *know* how to accessorise things to express my personality!' I wail. 'That's what I need *you* for.'

'Some fabulous, sexy peep-toe heels,' Jemima says desperately as her phone starts ringing. 'A long pendant? A gorgeous sequinned scarf? I can really see you in one of those, Isabel!'

'Great,' I say. 'Thanks.'

'So I'll put you down for Thursday the thirtieth at ten o'clock,' Jemima writes in her diary. 'We'll sort you out then, Isabel, I promise.'

I stamp about the shop floor for a while, scowling at a variety of little black dresses I can't possibly afford, until I see that Katriona has emerged from the cocoon of the changing room. She's at the till, watching eagle-eyed as one assistant folds her small mountain of clothes and the other carefully rings up the enormous total.

'Isabel! I thought you'd gone to the café to write.'

'I think I've just about reached my writing limit for the day. I was having a little look around for a party outfit myself.' Maybe this will remind her of the projected reason for our shopping trip. 'Just a little black dress or something.'

'My God!' Katriona lets out a shriek. 'I don't believe it!' She darts back into the changing room, and re-emerges a moment later with a piece of black fabric. 'I tried it on, but it was *much* too big for me.' She holds it up against me. 'Oh, Isabel, it's so *you*.'

It's a little black dress, all right. Actually, it's a Very, Very Little Black Dress. It's practically pure Lycra. The only bits that *aren't* Lycra are the bits with ruddy great slashes cut into them. The skirt is about twelve inches long from waist to hem, and the neckline plunges so low that the only good thing you can say is that there's absolutely no chance of this dress giving you belly-button fluff. I'm only surprised it doesn't come 2-for-1 with a matching kerb-crawler.

'I mean, I didn't even know Harvey Nicks *did* things like this,' Katriona is saying to the shop assistant, who just looks relieved to have finally shifted one of the ghastly things.

'Katriona, I'm really not sure . . .'

'Oh, come on, Iz! It looked terrible on me, skinny old thing, flat chest. Hung off me like a bin bag. You need your kind of curves for this dress, Isabel, glorious, Rubenesque curves!'

'Now, hang on a minute . . .' I begin. I mean, I may not be the size of an iron railing, but I draw the line at 'Rubenesque'. It's just another way for Katriona to tell me she thinks I look fat.

But Katriona is tapping her Patek Philippe. 'Now,

I've booked you in for Luc at three, darling, so you'll need to be getting a move on to Duke of York Square.'

'Luc?' Is he the matching kerb-crawler?

'My saint of a hairdresser,' Katriona says. 'He'll sort that mop out, Iz, don't you worry. And *please* treat yourself to a manicure with Belinda while you're there. Those awful bitten nails have to be sorted out before this evening. Belinda will do what she does for me.'

Great. So I'll have Alexis Carrington nails to go with my Moscow streetwalker dress.

But it's not like I can really complain. Katriona may be a bossy old body-fascist with terrible taste in clothes, but she's only trying to help me look my best for the most important introduction of my life.

'We'll get ready together before the party, yes?' asks Katriona, kissing me on both cheeks. 'It'll be super!'

It suddenly strikes me, as I leave behind the warmth of Harvey Nichols and hurry off down Sloane Street, that Katriona de Montfort may not have been looking for an assistant.

She may have been looking for a friend.

Chapter 17

I know Katriona called Luc a saint, but I want to know – *are* there sainthoods available to hairdressers? Because if there are, I really think Luc should be put forward for one.

After three hours in his swivel chair, my hair has transformed into what Lara and I call Super-Hair. It glows with rich, warm chestnut tones and glistens when it catches the light with delicate, caramel highlights. It's smooth but bouncy in all the right places, and it moves like it has a life of its own.

At the very least, I think Luc deserves to have my book dedicated to him.

For Luc,
Who fought the frizz, and won.

Best of all, he was really nice to me, when normally I get the impression hairdressers are sniggering behind my back. The salon was glamorous and buzzy, they brought me a delicious non-fat cappuccino, *and* I even got something really useful done! This month's *Marie Claire* had one of those 'How I Write pieces', interviewing loads of my favourite novelists, so I spent a good hour or so assimilating all the most helpful-sounding tips. An afternoon well spent, I have to say.

I'm just wondering how you go about recommending someone for sainthood – the Pope, I imagine, would be the man to call – when my mobile rings. I answer it for the first time in two full days, even though it's a withheld number. My Super-Hair is giving me amazing confidence.

'Hello,' I say. 'Katriona de Montfort's Special Assistant speaking. How may I help you?'

There's silence on the other end of the line.

'Look, if this is the *Sun*—'

'No! I . . . but . . . Katriona de Montfort?' the caller interrupts me. It's a young woman's voice. 'This is *her* number?'

'Not quite. I'm just her assistant.'

'I'm sorry, I . . . I had no idea this was anything to do with Katriona de Montfort.'

'Look, who's calling, please?'

'Oh, my name is Milly Barnsley. I'm an editor at Aadelman Stern. You know, the publishers.'

Oh Christ. My legs have gone a bit shaky. I sit down on a low wall outside somebody's (eight-million-pound, probably) Knightsbridge townhouse.

'I was only calling,' Milly continues, 'because this phone number is on a rather odd letter we've received. It came with a manuscript called . . . er . . . *Showjumpers*.'

'Please, Milly, just let me explain . . .'

208

'I'm going to have to speak to somebody more qualified to deal with this.'

'Not the press! Milly, please! I'm being hunted by paparazzi already . . .'

'We'll call you back.' The line goes dead.

What an absolute cow! She's probably already on the phone to the *Sun*, negotiating a fat fee for Mum's ridiculous covering letter, so that the entire nation can have a bit more of a chuckle about silly old Isabel Bookbinder over their breakfasts tomorrow morning. *Why* can't Aadelman Stern just chuck the stupid letters in the bin, like any normal organisation, instead of sitting there and actually *reading* the bloody things?

I feel like crying. But I'm not going to. I'm *not going to*. That stinging in my eyes is just the horrible icy wind. I'm going to get in a nice warm taxi, and go back to my wonderful new bedroom in Kensington, and get myself ready for my first ever launch party at Claridge's. I've got the chance of a lifetime to meet some seriously important publishers, and I'm not going to be put off by Milly Barnsley. *Or* five million *Sun* readers.

In the taxi home, I remember what Barney said. He's right. Today's headlines *are* tomorrow's chip paper. Not to mention the fact that Jennifer Thingy and Gordon Whatsit probably don't even read the *Sun*. If I dazzle them with my Super-Hair, talk them very carefully through the complimentary riding crops, and impress upon them the fact that I fully intend to use a pseudonym, my book deal needn't be in jeopardy at all . . .

I'm preparing so intently for my meeting with Jennifer and Gordon that I don't notice anything funny outside Katriona's at first. It's only when I get out of the taxi, and the driver pulls a face and says, 'Pal of yours?' that I see this strange girl, hanging about beside a dirty red Nissan on the opposite side of the road.

She's not making a mobile phone call. She doesn't appear to be watching out for anyone up or down the street, like you do if you're waiting to meet a friend. All she's doing is staring. At the house. At the taxi. At me.

OK, I'm trying not to freak out, but I know just what this is. They're back. MI5 are back!

Clearly they knew I'd rumble them for a second time if they sent an obviously ruthless-looking killer like the one they tried to bump me off with on the train. So this time, they've tried a double-bluff. She doesn't look ruthless at all, this girl. In fact, she looks pretty much . . . whatever the opposite of ruthless is. Ruthful? She's much younger, for starters, probably about my age. She's incredibly skinny, and wearing skin-tight Kate Moss-style jeans with a baggy T-shirt and a fur-trimmed khaki-green parka. Probably leftover from her army days. But if MI5 thought I wouldn't notice a mousy-looking girl, dressed like a million other girls, then they made a seriously big mistake. Because no one could fail to notice this girl. It's her hair.

210

Remember those pictures of Justin Timberlake before he cropped his hair and got all sexy? Now imagine what his hair would've looked like if he'd grown it to his shoulders? And if no one ever recommended that he pop to Boots for a bottle of Frizz-Ease. I mean, it's *that* frizzy.

And if she *is* MI5, then she ought to be a lot better at her job than just standing across the street from her target, staring, and looking a tiny bit . . . well . . . gormless. Is she what we pay our taxes for?

I bet this is all a ploy by MI5 to lull me into a false sense of security! I've no doubt whatsoever that she's armed to the teeth beneath that parka, and trained in any number of terrifying, undetectable assassination methods.

My hands are shaking so badly, I can't find my front door keys. I don't want to ring the doorbell, though, in case Katriona comes to the door and sees that I'm being stalked like this, and panics about her precious security, and . . . Thank God, I've found my keys.

I'm practically sobbing with relief as I stagger through the front door and hear the satisfying heavy sound of it clunking shut behind me.

Katriona is not best pleased with my Super-Hair.

Well, she doesn't actually *say* this, but the glances I see her shooting in my direction as I come downstairs for our party speak volumes.

She doesn't seem best pleased with the styling work I've done on the Very, Very Little Black Dress, either.

With the thickest black tights I own, I've managed to make the hemline hover on the right side of revealing, as opposed to practically gynaecological. I've also pulled it down as far as it will go on the top half. This has made it more of a high-waisted skirt than an actual dress, but with the little sparkly black sweater I'm wearing over the top, nobody will notice.

'Gorgeous hair,' Katriona says thinly, once we're in the cab and on our way.

I'm too distracted by looking out of the window for MI5 to answer. But neither Frizz-Hair nor her Nissan seems to be there any more, thank God.

'You know, with a long, thin face like yours, that fringe really works.'

Oh God, she's 'complimenting' me again.

I just smile. 'I can't thank you enough for inviting me tonight, Katriona.'

She looks put out that I'm not rising to her bait. 'Oh. Well. That's quite all right, Isabel. Jennifer and Gordon are *very* much looking forward to meeting you.'

'Really?' I feel my heart skip.

'Well, of course they are,' she says, applying apricot lipstick that's going to clash with her royal-blue dress the moment she takes her coat off. 'I actually spoke to Jennifer earlier today, and she practically dropped the phone when I told her more about *Showjumpers*.'

Milly Barnsley, do your worst, I think, as we pull up outside Claridge's, and a gold-braided doorman opens the door to let us out.

'Kat! Over here!'

It's Myles Salisbury-Kent. He's leaning against the wall, smoking, his tie loose around his neck as usual. It's probably partly the light, but he looks a lot less ginger than I remember.

'Darling,' Katriona kisses him, 'pay the cab man, will you? Neither Isabel nor I brought any money.'

'*Isabel*?' Myles's jaw literally drops. I don't know if it's gratifying or incredibly insulting. 'You look amazing,' he continues. 'I mean, my God! I hardly recognised you!'

All right. It's incredibly insulting.

'I sent Iz to Luc,' Katriona butts in. 'And I bought her this little dress. Sweet, isn't she?'

'*I'll* say,' says Myles, sounding posher than ever. 'Well, well, Isabel. Aren't *you* the belle of the ball?'

'Myles, darling! You know *I'm* always the belle of the ball.' Katriona gives her tinkly laugh. 'Now let's go in. I'm freezing!'

I have to say, Claridge's bar is just a teensy bit disappointing. The lack of cocaine-snorting celebrities in the toilets at the Wolseley should probably have given me a bit of a heads-up. But it could literally be *any* bar, in any hotel, pretty much anywhere. It's incredibly dark and stuffed to the gills with people knocking back booze like there's no tomorrow. The men are mostly dressed like Myles, in crumpled designer jackets and untucked handmade shirts. The women are smarter and glossier, but they're dressed down too, in slouchy Margaret Howell-type trousers and black cashmere.

Did Katriona *know* all the other guests would look as though they were on their way to a casual Sunday brunch? Did she deliberately make me wear the Very, Very Little Black Dress so I'd look gauche and trashy, and a little bit stupid?

But why would she want me to look gauche and stupid in front of Jennifer and Gordon? Anyway, look at Katriona herself. She's surrounded by an adoring gaggle of middle-aged men, clutching an untouched glass of champagne, all done up in her royal blue like the fairy on top of the Christmas tree. I'm sure she thinks wearing slouchy trousers and black cashmere to a party shows you're not making enough effort.

'Well,' I say brightly. 'This is nice! Whose party is it, by the way?'

'American literary wunderkind. Thinks he's F. Scott Fitzgerald.' Myles nods in the direction of a tubercular young man. He's wearing the most crumpled jacket and the scruffiest shirt of all, and he's standing in the corner by himself looking a bit desperate. 'Wait here, Isabel,' Myles adds, 'and I'll get us some champagne. Got a couple of people I need to have a word with while I'm at it.'

'OK. Oh, do you know if Jennifer Reilly and Gordon Scott are here yet?'

Myles stares at me. 'Friends of yours?'

'Well, it might have been Jennifer Scott and Gordon Reilly. They're some Lemper Snyde Brusoff people Katriona wanted me to meet. If you point them out, I'll introduce myself.'

'Ohhh. Jennifer and Gordon.' Myles glances around the bar. 'Sorry, Isabel. No sign of them as far as I can see. Why don't you just wait here, and I'll ask around?' Before I can agree, he leans down, gives me a peck on the cheek, then starts making his way to the bar.

I can't believe he just kissed me. Part of me is flattered, part of me . . . Well, all right. All of me is flattered.

'Another paid-up member of the fan club?'

I turn round to look at the man who's just spoken behind me.

He's tall, brown-haired, and unlike everyone else here, smartly dressed. A bit boringly dressed, actually, in a navy suit with a white shirt and a navy striped tie that's actually tied in a proper knot. He isn't knocking back champagne like it's orange juice, but sipping from a glass of . . . Yes. I think it actually *is* orange juice.

'Pardon?'

'Myles Salisbury-Kent,' he says. 'Seems like you're another big fan.'

I'm not sure I like his tone. 'Not a big fan,' I say stiffly. 'Not any kind of a fan, in fact. Just an acquaintance.'

'Right.' He sips his orange juice again. 'I didn't mean to offend.'

There's a sudden racket in the nearby corner, which turns out to be a gang of partygoers falling about with hilarity, and calling the waiter over for yet more champagne.

Now *that's* what launch parties are meant to be like. Chris Macbeth and Millicent Petersen started their torrid, baby-oil-lubricated affair after meeting at a launch party. How come I'm stuck with the juice-sipping, navy-clad dullard?

Actually, that's not nice of me. I've always hated those people who spend parties looking over your shoulder for someone more interesting to talk to. And I'm not about to start losing my manners just because I'm moving in top-flight media circles. Besides, his dress sense might be a little on the reserved side, but he's far from bad-looking, and he's got small creases at the sides of his eyes that *might* mean he's got a sense of humour beneath all that navy.

'So,' I say brightly, 'why are you here?'

He shrugs. 'I've asked myself the same question. Sitting at home watching water boil would be a better use of an evening.'

I stare at him. 'But . . . it's a book launch!'

He stares back. 'So?'

'Well, there's free champagne . . . and smoked salmon blinis . . . And all these glamorous people . . .'

His mouth gives a twitch. It's not exactly a smile, but it's as close as he's got so far. 'Well, I don't drink champagne. I can't stand the taste of smoked salmon blinis. And I have nothing to say to a single one of these glamorous people.'

'Well, why *have* you come, then?'

'Work,' he says.

'*You* . . . work for LSB?' I have a sudden sinking

216

feeling. 'Oh God, your name's not Gordon Reilly, is it?'

'No.'

'Gordon Scott?'

'*No*. And I don't work *for* LSB, as such. I *do* some work for them. I'm a solicitor in the City. Thomson Tibble Telford.'

'Oh . . .' Well, this explains the navy suit and the orange juice. 'How . . . interesting.'

Now there's a definite flicker of a smile. 'Yes, that's just the tone of voice all my friends use about my job.'

'No, no, I'm sure it's fascinating! And surely media law is . . . well . . . more interesting than other kinds of law.'

This is a bit of a field of expertise with me, by the way. A couple of years ago, when Dad was launching a sustained attack on my career choices, I did an enormous amount of research on this very area. Obviously, media law was the only kind of law I ever considered, no matter how keen Dad was on me becoming a tax lawyer, or something equally deadly. I even sent off for some glossy brochures that made being a solicitor look quite a lot like being a model for *Cosmopolitan*. (I think one of them might even have been from Thomson Tibble Thingy, come to think of it.) I really put my back into it. And my conclusion was that media law was *more* interesting than other kinds of law. Not *actually* interesting. But still, more interesting than tax law.

'You'd be surprised,' Mr Navy is saying now.

'People always think that, but actually I'm much more interested in tax law.'

Well, this does it. All hopes of a hidden sense of humour were clearly false. I'm going to make my excuses, politely, and disentangle myself.

'You see, media law is usually just very basic stuff about contracts,' he carries on, 'while *tax* law, on the other hand, presents with a surprising amount of interesting quirks . . .'

Hang on a moment. His eyes have suddenly glazed over – *his* eyes! – and he's staring over my left shoulder.

'Right,' I say. 'Well, I'm sorry to have bored you. Perhaps you'd prefer to speak to whoever's behind me.'

'Not really,' Mr Navy says, so stonily that I turn round to see who it is that's bothering him.

Oh. It's Joe Madison.

'My God,' Joe says. A National-Grid-blowing smile is breaking out across his face.

'Joe,' is all I manage to say. It's not particularly impressive.

'Isabel,' he says, which somehow sounds a lot more impressive. He leans down to give me a soft, slightly lingering kiss on each cheek, and I catch the spicy scent of Jo Malone again. 'You look absolutely sensational.'

'Thank you.' I can feel my face flame. 'So, is . . . er . . . is Gina here?'

'Not tonight. I'm flying solo.'

This is exceptional news.

1) Joe Madison is here!
2) Joe Madison is here *without Gina*!
3) Joe Madison just told me I look absolutely sensational!
4) Joe Madison had a certain look in his eye as he said it; a look that is hard to place exactly, but a look that seemed to hint at more, much more, than he's able to say . . .

'So, Isabel.' Joe interrupts my train of thought. 'Who's your friend?' He nods at Mr Navy.

'Oh God, sorry!' I completely forgot about Mr Navy, still standing there with his orange juice in his hand like a wet weekend. 'Joe Madison, this is . . .'

'Will,' says Mr Navy. 'Will Madison.'

So this is weird.

'The same surname!' I say. 'What a coincidence!'

'Not really,' says Joe, with a grin like a naughty schoolboy. 'We're brothers.'

'*Brothers*? *You* two?'

'I'm not sure which of us you're insulting,' says Joe, whose grin is getting even naughtier. 'But, yes. We share our parents' DNA.'

Odd way to talk about your brother. Mind you, they don't seem particularly close. Even aside from the fact that they don't look much alike – though now I look closely, I can see a *small* likeness around the mouth, and Will's eyes *might* be a similar shade of blue if they weren't being swamped by all that navy –

they're standing apart from each other like one of them might go off at any minute.

'I'm not trying to insult either of you . . .'

'Try harder,' says Will. He isn't smiling.

OK. I can see who got all the charm genes in the family.

'You can see who got all the charm genes in the family,' says Joe, stopping a passing waiter for two glasses of champagne, one of which he hands to me. 'And it ain't my little brother, Wills!'

I stare at them both. '*Little* brother?' I actually need to get a grip here. 'I mean,' I continue, hastily, 'Will's the one with the responsible job and all. I just assumed he'd be the older one.'

'Well,' Will says, 'I'm not.'

'I'm only a year older,' says Joe, giving me a nudge. 'And Will's not *really* more responsible than me.'

'Right,' says Will, through barely parted lips. 'When *was* the last time you managed to find a weekend to visit Mum, Joe?'

Joe just grins. 'Let's save the family drama for a time when we're not in the presence of a beautiful woman.'

5) Joe Madison just called me a beautiful woman!

It makes me sound like some kind of dusky Cuban señorita. Now, there's a Look I hadn't thought of. Heavy eye makeup, tight skirt, possibly some sort of ruffled blouse, a single bougainvillaea bloom tucked behind one ear?

Isabela Perón
Isabelita Sanchez-Vicario . . .

Well, I'll put it to Jemima on the 30th. I'm sure she'll have some suggestions of her own.

'I'll leave you two to chat.' Will Madison shoves his orange juice glass at Joe and stalks out of the bar.

'God, Iz, sorry about that.' Joe lets out a long sigh.

'That's OK.'

'Will and I try to keep our relationship purely professional these days.'

'That's a pity.'

'Anyway, my dear Iz-Wiz, glad to see you're out and about.' There's a distinct twinkle in his ocean-blue eyes. 'Not brought the paparazzi with you?'

So he knows. Of course he knows. But there's something about his smile, thank God, that makes me think he probably didn't read about it in the *Guardian*.

'I have nothing to hide.'

'Well, in that dress, I'm not sure you'd be able to hide anything even if you had to.' Joe's eyes go e-v-e-r-s-o-s-l-o-w-l-y down, then back up again. 'Good for you, Isabel. Don't let the bastards get you down. But tell me,' he leans close again, as though we're sharing a big secret, 'what *are* you doing here, anyway?'

'She's working for Kat,' says Myles, suddenly appearing at Joe's elbow. He's carrying two glasses of champagne, one of which he hands to me, after shoving my empty glass at Joe. He's also brought a small plate of smoked salmon blinis.

The effect of the pair of them in stereo is quite dazzling. I think I need a lie down.

Joe swipes two smoked salmon blinis from the plate. 'Working as Kat's *what*?'

'Hey, Isabel, why don't you give Joe one of your business cards?' asks Myles.

'I don't think so.'

'Go on! They're hilarious.'

'*No*,' I snap. It does the trick, because Myles shuts up. 'I'm Katriona's Special Assistant,' I tell Joe.

'And Isabel is something of a writer herself,' says Myles. 'She's got a cracking little bonkbuster under her belt.'

'Oh, I'll bet she does,' says Joe, softly.

OK, now I definitely need a lie-down.

'Well, if you need any help with it, Iz-Wiz, you know where to come.'

'I'll be helping Isabel with this project,' says Myles. 'Actually.'

'You can *both* help me with the project!' I announce, just in case they decide to have a row about it. 'Actually, *you* don't happen to know a Gordon Scott, do you?' I ask Joe.

'I don't think Gordon's here tonight, Isabel,' Myles says, before Joe can answer. 'I've had a good look, but I can't see him or Jennifer anywhere.'

This is typical. I sorted out the Very, Very Little Black Dress. I've got my Super-Hair. And Gordon Thingy and Jennifer Whatsit aren't even here! What a waste.

Although Joe did tell me I looked absolutely stunning. So not a *total* waste, perhaps.

'Well, I've got to dash, my darling,' Joe suddenly says, leaning down to give me a kiss on both cheeks. 'People to see, places to go.'

'There's no need to look so gutted, Isabel,' Myles says irritably, as we watch Joe leave. 'It's not like he's abandoning you with Quasimodo.'

'No . . . I'm sorry . . . I'm just a bit disappointed that Jennifer and Gordon aren't here.'

Myles grabs another glass of champagne, and downs it in one large, grouchy gulp. 'Didn't anyone warn you, Isabel? Launch parties are shit.'

'What a hit *you* were,' says Katriona, in the taxi going home.

I'll be completely honest: the launch party wasn't *quite* the fun I'd been expecting it to be. I mean, don't get me wrong, it was nice to see Joe again. And Myles's attention was very flattering. It's just . . . I don't know. The smoked salmon blinis were there, after all. And the champagne. There just seemed to be something missing.

'Quite the little star,' Katriona continues. 'Though you know, Iz, darling, you ought to watch out for Joe Madison.'

'What? No! I mean, I don't have to watch out for him. I've got no interest in him. No interest at all.'

'Isabel.' She puts a chilly, jewel-laden hand on top of mine. 'He eats girls like you for breakfast.'

'Girls like me?'

'Sweet. Naïve. Hopeless romantics.'

'I can assure you, Katriona,' I say, 'that there is nothing hopeless about me.'

We ride along in silence for a few minutes.

'Well, did you have a good time?' Katriona suddenly asks. Her voice is warmer now. 'I'm sorry, Isabel, that I lost track of you. There are always so many people who want to talk to me at these things. I'd have introduced you to Jennifer and Gordon, but time just seemed to slip away . . .'

'You mean they *were* there?'

'Of course they were! Didn't Myles introduce you to them?'

'Myles said they weren't around.'

'God, that lying shit! Oh, poor you, Iz. Just because Myles is a miserable old git, that doesn't mean he can get in the way of your career. Well, you'll soon show him. Just you wait until he gets a sneak preview of your . . . what was it called again?'

'*Showjumpers.*'

'*Showjumpers,*' she repeats with satisfaction. 'I can hardly wait to read it myself! When do I get my sneak preview?'

'Er . . . you might need to wait just a tiny bit longer . . .'

She's staring at me. 'But at the Wolseley, you said you'd almost finished.'

This isn't fair. At the Wolseley, *she* said I'd almost finished. I avoided the issue entirely.

'Well, there's been a bit of a hiatus recently,' I begin. 'All the stress of the political scandal . . . I've got two or three chapters, though!'

'Isabel,' she gives me a sharp look, 'I am not about to let you approach people as important and as busy as Jennifer and Gordon with *two or three chapters*.'

Great. Working for Katriona was meant to be speeding up my book deal, not slowing it down to a grinding halt.

'Look.' She must have noticed my crestfallen face, because she squeezes my hand, rather hard. 'I do understand, Isabel, how difficult writer's block can be. I tell you what,' she squeezes my hand again, 'I can manage without much help for a few days. Why don't you take the time to push on with *Showjumpers*? Turn your two or three chapters into something we can actually show Jennifer and Gordon?'

'That's really kind, Katriona, but what about your diary . . .?'

'Selma can help me out if I need it. And I'm hardly incapable of sorting out my own diary! I'll even set up that meeting with Jennifer and Gordon myself, for a couple of weeks' time. Give you some real motivation.'

'But honestly, Katriona, I really think once Jennifer and Gordon hear about the complimentary riding crops –'

'Don't you worry about me,' she carries on, as if I haven't even spoken. 'You just focus on *your* work, Isabel. It's time for you to take yourself seriously for a change.'

HOW I WRITE

by Isabel Bookbinder

Chapter 18

God, I feel inspired.

I woke up *before* the dawn this morning, then sat by the window, gazing across Kensington Gardens. It was an awful lot more inspiring than the gazing I was doing back in Hammersmith. I mean, watching the sun come up over a billion pounds of prime W8 property has a really invigorating effect. I don't know why more novelists don't do it.

Anyway, then I pottered down to the huge basement kitchen and made myself an invigorating coffee with Katriona's swanky Italian espresso machine. I can't say the coffee was the very best I've ever tasted – sort of like hot, bitter grit suspended in pond water – but it was already an improvement on the ones I've made every other morning this week. I'm sure it will come right eventually.

Then I assembled my Inspiring Outfit. I may not have my cashmere tracksuit yet, but after a bit of trial and error, I've cleverly *combined* cashmere and tracksuit to devastating effect. M&S trackie bottoms, my lemon-yellow C&C California vest, and my cashmere (mix) shrug from Marley's wedding. I've dabbed half a bottle of Envy behind my ears, popped on a dab of volumising mascara and some Touche Éclat, and now I'm all ready to go.

I can't believe how much I've achieved in just one morning!

The only thing I'm having a bit of a hard time cracking is the part where you actually sit down and write stuff.

There are lots of really good reasons for that, though. For one thing, being a Novelist is proving to be a very messy activity. I seem to wake up every morning in a bit of a slum, with empty biscuit packets and old teacups littering every available surface. Tidying up enough space to work in takes a good chunk of the morning, by which time the most valuable hours of the day have gone. Plus, being a Novelist is much more tiring than you'd think. I know it *looks* like you're just sitting about on your bottom all day, but the brain needs to be constantly alert, in case inspiration should suddenly strike. I think that's why I've been spending so much time napping recently – I just want to be prepared to spring into action the moment I need to.

But this morning has gone so well already, I think the time has actually come to start the writing part.

OK.

Let's just sit down at the desk, for starters. Try it out for size.

Very comfortable. Very nice.

Perhaps I should do a few yoga stretches to get myself warmed up. Less chance of a horrific desk-related injury that way. And everyone knows you need to be fit in order to think clearly. *Mens sana in corpore . . . senex?*

Now. What yoga poses do I know? Well, there's definitely something about saluting the sun, but that sounds a bit Stonehenge-druid for my taste. What about . . . the Warrior? A deep lunge, then you lift your arms as though you're holding a bow and arrow, then arch your back . . .

Ow. *Ow.* I knew there was a reason I was hoping yoga wasn't compulsory.

Well, this is great. How am I supposed to write anything when I'm flat on the floor waiting for my spine to come out of a spasm? I bet this never happens to Madonna.

Perhaps the pain would ease a bit if I had some sort of distraction. Like *This Morning* with Phil and Fern.

I prop myself up at the side of the bed, switch my portable TV on and settle down to a low-fat cookery demonstration with Fern's lovely hubby. I feel better already.

Now there's someone knocking at the door.

'I come in?'

'Oh, yes, Selma! Please do.'

Selma backs into the room, holding a tray. 'Is-a-bell?'

'Yes, Selma, I'm down here!' I wave at her from behind the bed.

She stares down at me. 'You are unwell?'

I haul myself halfway up. 'Actually, I'm feeling a bit better now.'

'Miss de Montfort say you are working very hard on your book about horses. But I think maybe you like some refreshing.'

'Oh, that's really kind, Selma, thank you!'

She starts to unload her tray onto my desk: a cafetiere of fresh coffee and a plate of assorted McVitie's biscuits. She must have popped out specially to get the biccies from the shop, because Katriona won't allow them to be kept in the house.

'Why don't you stay,' I ask, 'and have a coffee with me?'

'But Miss de Montfort say you must work.'

'Oh, that can wait.'

Well, all this inspiration isn't *going* anywhere, is it? I'll be just as inspired in twenty minutes' time. Anyway, poor Selma just seems to spend all day floating about this giant house, looking bleak. I can't tell if it's suppressed memories of the horrors of her homeland, or just the effects of daily battle with Lysander, but she looks as though she could do with some cheering up.

For Selma,
Who could do with some cheering up.

'Come on, Selma. It'd be nice to have a chat.'

I can see her face soften, just a little bit.

'All right,' she says. 'Five minute.'

She sits down on the edge of the bed while I rinse out the tooth-mug in the bathroom. I pour two cups of coffee, hand her the nice one and take a sip from the tooth-mug myself.

'Well,' I say. 'This is lovely!'

Selma helps herself to several biscuits.

I can see this is going to be hard work. 'Tell me about yourself! Where are you from?'

'Ljubljana.'

'Beautiful,' I nod. 'Beautiful country.'

'Is a *city*. In Slovenia.'

'Oh, of course! I am sorry, Selma. You'll have to forgive me. My knowledge of Balka is a bit limited.'

Selma stares at me. This isn't going quite as well as I'd hoped.

'So! How long have you worked for Katriona?'

'One year.' She stares at the floor. 'She is good employer. I very, very happy here.'

Is it just me, or has her voice gone a bit robotic?

'Well, who wouldn't be? Living in this beautiful house . . . got to be better than back home!'

Her face has gone stony. 'Back home is not a dump.'

'Oh, Selma, I didn't mean anything by that! I've heard the most *wonderful* things about Slovakia . . .'

'*Slovenia.*'

'. . . *and* Slovenia,' I add smoothly. 'Friendly locals, great nightlife . . .' I'm racking my brains for any information I might have accidentally picked up from *A Place in the Sun*, '. . . fascinating history . . .'

I think I've succeeded in mollifying her a little bit because she nods. 'You good person, Is-a-bell.'

'Well, thank you, Selma.'

'Funny person, but good person.'

'Er . . . again . . . thank you.'

'I like you more than Becca.' She stops.

'Becca? You mean Lysander's babysitter?'

'Who say she was Lysander babysitter?' Selma has turned very pink, and her top lip has started sweating.

'Er . . . Lysander said so, I think. Well, he said she was fun. And that she wore old jeans and T-shirts. I assumed that was to join in with his spreading game.'

'Then, yes.' She nods unconvincingly. 'Yes, OK, Becca was Lysander babysitter.'

There's something odd going on here. And I think I know what it might be. 'Selma,' I begin carefully, 'Myles Salisbury-Kent mentioned something the other day about not liking Katriona's assistants in the past. This Becca girl wouldn't, by any chance –'

'Miss de Montfort has never had assistant until you,' Selma says, getting to her feet. 'I go now.'

'Oh, please don't go, Selma! Stay and have more coffee!'

'I have much washing and cleaning to do.' Selma closes the door very firmly behind her.

Now this is just plain weird. If this Becca person *was* Katriona's assistant, and not some babysitter of Lysander's, what's the big deal? I mean, does everyone think I'll be upset if I'm not Katriona's first, or something? It's hardly like lying about how many people you've slept with. I'm not trying to be melodramatic or anything, but there's something a bit creepy about it.

But I haven't put in all this morning's hard graft

to sit around here worrying about mystery Beccas.

I sit down at my desk.

I pick up a pen.

I open my notebook.

'Barrington

Bosworth-

B—'

My phone starts ringing. I snatch it up and flip it open. 'Hello?'

'He*llo*,' says a very friendly man's voice. 'This must be Katriona de Montfort's assistant.'

'Yes. Who's this?'

'Paul Gardner speaking.' He says the name as though I should recognise it. Then, when I obviously don't, he adds, 'I'm the Managing Director of Aadelman Stern.'

So. That cow Milly Barnsley *has* done her worst, after all. 'Look, Mr Gardner, you should know that I don't take kindly to being harassed. I've already written to my MP about the matter, and—'

He isn't listening. 'So, everyone here at Aadelman Stern thinks this manuscript is something pretty special.'

I nearly drop my phone. 'Pardon?'

'*Showjumpers*,' he says, slightly louder, as if he's talking to an idiot. 'It's sitting in my desk in front of me right now, and I have to say, I'm very excited.'

'You . . . you *like* it? You like *Showjumpers*?'

'Love it,' he says. 'Terrific stuff.'

I'm finding it very difficult to digest what he's

saying. 'So . . . you didn't see any kind of . . . er . . . covering letter?'

Paul Gardner lets out a low chuckle. 'Well,' he says, 'that *is* one of the things we were going to ask about.'

'Oh God.'

'Brilliant joke. Brilliant.'

'Yes!' I gasp. 'Yes, it *was* a joke!'

'*So* funny. Now, how quickly can we see you? We'll clear our schedules if that helps. You're incredibly busy, obviously.'

'Incredibly . . .'

'But you'll make time for us?' He sounds anxious, all of a sudden. 'How does tomorrow sound?'

I can't wait until tomorrow! 'Today!' I squeak. 'I could do today!'

'Oh, jolly good. Half-three suit you?'

'Half past three . . .' I pretend to be considering. Paul Gardner doesn't know I'm not checking out some state-of-the-art BlackBerry-type personal organiser. 'Yes. That will do just fine.'

'Lovely! Can you come to the office? In St James's Square? Or we could come to you, if you'd rather . . . you know . . . keep a *low profile*.'

Oh God. He's obviously referring to the *Saturday Mercury* scandal. Still, if they're this desperate to meet me, they can't be all that worried about it.

'Just so you know,' I say, 'I have already started thinking about possible pseudonyms.'

'Pseudonyms?' he echoes. 'Well, I don't think we'd necessarily want to do that. You do realise, don't you, that this *Showjumpers* thing could be a million-seller?'

'Fucking hell.'

'What?'

'I mean, well, well, well.'

'Looking forward to an extremely productive meeting, Liz!'

'Iz,' I say, but he's already gone.

It's been a frantic couple of hours, but the outfit is good. Black cigarette pants and a graphic-print black-and-white tunic, belted on the hips with my skinny black Marni belt, all finished off with the red platform Mary-Janes I bought in the Kurt Geiger sale last January.

All right. Full price last March.

Topped off with my brand-new Super-Hair and an extra-generous spritz of Envy, I feel ready to take on Aadelman Stern.

A million-seller, Paul Gardner said. He didn't *sound* like he was taking the piss.

I bundle myself up in my warmest coat and start to head down the stairs. I'd better let Katriona know I'm going out. All I have to do is follow the sound of 'Axel F' to the fitness studio.

Clad in eye-poppingly tight pink Lycra, Katriona is bouncing up and down to the music. An extremely bronzed man with a rippling six-pack and white-blond dreadlocks is bouncing with her.

'Sorry to interrupt!' I yell. 'I'm just nipping out, Katriona.'

Katriona stops bouncing, and puts her hand on her hips. 'Out?'

'Only for a couple of hours. I've been writing *so* hard these last few days, I just feel like I need a little break.'

'A break?' She folds her arms. 'Proper writers don't take breaks, Isabel.'

This is a bit unfair. I'm not the one body-popping around my private yoga studio at one in the afternoon.

'I know, but this is work-related.' Now I'm a bit stuck. I don't actually want to tell her about my conversation with Paul Gardner. She's doing so much to engineer matters with Jennifer and Gordon at Lemper Snyde Brusoff, I really can't risk offending her until I'm certain things will work out with Aadelman Stern. 'It's . . . research! Yes! Research is what it is.'

'Research?' She wrinkles her tiny nose. 'What kind of research?'

Oh God. What kind of research might *Showjumpers* need?

'Horses,' I hear myself say. 'I'm off to the park. To look at horses.'

Now even the blonde Rastafarian has stopped bouncing.

'Horses are tricky things,' I say. 'It's very hard to capture the . . . the *spirit* of a horse on paper.'

'Horses,' echoes Katriona. Then all of a sudden, she bursts out laughing. 'I don't believe a word of it!'

Shit. 'Look, Katriona, the truth is—'

'*We* know what kind of research Isabel's *bonk*buster

236

needs, don't we, Merlin?' She nudges the fake Rasta.

That's Merlin? But Merlin's meant to be a wizened-up old yogi. Ben Kingsley. Not Jean-Claude Van Damme.

'Off you go,' Katriona shoos me, 'and whoever . . . I mean, *whatever* you're off to do, you just make sure you write *all* about it in your bonkbuster!'

'Er . . . OK . . . I won't be long . . .'

She waves a dismissive hand, already bouncing again as Olivia Newton-John urges her to get physical. 'This book won't write itself, remember, Isabel. Take as long as you need!'

Chapter 19

I'm far too early for my meeting. Still, I'm not going to stand around freezing in St James's Square. I push the revolving doors and go on into Aadelman Stern's reception.

God, it's already everything I'd hoped a top international publishing house would be. Lots of blond wood and stainless steel, which is always reassuring. The young man behind the big blond wood desk doesn't seem the slightest bit interested in the nature of my meeting, not even when I tell him what Paul Gardner said about it selling millions. He just sends me over to wait on some huge squashy sofas until it's time for me to go up.

There are a couple of other people waiting on the sofas too – two middle-aged men in grey suits who don't look like novelists at all. They're both engrossed in big broadsheets (headline – 'CAROLINE MACBETH FORCED TO ABANDON ANTI-SLEAZE INITIATIVE') and there's no paper left on the table for me. So I decide to get out my phone and give Mum a call.

She picks up after several rings. 'Hello?'

'Good afternoon,' I say, neutrally, just in case the men are listening in. They don't look the sort to phone their mothers before an important meeting.

'Iz-Wiz! I was just about to call you!'

'I don't have long, I'm afraid. I've got a meeting at Aadelman Stern. You know, the publishers.' I raise my voice slightly. 'I'm here to see what kind of a book deal they want to offer.'

The men don't even look up.

'Oh, Isabel, that's wonderful! I *told* you Mr Aardvark-whatsit would snap you up!'

'Well, it certainly seems that way.'

'I'm so proud of you, darling. Dad will be too.'

'Yes . . .' I lower my voice. 'Actually, Mum, can you not tell Dad until I actually have a *definite* offer on the table? I just . . . I don't want to jinx anything.'

'My lips are sealed. Actually . . .' now *her* voice is lowered, 'I'm keeping a few secrets from him myself at the moment.'

'Oh?'

'But you must promise not to tell, Iz-Wiz.'

'Of course I won't tell.'

'Because your dad didn't particularly like Nathan when he was round here the other day, so if he knew what was going on . . .'

Oh my God. 'Mum,' I croak, 'you're having an affair with a cub reporter.'

'Isabel Bookbinder! I am doing nothing of the sort.'

'So what's Nathan got to do with it?'

'Because it's thanks to Nathan that I have *become* a cub reporter.'

I don't think I've heard this right. 'I'm sorry, it's quite noisy in here . . .'

'A cub reporter,' repeats Mum. 'On the *Central Somerset Gazette*. They have a wonderful training scheme. Nathan's specialising in investigative journalism, but I thought *I* might like to try something a little bit less *nosy*. So I was thinking of arts and features, darling, like you used to do. Well,' she corrects herself, 'like you told us you used to do.'

'But, Mum, you don't *know* anything about arts and features.'

'Well, neither did you.'

'But my career was all a lie!'

Now, of course, the businessmen have started eavesdropping.

I lower my voice again. 'I mean, arts journalism is harder than you think. You'll need contacts, for starters.'

'Well, I've got you. And I was thinking, darling, for my first interview . . .'

'Oh, I don't know, Mum,' I say. 'I'd have to check with the press office at Aadelman Stern before I could agree to anything like that.'

'Not *you*,' says Mum. 'Your boss. You did say it was that de Montfort woman, didn't you?'

I open my mouth, but nothing comes out.

'The editor would be really impressed if I got such a big interview the first time out,' Mum is continuing. 'It would really help my chances of being kept on after the work experience.'

Ask Katriona de Montfort to do an interview with a fifty-seven-year-old cub reporter from the *Central Somerset Gazette*? 'Mum, I'll see what I can do, but—'

'Thank you, darling. Look, I'd better go. Nathan is coming round to test me on my shorthand.' She hangs up.

OK. This is all I need. I mean, I'm genuinely thrilled for Mum that she's finally found a career for herself. And it's something she's always wanted to do, if her years spent writing letters to newspapers are anything to go by. But Dad is going to go mental when he finds out. He's never wanted Mum working. Like one of those Communist dictators, he fears the freedom it might give her. And thanks to the *Gazette* connection, he'll doubtless seek a way to blame me.

Anyway, there's no time to worry about that now. The bored receptionist is waving me over to the lifts.

'Fifth floor,' he tells me. 'They'll meet you up there.'

The lift is all blond wood and stainless steel too, which bodes well, and there's a girl travelling up in it carrying a gorgeous, brand-new Mulberry Roxanne, which bodes even better.

Another girl leaps at me as I step out of the lift on the fifth floor. 'Liz? I'm Milly Barnsley.'

I don't know why I ever imagined Milly was the kind of girl who'd sell stories to the gutter press. She's ever so earnest-looking, with an air of medium-level anxiety.

'So,' she continues, 'it's . . . it's just you?'

I'm not really sure what she means. 'Yes. Just me.'

'Well . . . that's fine! That's good, in fact!'

Oh. *I* get it. She's probably used to seeing all the top novelists arrive with all kinds of entourage and hangers-on. Agents and lawyers and publicists and hairstylists . . . I mean, Katriona probably takes Merlin to every meeting, in case she's suddenly in need of spiritual guidance, or strenuous cardiovascular activity. I make a promise to myself here and now to smash this stereotype. 'Such a nice, normal girl,' everyone will say about me. 'We've never known a bestselling Novelist so delightful to work with. Apart from the fame, the money, and the phenomenal wardrobe, she's really just like anybody else! You don't get diva antics from Isabel Bookbinder.'

I should probably rethink that pseudonym too. Isabel Bloggs? Izzy Smith? And maybe my trademark could be that I travel everywhere on a simple bicycle, shunning chauffeur-driven Bentleys. Or that I turn up to meetings with my own little Thermos flask of coffee, and hand round some delicious home-made sandwiches, wrapped in tin foil.

But I don't want to take things *too* far.

'I think in general, it's best to keep things low-key,' I tell Milly as she leads me down a long corridor. 'No special treatment. No starry behaviour.'

'Well, certainly,' says Milly, looking a bit confused. 'We just want things to be comfortable. However you generally prefer to work. We're all pretty nervous about this, as I'm sure you can imagine!'

I pat her on the hand. 'Please, don't worry. I'm sure

this association with Aadelman Stern is going to be a long and profitable one.'

'*Really*?' She looks ready to cry. 'Oh God, Liz, that's the most fantastic news!'

'Actually, my name's . . .'

But Milly is already opening a door at the end of the corridor and waving me through.

'Everyone, this is Miss de Montfort's Special Assistant.'

It's a large, bland boardroom, with more of the same blond wood and – oooh, lovely – a nice pot of coffee and some fig rolls on the table. There are three people already sitting there: a red-faced middle-aged man who must be Paul Gardner; a freckled girl of about my age, dressed all in brown; and a woman of about forty wearing a Margaret Howell trouser suit, natch, with a chic blonde bob and lightning-bolt earrings.

'Hello,' I say, with a big, friendly smile, just to reassure them about what a delight I'm going to be. 'It's wonderful to meet you all!'

The middle-aged man springs up from his seat. 'Paul Gardner. Welcome!' he says, clasping my hand between both of his, and shaking it warmly. 'Er – all alone?'

'Please,' I say. 'Let's get one thing straight from the outset. I don't need an entourage. I'm not going to be a diva. In fact, that kind of behaviour makes me sick. We're all the same underneath it all, aren't we? Why should anyone feel they're better than somebody else, just because they're a mega-million-selling international sensation?'

You know, maybe I should think about getting into politics after all. I'm sure the Socialist Workers Party would welcome a few more millionaires with social consciences like mine.

'Liz has come by herself today,' Milly says, holding out a chair for me. 'Probably best, don't you think, for our initial meeting?'

'Oh, of course, of course,' says Paul Gardner, clapping his hands together. 'Jolly good.'

I like him already. If he's going to be editing *Showjumpers*, I'll be in for a treat. He looks like a man who understands the serious side of this business. If that glow around his nose means anything, he's seen a few wild launch parties in his time.

'You must meet everyone,' he's saying. 'You already know the lovely Milly, junior commissioning editor extraordinaire. And this lovely lady to my left is the lovely Shonagh McDermott, our lovely head of Legal.'

'Hello,' says the freckled girl in brown, barely looking up, and scribbling in an intense way on a yellow pad of paper.

'And this,' Paul Gardner turns to the chic, blonde woman, 'is Penelope Bright, our senior publisher.'

I can't help noticing that he's dropped all the 'lovely's.

'Welcome,' says Penelope. She isn't smiling.

'Penelope is *particularly* excited about this project,'

Gardner says, pouring me coffee and shoving over the fig rolls. 'Aren't you, Penelope?'

I have to say, she doesn't *look* particularly excited. She's looking at me across the table like Dad looks at errant third-formers. My fingers are itching to reach down beneath the table and pull my socks up.

'If we're lucky enough to sign up this book, Penelope will be the one editing it,' Gardner adds.

Oh, great. Penelope Bright looks like she wouldn't even authorise a search party for me, let alone a launch party.

'Well, Liz has given me a major hint that we *are* going to be lucky enough to get the manuscript.' Milly flushes.

Gardner bashes his palms together again, with a beam that threatens to crack his mottled cheeks. 'Great stuff!'

God, it's *so* nice to meet people who are thrilled to be working with me.

To Paul,
Who was thrilled to be working with me.

'So, Liz, let's get down to brass tacks. You must be far too busy to sit around here listening to us pontificate. We all know how busy your boss is.'

'Er – yes.'

'Why don't you start by telling us a bit more about *Showjumpers*.'

'Of course!' I can't wait to see his face when I

245

mention Bring Back the Bonkbuster, and tell him about the complimentary riding crops. 'What kind of thing do you want to know?'

'Do you know how it will develop?'

'Well, I see it developing very much into a proper book,' I say. 'With chapters, and everything.'

'Er . . . I meant, how does the *plot* develop?'

Oh God, this blasted plot nonsense again. 'Well, there will *be* a plot, of course. But wouldn't you rather concentrate on other things for the time being? The characters, for example? The title?'

From the silence around the table, I think maybe I've said something wrong.

'I mean,' I continue, 'that . . . well . . . plot-wise . . . the – er – sky really is the limit.'

Milly suddenly leans forward. 'Are you talking about a series?'

I stare at her. 'Are *you*?'

'Naturally we'd like to take the project as far as it can go. Three books.' Milly says. 'Maybe four.'

I'm trying very hard to maintain my cool, professional façade. But inside, I'm doing cartwheels. *Three books! Maybe four!* Well, yah, boo, sucks to you, Gina *Wave/Lengths* Deverill.

I notice that everyone is staring at me across the table, as though they're waiting for me to speak.

'Well,' I say, 'I think a series is possible.'

Gardner lets out a little bleat. 'Wonderful. Wonderful!'

'We certainly would love to see more in the same

vein,' says Milly. 'The first volume is *so* fun, *so* amusing.'

'Mmm.' Penelope is pressing her lips together. 'It's odd, isn't it?'

'Odd?' Gardener, Milly and I say, in unison. See? We're working in harmony together already!

'Well,' Penelope continues, 'from the little I know about Katriona de Montfort, I've never imagined her as a woman with a highly developed sense of humour.'

I'm not really sure where this is leading. 'Oh, yes,' I say. 'She's a very funny woman.'

Gardner bangs the table. 'I thought she must be! There was that terrific joke with the covering letter, for starters. "Isabel Bookbinder". I mean, wasn't that the name of the girl who's just exposed the Home Secretary's husband's affair?'

'Er . . .'

'*So* witty. I didn't really understand it, but hilarious, obviously. Katriona does see the rest of the *Showjumpers* series as comic works too, yes?'

I stare at him. 'Pardon?'

'Those snogging scenes for example – I mean, we roared! We'd probably have to think about raunching it up a bit, but maybe it's best not to communicate that to Katriona right away.'

'So you think . . . it's *Katriona's* work?'

'Well, I must say, we'd never have guessed if Milly hadn't made that phone call to you! Quite a risk Katriona was taking, sending it out anonymously like that. And that hilarious letter – priceless!'

247

I can feel Penelope's eyes boring into me from across the other side of the table.

'Yes,' I manage to say. 'Well, like I said, Katriona's a funny woman.'

'You know, people think these epic bonkbusters are terribly out of fashion these days, but who better to inject some life into the genre than Katriona de Montfort?'

'Twenty million books sold worldwide,' mutters Penelope, as if to boost her own morale.

'Exactly,' says Gardner, attacking a fig roll with gusto. 'So we have very high hopes for *Showjumpers*, Liz. Very high hopes indeed.'

'Great,' I say. 'Really . . . great.'

Everything is starting to make a bit more sense now, to be honest. Milly's surprise that I'd come on my own – that is, *without Katriona*. The *frisson* around the table when I confirmed the possibility of a series. Paul Gardner's manifest delight to be working with me. Except, of course, not me. Katriona. I mean, what publisher in their right mind wouldn't be falling over themselves with excitement at the thought of signing Twenty-Million-Books-Sold-Worldwide Katriona?

I have a horrible feeling that if I own up right now, they aren't going to be quite so interested in *Showjumpers* after all. But how the hell am I going to pretend that it's really Katriona signing the book deal? I can't exactly *forge* her signature. Can I?

'Well, *my* hopes will be higher once I've actually seen a little more of the manuscript.' Penelope is opening up a slim file. She takes out a sheaf of paper, a photocopy of familiar handwriting. The pages are stapled in one corner. 'This is only the first three thousand words. We can't possibly go ahead with a contract until we have more idea how the book is progressing. For a start, we can't set a publication date until we know just how much editorial work there is to do. And I'm sure Sales and Marketing are going to want a good idea of how much they should start budgeting for a suitable publicity campaign.'

This is all a bit technical-sounding. But I think what Penelope is saying is 'no manuscript, no deal'.

'I tell you what,' I say hastily. 'Why don't you concentrate on getting the contract all written up, and I'll concentrate on putting together some more of Katriona's . . . er . . . material?'

That sounded promising enough to keep them happy, I think. while still being vague enough that I don't have to do anything mad, like go away right now and write the entire thing.

'More *material*?' Penelope snaps. 'What *kind* of material?'

Bloody Penelope. 'God, I hardly know where to begin . . .' I turn my attention to Milly and Paul. 'Loads more chapters, obviously . . . er . . . a synopsis . . . oh!' I've just remembered. 'Some *amazing* publicity and marketing ideas!'

That's it! My Bring Back the Bonkbuster campaign! That's what I can give them! And then they'll be so bowled over that they'll call me in to see them a few days later, and say, 'We don't even need to see another chapter. This is going to be the biggest hit since *Riders*. If only the author were in the room, we'd make her sign that contract this very day!' And I'll give a little smile, and say, 'Actually, the author *is* in the room . . .' And then they'll gasp, and laugh, and I'll sign the contract, and they'll crack open some champagne, and take me to a celebration lunch down the road at the Wolseley.

It's going to be brilliant!

'We have a publicity department for that kind of thing,' Penelope says. 'They'll do all that. What we want Katriona to do is provide us with more than just one per cent of the final book!'

One per cent? 'You want *Showjumpers* to be . . . three hundred thousand words?' I stare at her. 'Won't that be an awfully *long* book?'

'An epic bonkbuster,' says Penelope, 'ought to be epic. Surely.'

Are these people completely insane? When am I going to find the time to write *three hundred thousand words*, for God's sake?

'Well, I'm not so sure,' I tell her. 'I mean, surely most people read a bonkbuster on the beach. A big, heavy book just isn't convenient! Especially when it gets all slippery with sun lotion.'

Now even Shonagh looks up from her yellow pad.

'Not to mention the environment!' I add. 'Just how much extra fuel will all the planes and trains use up, transporting people who are reading a copy of

Showjumpers? I'm just not sure Katriona will be comfortable with that kind of carbon footprint . . .'

Paul Gardner interrupts me with a long, loud laugh. 'I think we've got our advertising campaign right there! "Are you too green for *Showjumpers*?" Brilliant!'

'I prefer "Bring Back the Bonkbuster",' I mutter, defeated, folding up the photocopy of *Showjumpers* and shoving it in my bag. 'And tartan taffeta.'

'Well, exciting though that all sounds,' Milly is glancing nervously from Gardner to Penelope, and back again, 'we should probably leave the advertising campaigns until we've got a contract all signed. Now, Shonagh will get a draft drawn up over the next week or so, and we'll put a copy in the post to Katriona.'

'God, no!' I can't risk Katriona opening up a draft contract from Aadelman Stern for a book she hasn't written. 'I mean . . . er . . . there's no need for that. Just give me a call when it's ready, and I'll swing by and pick it up. I can drop Katriona's material off at the same time. It would be so nice to see you all again,' I add, in case they're unconvinced. 'Sort of like a reunion!'

'Er . . . lovely . . .' says Gardner. 'Now, of course, we come to the . . . er . . . difficult bit.'

Shonagh tears a piece of paper from the top of her pad, and Gardner passes it across the table to me.

'Tell us what you think Katriona will think of this number.'

I stare dutifully at the long number written on the yellow paper. 'I don't know,' I say truthfully. I mean, it's a slightly weird question. How am I supposed to know what kind of numbers Katriona likes or dislikes? 'I don't think Katriona will have any particular feeling about it one way or the other. Is it her *lucky* number, or something?'

Gardner and Milly both give uncertain little laughs.

'It's what we're offering for *Showjumpers*,' Penelope says, her voice heavy with disdain. 'That's pounds, by the way, not dollars.'

'*Ohhh.*' I stare again at the number. It's mostly zeros, apart from the number one in the front, and there's no decimal point where you'd think there should be. 'I'm sorry,' I say. 'This number can't possibly be right.'

Paul Gardner swallows visibly. 'Right. Oh God. Well, of course . . .' He grabs Shonagh's pen, scribbles out the *one* and puts a *two* in its place.

He's just doubled the amount they're offering.

'Now that we know it's definitely going to be a series,' he says, in a very small voice. He's not meeting Penelope's eye.

'Oh,' I say, rather faintly. 'Well. This is . . . certainly going to be a very popular number with Katriona.'

'Oh, well, obviously, you'll need to put it to Katriona herself.' Gardner is looking very nervous. 'And of course, we're very flexible on the royalty rate, and we can build in some generous bonuses for—' He stops, very suddenly. I think Penelope has kicked him under the table. 'Naturally this is all the kind of stuff we'll need to start discussing with Katriona's agent,' he finishes.

'Myles Salisbury-Kent,' Shonagh suddenly utters. Above her brown suit, her pale cheeks are suddenly glowing. Another paid-up member of the fan club.

'Yes,' I say hastily. 'And I'm sure Myles will really look forward to that. However, for the time being, I'm afraid I absolutely must insist that you contact me and me alone about this project.'

'That seems extremely unusual,' Penelope snaps.

'Katriona,' I say, 'is an *extremely unusual* author.'

'Many of my authors are unusual.' Penelope regards me coolly across the table. 'I am accustomed to all kinds of eccentricity. I can see why Katriona prefers to work without us bothering her, but surely it won't matter if we start talks with her agent?'

I see that handling Penelope is going to be tricky.

'Well,' I sigh, 'I didn't want to have to say anything about this. But actually, Myles and Katriona haven't been getting on awfully well of late.'

'Ah.' Gardner nods sagely. 'I see. Well, of course, there have been rumours.'

There *have*? I thought Katriona and Myles kept their little squabbles private.

'Exactly,' I say. 'So you can see why Katriona isn't sure she wants Myles muscling in on *Showjumpers*. Taking his percentage. If she's thinking of getting rid of him.'

Gardner and Milly are practically licking their lips.

I think they'd like nothing better than some good, juicy gossip.

'I'm afraid I can't say any more than that right now,' I tell them. 'And obviously, this is all strictly off the record.'

'Oh, obviously,' says Gardner, whose eyes are like saucers. 'Katriona has our total reassurance. Not. A. Word.' He leans across the table and clasps my hand again. 'Let's hope this is the start of a long and productive relationship, Liz.'

'Yes,' I say. 'Let's hope.'

'Great! Lovely! Well . . .' He pushes back his chair and stands up. 'Milly will walk you back to the lifts.'

'Don't worry. I'll do that.' Penelope comes to open the door, and holds it for me to go through.

I march as fast as I can back down the corridor towards the lifts, hoping Penelope will have difficulty keeping up. No such luck, though.

'You will convey my regards to Katriona?' she says, as she marches up alongside me.

'Of course.'

'*Showjumpers* is not at all the kind of book I normally work on,' she continues. 'I've edited four out of the last ten Booker Prize winners, you know.'

'Well, good for you!'

'But Katriona de Montfort being such a high-profile individual and everything . . .'

'She'll be thrilled to know you're at the helm,' I say, pressing the lift button several times.

Penelope narrows her sharp little eyes until they're

barely more than slits. 'I would just like it to be known that this is an arrangement I find *highly* irregular.'

The lift makes a pinging noise as it reaches our floor. Not a moment too soon.

'Well, 'bye then, Penelope!' I hurry through the open lift doors and reach for the button to close them. 'I'll be in touch!'

'I shall certainly look forward to hearing from you, Liz,' she says. 'You'll get that material to us as soon as possible, yes?'

'Oh, yes,' I say. The lift doors are closing. 'Absolutely.'

Once I know I'm out of view, I fall back against the lift wall, my heart racing like I've just run a marathon. Or maybe it's some kind of physical shock. I mean, I've never been offered anything like that much money before. For a book I haven't even written yet. A book that they think is being written by Katriona de Montfort.

But at the end of the day, really, those are just details.

I take a deep breath, then another. It's very important to stay calm right now. Very important indeed.

I've got a three-hundred-thousand-word epic bonk-buster to write.

BOOK OF THE WEEK

~~Isabel Bookbinder's debut novel is a heart-breaking work of staggering genius~~

~~Run, don't walk, to buy your copy of Isabel Bookbinder's Showjumpers~~

Showjumpers looks at first like the kind of old-school epic bonkbuster that is so out of fashion these days. But who better to inject some life into the genre than stunning Isabel Bookbinder, *27*?

Although a regular on the London party circuit, Ms Bookbinder is known to have put gruelling hours of work into completing this, the first volume of the *Showjumpers* Trilogy, even turning down glamorous launch-party invitations when absolutely necessary.

But every minute was well spent. This is, quite simply, the most exciting literary debut for many years. The first three thousand words, in particular, are simply gripping. Laetitia Lovelock proves a feisty heroine, Barrington Bosworth-Bounder is a truly fantastic womanising cad, and all the other characters are really interesting too.

A single complaint would be that the book really is just that bit too heavy for comfortable beach reading. Hopefully Ms Bookbinder's publishers will take note of this, and allow her to write a significantly shorter epic bonkbuster next time.

But all in all, a superlative debut that will deserve its

undoubted status as a world-wide bestseller. Isabel Bookbinder has proved that she is more than just pretty and stylish, with a gym-honed size-eight figure. Rivals, such as Gina Deverill (whose promised novel *Wave/Lengths* has sadly never materialised) will be left quivering in her wake.

Richard and Judy, Thursday 3 April, 5.15 p.m.,
Channel 4

RICHARD We're really thrilled to be able to welcome
our next guest. Her epic bonkbuster, *Showjumpers*, has
rocketed to the top of our Book Club bestsellers, hasn't
it, Judy . . .?
JUDY Yes . . .
RICHARD . . . and she's already hard at work on the next
book in the trilogy. She's been fêted both here and over
in the States as the best thing to happen to the genre in
years. She is . . . Isabel Bookbinder! Isabel, lovely to
meet you.
ISABEL Thank you, Richard. I'm thrilled to be here.
RICHARD Now, you've got quite an amusing story about
how the book was originally spotted, haven't you?
ISABEL I have, Richard.
RICHARD A little bird has told us that your mother was to
blame!
ISABEL That's right, Richard.
JUDY Oh, how—
RICHARD Anyway, Isabel, tell us the story. Your mum
sent the manuscript off to the publishers, didn't she? But
– and here's the really funny bit – somehow the publishers ended up believing that the manuscript had
come from Katriona de Montfort, is that right?
ISABEL Completely right, Richard. I was working for
Katriona at the time, and there was a little mix-up, and
yes, the publishers did think for a short time that Katriona
was the one who'd written the book. I soon set them

straight, though. The ~~deception~~ misunderstanding really only lasted for a couple of weeks.

RICHARD But by then, the publishers were so thrilled with the plans for the rest of the series that they stuck to the original deal, didn't they?

ISABEL They did, Richard. Which was a jolly good thing, as I'd already gone out and spent most of the money in advance!

RICHARD Ha ha ha! On what?

ISABEL ~~Two Mulberry bags, a cashmere blanket and an Inspiring Outfit from Harvey N~~ Basic writing necessities, Richard.

JUDY So, Isabel, tell us about—

RICHARD So, Isabel, tell us about your new life as a best-selling novelist. Is it everything you dreamed it would be?

ISABEL It is, Richard. In fact, I'd like to send out a personal message of hope for any of your viewers who hope to be novelists one day: Viewers, it really *is* all it's cracked up to be.

RICHARD Ahh, that's nice, thank you, Isabel. But it's a lot of hard graft too?

ISABEL Yes, indeed, Richard. I'm up at six most mornings for my run in the park, and hardly a day goes by when I don't work out with my personal trainer, Merlin. That's one thing I learned from working with Katriona – a novelist's development must be physical, as well as spiritual.

RICHARD Judy, perhaps we should add a compulsory grooming and personal fitness element to our short-story competition?

JUDY Well, I think—

RICHARD And you've got some really exciting events coming up in your personal life, haven't you, Isabel? Your huge society wedding to top literary agent Joe Madison, for one.

ISABEL That's right, Richard. [*Displaying 2-carat diamond and aquamarine engagement ring.*] Joe and I are getting married in Venice this summer. I'll be wearing ~~Monique Lhullier Amanda Wakeley~~ custom-made Vera Wang.

RICHARD We'll look forward to the invite! A pleasure to meet you, Isabel. We, and our millions of viewers, eagerly await your next volume.

ISABEL Thank you, Richard. And thank you, Judy.

JUDY Yeah. Whatever.

Chapter 20

God, I feel inspired.

I mean, this place is *amazing*. It's not the biggest flat in the world, obviously. You don't get an awful lot of space for only three-quarters of a million pounds in Kensington. But it's got two bedrooms, two bathrooms, a gorgeous open-plan kitchen/dining room, and a beautiful Kelly Hoppen-style living room with big French windows that open out on to a decked terrace, with views of Kensington Gardens. Well, views of Kensington Gardens if you stand on a chair in a pair of extremely high-heeled Kurt Geiger platform loafers. I know, because I tried it as soon as we arrived.

I have to say, I'm feeling really good about my decision to invest my advance in property. Jeremy, my estate agent, says I have one of the best natural feels for the Kensington property market he's ever come across. It's because I'm prepared to overlook petty considerations like, say, how many square feet you get per hundred grand, or whether or not something counts as a bedroom simply because there's very nearly space for a single futon. Jeremy says this kind of open-minded outlook will mean I reap serious rewards in the property game.

To Jeremy,
Who helped me reap serious rewards in the property game.

'The kitchen is Poggenpohl, of course.' Jeremy has gone back into the kitchen for a closer tour, opening up a selection of cupboards to show the current owners' collection of hand-made pappardelle and Maldon sea-salt. 'You've got your granite worktops, slate flooring, ample cupboard space . . . I'm getting the impression your boyfriend is quite the amateur chef,' he adds, nodding over at Barney, who's gazing at the Smeg refrigerator like he's just found the Holy Grail.

'Oh, he's not my boyfriend,' I say. 'He's just taken the morning off work to come flat-hunting with me. He will be living with me here, though. As my personal chef.'

'Personal chef!' Jeremy's obviously impressed. 'You know, my great-uncle wrote books, but he didn't seem to enjoy half as many perks as you do.'

'Did he write epic bonkbusters?'

'No. Military books, mostly. A lot of stuff about Sopwith Camels.'

'Ah.' I nod. 'Well, that explains it. I don't suppose there's very much glamour involved in writing about wildlife.'

Jeremy just blinks. He's got that contact lens problem back again.

'Anyway, writing epic bonkbusters isn't *all* glamour

and fun,' I say. 'There's a lot of hard graft too. I've been working completely flat out all week.'

Which is one hundred per cent true, by the way. I mean, there's tons of stuff I have to be doing if I'm going to be ready in time:

1) I have to lose half a stone (in fat) while at the same time putting on several pounds (of muscle, mostly in the tricep and gluteus maximum area).

2) Flat-hunting. I mean, any day now, I could be doing a photo-shoot with *Hello!*, and welcoming them into my stunning home. And obviously, I'll be needing a stunning home to welcome them into.

3) I've been putting in the hours at Waterstone's on Kensington High Street, making (if I say so myself) a meticulous, high-level research study into book-jacket photographs, and how to pose for them.

4) Not to mention all the time I've had to spend sorting out my Look, without a qualified personal shopper to help me.

And then, of course, there's the other stuff. The writing part. Which is coming on in leaps and bounds, I have to say. I mean, I'm *miles* beyond the creative visualisation stage now. My publicity and marketing strategy is really starting to take shape. Only yesterday morning, for example, I nipped into Smythson and bought a really stunning conference file. It's pale blue leather, and I got them to put 'Operation: Bring Back the Bonkbuster' on the front, in silver letters. And I got all this fantastic stuff at Ryman's, too – clear plastic files, coloured pencils, even a protractor and compass set, because it comes in a gorgeous little tin, which is bound to be useful. I can hardly wait to start! In fact, I'm all geared up to crack on with it right after flat-hunting today.

'So . . .' Jeremy's looking at me. 'Interested?'

'God, yes.'

'Terrific!' Jeremy claps his hands. 'You'll have to hit the asking price, though, I'm afraid. They've turned down every lower offer.'

'Jeremy.' I look him in the eye. 'This is me you're talking to, remember? I'm the one with the exceptional feel for the Kensington property market. I hit whatever price I need to.'

'Well, I'll give them a call and see what they say. Now, if I remember correctly, you did say you were looking at a mortgage-free purchase?'

'Oh, yes.'

'So you'd be looking to exchange . . . er . . . when, exactly?'

I hold back a sigh. I like Jeremy, I really do, but he doesn't seem to be able to retain the most basic information.

'I don't have anything *to* exchange, Jeremy. I've told you already, I'm a first-time buyer. The people selling this place are just going to have to find their own new flat to buy.'

Jeremy's contact lens problem suddenly gets really

bad, so he has to go outside to sort them out while he makes his phone call.

'Come on, Barn,' I say. 'Let's have another look at the living room.'

I flop on the gorgeous cream sofa while Barney channel-hops on the plasma TV to find UKTV Food.

'Don't you think it's perfect, Barn?'

'Perfect.' Barney's in a bit of a daze. I think he might have been hypnotised by the gleam of the granite worktops. 'Completely perfect. I can't believe you're really going to be able to buy a place like this. I mean, those Le Creuset pans . . . that Pavoni coffee machine . . .'

'Barney,' I say sternly, 'swanky accessories don't influence me. That's the way bad property decisions are made. It's about bricks and mortar, not Le Creuset and Pavoni. Donald Trump doesn't expand his property empire going all swoony over saucepans, you know.'

Barney looks impressed, though whether that's about my new-found hard head for property or the bouillabaisse Rick Stein is boiling up on the plasma screen, it's quite hard to tell.

'This place is a sound investment, that's all, Barn. You can't go getting seduced by a lifestyle.'

Still, as lifestyles go, this one hasn't got a lot wrong with it. The owners look pretty content, grinning down at me from black-and-white photographs on the walls. He looks rugged and chiselled, like some kind of posh artisan, somebody double-barrelled who makes a fortune carving traditional English furniture for all his old school chums. And she looks like a part-time model, possibly with her own boutique clothing line. There are hints of their fabulous existence dotted about the place – invitations to summer parties at Babington House propped on the mantelpiece, *Harper's Bazaar* and *Vogue* fanned out on the cherry-wood coffee table, someone's yoga mat rolled up in the corner by the French windows . . .

Not that I'm buying into the lifestyle for a minute, obviously. But you just know this is the kind of place where life would be great. You'd cook up amazing, seasonal, locally sourced meals in the kitchen, while good-looking friends with great outfits and extremely white teeth gathered around, sipping fresh peach bellinis and listening to experimental jazz on your sound system. (Isabel Palmer-Tomkinson . . .?) And in the summer, you'd do your daily Ashtanga on the decked terrace, before whizzing up a smoothie and an egg-white omelette and settling down to read a selection of edifying periodicals. My God, you'd be a honed size eight in no time! Not to mention the self-improvement from all those edifying periodicals and all that experimental jazz.

I wonder if Barney would ever consider getting his teeth whitened.

'Barney . . .'

'God, I wish you'd let me tell everyone in the office all about all this, Iz. They're all so keen to bad-mouth you about the email bugger-up, they'll be eating their words if they hear about your book deal.'

Knowing I'm still Public Enemy Number One at the *Saturday Mercury* has taken the shine off my morning ever so slightly.

'You can tell them soon. But you have to keep quiet for now, Barn. I don't want people knowing anything about Aadelman Stern until the contracts are all properly signed.'

Barney averts his eyes from the screen, where a heroic crab is making a break for freedom across Rick Stein's worktop. 'But you haven't even told *me* much about it! All I know is, you're getting a three-book deal and squillions of pounds.'

I grab one of the *Harper's Bazaars* and start flicking through it, very casually. 'Well, Barn, that's about all there is to know . . .'

I mean, don't get me wrong. *I'm* not all that concerned about the fact that I've temporarily misled Aadelman Stern into thinking they're about to sign Katriona. But I have a kind of funny feeling that other people might be.

It's partly why I haven't mentioned anything about the book deal to Lara yet, even though she's been back from her conference for a few days now. I'm not sure I'll get away with giving her a slightly . . . *edited version* of the truth, like the one I've given to Mum and Barney.

'But I want to hear *everything*. Who you met, what they said . . . this is the biggest thing that's ever happened to anyone I know, Iz!'

'Oh, you know I don't remember that stuff!' I'm pretending to be completely engrossed in my magazine. 'It's all a bit of a blur . . .'

Oh my God. Oh my *God*.

'*Bloody* Gina Deverill!'

Barney is looking at me like I've gone mad. 'Where?'

'Here!' I thrust the magazine at him. 'She's only gone and got herself in *Harper's Bazaar*!'

It's actually only a teeny-tiny picture, in the section at the back where they print photos of people at parties. This one looks like a fashion party to launch some new It-bag by a Danish designer. There are lots of those yummy-mummy West London models I can never tell apart, and American heiresses, factoring high on the glossy scale. And then there's Gina. It practically kills me to say it, but she's out-glossing them all. Thinner than I've ever seen her look, but in a good way, in skin-tight jeans and those same irritating flat pumps she wore at the wedding, with a glowing tan and the kind of super-shiny ponytail that makes you want to reach for the scissors. The handbag she's holding is completely drool-worthy – a giant, soft pouch in quilted sage-green leather, hanging on a long strap against her non-existent hips.

Barney reads out the tiny caption. ' "It-girl novelist Jenna Deverill poses with her Mikkel Borgessen 'Yoko' bag . . . 'It's the perfect size for carrying around huge manuscripts,' says Jenna, 'and big enough to sling in a few key pieces if I'm suddenly called to a meeting in LA at a moment's notice.' " Well, you've got to look on the bright side, Iz. They've spelled her name wrong.'

This is the *only* bright side. And it isn't a big enough bright side to make up for the fact that Gina Deverill is in *Harper's*, that Gina Deverill goes to fancy-schwancy fashion-y parties, and out-glams famous models, that Gina Deverill has to head off to meetings in LA at a moment's notice *or* that Gina Deverill dresses in 'key pieces'.

Right. One thing, and one thing only, has just gone rocketing to the top of my to-do list: 'Get Mikkel Borgessen Yoko bag A.S.A.P.'

Oh, and 'Start dressing in key pieces', I suppose.

'I bet she got the handbag for free, as well,' Barney says.

'*Free?*'

Barney shrugs. 'They give these things out at parties like that all the time. When I blagged my way into that launch party for Gordon Ramsay's new gastropub, they were giving out copies of his cookbooks *and* free kitchen stuff with his name on it. That's where I got my blowtorch and my asparagus peeler.'

Right. Well, I've got to have an urgent word with someone at Aadelman Stern about this. Surely they have some kind of . . . Head of Freebies, or something. Maybe it's that girl I went up in the lift with, the one with the Mulberry Roxanne! *Somebody* in a big publisher like that has to be in charge of handbag procurement. I mean, quite obviously, it's a basic Novelist's essential!

Jeremy's coming back in, closing up his mobile.

'Can't get through to the vendors right now,' he says. 'They'll call back when they get my message. Now, do you want to look at anywhere else, or are we all done here?'

I've really got to be getting on with my publicity and marketing strategy this afternoon. Not only that, but if I leave here now, I could be in Harvey Nichols' handbag department in fifteen minutes, and back home with my new Yoko bag in less than an hour. There'll be plenty of time for Operation: Bring Back the Bonkbuster then!

'We're all done here, I think, Jeremy!'

'Excellent.' He strides over and gives each of us a firm handshake. 'I'll be in touch, Isabel. Always nice to leave behind a satisfied customer!'

I'd be more of a satisfied customer if Harvey Nichols hadn't completely sold out of Yoko bags. I mean, talk about flying off the shelves! The sweet salesgirl who's helping me, ringing around all the other Harvey Nichols stores in the country, says they only went on sale at ten o'clock on Tuesday morning, and by twenty past, not a single one was left.

'Not even the horrible sage-green one,' she told me. 'We couldn't believe *that* one sold at all! It looks like someone's sneezed on it.'

So I feel a bit better about that.

But things aren't looking good, as she puts her phone down now. 'Leeds are already sold out.

Edinburgh too. Manchester are getting back to me, but it isn't looking very good at the moment.' She sighs. 'I'm really sorry.'

'It's not your fault. Obviously you've been completely overrun with top Novelists.'

'Top novelists?'

'For the Yoko bag. I mean, there's really no other bag big enough to carry our manuscripts in. And to squeeze in a few key pieces, if we need to dash off to LA at a moment's notice.'

She looks confused. 'I don't think *any* novelists have been buying them.'

Damn it. 'Well, that's probably because all the freebies co-ordinators got here first!'

'Right . . . Well, if it's something really big you're after, have you considered something from Balenciaga?'

'No.' I shake my head. 'I'm afraid only the Yoko will do.'

'Oh, I'm sure we can find you something else!' She starts to lead me off through the handbag stands, picking up various gigantic totes along the way. 'This Louis Vuitton's even bigger than the Yoko, you know. Plenty of room for everything in there . . .'

'No, honestly, it really does have to be the—'

Hold on a minute. Now, *that's* what I call a handbag.

While the salesgirl is fussing over a Louis Vuitton, my eye has been caught by a vision in emerald green. It's quilted leather, like the Yoko, with a proper old-fashioned clasp that you can open to reveal . . . oh God, hot-pink silk lining the inside.

'It's gorgeous,' I breathe.

'*Isn't* it?' says the assistant. 'That's the Marianne. That's a Mikkel Borgessen too, you know. But it's just a clutch bag, of course, so not the kind of thing you were after . . .'

Oh, did I not mention that? The jewel-green bag is a clutch.

Actually, I think calling it a clutch is being a little bit unfair. I mean, obviously you *would* clutch it, as it doesn't have any handles, but it's hardly a traditional clutch. Most clutch bags barely fit a lipstick. Whereas this one is positively roomy! Miles of space for all your necessities! As long as you prune your necessities down a bit. I mean, who needs to lug around half their life with them in a handbag, anyway? All this bottle-of-Evian-and-a-small-Chihuahua nonsense. All I ever really need is my notebook, one credit card and a small mobile. A *very* small mobile.

'You'd never get your manuscript in there,' the girl is saying. '*Or* your key pieces.'

Actually, I think she's wrong about that. You could get a manuscript in there quite easily, for example, *a few pages at a time*. And let's face it, am I really going to need to lug an entire epic bonkbuster and my key pieces around with me every single time I step outside the front door? I mean, what if I'm *not* going to LA at a moment's notice? What if I'm just dashing out for a pint of milk and a KitKat, or something?

'I'll take it,' I say, shoving the Marianne bag into the

assistant's hands. 'In fact, don't even wrap it up. I'm going to start using it right now.'

'Are you sure? I don't think there's room for all your stuff . . .'

I peer into my over-filled shoulder bag, whose current contents are:

1) wallet
2) phone
3) Mac eye-pencils (assorted)
4) Stila lipgloss (splurging)
5) old black Smythson notebook
6) new blue Smythson folder
7) family-pack of Revels (open)
8) six or seven tissues (used)
9) one tissue (unused)
10) *heat* magazine
11) *Grazia* magazine
12) *A Woman of Substance* (the book, not an actual woman)
13) my photocopy of *Showjumpers* (first three chapters)
14) a wide selection of estate agents' particulars
15) and something squashed that could be a prune . . . no, hang on, it's a black fruit pastille.

She may have a point.

You see, *this* is why I actually need to get this Marianne bag. I mean, what does it say about a person if they go about the place with an cheapo Accessorize handbag like this, all bent out of shape and stuffed to the gills? I'm almost ashamed I didn't realise before. Well, it stops right here.

'Tell you what – why don't you give me the biggest carrier you've got?' I'm not about to lessen the impact of the brand new Marianne bag I'm carrying by lugging about a battered old Accessorize, too. But a Marianne bag plus a posh Harvey Nichols carrier . . . now *that's* the kind of Look that gets you into swanky fashion parties in Notting Hill. 'I'll put all my bits and pieces in there until I get the chance to sort them!'

While she's running the purchase through, I empty the contents of my handbag into the huge white carrier she's given me. I'm just wondering if it's worth stopping off at a charity shop on the way home to donate them my shameful old Accessorize bag, or if the Gucci-filled charity shops of Kensington will simply turn me down flat, when my phone starts to ring. It's Mum. She's called me three times a day since I told her about the book deal, badgering me with silly questions, like have I started planning my launch party yet.

(Cucumber mojitos at Soho House, I was thinking, or raspberry Bellinis and bruschetta at the River Cafe. It wouldn't do to go getting any more definite at this stage.)

'Iz-Wiz? Great news! The editor's approved my piece about Katriona de Montfort, Iz-Wiz! It's going to be published in the *Gazette*!'

'Mum, that's great!'

'Both of us, Isabel, published writers! And it's going to be the perfect way to announce the job to your father. I'll just put the paper down in front of him when he's having his breakfast.'

'Mum, you know Dad's not all that keen on finding things out about his family in the newspapers . . .'

Mum ignores me. 'So, have you got a date from Katriona yet?'

'A date?'

'For my interview!'

Oh, damn. What with the excitement of the book deal, plus all the hard graft I've been doing lately, I haven't given Mum's interview a moment's thought.

'That could be a bit tricky . . .'

'*Iz*-Wiz!' Mum sounds dismayed.

The salesgirl is waiting for my credit card, so I jam the phone between my shoulder and my ear while I open my wallet. 'Well . . . can't you just cobble together an article from old press cuttings about Katriona?'

She tuts. 'No, Isabel, I can't. Nobody has ever written about Katriona from the Somerset angle before.'

'*Does* Katriona have a Somerset angle?' I key in my PIN, trying not to feel too light-headed at the amount I've just spent on a tiny piece of leather. It's more than an entire month's rent at Russell's. Mind you, when you look at it like that, it suddenly seems like a total bargain.

'Well, of course she has a Somerset angle, Isabel!

That's why the editor is so keen. Katriona used to live in Yeovil. Hasn't she mentioned it?'

'No, she hasn't.'

Actually, she's never mentioned anything about her past at all. I have my suspicions that she was dropped, by a stork, fully clad in Chanel bouclé, right outside Harvey Nichols, in time for opening. It's hard to imagine her in any other life. Let alone one in Yeovil.

'You promised, Iz-Wiz.' Mum is sounding tearful. 'You promised you'd get me this interview.'

'All right. I'll speak to her, OK? But on one condition. You do realise you can't say a *single word* about Aadelman Stern, don't you?'

'Edelweiss who?'

Actually, this could be easier than I thought.

'I'll call you when I've asked her, OK? 'Bye, Mum.'

The salesgirl helps me empty the contents of my shoulder bag into the giant carrier she's found for me, and holds the doors open for me as I leave.

'Thank you,' I say, as she waves me goodbye. 'You have no idea what this bag is going to do for my career.'

'Well, I'm very glad to hear that,' she says. 'It's nice to be of service!'

Isabel Bookbinder
Kensington
London

Mr Mikkel Borgessen
Borgessen House
~~Wonderful, wonderful~~ Copenhagen
Denmark

16 January

Dear Mr Borgessen

Let me start by saying what a huge fan I am of your ~~bags~~ Work. Even though I had never really heard of you until today, I instantly recognised a master. Not half an hour after spotting one of your pieces in a magazine, I instantly dashed to Harvey Nichols, where an extremely helpful assistant (Mara – you may want to start employing her on some sort of commission basis) furnished me with a truly fantastic emerald-green Marianne bag.

However, I cannot say I am entirely happy with this state of affairs. Although I am soon to be a millionaire novelist, I am a ~~woman~~ person of social conscience, even considering at one stage standing for the Socialist Workers' Party, so you will understand my extreme disappointment at being forced to *buy* this bag, when others are simply given it.

Is this really fair, Mikkel? I thought Nordic people were supposed to have a long tradition of fairness and equality. So as a Nord, tell me this: why should we live in a world full of Haves and Have-nots? Or, at the very least, why should I have to be one of the Have-nots when Gina Deverill is one of the Haves?

As I am just as willing to give your bags free advertising as she is, I wonder if it might be possible to arrange some sort of reimbursement for my Marianne bag, purchased today? If not, then my other suggestion is that you make amends by sending me another bag. A Yoko would be nice. Or any others you have ~~knocking about~~ to hand. Or perhaps a really nice gesture would be to *design me a brand-new bag*, which I could then promote all around the world for you! Something fairly large, in case I need to fly to LA at a moment's notice. And I've already got a new clutch bag now, so I'd really like something a bit more practical.

Yours, in admiration,

Isabel Bookbinder

PS. If you do make me a bag, please could you call it the Isabel?

PPS. I would also like it to have a hot-pink silk lining. Thank you.

ON THE TOWN! The parties, the people, the places to be seen . . .

The party of the year was thrown at Soho House, to celebrate the launch of Isabel Bookbinder's exciting debut novel, *Showjumpers*. Miss Bookbinder (pictured) looked simply stunning, out-glossing everyone else present in skin-tight jeans and flat pumps, with a glowing tan and a super-shiny ponytail. She also sported a unique touch – a handbag designed and named especially for her by designer-to-the-stars Mikkel Borgessen.

'I just love my Isabel bag,' Miss Bookbinder, 27, told us, in between sips of ~~cucumber moji raspberry Bellini~~ champagne and morsels of smoked salmon blini. 'It's the perfect size for carting around all my basic novelist's essentials, and yet chic enough to take out to a fabulous launch party. I can even squeeze my key pieces in it if I need to jet off to LA at a moment's notice. Really, every Novelist should have one.'

Isabel was accompanied to the star-studded bash by her adoring boyfriend, Mr Joe Madison, looking dashing in his customary Paul Smith. After Mr Madison's touching tribute to 'his perfect Isabel', partygoers David Furnish and Elton John proceeded to dance the night away with an unusually laidback Johnny Depp, while spontaneous entertainment was provided by Nicole Kidman and Robbie Williams, who grabbed the micro-phone for some Sinatra classics.

Revellers leaving the party at dawn were heard to say,

'It was so much better than the fancy-schwancy West London fashion-y parties we normally go to.'

Roll on *Showjumpers* #2!

Chapter 21

Now I've got my gorgeous new Marianne bag, I feel more geared up than ever to get on with my publicity and marketing strategy for Aadelman Stern. I knew a little bit of incentivising was all I really needed! Lara's always advising her clients to treat themselves to something nice when a tough time is ahead, so the bag wasn't only a basic Novelist's necessity, it was actually a basic *human right*. No wonder I feel so energised and motivated! No more faffing. And to be honest, there isn't really any time for faffing. I've got my meeting with Aadelman Stern tomorrow, and they're expecting all that material I promised them. So I'm just going to shut my bedroom door, sit down at my desk, and . . .

Shit. MI5 are back.

I can see the dirty Nissan the minute I turn off Kensington Church Street. It's parked a few doors down from Katriona's, and . . . that's weird. It's empty.

You know, the only thing scarier than knowing MI5 are watching you is knowing they're watching you *when you can't see them*. I have a quick look up and down the street, clutching my Marianne bag to my chest in case Frizz-Hair suddenly decides to take a shot at me. God, what a great free advert for the bag *that* would be. 'DESIGNER CLUTCH SAVES NOVELIST FROM BULLET. SUPER-SOFT QUILTED LEATHER ABSORBS IMPACT: "IT'S FAR BETTER THAN THE YOKO," SAY EXPERTS.'

Oh Jesus, now I can see her. Frizz-Hair. But this time, she isn't alone. There's a man with her. It isn't the guy from the train, the old, tweedy one. If anything, he's even *more* ruthless-looking. He's young and sly, with hips like Pete Doherty, and a similar line in skanky-looking denim and leather.

And they're right outside Katriona's house!

It looks like they've just been speaking to someone at the door, and now they're turning away and heading back to their car. Were they *asking* about me? Enquiring as to my movements, my routine, the times when I'm most likely to be in the house alone?

I flatten myself back against the privet hedge of the house next door, which – thanks to the Super-Riches' need for total privacy – provides enough cover to conceal me while they get into the Nissan. They seem to be having a row as they drive away. He's waving his hands a lot, and she's looking upset. Did they not get the information they wanted? Are they going back to Caroline Macbeth, heads bowed, admitting their quarry has outsmarted them after all? And Caroline Macbeth will swivel round in a big leather chair, and stroke a small cat with a gloved hand . . .

Anyway, I'd better go inside, and find out who answered the door to them. Please, God, let it have been Selma. The last thing I need right now is Katriona getting all jumpy about her precious security. I mean, OK, I probably should have told her I'm a target for political assassination before I moved in. But on the positive side, the fact that her house has been under surveillance by MI5 means there's far less likelihood of one of her dreaded burglaries happening.

There's no sign of Selma, though, when I get inside, and I can hear Katriona's voice coming from the living room. It sounds . . . shit. It sounds high-pitched, and slightly shrieky, and upset. And now I can hear another voice, a male one, almost as bad-tempered. Myles? It sounds like they're having a row.

The living-room door is too thick for me to get a good listen from this distance, so I tiptoe a little bit closer, then tiptoe back again in a very big hurry when I hear heavy footsteps stamping towards the door.

It *is* Myles.

'Isabel,' he snaps in greeting, marching right past me and out of the front door before I can say a word. He slams it behind him so hard, you can practically feel the house shake.

'Isabel!' I hear Katriona sing out. She comes running out of the living room, pink-cheeked and breathless. 'Did you just get back? I'm *so* sorry you had to witness that!'

She's not giving me any grief about suspicious visitors. I guess maybe she didn't answer the door after all. 'Oh, I didn't witness anything.'

'We have these little fall-outs from time to time.

Myles can be such a . . .' She exhales, hands on her minuscule hips. 'Oooh, been shopping?' Her luxury-goods radar is up like a shot at the sight of my Marianne. '*That's* rather lovely.'

I don't want Katriona wondering how I can suddenly afford to buy things like this. 'Well, I've been saving up for a while . . . and I had to get a new bag to put *Showjumpers* in.'

'A *clutch* bag? Is that big enough for *Showjumpers*? I thought you'd been writing non-stop for days!'

That's an excellent point. 'Er . . . well, it just got *so* big, I've had to . . . transfer it all to microfiche!'

She shakes her head. For a moment, I think she hasn't believed me, but then she says, 'Isabel, your work ethic puts me to shame. Your parents must be so proud of you.'

Oh. This reminds me. 'Katriona, I know how busy you are, but would you be able to spare five or ten minutes to do a little interview some time?'

'Interview?' Her arched eyebrows shoot upwards.

'It's just my mother,' I carry on. I'm hoping the more pathetic I make it sound, the more she'll take pity on me and agree to do it. 'She's got herself this traineeship on a newspaper, and she'd really love to write an article about you.'

'Well, of *course* I can spare five minutes! I can spare a lot more than that, for your mother, Isabel!'

'Really? That's brilliant, Katriona! She'll be thrilled.'

'She can come up to town! Take me to lunch on her expense account!'

'Well, it's only the *Central Somerset Gazette*, so it may not be quite what you're—'

'*What?*'

'The *Central Somerset Gazette*,' I say, less certainly. 'It's a local paper that covers . . . er . . . central Somerset . . .'

'I am *aware* that it is a local paper.' Katriona's eyes are like tiny darts. 'What I cannot understand, Isabel, is why you are asking *me* to be interviewed for it.'

'I know it's very small potatoes,' I begin. 'I just thought, seeing as you used to live in Yeovil . . .'

'That was a very, *very* long time ago,' she spits.

God, it's like I've unearthed the discovery that she used to wear a beard and answer to the name of Keith, or something. I mean, I'm not a huge fan of Yeovil myself, God knows, but I'm amazed she's being quite so prickly about it.

'I'm really sorry, Katriona. I'll tell Mum you'd rather not.' *That's* going to be fun.

'Good!' She's already stamping off up the stairs. 'I'd appreciate it if you didn't waste my time with any more of these enquiries, Isabel. It's not as if I don't have enough on my plate right now. I will be working in my study for the rest of the day.' She spins around on the top step, and glowers back down at me. 'Needless to say, I do *not* want to be disturbed.'

Isabel Bookbinder
Kensington
London

The Home Secretary
The House of Commons
The Houses of Parliament
Big Ben
London

16 January

Dear Home Secretary

~~Look. This has really got to stop.~~
~~I've had just about~~

May I start, once again, by apologising for the ~~myriad~~ problems I seem to have caused you. Though not a political person by nature (the recent lure of socialism aside) I assure you that I am *seriously* considering voting for you in the next election. This will make me feel less guilty about wrecking your Stop the Sleaze initiative, and will give you a much-needed extra vote. I think you will agree that we both win.

However, I am afraid I must take task with your continued aggression towards me. It is most unpleasant to come home to ruthless political assassins on my doorstep. I fear that their continued presence will start to alarm my employer, who is a highly strung woman at the best of times. Not to mention the fact that I can scarcely enjoy my day-to-day tasks, worrying about sudden violent death the whole time. The shine was almost completely taken off the purchase of my new Mikkel Borgessen handbag today – what will it be tomorrow?

I would appreciate it if you would tell Frizz-Hair and the Grubby One (my code names, though they may also be yours) to BACK OFF AND LEAVE ME ALONE. As I have said before, there is nothing to be gained from revenge, and everything to be lost. Think of that extra vote, ~~Caroline~~ Home Secretary. Think of it.

Yours, in exasperation,

Isabel (Bookbinder)

Chapter 22

I'm a tiny bit late for my meeting at Aadelman Stern this afternoon. First of all, Katriona nabbed me on my way out the front door, all contrite about losing her temper yesterday. She was just in a bad mood about the row with Myles, she told me, which is why she reacted so badly to the *Gazette* interview. Mind you, I suspect she minds about it being a crappy local paper just as much as she said yesterday, because she's promised to call some of her friends at *Marie Claire* and *Tatler* to see if they'd like Mum to write the piece for them. So the interview's going ahead next week after all! Mum will be thrilled.

The other reason I'm late is because my publicity and marketing strategy took a little bit longer than I thought. I should probably have started it earlier than I did last night, but I got side-tracked by a couple of other important issues. Today's outfit, for one thing. And how to achieve the perfect blow-dry without Luc, for another. So in the end, I didn't really get started on the actual paperwork until nearly midnight, and it's been nose to the grindstone ever since.

Anyway, it's paid off. Operation: Bring Back the Bonkbuster is fantastic. I don't think there's a single

publicity avenue I've left unexplored, a single marketing stone I've left unturned. It's about fifty or sixty
pages thick, and it's all laid out in my delicious pale
blue Smythson file. Aadelman Stern are going to
love it!

It doesn't really seem to matter that I'm a few
minutes late. Milly tells me as soon as I arrive that
Penelope won't be joining us. She's conducting some
kind of finance meeting in the boardroom, so it's just
me and Milly and Paul Gardner in his office on the
fourth floor.

'Lovely bag,' Milly tells me, as we settle down
around the desk.

'Isn't it?' I give her a meaningful look. 'Probably
your freebies co-ordinator would like a look. Might be
the kind of thing her department would be interested
in.'

There's a bit of faff for a few minutes while a junior
assistant brings in coffee and mugs, then Paul Gardner
claps his hands together. 'So! Lovely to see you again,
Liz!'

'You too!' God, it's *much* nicer now Penelope's not
around.

'I see you've brought that little something for us,' he
beams, pointing at my file. 'And we've got a little
something for you too!'

Milly pushes a brown A4 envelope across the desk.
'Katriona will want some time to peruse the various
clauses, of course. It's all fairly standard, but her
lawyers will want to check it out . . .'

I peel open the envelope and peek inside. 'My contract!' This is incredible! What a moment. I don't even mind that it's got Katriona's name on it instead of mine. I mean, fixing a little thing that is only going to take a couple of minutes with some Tipp-ex. Not that I'm going to mention that to Milly and Paul just yet, obviously. They're already looking at me in a slightly peculiar fashion.

Oh. I get it.

'*Katriona's* contract,' I correct myself, hastily. 'Sorry about that. I just get so excited on her behalf.'

'How nice!' Gardner reaches for my Smythson file. 'So! Do you mind if I look?'

'Please! You go right ahead.'

'Operation: Bring Back the Bonkbuster!' he says, reading the front. 'Well! How . . . novel.'

I nod happily, and watch them start to leaf through the file. Neither of them says anything for a few moments. Milly is the first to speak.

'Complimentary riding crops?' she says. 'I'm . . . not sure I understand.'

'That's just the kind of question you *should* be asking, Milly!' I beam at her. 'But it's actually a very simple concept. In essence, what we're really talking about are *riding crops* that are *complimentary*.'

There's silence again.

'Anything else?' I ask.

'Er . . . are these . . . *pie charts*?' Gardner asks.

'Oh, yes! I should talk you through those.' I take the file back from him. 'Now, Pie Chart 1A shows the proportion of time we'd like to spend on different types of publicity. For example, the largest shaded area, in the blue, denotes television appearances. Now, if you cross-reference that with Pie Chart 1B, on the following page . . .' I turn the page for them myself, 'you'll see that here, Pie Chart 1A has been broken down into several sub-categories. *Richard and Judy* is the yellow chunk, *This Morning* is right beside that, in the shaded green area. Now, *Loose Women*'s a smaller slice, unless they decide to offer a regular presenter's slot . . .'

I glance up. They're both staring at me.

'Well, I wouldn't worry too much,' I say. 'This is probably something for your publicity people. Obviously, *your* involvement will come a bit later, when I bring you more of the actual book.'

Milly and Gardner exchange glances.

'But wasn't that what you were *meant* to be bringing us?' Milly asks. 'A few more chapters? A synopsis? Some information about the other books in the series . . .'

'Well, of *course* I've brought a synopsis!' If I'm enthusiastic enough, hopefully she'll forget I'm not mentioning the extra chapters. '*And* some information about the other books in the series!'

'Oh, thank heavens for that!' Gardner gives a bark of laughter. 'We were starting to get worried there!'

I flip right to the back of the file. 'Here – look. "Book One, *Showjumpers*, follows the sexually charged exploits of Barrington Bosworth-Bounder and the other characters as they showjump in the county of Cocklesmore." Is that enough of a synopsis for you?'

'Er . . .'

' "Book Two will be entitled *Rockclimbers*, and will follow the sexually charged exploits of Barrington Bosworth-Bounder and the other characters as they climb rocks in the county of Cocklesmore." '

'Liz . . .'

I hold up a hand. ' "Book Three will be entitled *Ice-Skaters*, and will follow the sexually charged exploits of Barrington Bosworth-Bounder and the other characters as they skate at the Cocklesmore County ice-rink." ' I slam the file triumphantly shut, and I hand it back. 'What do you think?'

'I don't know what to think,' Gardner murmurs. 'Is this . . . er . . . something Katriona does for *all* her books?'

I take a deep breath. 'Well, it's funny you should ask that . . .'

The thing is, though, I'm not sure this is quite the right atmosphere for my Big Revelation. I mean, nobody's said anything yet about this out-selling *Harry Potter*. Or cracked open a bottle of champagne.

'I think we're going to have to show this to Penelope,' Milly is saying, playing with her glasses and looking nervous.

Oh, *I* get it. They don't want to get in trouble with the Queen Bee by excluding her from the celebrations. Well, that's fine. The champagne can wait a couple of days.

'Of course. You show Penelope as soon as possible. And then . . .' I give them a special, mysterious smile, 'you may just find there's a little surprise in store!'

'*Another* one?'

Gardner is looking very pale. I think I should probably leave now. He's obviously drained by all this excitement. And I'm due to meet Lara halfway across town in less than an hour.

'Well, I'll be off,' I say, getting to my feet. 'Katriona and I will just . . . *peruse* this contract for a couple of days, with our team of lawyers, of course. And you can peruse our publicity and marketing strategy! There should be plenty of food for thought in there!'

I have a bit of a peer about, on my way back to the lifts, but I can't see the girl with the Mulberry bag anywhere. Oh, well. I'll set up a proper meeting with the freebies co-ordinator just as soon as everything's out in the open.

I wish I had another copy of Operation: Bring Back the Bonkbuster, because I'd love to be able to show it to Lara. I'm trailing all the way to the City to meet her, because she's giving some seminar on how to manage stress at work. Normally when I meet her after work we go to this fantastic tapas place on Marylebone High Street, where I'd have been able to have these bowls of sugar snap peas that would have fitted in perfectly with my diet. But all the restaurants in the City serve up giant portions of boarding-school comfort food for sleep-deprived investment bankers, don't they? And steak-and-kidney pud and jam roly-poly might be tastier than peas, but they aren't exactly going to help me make it to a honed size eight. So we're meeting in a pub instead.

In honour of my new contract, and because none was forthcoming at Aadelman Stern, I order two glasses of champagne and slip into a booth to wait for Lara. She's running a couple of minutes late, which is unusual for her but fine by me. I nipped into the WHSmith two doors down before I came into the pub and picked up that Tipp-ex I was after. I just can't wait to see how this contract looks with my name on there! Now, a blob or two over the words Katriona de Montfort, blow on it to dry, then carefully print my own name on the front page instead . . .

Wow.

I mean, look at this: '. . . *the agreement made this day between Aadelman Stern (hereafter known as "The Publisher") and Isabel Bookbinder (hereafter known as "The Author") . . .*'

I'm hereafter known as The Author!

God, I'm going to have to make some copies of this. Maybe Mum and Dad could use it for the front of their next Christmas card. Or maybe . . .

Oh, hang on, I can see Lara pushing her way through the crowds by the pub entrance. I wave her over with my glass of champagne and turn my contract over so that she won't be able to see what it is until I do the big reveal. She's going to go insane with excitement!

'Sorry, Iz-Wiz, sorry!' Lara reaches the booth, all pink in the cheeks from running. 'Wow – Super-Hair!' She gives me a hug and collapses onto the seat opposite me. 'God, what a day! Never try to teach a bunch of solicitors the value of de-stressing at work. They kept dashing out to take phone calls in the middle of deep relaxation techniques. Still, I got you a nice corporate freebie out of it.' She pulls a blue baseball cap out of her bag and chucks it across to me.

'Thomson Tibble Telford? I know them!' It's Will Madison's firm. 'Hey, was there a dark-haired guy in your seminar? Mid-thirties? Tall? Bit irritable? Wearing a navy suit?'

'No, Isabel,' Lara snorts. 'There was no one matching that description at the solicitors' firm at all.'

It's a fair point.

'So! It's champagne we're drinking then, is it? What's the occasion . . . ?' Suddenly Lara lets out a little cry. 'What's *this*?'

For a moment I think she's seen my contract, but actually it's my Marianne that's caught her eye.

'Oh, just a little treat I bought myself.'

Lara takes it from my hand and strokes the soft leather reverentially. 'I've seen these bags in *Grazia*, Iz-Wiz! They cost a *fortune*.'

'It was an investment buy.'

'Investment buy,' she repeats sceptically.

'Yes! This bag is a basic Novelist's necessity, Lara, just like paper and pens. Anyway, I thought you were always telling your clients to treat themselves, when they've achieved something they're really proud of.'

'Yes,' says Lara, 'but I mean a new lipstick or a big bar of Whole Nut. Not seven hundred quids' worth of handbag.'

I hadn't actually realised that.

'You can't keep this, Iz. I mean, it's gorgeous, but you'll have to starve when the credit card bill comes in.'

I let out a long exaggerated sigh. 'You're right, Lars. Maybe I'd better call Aadelman Stern and ask them to advance me some money from my seven-figure book deal.'

'I mean, you have to be –' Lara stops and stares at me. 'What did you just say?'

I can't keep a grin from breaking out across my face. 'A book deal. A *three-book* deal, in fact. With Aadelman Stern. For *Showjumpers*.'

All the blood has drained from Lara's face. 'You're joking.'

'Uh-uh.' I shake my head. 'I'm not.'

'But . . . how . . .'

'Well, remember I told you Mum sent them *Showjumpers*?'

'Oh my God!' Lara covers her mouth with her hands. 'They *liked* it?'

'Thanks,' I say.

'No, no, I mean . . . *I* like *Showjumpers*. I love *Showjumpers*. But it's only a few pages, Iz-Wiz. I didn't think a publisher would offer you a . . . a *what* did you say?'

'Seven-figure, three-book deal,' I say happily, picking up my contract and lifting it above my head like a Wimbledon champion. 'We're signing it any day now!'

'Iz, this is incredible! My best friend, superstar novelist!'

'I know!'

'So tell me everything! Have they given you a deadline? How much more do you have to write?'

'Well, they're saying three hundred thousand words,' I say, 'but I think they'll be open to negotiation further down the line.'

Lara actually chokes on her mouthful of champagne. '*Three hundred thousand words*,' she echoes. 'Fucking hell, Isabel! If I knew I had to write a whole three-hundred-thousand-word novel, I'd completely flip.'

'You would?'

'Oh God, don't *you* worry, Isabel! I mean, Aadelman Stern wouldn't be throwing all that money at you if they didn't think you could do it.'

I don't say anything.

'Would they?'

I take a gulp of champagne.

'*Isabel?*' Lara is watching me. 'I know that look.'

'All right. But you have to promise – *promise*, Lars – that you won't get cross. You won't judge. You won't analyse. And you won't try to talk me out of it.'

'Oh God. What have you done?'

'They think *Showjumpers* is being written by Katriona de Montfort,' I say.

Lara just stares at me.

'It wasn't my fault,' I carry on. 'They called, thanks to Mum's bloody covering letter, and I said I was Katriona's assistant. I didn't *tell* them *Showjumpers* was by her.'

Lara frowns, the way she does when she's concentrating very hard on something. 'But . . . you didn't tell them they'd made a mistake?'

'It would've been really awkward!'

'More awkward than this?'

'Anyway, by then they'd started talking about how they want a series and everything. They said it could sell a million copies!'

'If *Katriona's* name is on the cover,' says Lara, faintly.

'Well, yes, but Katriona didn't write it, did she? *I did*. Why should I give up the chance to get this amazing deal, just because I haven't already got a big, famous name to put on the cover?'

Lara is massaging her temples. 'Jesus Christ, Isabel, have you thought this through at *all*? When are you going to tell them the truth? You can't sign in Katriona's name, you know!'

'I *know* that,' I sigh. 'I've got all that sorted, Lara.'

'*How?*'

I don't think that now is the time to show her the fruits of my careful Tipp-exing.

'Well for one thing, I've just given them this

298

amazing publicity and marketing strategy. I mean, it's brilliant, Lars. I've done sales projections, a whole campaign . . . So when I go back to them with the contract signed in my name, they won't mind when I tell them who it's really by!'

Lara's eyes are closed, as if she's in pain. 'And in the unlikely event they *don't* like your publicity and marketing strategy?'

I swallow hard. 'That won't happen. But if it does, well, I've already signed the contract by then, haven't I? They can't go back on it then.'

'Oh, *Isabel*.' Lara buries her face in her hands. 'Isabel, Isabel, Isabel.'

This isn't particularly supportive. I only hope this isn't how she handles her clients.

'Come on, Lars! It's not like I'm telling them a lie, exactly. It's more of a . . . half-truth! And it's not like I'm stealing Katriona's *work*, or anything. I would never do something like that . . .'

'Isabel, you're stealing Katriona's name. You're stealing her reputation.'

'*Borrowing*,' I say. 'Anyway, it's only for another few days.'

'But you could get into terrible trouble!' Lara grabs my hands. 'You only just got away with all that stuff at the *Saturday Mercury*. And that was just a silly mistake. This is *fraud*, Iz!'

'It's nothing of the sort!'

'Well, I'm not sure Aadelman Stern will see it that way. *Or* Katriona de Montfort. God, Isabel, these people have whole teams of lawyers dedicated to this sort of thing!'

'But it'll all be out in the open very soon, Lars. And then everything will be OK. I promise.'

Lara doesn't say anything.

I feel cut adrift. I wanted her to be excited about all this. I wanted it more than anything.

'Well, it's great to have you on board, Lara. I really appreciate the positive thinking.'

'Look, Iz-Wiz—'

'Don't Iz-Wiz me!' I can feel my throat tightening. 'It's all right for you, Lara. You're already doing what you've always wanted to. All you had to do was get on the right course at university, then do your Ph.D. –'

'A mere six years of hard slog and financial sacrifice,' says Lara, coolly.

I think I'll ignore that. 'But getting my dream job isn't that easy for me! So I saw an opportunity, and I took it! And all you can do is bang on about theft and fraud.' I'm already pulling on my coat. 'Well, you're entitled to your opinion, *Dr* Alliston. But I *won't* be dedicating this book to you.'

'Iz, wait . . .'

I hear her calling after me as I stamp out of the pub and into the freezing January air. But I'm not going back in there. I knew Lara might have a little bit of a go at me, but I never thought it'd be that bad. And she wasn't even helpful! All she did was bandy around scary-sounding crimes she knows nothing about!

I grab a passing middle-aged man in a pinstripe suit.

'Excuse me, sir, could you tell me exactly how I can find Thomson Tibble Telford?'

Chapter 23

I realise now that I should have come to Will Madison right from the start. I mean, I bet even the security guards at Thomson Tibble Telford know more about law than Lara does! Certainly the way they apprehended me when I tried to get in the lift without a security pass shows they know a lot about trespassing. Not quite so much about human rights, though.

I'm still rubbing my bruised bicep when Will Madison puts his head around the door of the security guards' office.

'Isabel?'

'Will!' I beam at him. 'I *thought* you'd still be here.'

'They called up to say a friend of my brother's was downstairs . . .' He's looking less irritable than I thought. Other than that, he looks exactly the same as he did at Claridge's, except this time his tie is light blue. It's quite nice, actually. It brings out his eyes, and makes them look a bit more the colour of Joe's.

'I'm really sorry to disturb you at work. But I was in the area, meeting a friend, and . . . well, there's a legal matter I'd like to discuss with you. If you've got a few minutes . . . ?'

'Right . . . well, you'd better come up to my office, I suppose . . .'

'Thank you!' I give the security guard a dirty look as Will holds the door open for me. 'I *told* them I knew someone in the building!'

I'd expected a solicitor's office to be all wood panels and leather armchairs, with fancy framed degrees and diplomas on the walls. But it isn't like that at all. We get out of the lift straight onto an open-plan floor that looks a lot like the *Saturday Mercury*, right down to the recycling bins. A few stalwarts are still at their desks, but it's mostly empty now, apart from the cleaners pushing big Hoovers around.

'My favourite time of the day,' Will says, leading me across the floor. 'No one around to disturb, with nattering and gossip. It's the best time for getting actual work done.'

I don't mention that, in every office I've ever worked in, the nattering and the gossip was by some distance the best part of my working day. 'Will, I'm really sorry to disrupt your work.'

'Not at all,' Will says, a bit stiffly. 'It's very nice to see you again. And I wanted to apologise for the way I behaved at that launch party.'

'Oh, don't worry about that! Joe explained that you two don't really get along. Honestly, if I had a fiver for every time I've stalked off from a row with my brothers in a huff—'

'I didn't mean that,' he interrupts. His cheeks have turned just a little bit pink. 'I meant the way I wittered on about tax law. I just feel like such a fish out of water at those kinds of dos; sometimes I find myself talking too much . . .' He stops himself as we reach his office door and looks down at me. 'I'll try not to bore you as much today, I promise.'

'You didn't bore me at all,' I tell him.

He almost smiles. 'Come on in.'

There are two desks. One, by the inner window, the one that looks out onto the open-plan area, is totally, anally tidy. There's nothing on this one but a yellow legal pad and a pen tidy, filled with rows of perfectly sharpened HB pencils. The other, by the outside window, is a complete tip, with papers piled in lurching towers and day-old coffee mugs gathering dust.

'Have a seat,' Will says, pulling out the chair for me at – surprise, surprise – the anally tidy desk. 'I . . . er . . . do apologise for the mess. My trainee, Chrissie, is so untidy. I was in a seminar most of the afternoon, so I'm afraid she really let things slide today.'

'That must have been in Lara's seminar! Dr Alliston,' I add, when he frowns uncomprehendingly. 'She gave a seminar on stress here this afternoon.'

'Yes, that was it! She was a very good speaker, actually.'

'She's brilliant. We've been best friends since we were seven,' I say, before I remember that I'm annoyed with Lara.

'Well, tell her from me, I thought she was excellent.'

'I will.' Actually, Will and Lara would make a good

304

couple. Both highly ambitious, focused solely on their jobs, to the detriment of their personal relationships. It could be a match made in heaven! And then, if they got married, I'd be the bridesmaid, obviously, and Joe could be the best man, and then we'd have to walk back down the aisle together at the end of the service, and Joe would look across at me and realise what he's been missing –

'So.' Will interrupts my thoughts. 'What was it you wanted to talk to me about? A problem with Miss de Montfort?'

My heart thuds. 'What?'

'Well, you work for Katriona de Montfort, don't you?' He's turning a little bit pink again. 'Didn't you . . . er . . . tell me that at the party?'

I'm not sure I did, to be honest.

'Or maybe Joe mentioned it when I spoke to him the other day,' he mumbles.

Is Will Madison checking up on me? Or – and this would be so much better – is *Joe* Madison simply unable to stop talking about me?

'It's nothing to do with Katriona de Montfort, actually,' I say. 'It's to do with my own writing career.'

'You're a writer too?' Will actually looks gratifyingly impressed. 'Wow.'

'I thought you hated writers,' I say. 'I thought spending an evening with them was like watching a kettle boil.'

He looks surprised. 'I never said I hated writers. I said I hated publishing parties. I don't hate writers. I'd be one myself,' he pulls a wry face, 'if only I had the talent! Not that talent's all you need, of course.'

'Of course.' I give him a sympathetic smile. 'I imagine you'd struggle with the creative visualisation aspect too . . .'

Will just blinks. 'I meant the discipline.'

'Discipline?'

'Yes. Getting up every morning, when you have no place you have to be, and sitting down at a desk to write every day, all by yourself . . . I'm really impressed you can do it, Isabel.'

'Well,' I say, 'discipline *has* always come easy to me. Most days I just can't *stop* writing!' I reach into my Harvey Nichols bag for my Smythson notebook, hiding the front cover. 'This is where it all happens.'

Will looks genuinely impressed. 'Well, if you ever find your inspiration drying up, maybe you'd like to go down and stay on my mother's farm in Dorset.' He turns even more pink, as if he's just been taken aback by his own spontaneity. 'She often has writers to stay, is what I mean,' he adds. 'You know, for the solitude.'

'Oh, I *love* solitude.'

He smiles, but whether at me or at the thought of his mum's farm, I can't be sure. 'I keep telling her she should make a little business out of it. What with all Joe's contacts, and everything . . .'

'Yes. Gina must go there a lot.'

'You know Gina?' He pulls a face. Briefly, but not so briefly you could miss it. 'Actually, Mum doesn't seem to like Gina all that much. I don't think they'd last two minutes in each other's company down on the farm.'

This is the best news I've had all day! Well, apart from getting my contract, obviously. Joe's mum doesn't like Gina! I bet she'd like *me*. I bet she and I would have a ball down on the farm together. I'd help her milk cows, and herd sheep, and . . . do whatever it is you do with chickens. And we could bake bread together in the big country kitchen, and wash clothes with carbolic soap and a mangle, and fry up delicious hearty farm breakfasts for the menfolk returning from the fields. And I could wear a fetching little headscarf and a checked shirt, like one of those landgirls. And the country air would make my cheeks all rosy, and Joe Madison would come down to visit for the weekend with Gina, and take one look at me, and realise his mother was right all along, and then we'd go and find ourselves a nice, quiet little haystack, and –

'So!' Will is clearing his throat and picking up a legal pad. 'We should probably get on. My rate is five hundred pounds an hour, so . . .' he taps his watch, 'I'd try to keep the questions brief, if I were you.'

I stare at him. 'I . . . I didn't think . . .'

'Isabel. It was a joke.' He's still dead-pan.

'Oh! How . . . how funny . . .'

'Sorry. I don't do jokes all that often.' His set face gives way to a sheepish grin. 'And as you can see, I don't do them all that well, either.'

'No, no! It was very funny . . .'

'It wasn't, but thank you. Now, what can I help you with?'

I think I'd better keep all this nice and vague. I don't want him getting wind of what I'm doing and mentioning it to Joe in his next phone call.

'Well, it's just that after that chat we had at the party the other week, I simply have not been able to stop thinking about contracts,' I say. 'And I realised what a terrible gap in my knowledge there is.'

Will glances up from his pad. 'Do you find you *need* a lot of knowledge about contracts?'

'Well, one day – *in theory*, of course – I could be signing a book deal of my own. I just thought I ought to get a handle on the basics, so I'm all prepared.'

To my surprise, he nods approvingly. 'Good for you, Isabel. More people should take an interest in the basics of contract law. It would solve a lot of problems for us lawyers if people had an idea about what kind of mess they can get themselves into.'

'Exactly.' I beam at him. 'Just simple stuff, really.' I turn to a new page in my Smythson, to look as if I'm making notes. 'Like, whether it matters if you sign a contract that's meant for somebody else. That kind of thing.'

He glances up, more sharply this time. 'Sorry?'

'Well, could I sign a contract that's meant for, say, my friend Bob, without Bob knowing about it? Like a . . . a surprise contract!'

'There's no such thing as a surprise contract.'

'Are you sure? It could just be an incredibly rare point of law that you haven't heard of.'

'Isabel.' He puts down his pen and stares right at me, across the desk. His eyebrows are very high on his forehead. 'I've been practising law for thirteen years. And I've never heard of a surprise contract before.'

'Well, I may have the terminology wrong,' I say hastily, before he gets suspicious. 'All I really mean is, could I sign a contract that's in someone else's name?'

'Oh, *that's* perfectly all right. Although you'd need a power of attorney, obviously.'

'Obviously,' I say. 'A powerful attorney. I think *all* our lives would be easier if we had one of those.'

He seems to be hiding a smile. 'Not a powerful attorney. A power *of* attorney. It's a document that gives you the right to sign on your friend Bob's behalf, if Bob can't be there to sign it himself.'

'Oh. But it makes it all legal, yes?'

'Yes . . .'

'That's great!' I *knew* it was OK. This will shut Lara up.

'But of course, the *contract* is still Bob's,' Will is continuing. 'Therefore everything promised to Bob in the contract is still Bob's, even though your signature is on it.'

Bloody Bob. 'Right.'

'I mean, anything else would be unlawful. Even illegal.'

I swallow. 'Would it?'

'Absolutely! White-collar crime isn't my field, of

course, but I believe at worst you could be charged with obtaining a pecuniary advantage by deception. Very serious indeed. A hefty fine, probably, but I can't imagine that a prison term is out of the question.'

'*Prison?* I . . . didn't think . . .'

So Lara was right. If Aadelman Stern *don't* like Operation: Bring Back the Bonkbuster, I can't just sign the contract anyway. Not unless I want to be overseeing the distribution of the complimentary riding crops from Cell Block H.

'So you're telling me nothing can be changed on a contract once it's been drawn up. Nothing at all.'

'Well, not *nothing*.' Will loosens his tie, slips it over his head one-handed and absent-mindedly undoes the top button of his shirt. I think all this talk of contracts is relaxing him. Certainly he looks better less buttoned up. I can even see just a tiny hint of lightly tanned chest. 'I mean, there are sometimes errors, even in a final draft. It's perfectly fine to change those.'

I must stop staring at his second shirt button and pay attention. 'Errors?'

'An ambiguous word here, a misinterpretation there . . . Contracts don't have to be sacrosanct, you know, Isabel. If there's a word or two you're not that happy with, you can just cross it out and write in the exact meaning you're after, initial the changes, and then the contract can be signed.'

OK. *This* is more like it. I'm just about to ask whether Tipp-ex is considered a reasonable alternative to crossing-out when he goes on.

'Of course, nothing that changes the basic sense of the contract,' he adds. He slings his tie into a desk drawer. 'I mean, you can't go around adding zeros to the amount of money changing hands!'

I'm just wondering if changing Katriona's name to mine could be construed as 'changing the basic sense of the contract'. I don't think it could.

'You know, Isabel, if you ever need more advice – or someone to look at a contract for you – I'd be happy to help.'

'I will, Will. You've been so helpful already!' I want to give him a hug, but I'm not sure it's the kind of thing you do in a solicitor's office. 'You must let me buy you a drink sometime.'

'OK. How about now?'

'*Now?*'

He fixes his deep blue eyes on me. For just a moment, it's like being in the room with Joe instead. 'Why not? I've had a long, hard day. I'm sure you have too. Liquid refreshment might be just what the doctor ordered.'

'Well . . .'

'It's either that,' he says, getting up and pulling his jacket on, 'or I have to bill you for the time you've just taken.' He must realise I'm looking a bit put out, because his face suddenly breaks into a grin. 'That was another joke.'

Well, I suppose there could be worse things than having a quick drink with Joe Madison's brother. He isn't as boring as I thought he was. There really is a sense of humour lurking beneath that solicitor façade, and I'd have to take issue with the view that Joe's the one who got all the charm genes in the Madison family.

And talking of Joe, I'm sure there are all kinds of stories Will can tell me about him.

'All right!' I say. 'Let's have a drink! It'll have to be just the one, though.'

For one thing, I've got to be up bright and early for Katriona's book signing in the morning. And I really want to have a read of my brand-new contract before I go to bed tonight.

I mean, I have to know *exactly* what I'm signing. People can be very unscrupulous.

SOLITUDE IN DORSET TIMETABLE

6 a.m. – Wake up; spring out of bed; enjoy solitude

6.30 a.m. – ~~5 mile run 3 mile run~~ Hearty country ramble (o'er hill and down dale?)

7.45 a.m. – Dry body-brushing; energising face-mask; brisk shower

8 a.m. – Select fetching landgirl-style checked shirt; no need to apply light makeup as skin will already be taking on a creamy countryside glow; go into battle with hair

~~8.30 a.m.~~

~~8.45 a.m.~~

9 a.m. – Breakfast (full English if absolutely necessary)

9.30 a.m. – Wholesome farm-related duties with Mrs Madison

11 a.m. – Work on *Showjumpers* OR morning coffee break

11.15 a.m. – Enjoy solitude

1 p.m. – Lunch break: read improving book OR *Farmers Weekly*

1.15 p.m. – Wholesome farm-related duties with Mrs Madison

3 p.m. – Enjoy solitude

4.30 p.m. – Work on *Showjumpers* OR afternoon tea break

4.45 p.m. – ~~Wholesome~~ Farm-related duties with Joe Madison

6 p.m. – Dry body-brushing; energising face-mask, brisk shower

6.30 p.m. – Select fetching landgirl-style cotton dress; no

need to apply makeup as cheeks should be really glowing by now; go into battle with hair

~~7.30 p.m.~~

~~8 p.m.~~

8.30 p.m. – Tractor to Barn Dance

11 p.m. – Tractor home

11.30 p.m. – Work on *Showjumpers* OR have a nice early night, to maximise chances of progress/solitude tomorrow morning

Chapter 24

Where is it? *Where is my contract?*

God, I should have *known* it was a mistake to carry important things like that in a huge Harvey Nichols carrier bag, without a clasp or anything. My stuff is strewn all over the room. There's my Smythson notebook, soaking in a pool of Stila lip gloss. There's that fruit pastille, and the half-empty packet of Revels. My mobile is safe, of course, inside my Marianne bag, which is perilously close to the lip-gloss slick. But no contract.

OK, let's not panic. It's probably under the bed . . . Or under the pile of clothes I can't precisely remember taking off when I got in last night . . .

No. It isn't.

Bloody Will Madison. I mean, all this is his fault. Turning out to be surprisingly good company, and making me laugh (no, really) with stories about his job (no, *really*), and suggesting we taste-test the six different flavours of mojito on offer at the bar. Well, all right, the mojito testing might have been more my idea (launch party research; I never rest), but it's basically his fault. His stupid fault I've lost this fucking contract.

It couldn't have fallen out of the carrier somewhere *outside* my room, could it? Like . . . somewhere Katriona might find it?

Oh Jesus.

I know I Tipp-exed out her name, but I can't have Katriona thinking *I've* got a book deal with Aadelman Stern either. She'll start asking all kinds of awkward questions, and she'll be offended about the snub to Jennifer and Gordon . . . God, she could even call up Paul Gardner himself and demand to know why he was poaching her own assistant from under her nose! I've got ice down my spine just thinking about it.

I sling on a T-shirt and my new cashmere tracksuit bottoms, and peer out onto the landing. I can't see anything on the floor out there . . . Maybe on the stairs . . .

Lysander is sitting halfway up the staircase. He's running some grotty old toy ship up and down a section of gold banister, and his lips are smeared with chocolate from the things he's popping in his mouth and chewing. Things that look like . . . They are! Revels!

'Hi, Wizzy,' he says. 'Want to play?'

'Not now, Lysander. Where did you find the sweeties?'

'On the stairs. Why?'

I knew it. 'Oh, no reason!' I say casually. 'I was just wondering, did you find anything else on the stairs when you found the sweeties? A brown envelope, say?'

He scrapes his little ship up and down the banister a few more times before he answers. It looks a bit like a wooden version of the super-duper Captain Kidd ships you see advertised on TV, but this one's a right old wreck. It's just some home-made thing cobbled together out of bits of old plank, but Lysander's gazing at it like it's the top treat from his Christmas list. 'Maybe,' he says.

He's got it. The little sod has got the contract, hasn't he?

What would Fun Nanny do in this situation?

'I tell you what, Lysander, if you give me back that special envelope without showing anyone, I'll give you . . .' What *do* you give a spoiled multimillionaire's son? '. . . Nutella! And I won't tell Mummy!'

Now he stares at me, with wide eyes. 'You would *lie*?'

I grit my teeth. 'It isn't lying, Lysander. It's just keeping a secret. Nothing wrong with that. Nothing wrong with that at all.'

He seems to be contemplating this for a moment. 'I don't like secrets.'

'Oh, come on, Lysander, everyone likes secrets!' I give him my Fun Nanny thumbs-up. 'Keeping secrets is fun!' I'm changing my mind about this a bit, though. Keeping *this* secret is starting to get stressful.

'Mummy has *lots* of secrets,' he's carrying on, more to himself than me.

'What's that, darling?' Katriona is coming up the stairs. 'Oh, Isabel!' She stares at me. 'Have you forgotten the book festival? The car's coming to take us to Hyde Park in twenty minutes! Were you planning on having a shower this morning? Using a hairbrush?'

'Yes, Katriona, of course . . .'

'Then chop-chop!' She claps her hands. The sudden noise – and today's bright violet Chanel – does nothing for my hangover. 'If you aren't in that shower in one minute –'

'But—'

'No buts!' She pushes my bedroom door open herself, and points a finger. 'Go.'

I can't leave Lysander behind without getting my contract back! 'Don't forget that little treat we talked about, Lysander,' I say, desperately giving him a meaningful look.

'Darling, *don't* play with this horrid old ship,' I hear Katriona say, as I trudge towards my shower. 'Mummy's bought you a lovely new one!'

In the shower, I work out a strategy. I'll suddenly 'forget' something, just before the taxi pulls away, then I can shoot back inside and dash into Lysander's nursery. That should be around the time Selma's giving him his mid-morning rice cakes and organic soya milk, so the coast should be clear . . .

Hold on. I've just gone back into my bedroom to get dressed, and the envelope is there. It's just sitting on the desk, as pristine as before apart from a small, child's finger-shaped smear of chocolate. I glance inside to check the contract is there. Yes, it is, along with . . . Oh. That's odd. I don't remember putting my photocopy of *Showjumpers* in the envelope as well. Still, that's got a small chocolatey smear on it, too, so it was probably just Lysander trying to be helpful. Well, thank God for that. Thank *Lysander* for that. I think Fun Nanny's approach paid off. Either that, or Lysander's not such a little monster after all.

I'm not relishing the prospect of another of my taxi rides with Katriona. And it turns out I was right.

'Lovely outfit, Isabel.' She looks over my leggings and sweater dress, and the ironic patent stilettos I picked up from this cut-price, hard-to-find Kurt Geiger outlet store . . . All right. The flagship on South Molton Street.

'Thank you . . .' I just sit back and wait for the anti-compliment to kick in.

'Very *Desperately Seeking Susan*.'

Right. That's the last time I try the layered look, then.

'God, I loathe these events.' She slumps back in her seat and gazes balefully out at the Albert Hall. 'Thousand, of hysterical kids. Face-ache from smiling. *Tap water.*'

I make a non-committal soothing noise.

'I wouldn't do them at all, but Myles has always made me. Well, it's the *last time.*'

She says this with such obvious meaning that I obviously have to ask. 'Oh?'

'I'm leaving Myles,' she says simply. 'I'm dropping

him as my agent, and working with Joe instead. We worked it all out this week. What do you think of this lipstick, Isabel? Does it suit me?'

'You're *dropping* Myles?'

'No, it's too sickly,' she decides, peering at the lipstick in her compact mirror. 'Lovely on *you*, though, Isabel. Have it.'

I don't pay much attention to the brand-new Guerlain lipstick she slings across at me. There's no room for it in my Marianne bag, apart from anything else. 'But you've worked with Myles for years!' And made him millions, which I doubt he'll take too kindly to missing out on. 'Won't he mind?'

'Oh, he'll get over it.'

'But . . . why are you getting rid of him?'

She shoots me a very sharp look. 'You know, some people would think that's none of your business, Isabel. But it's hardly a big secret. You've heard us rowing. And we've been getting on so badly lately that I just don't think either of us could stand any more bickering. *When's the new book going to be finished?'* She does a sudden, startlingly accurate impression of Myles at his poshest. *'We cahrn't keep them waiting for-evah.* Well, it's all *his* fault I've had that horrid writer's block. Bullying me like that all the time. Do you know, it's only been a couple of days since I made my decision to go with Joe, and already my block is lifting? I've written *oodles*!'

'Well, Joe is very . . . inspirational.'

'Yes, I *knew* you'd like me working with Joe!'

Katriona lets out a cackle. 'Well, it won't just be a chance to feed your obsession, Isabel. This move is going to be very good for you in other ways, you know. Joe is even better connected than Myles for your kind of novel. Oh! That reminds me,' she carries on, before I can disabuse her of the notion that I'm somehow obsessed with Joe Madison. 'I really *must* fix up that meeting with Jennifer and Gordon for you. I'd forgotten all about it! I'll arrange something for next week.'

'Well, no rush . . .'

'But you must want them to see it! All that research you were doing, you must be almost finished.'

'Er . . . almost.'

Katriona lets out a long, theatrical sigh. 'Lucky old you, Isabel. Even now my block's lifted, I'm going to have to chain myself to my desk if I'm ever going to get this new Kidd in on time.'

As far as I know, the new Kidd is already months overdue. Still, I suspect Katriona's version of 'on time' is quite different from everyone else's. Even mine.

Chapter 25

Looking at the queues in Hyde Park for Katriona's book signing, I can't understand why she hates them. It looks fantastic! I can hardly wait for my own. My fans will probably have camped out all night to meet me, just like people did when Charles and Lady Di got married. Then I'll roll up in a chauffeur-driven Bentley, and everyone will cheer and wave flags, and a small girl with ringlets will come forward and give me a little posy, and she'll curtsy . . .

Well, it may not be quite so much like a royal wedding as that. But it's going to be great.

I mean, look what they've done here! An entire marquee has been turned into the *Tiki-Trekker*, Captain Kidd's ship. There's netting all over the ceiling, old-fashioned cannon lining the walls, and an array of plastic barnacles and fake seaweed that even Mum would be proud of draped over every available surface. And there's an actual little ship's cabin, faux-ramshackle Cath Kidston-style, with the front two walls cut out, where Katriona has already started signing her way through thousands of Captain Kidd books for the long queue outside.

There're about fifteen staff members, dressed up in

sailor suits, flapping nervously around Katriona, proffering pens, and cushions, and water, and Thai-style foot massage, for all I know. She's lapping it up like a pampered pet, commanding several of them to open her books at the front cover for her, so she can sign faster, and dispatching several more to various coffee shops way over the other side of Park Lane to bring back sample espressos, most of which she'll reject.

I knew I'd learn a lot from today. Katriona's behaviour is just making me even more determined never to turn into that kind of a diva. People will *beg* to be allowed to come and work at my signings. Word of my simple, unassuming nature will spread through the booksellers of the nation like wildfire. I'll offer to fetch *my own* coffee, and then I'll buy mocha Frappucinos as a surprise treat for everyone. And I'll be charm personified to every single fan who's queued to meet me. Probably some of them will break down in tears with the emotion of it all, and I'll come out from behind my desk with open arms and a heart-breaking smile, and dab their tears myself . . . well, unless it's one of the ones who's camped out all night. I might ask them to go and have a bit of a wash first, before I start dabbing anything.

Anyway, I'll be a sight more popular than old Katriona, anyway. I heard some *very* disgruntled conversation between the two poor souls being packed off to find the perfect espresso. You can hardly blame them. It's barely three degrees out there. I, on the other hand, as Katriona's *personal* assistant, have been given the relatively cushy job of selecting a shortlist for the 'Best Fancy Dress' prize, to be awarded by Katriona herself at the end of the signing. This really just means I have to wander around the festival's various heated marquees, slapping a red sticker on a dozen kids dressed up as parrots and pirates.

Which is making me pretty popular right now, I have to say. Once word of my mission leaks out, I'm inundated with bribes and backhanders. From the children at first – shares in pocket money, Opal Fruits – and then, as the red stickers dwindle to a coveted two or three, their parents get in on the act. But I have to be squeaky-clean, of course; whiter than white. By the time I've off-loaded my final sticker on a very impressive Kevin the Kipper outfit, I've turned down a day at Champneys, a week in San Gimignano, and (regretfully) a brand-new Smart car with personalised numberplates.

I couldn't say no to the Opal Fruits, though.

Anyway, once the frenzy had started, it all took a lot less time than I'd expected. I've got the rest of the morning to myself now. There's a bookshop area set up in one of the other large marquees, with a nice little Costa coffee concession (espresso rejected by Katriona on grounds of . . . well, the grounds. They're not fine enough, apparently). I'll head over there and pick myself up something to read and a nice cup of coffee! I think there's a new Joanna Trollope out in paperback . . .

Oh. The bookshop area appears to be closed.

The tills are unmanned, and instead of people browsing at the makeshift shelves, there's just a few women sitting in a half-empty semi-circle of orange chairs, sipping from polystyrene cups of tea, and nattering at each other. Hmm. That looks horribly like a book group to me. I've always given them a wide berth, even though Lara's a big fan. I mean, the only book group I've ever liked the look of is Richard and Judy's.

'Hello, there!' One of the women has spotted me, and darted over. 'I'm Rhoda. Come to join us?' She's got a gleam about the eyes that could be messianic fervour, or could just be desperation. 'We were hoping for a few more bods before we start!'

'Oh, that's all right, thank you. I'm not really into book groups.'

'Oh, this isn't a book group. It's a *workshop*.'

Pah! as Hercules Poirot would say. You can't go fooling me with workshops. A book group, by any other name, is still a book group.

'*How to Get Your Novel Published*,' Rhoda adds, pointing out the big sign propped up on one of the orange plastic chairs. 'The festival runs it every year. You wouldn't happen to be an aspiring novelist, would you?'

'Actually, I *am* a Novelist.'

'Oh! What's your name? Have I read you?'

'I'm Isabel. And you won't have read me yet. I'm just in the process of signing this really big three-book deal.'

'How super!' She looks genuinely, gratifyingly impressed. 'Gosh, I don't suppose you'd be prepared to come and speak to us, would you? The speaker we'd arranged is running late, and I really don't want these ladies to miss out.'

'I don't know . . .'

'Someone who's navigated the obstacle course, and triumphed. You'd be an inspiration to them, Isabel!'

Actually, I quite like the sound of that. As inspired as *I've* been lately, I don't think I've ever been an inspiration to *anyone else* before.

To Rhoda's Book Group,
Who found me inspiring.

'Well, I suppose I could talk through a few of the basics. How to approach a publisher. How to perfect your Look. That kind of thing . . .'

'Super!' Rhoda takes me by the elbow and steers me towards the circle of chairs. 'We can get started!'

I have a look around the group while Rhoda fusses with finding me a cup of tea. I don't want to be funny, but I'm finding it a bit hard to believe this lot are *proper* aspiring novelists. I mean, seriously, there's not a single half-decent Look between them! One woman, right across from me, is wearing – actually *wearing* – purple Aladdin pants, a pink cloche hat, and the weight of a small child in bangles. Elsewhere, it's an odd mix of tie-dye and polyester twinset. They all look jolly enough, though. Apart from Aladdin Pants, who's scowling across the semicircle like I've brought a bad smell with me or something.

'Ladies, we can begin now.' Rhoda taps her fingernails on an empty seat to get people to quiet down. 'A bit of a change from what was advertised, but I know you'll all be thrilled with the guest speaker we've got for you today. She's just in the process of signing her first three-book deal, so she comes to you battle-hardened from the front lines, so to speak!'

There's a little titter of laughter, which I don't join in. I'm trying to look battle-hardened.

'She's happy to answer any questions you have on the perils and pitfalls of finding a publisher. So without further ado, I give you . . . Isabel . . .'

'Thank you, Rhoda,' I say, before she can ask me my last name. 'And hel-LO, Hyde Park!'

I didn't think it would sound quite that silly. It always sounds good when you hear Paul McCartney or Robbie Williams say it.

'Right!' I try again. 'Let's get this ball rolling! I'll start with some basics, and then you can ask me anything you like, OK?'

There are a few nods.

'Well, first and foremost, you all need to be thinking about finding a personal shopper. Now, I know you probably think that can wait, but I can't tell you the difficulties I've had trying to find a personal shopper who could squeeze me in at short notice. In fact, I would advise all of you here today who are even *thinking* about writing a novel to book an appointment with a qualified personal shopper before you even start.'

Everyone is just staring at me. Shouldn't they be writing this down?

'Er . . . perhaps you could explain what you mean, Isabel.' Rhoda is frowning. 'I'm not sure any of us is really sure what you needed a personal shopper *for*.'

I beam at her. 'That's sweet, Rhoda! But just like all of you, when I started out, I did not have the faintest idea what Look to aim for. This –' I stand up, to display my new Sass&Bide sweater dress and my ironic stilettos, '– is the result of careful thought, and a good deal of trial and error.'

Aladdin Pants has put up her hand.

'Yes!' I say. 'You in the . . . Aladdin pants.'

'I didn't come here for advice about my Look,' she snaps.

'*Really?* Are you sure you wouldn't like some, anyway?'

'I just want to know how you got this book deal of yours. Because I've just been stuck in the slush for months.'

I nod sympathetically. 'I can see that. That's why I thought, some basic style advice, you see . . .'

'The slush *pile*,' she snaps. 'You know? The pile of manuscripts publishers get from people who don't have an agent?'

'Well, *I* don't have an agent,' I begin.

328

It might have been the wrong thing to say. There's a collective gasp of fury, led by Aladdin Pants.

'You got picked up from the slush pile?'

'Well, Isabel's been very lucky, obviously!' Rhoda interrupts. I think she's worried things could turn nasty. 'But I'm sure she deserves her success! Tell us, Isabel,' she turns to me, a bit desperate for a subject change, 'does it take a real core strength to do what you've done?'

'Oh, yes!' I'm as happy to move on as she is. 'Core strength is *extremely* important. A little bit of Ashtanga yoga will do wonders for sluggish stomach muscles . . .'

My eye is suddenly caught by someone walking into the marquee, at the far end. Oh my God. Is it . . . ? Yes. It's Penelope Bright, coming over this way. And I'm talking about my three-book deal! And calling myself Isabel!

I'm not sure I can pull off a faint again. I just sit back in my seat and scrunch down as far as possible.

'Well, I think that about wraps things up,' I whisper. 'Thank you for coming!'

'You've still got another twenty minutes, Isabel,' Rhoda says. 'I'm sure there are more questions.'

'There are always more questions, Rhoda,' I say, scrunching down even lower. 'A good writer never stops asking questions. Unfortunately, I don't have all the answers.'

'Well, they've paid for a half-hour workshop,' Rhoda is sounding ever so slightly stroppy, 'so perhaps you could see if you have *any* of the answers?'

'I . . . er . . .'

Rhoda suddenly seems to notice what I'm staring at. 'Oh! Penelope's made it after all!'

Penelope is their speaker? The one who was running late?

'You carry on for a few more minutes, Isabel.' Rhoda is already getting up to go and greet her. 'I'll just explain to Penelope where we're at, and she can take over. I think maybe that would be better for everyone,' she adds, not quite under her breath.

She doesn't have to tell me twice.

'Let me finish,' I tell the workshop, 'with a bit of that yoga I was just talking about.' I slide off my chair and onto the floor, flattening my hands out and touching my forehead to the floor like a Muslim praying. 'I find this pose the most effective way to strengthen the stomach.' I glance up. Nobody is copying me. 'Actually, this is a trick Joanna Trollope passed on to me . . .'

Well, *that's* done it. Even Aladdin Pants has hurled herself to the floor so fast you can practically see the dust rising.

'Excellent! Now, stay down as long as you feel comfortable! Embrace the silence . . .' I start to edge out of the semicircle, sideways on my hands and knees, like a crab. Rhoda is still engaging Penelope in energetic conversation near the café. If I can just make it behind one of those big bookshelves . . .

Perfect!

'Hey!' Surprise, surprise, it's Aladdin Pants. I should've known *she* wouldn't embrace the silence. 'Where's she gone?'

Now all I have to do is wait until Penelope's half of the workshop is over. And then I'm home free!

Chapter 26

God, my half of the workshop was so much better than Penelope's half. I mean, I was offering proper, practical advice. Penelope just wittered on about 'finding the right audience' and 'taking constructive criticism'. Aladdin Pants and co seemed to like it, though. Well, that'll be why they're the ones in the slop pile and I'm the one with the three-book deal!

Anyway, the good news is, nobody mentioned my talk to Penelope, which is why, now she's finished, I'm going to go and nab her. I've got every right to be here, after all, thanks to Katriona. Actually, it's thanks to Katriona that I've *got* to go and nab Penelope, even if I don't want to. I don't want her getting any funny ideas about collaring Katriona about *Showjumpers*. Plus I'm dying to learn if she's had the chance to look at Operation: Bring Back the Bonkbuster!

Once Penelope's safely in the café, and Rhoda has gone off for her lunch break, I dust myself down, emerge from my hiding-place, and wander over to Penelope's table.

'Oh, hi there!' I say casually.

She looks up, with a smile, then scowls when she sees it's me. 'Oh. Liz. I suppose I should have known you'd be here today.'

'Well, where Katriona goes, I go! Mind if I join you?'

'It's a free country,' she says, sounding as though she'd rather it wasn't. 'Actually, I'm glad I ran into you, Liz. I was having a little look at this on the tube over here.' She reaches into her handbag and pulls out my pale blue leather file.

'I bet that livened up your tube ride!'

'It certainly did.'

I can feel my heart starting to race. This is it! This is going to be that moment! The one where Penelope says, 'I've never seen anything quite like this'. And I say, modestly, 'I know . . .' And she says, 'With a publicity and marketing strategy as incredible as this, *Showjumpers* could be the biggest literary hit since *The Da Vinci Code*.' And I say, 'Well, actually, Penelope, there's something I have to tell you . . .'

'I've never seen anything quite like this,' begins Penelope.

'I know,' I say modestly.

'I mean, what *is* this shit?'

'Well, actually, Penelo—' I stop. 'Sorry?'

'When I said we couldn't sign a deal without more to go on, I did *not* mean I wanted this *school project*.'

'I don't understand.'

'Well, have you *seen* it?' Penelope leafs through it. 'A list of Katriona's favourite chat-show hosts . . .

What I can only call an *essay* on the merits of Johnny Depp versus Daniel Craig . . .'

'Oh, that's to play Barrington Bosworth-Bounder in the movie,' I say helpfully. 'It's a tricky decision. Katriona thought people might like a bit of guidance.'

She's ignoring me. '. . . and what are *these*, for God's sake?'

'Pie charts.' Isn't it sort of obvious? 'They're pie charts.'

'I see you two have met, then,' a voice suddenly pipes up behind me. Rhoda's voice. 'Well, I hope you're discussing your very different approaches to the workshop.'

Go away, Rhoda, please go away.

'I must say, though,' Rhoda turns to me, looking peeved, 'I wish you'd told me your approach was quite so . . . unusual. I've had a lot of people complaining that they put their backs out.'

Penelope's intake of breath is audible. '*You* were giving Rhoda's workshop?'

'Just a little yoga demonstration,' I say desperately. 'I'm a qualified instructor, you know!'

'Well, I've got several unhappy customers to placate. They didn't pay thirty pounds for some tin-pot yoga class.'

Rhoda, mercifully, bustles back across the marquee, where Aladdin Pants and several others are still standing.

I hardly dare look at Penelope.

'Yoga,' she says.

'Namaste.' I bow my head. 'Anyway, I really should be getting on . . .'

Penelope grabs my arm as I get up to leave. '*I. Know. What. You. Are. Up. To.*'

Oh God.

I can hardly breathe. 'Look, Penelope, I can explain—'

'This whole thing has gone beyond farce,' she hisses. 'You will not allow any contact with Katriona. You refuse us permission to contact her agent. And now I find that you lecture writers' workshops on *how to get a publisher*. I should have known you were a professional, Liz, right from the start.'

I blink at her. 'A professional *what*?'

Her eyes are glittering with fury. 'If Katriona wanted to get the highest price for *Showjumpers*, she should just have had her agents auction it, out in the open. Not hire a mercenary like you to go around shoring up rival bids and playing us all off against each other. How many other publishers are you taking for a ride right now? Three? Four? You're just holding out on us with the manuscript, aren't you, to see if anyone else is going to jump in with a better offer.'

'God, no, Penelope, you've got this all wrong—'

'Well, enough is enough, Liz.' She gets to her feet. 'You know, I don't even believe she's *written* the book yet. Everyone knows Lemper Snyde Brusoff have been waiting for the latest Captain Kidd for the last six months.'

'She *has* almost finished the book, honestly, Penelope! She could give it to you tomorrow, if you wanted!'

'Fine.' Penelope folds her arms. 'I do want.'

'Well, that might not be possible . . .'

'Then nor is my continued co-operation.'

'All right!' I have to stop Penelope before she can stalk away, and out of my life, taking my book deal with her. 'All right, Penelope, I'll get you the manuscript!'

She stops. 'The whole thing?'

'The whole thing!'

'Before we sign the contract?'

I swallow hard. 'Yes. If that's what it takes. Before we sign the contract.'

She thinks about this for a moment. 'Fine. I mean, I never wanted to do this project in the first place, but the money men are keen. I'll expect it first thing Monday morning.'

'*Monday?*'

'Let me guess – there's some kind of a problem with that,' Penelope snaps.

'No, no . . .' I have to talk her out of this insanity. 'It's just . . . well, today's Saturday, and I won't make the late post, and then it's Sunday, so really . . .'

'Fine. Put it in the post on Monday. And I'll expect it on Tuesday.'

That's no good! 'Yes, but—'

''Bye, Liz.' Penelope doesn't even let me finish. 'Give my regards to Katriona.'

The minute she's out of sight, I sit back down at the table. My legs are shaking.

A three-hundred-thousand-word epic bonkbuster. In two days.

You know what this is, don't you?

This is an Absolute Worst-Case Scenario.

Seriously.

EMERGENCY TIMETABLE

6 a.m. –

5 a.m. –

4 a.m. – Wake up; spring out of bed; drink ~~lemon and hot water~~ double espresso

4.05 a.m.– Write 20,000 words of *Showjumpers* AND do some light warm-up stretching

6.30 a.m. – ~~5 mile run 3 mile run~~ Jogging in Kensington Gardens

7.00 a.m. – ~~Dry body brushing; instant face mask~~; Extremely brisk shower

7.10 a.m. – Select outfit; apply light makeup; wear baseball cap to hide hair

7.30 a.m. – Write 50,000 words of *Showjumpers* AND eat breakfast (five scrambled eggs, grilled tofu, energy bar)

11 a.m. – Energising ginseng tea break and power nap

11.15 a.m. – Write 20,000 words of *Showjumpers* AND spellcheck

11 p.m. – Lunch break: read *Showjumpers*

1.05 p.m. – Write 30,000 words of *Showjumpers* AND phone Lara for support and encouragement

5 p.m. – Energising yoga stretches and power nap

5.15 p.m. – Write 30,000 more words of *Showjumpers* AND order gourmet take-away dinner (lean meat, super-food salad, energy-packed flapjack)

11 p.m. – Have a nice early night, to maximise chances of easily getting another 150,000 words done tomorrow!

~~EMERGENCY~~ COMPLETE AND UTTER CRISIS
TIMETABLE

~~4 a.m. Wake up; spring out of bed; drink lemon and hot water double espresso~~

~~5 a.m. Wake up; spring out of bed; drink lemon and hot water double espresso~~

~~6 a.m. Wake up; spring out of bed; drink lemon and hot water double espresso~~

~~10 a.m.~~

~~10.30 a.m.~~

1 p.m. – Lunch (Domino's delivery, extra double pepperoni, ~~one large beer~~ two large beers

1.05 p.m. – Phone Lara for support and encouragement

1.06 p.m. – Wait for Lara to get message and return call

1.32 p.m. – Wait for Lara to get message and return call

1.47 p.m. – Wait for Lara to get message and return call AND power nap

6.18 p.m. – Speak to Lara who has returned call AND interrupted power nap

6.22 p.m. – Write 150,000 words of *Showjumpers*

7.13 p.m. – Write 149,998 words of *Showjumpers*

7.56 p.m. – WRITE 149,998 WORDS OF *SHOWJUMPERS*

9.43 p.m. – STOP STARING INTO SPACE AND WRITE 149,998 WORDS OF *SHOWJUMPERS*, FOR THE LOVE OF GOD!!!

11.31 p.m. –

12.08 a.m.

01.4

Isabel Bookbinder
Bolivia

Ms Penelope Bright
Lovely Senior Publisher
Aadelman Stern
Piccadilly (opp. Wolseley)
London

21 January

Dear Penelope,

May I start by saying how nice it was to see you at the book festival the other day. What a great opportunity it was for ~~you and I~~ ~~you and me~~ us to get to know one another better, and to laugh together over that silly misunderstanding with my yoga workshop! I really feel that now we can call each other friends, and not merely colleagues.

On that note, I am writing to inform you that it may be some time before we are able to enjoy each other's company again. I am moving to Bolivia, at exceptionally short notice, and henceforth communication between us will of necessity be rather slow. Although Bolivia is an extremely beautiful landlocked country in central South America, bordered by Brazil on the north and east, Paraguay and Argentina on the south, and Chile and Peru on the west, I have heard only poor reports of their postal service. For this reason, it may be a few ~~days~~ weeks before you receive Katriona's completed manuscript, which is so completely fantastic that I simply had to bring it out with me

340

to read on the plane. I have given up caring about carbon footprints.

I am sure that the anticipation will make *Showjumpers'* arrival all the more exciting, and

Chapter 27

All right. Let's not panic here.

So it hasn't been the most productive two days of my life. All top novelists go through periods like these sometimes.

I mean, I may not have written a huge amount, but I think what I *have* written shows very much the direction I'm heading in: onwards and upwards. You don't even *need* three hundred thousand words to tell you that! You can work that out from just a couple of words, if you really want to. Which is good, because a couple of words is all I've actually written: 'Chapter Four'.

But I'm not panicking. I'm too exhausted from lack of sleep to panic, apart from anything else. All I need to do is beg and plead with Penelope to give me a few more days. Or rather, I need to persuade Paul Gardner to beg and plead with Penelope to give me a few more days. I've already called and left a message for him this morning, so I just need to work out the best way to get him onside when he calls back. It shouldn't even be that big a deal. At the end of the day, it's just like asking for an extension on your school project. And Gardner won't let Aadelman Stern walk away from the chance of signing Katriona for the sake of one measly week. I'm sure he won't.

And I'm not going to panic about the next step, either. *Obviously* I froze in the face of having to get an entire epic bonkbuster written in little more than a single weekend. But if I can just get an extension for a week, there's really no reason to freeze at all. I know forty-two thousand eight hundred and fifty-seven words a day *sounds* like quite a lot, but really, all you have to do is break it down into manageable chunks. Five thousand words before breakfast. Five thousand words *after* breakfast. Five thousand words before lunch. Five thousand words *after* lunch . . .

What am I talking about? That will never work.

Ten thousand words before breakfast. Ten thousand words *after* breakfast. Ten thousand words before . . .

My phone is ringing. It's Paul Gardner.

'Paul! You got my message.'

'Yes. I called back as soon as I could.' He sounds worried. 'I think I know what you're calling about, Liz. Is it true? Is Katriona really dumping Myles Salisbury-Kent?'

I almost drop the phone. 'You *know* about that?'

'Milly saw her having lunch with Joe Madison at Le Caprice yesterday. They were going over contracts, Mills said, and drinking champagne.'

'Milly didn't *say* anything to them, did she?'

'Oh, no, no! Milly is fully aware of Katriona's desire for privacy, Liz! We *all* are.'

'Well, Milly's right. Katriona and Myles *are* parting ways.'

'I knew it! So how is everything there? How's Katriona handling it?'

Hang on. I think I've just spotted the most fantastic way to get the week's extension I need.

I sigh sorrowfully. 'Well, Paul, she's pretty upset, actually. It's all very unsettling. And it's had a *terrible* effect on her work.'

I can actually hear him swallow. 'Right . . . Er . . . she'll still be able to get the manuscript to Penelope today, like you promised, won't she?'

'I have to be honest with you, Paul, I just don't know if that's a possibility right now.'

There's a short silence. 'But . . . Pen's expecting it this morning,' he squeaks.

'I'm as worried about that as you are, Paul. But I'm afraid Penelope may just have to wait it out a little bit longer.'

'But . . . Liz . . .' He sounds like he might be about to have a heart attack. 'I know Katriona's a bit upset about all this, but if the book's ready, she doesn't have to do anything but get you to bring it over.'

I hadn't actually thought about that. 'Well . . . er . . . it's not actually that simple, Paul. I'd need to actually *get hold* of the manuscript to do that, you see. And Katriona's locked herself in her room. *With Showjumpers.*'

Now there's a longer silence.

'I know it sounds strange,' I say hastily, 'but her writing gives her comfort in stressful times like these. I've spent hours hammering on her door, pleading with her to let me bring you just one chapter. But I just didn't think you'd want to feel responsible for – you know – pushing her over the edge or anything.'

'Oh, no, no!' He sounds a bit strangled. 'Well, how long do you think it'll be before she . . . er . . . unlocks the door?'

'I would say about a week should do it.'

'A *week*?'

'You can keep Penelope off my back for that long,' I plead, 'can't you?'

'God, Liz, I don't know. I can try. But Penelope's a bit stressed too, to be honest with you. I mean, the lawyers are already trying to talk us out of the whole deal –'

My heart gives a nasty lurch. 'That's ridiculous! What are lawyers sticking their noses in for, anyway?'

Gardner lowers his voice. 'Look, this is off the record, Liz, obviously, but there is a slight feeling around here that Katriona de Montfort isn't . . . well, isn't the most *stable* person we've ever worked with. Pen's a bit worried that if Katriona mishandles this bust-up with Myles, maybe he'll have grounds for legal action against Aadelman Stern. We did go ahead with negotiations for *Showjumpers* without telling him, you know. That could be against the terms of his original contract with Katriona.'

'She won't mishandle it! She's completely in control of it all.'

'But you just said she's barricaded herself in her room.'

'Well, yes, but that's just *her way* of handling it. There's no need for your legal department to go wasting their time on this!'

'Oh, we're using our specialist legal consultant, actually. Shonagh's only responsible for drawing up contracts. Pen thought we needed an expert for this. Though I've got a few doubts about it.' He lowers his voice again; he's practically whispering now. It almost makes me wonder if Penelope has his office bugged or something. 'We've used him lots of times in the past, but given that he's Joe Madison's brother, I'm not sure whether there isn't a bit of a conflict of interest going on.'

'*Will Madison*?' I sit down on the edge of the bed. '*He*'s your specialist consultant?'

'Do you know him?'

Oh, yes, he's my future boyfriend's brother!

Who knows I'm Katriona's assistant.

Who knows what kind of questions I've been asking.

'Just slightly,' I croak.

'Well, Pen saw him this morning – I wish she'd known before she'd gone. He might be more amenable to Katriona's cause if he's a pal of yours.'

'Look, Paul, I have to go.'

'But what am I going to tell Penelope about *Showjumpers*?'

346

'A week, Paul. That's all I need. Just get me that week.'

Will's secretary told me he was in meetings all day, but he'd call me back if he got five minutes. Well, that's not good enough. I need to deal with this fast. Which is why I'm in this taxi right now, heading to Thomson Tibble Telford.

Well, I'm trying to head to Thomson Tibble Telford. The traffic on Kensington Church Street is conspiring to stop me. There must be some kind of blockage at the High Street end, because we haven't moved more than five metres in five minutes. This isn't helping my shredded nerves recover, I have to say.

'Love?' The driver is trying to get my attention. 'Know this bloke in the Porsche, do you?'

On the opposite side of the road, which is also gridlocked, Jeremy the estate agent is grinning at me, and giving me big thumbs-ups, and signalling me to wind down my window.

'I left you a message on Saturday afternoon,' he says, once I've grudgingly wound it down. 'Didn't you get it?'

'I had a deadline,' I tell him, entirely truthfully. 'I wasn't returning calls. I didn't even pick up my messages.'

'Well, you should have! Congratulations, Isabel! You're the new owner of a prime piece of W8 property!'

'I . . . you . . . what?'

'The vendors got back to me about your offer. They were happy with the asking price, so,' he gives another thumbs-up, 'away we go!'

I think the taxi has started moving again. Oh, no. It just *felt* like the ground was shifting from under me.

'But I never put in an offer!'

Jeremy frowns. 'Sorry?'

'I didn't say I wanted to buy the place!' I'm well aware the taxi driver – and most of the other occupants of the traffic jam probably – are listening to this with ears on stalks. 'I mean, I really liked it, but I didn't tell you to go around making offers for me!'

'You said you'd hit whatever price you needed to. You saw me go outside to make the call to the vendors . . .'

'I thought you were going to tell them how much I liked it! I thought you were just passing on my compliments!'

'Isabel . . .' Jeremy's contact lenses are troubling him again. 'The vendors have made an offer on a new place dependent on *your* offer. They're instructing solicitors. I thought you were all ready to move on this!'

'Well, I am, I just . . .' I just don't happen to have three-quarters of a million pounds in my bank account, yet, like I was supposed to.

'You can't just back out,' he's carrying on, looking more and more cross. 'They'll be terribly upset.'

'I didn't want to upset anyone!'

'So you're still in?'

My taxi is starting to move properly this time. 'I . . . maybe . . .'

'Call me!' he yells, as we start to move away from each other. 'For Christ's sake, Isabel . . .'

The taxi driver gives me funny looks in the rear-view mirror the entire rest of the way across town.

'Don't you worry about that, love,' he says, when I try to tip him as we pull up outside Thomson Tibble Telford. 'Sounds like you'll be needing every penny you've got.'

Like I thought, the security guards are on the internal phone to Will practically the minute they see me walk through the revolving doors. And he comes hurrying out of the lift about thirty seconds later, so his meeting can't have been all *that* important.

'Isabel?' He strides over to the reception area, looking purposeful in – surprise, surprise – navy. It's a different suit than before, though, with a fabulous sleek cut, and a beautiful (albeit blue) Armani tie. For a moment, I think he's going to greet me with a kiss on the cheek. After our mojito-sozzled evening out, it wouldn't be inappropriate or anything. But he doesn't kiss me. He just stops, a couple of feet away, looking puzzled. 'Did you come with Joe?'

'Why . . . er . . . why would I?'

'Because Joe's coming over here today to drop off a present for Mum.' Will's mouth pulls into a thin line. 'He can't make it to her birthday dinner this weekend.'

'Joe's coming here? *Now?*'

Will glances at his watch. 'Any minute. That's why I assumed you must be here with him.'

'God, no. No, I'm here about something much more important. Not that your mum's birthday present isn't important, I just mean –'

'Hang on. This isn't anything to do with Katriona de Montfort, is it? Because I was just speaking to someone this morning who knows you. Well, she *claims* to know you. She kept calling you Liz, so I think maybe she was speaking about another of Miss de Montfort's assistants . . .'

I'm not sure there's any way to do this other than the truth.

Well, half the truth.

I take a deep breath. 'Will. Look. I need you to do something for me. You have to stop telling Penelope Bright to back out of the deal with Katriona.'

Will's eyebrows look like they're about to launch themselves right off the top of his forehead. 'How do you even know I've been talking to Penelope Bright?'

'I can't tell you right now. But please, Will, can you just do what I ask? Just for another week or so?'

'Isabel, I absolutely can't do that.' He stares at me. 'It's a matter between me and my client.'

'All right, all right.' I'm going to try a different tack. 'Can you do something else, then? Can you *please* not mention anything about Katriona's new book deal to anyone just yet?' I swallow hard. 'Particularly not to Myles Salisbury-Kent. Or to Joe, for that matter.'

'But, Isabel, this directly concerns Myles Salisbury-

Kent! Katriona has gone right over his head with this, and they have an agreement . . .'

'Please.' Out of nowhere, I can feel tears prickling the back of my eyes. 'Just for one week.'

'Oh God . . .' Will looks agonised. I'm embarrassing him in front of the security guards again. He takes my arm and pulls me gently over to a quieter corner of reception. 'Please, don't cry, Isabel.'

'Sorry,' I gulp. I start scrabbling in my pocket as though I've got a tissue in there, which obviously I haven't. 'It's just that . . . I'm having a bit of a horrible day . . . and then this estate agent . . .' No, Isabel, *don't* blub to Will Madison about how you might have accidentally bought a prime piece of Kensington property. '. . . and you're being very sweet, and . . .'

'What on earth is going on, Isabel? I'll do anything I can to help, but you have to tell me. Hang on.' He's staring over my shoulder, out of the huge panes of glass, on to the street. Suddenly he swears under his breath. 'Joe's here.'

Joe's stepping out of a taxi, carrying a huge Jo Malone bag, and he's already spotted us. He speeds up and jogs through the revolving doors.

'Isabel? Are you all right?' Joe looks from me to Will and back again. 'What the fuck are you doing to her?'

'I'm not doing anything.' Will lets go of my arm, but doesn't move away from me.

'Yeah?' Joe actually squares up to him. 'Then what's she crying for?'

'I'm not crying!' I say hastily. I plaster a big, toothy,

351

fake smile on my face, which seems to alarm Will even more than the tears did. 'It was just . . . just the air-conditioning. It makes my eyes sting.'

'But—'

'So everything's fine!' I give Will a pleading look. 'Let's just forget about everything. *Everything*. All right?'

'All right . . .' Will says slowly, fixing his deep blue eyes on mine. I think he's trying to work out if I'm sending him secret messages. 'If that's what you want.'

'Yup!' I beam at him so brightly, he really must think I'm a lunatic now.

'Poor Isabel.' Joe puts an arm around me. 'Horrible air con. I always knew places like this were bad for your health.'

Is it my imagination, or is Will looking a little bit . . . well . . . furious? 'Did you bring Mum's present?' he snaps.

'Yeah.' Joe shoves the Jo Malone carrier bag in Will's direction. 'I bought up half the shop. Candles, bath oil, perfume . . . Oh, and I couldn't remember if she likes Roses or Gardenia, so I got both. I thought you might know.'

'And what do I do with the one she doesn't like?' Will asks. His tone of voice is a bit cold, I have to say, especially when Joe's been so amazingly generous with the present. I mean, he must have spent five hundred quid, at least!

Joe shrugs. 'Give them to your girlfriend?'

I didn't know Will had a girlfriend.

'What's her name? Chrissie?' Joe adds, with a cheeky grin.

Chrissie? The trainee who leaves Will's office so messy? From the scarlet hue of Will's cheeks right now, I'd have to say Joe was right.

'And don't forget,' Joe adds, 'give Mum a huge kiss from me.'

'Fine. I'll do that. Mum will be thrilled. Just like she was at Christmas.' Will starts walking back towards the lifts.

I can't just let him go without explaining.

'Hold on,' I tell Joe. 'I'll be back in one moment.'

I catch up with Will before the lift doors close. 'Will, wait! Look, I'm really sorry about all that. I can explain everything.'

He shrugs. 'Don't worry about it.'

'But I really do need to talk to you,' I say desperately. 'About Penelope . . .'

Will's face softens. He reaches for his wallet and pulls out a business card, then scrabbles for a pen and writes two numbers on the back. 'Here's my work number, my mobile and my home phone number. Call me this evening. I'll be on one of those. We'll have that talk then, yeah?'

'Thank you, Will. Thank you so much.' I would give him a little kiss on the cheek, but, well, Joe's watching. 'It was really nice to see you.'

'It was nice seeing you too, Isabel,' he says quietly. 'It always is.'

Joe's still standing near the revolving doors,

watching me with a quizzical look on his face. 'Mysterious,' he says, as I go back over.

'Oh, that was nothing.' I flap a dismissive hand back in the direction of the lifts. 'I was just giving him some advice about the Jo Malone stuff.'

'Right.' He moves a tiny bit closer. 'Well, it's very nice to have run into you like this, Iz-Wiz. Amazing, in fact, because I was going to call you this afternoon anyway.'

'Oh?'

'Oh?' He mimics me, with another of his devastating grins. 'Tell me, Isabel, what do you like to do of an evening?'

I need to sound sophisticated here. Sophisticated and intelligent. 'Well, regular visits to the theatre, obviously. I'm a huge fan of the Globe . . . European cinema . . .'

'I didn't see you as a subtitles sort of girl.'

'Oh, absolutely! The more subtitles, the better, in fact!'

He grins. 'Well, when you're not hot-footing it to the Globe, or hanging out at the Institut français, do you ever eat?'

'Eat?'

'Isabel,' his voice is very soft, and slightly deeper than usual, 'I'm asking if you'd like to have dinner with me.'

I can't think of a single thing to say. Not something sophisticated and intelligent. Not even something unsophisticated and dim. Just nothing at all.

'So?'

I find my voice, somewhere around my knees. 'I . . . but . . . what about Gina?'

'Gina and I have broken up,' he says softly.

'She *dumped* you?' I've blurted this out before I could stop myself. But it's *always* been Gina doing the dumping.

Joe just smiles. 'Other way round, actually. I didn't think it was fair to string her along. Not when I've had my eye on someone else.'

I'm about to ask who. Then I realise.

'*Oh*.'

'Come out to dinner, Isabel.' His eyes are fixed on mine. 'I promise, I'll be more fun than subtitles.'

I just give a little smile, even though what I actually feel like doing is a Viennese waltz across Thomson Tibble Telford's shiny marble floor. 'I'd love to.'

'Excellent.' He grins. 'Shall we meet at the Ivy? Eight o'clock? I would do the chivalrous thing,' he adds, 'and pick you up from your front door. But I don't think either of us are particularly keen on the idea of being waved off on a date by our boss.'

'God, no.'

He leans forward and gives me a kiss – a very soft kiss – right on the lips. 'Looking forward to it, Isabel, darling. Looking forward to it very much indeed.'

Chapter 28

After the disappointments of the Wolseley, I have to say that the Ivy seems *far* more up my street. Everyone either *is* a proper celebrity, or *with* a proper celebrity. At the very least, they look like they're only one reality TV show away from becoming a proper celebrity. Even the waiters look like celebrities. The room is stunning, all leather banquettes and dimmed lights. The menu is amazing. I've just polished off a plate of crispy duck salad, which was possibly the best thing I've ever eaten, and will certainly be the usual starter I have whenever I come here in the future. And best of all, I'm here with Joe, who's ordered expensive pink champagne, and who keeps holding my hand across the table and telling me how gorgeous I look.

You know, I think I ought to be enjoying it quite a lot more than I actually am.

The thing is that being out with Joe at a restaurant like this seems to require quite a lot of effort. All the waiters stop to exchange a word with him, and loads of the other regulars want a chat. He's just spent the last ten minutes, for example, chatting to a table of six in the middle of the room, including two ex-Spice Girls and one of the anonymous ones from that Irish boyband.

I mean, I'm not being picky. I'm really not. I'm happy to be here. I just think it's a tiny bit rude of people at a table of six to monopolise Joe so completely when they can see he's left his date behind all by herself.

Well, heigh-ho. At least there's plenty of this fabulous pink champagne to keep me happy. A few glasses have just started to take the edge off my nerves. Maybe a few more will start to obliterate the knowledge that I've still got the best part of a three-hundred-thousand-word bonkbuster to write.

'Sorry about that, darling.' Joe scoots back into his seat just as our main courses arrive, and grabs my hand across the table again. 'Everyone's planning an autobiography. God, I should *never* have picked the Ivy for our first date.'

'Don't be silly! I'm having a fabulous time.'

'I thought you would,' says Joe. 'Enjoying the food?'

'Mmm,' I say, tucking into my roasted salmon with a dill butter sauce. 'It's amazing.'

Actually, I think I spoke a bit too soon. This salmon is completely disgusting.

'Isabel? Are you all right?'

'I think it's off,' I gasp, washing down the giant piece of revolting salmon with a huge swig of champagne. Damn, that's another empty glass.

'Off?' Joe echoes. 'Isabel, I've eaten here at least

once a week for the last five years, and I don't think I've ever eaten anything that's tasted *off*.' He spears a piece of my salmon while I try very hard not to be sick over his fishcakes. 'That tastes completely fine!'

'No, it doesn't! It tastes like it's been left outside on the patio . . .'

'Dill,' laughs Joe. 'You're tasting *dill*. The herb they put on the top of smoked salmon blinis?'

This is what smoked salmon blinis taste like?

'But . . . it's horrible!'

Joe stops laughing, and beckons over one of the waiters. 'We've had a bit of a disaster with the salmon. Could you possibly bring Isabel a plate of the fishcakes instead?'

'Of course, Mr Madison,' says the waiter smoothly, whisking away my plate before I can say anything. 'It'll just be a few minutes.'

'I would have eaten it, you know,' I say in a small voice.

Joe shoves his own plate towards me so I can help myself to his chips, then refills my champagne glass again. 'Isabel, I've been looking forward to this far too much to have a nasty old salmon ruin the evening.'

His clear blue eyes are fixed right on mine. I can feel my heart pounding extremely hard in my chest.

'I . . . er . . . I hope you left things OK with Gina,' I hear myself say. I'm kicking myself under the table before the words have even left my mouth. I mean, that was a lovely romantic moment we were having just there. What on *earth* possessed me to bring up his ex-girlfriend? Have I really drunk *that* much champagne?

Joe shrugs. 'I don't think she was all that happy. And I do feel bad. I mean, Gina's a lovely person, obviously . . .'

'Oh, obviously.'

He leans across the table, and brushes the tips of his fingers, very, very lightly, across my cheekbone. 'But I couldn't stay with the wrong person when . . . who knows? . . . I just might have met the right person.'

OK. Play it cool, Isabel. Don't blush. Don't gush.

'Oh, *Joe* . . .'

'God, Iz-Wiz, can you excuse me just one moment?' Joe's eyes have flickered over my shoulder. A big group has arrived at a nearby table, and one of the women is waving frantically at him. 'Hi, Valerie!' he calls, before lowering his voice to talk to me again. 'An old client. I should say hello . . .'

I watch him as he heads across the room to back-pat and shoulder-squeeze. God, he's *gorgeous*. Even better-looking after . . . how many glasses have I had? Just two. Maybe three. Oh, and there was that champagne cocktail we had in the bar before we came to our table . . . Right, I really have to sober up now. I want to remember every detail about this evening for ever. And I'm already having a bit of trouble remembering the detail of the last two minutes. Now, what was it that Joe just said to me? That I'm the right person? That Gina was the wrong person? Definitely one of us is some kind of a person . . .

A waiter is hovering. 'Another bottle of the Bollinger, madam?'

I beam up at him. 'Yes!' I say. 'Yes, I think we will have another bottle. How lovely. Thank you so much.'

You know, in some ways, I've never been on a better date.

1) Joe not only didn't mind about the second bottle of Bollinger, but he ordered a third one as well.
2) When they brought the third bottle, Joe leaned across the table and whispered in my ear that we really should have ordered it to take away.
3) The taxi ride back to Joe's place was just about the most erotic fifteen minutes I've ever spent in my life. And all we did was hold hands.
4) Which geared me up all nicely for what was going to happen the minute we walked through his front door.

Except there's one very, very important reason why this was, officially, the Worst Date in the Entire History of the World.

1) I passed out on the sofa three minutes after Joe Madison started kissing me.

Bloody Bollinger! Bloody three bottles! Bloody *four* bottles, while I'm at it, because I have a dim memory of Joe cracking open yet another the moment we got back to his flat, though I have no memory at all of making any serious inroads into it.

I don't even know how I ended up in his bed. I suspect he probably carried me, which sort of makes me swoon and cringe in equal measure. And I'm semi-undressed, and wearing what looks like . . . yes, it's a Chelsea football shirt, which makes me cringe even more. I mean, I'd sorted the underwear issue very satisfactorily before I came out last night. But the idea was that Joe would discover tantalising scraps of black lace after I went into his bathroom and removed the necessary outer garments. The thought of him wrestling with the gusset of my tights himself is making me feel positively nauseous.

Oh God. Was I snoring?

But from the unrumpled bedclothes on the opposite side of the bed, it looks like Joe was a gentleman and slept downstairs, so with any luck he was spared the worst of any snoring. And . . . hang on – he's left a note!

Hi Iz-Wiz,
    Sorry to leave you – have breakfast meeting. Let's have a second stab at this tomorrow night, shall we? And don't worry – we'll stay off the Bolly this time.
J xxx

He wants to do it again? After I passed out the minute he started his moves? He's giving me a second stab?

To Joe,
Who gave me a second stab.

I sit up groggily and turn to look at the alarm clock. It's already 8 a.m., and I'm meant to be meeting Mum at Paddington at half ten. I'll need a hot shower back at Katriona's, and a change of clothes, and a strong black coffee to dislodge the pounding in my head, and –

What was that noise?

It was a thud, a definite thud. And it isn't coming from my hungover head. It's coming from down the stairs. There's somebody in the house.

There are two possibilities here.

1) It is Joe, coming to tell me he loves me.
2) It is a rapist/murderer, coming to rape and murder me.

I pull the Chelsea shirt back on and scurry to open the bedroom door a tiny chink. 'Joe?' I hiss.

There's no answer. Only heavy footsteps. They're a bit like the kind a rapist/murderer might make.

Right. I need a weapon. There must be something in here I can use to ward him off with. They always do it in *Poirot*. But annoyingly, Joe doesn't seem to have any Victorian fire-irons or heavily jewelled Indian statuettes hanging around.

I'm trying to remember what they taught in the personal safety classes Lara dragged me to a couple of years back. Never leave your drink unattended . . . don't use an unlicensed mini-cab . . . um . . . use the heel of your hand to strike your attacker firmly beneath the nostrils . . . Well, what *is* the heel of your hand? Didn't they mean the heel of your foot?

Anyway, I'm weaponless. I grab my Smythson notebook out of my Marianne bag: 'To whom it may concern. If you are reading this, I have been brutally . . .'

Oh God. The footsteps have started creaking up the stairs.

'Stop right where you are!' I shout. 'I've called the police, and they'll be here any minute!'

The footsteps stop.

'That's right,' I call out. 'Walk away while you still can! I've got a . . . a Victorian fire-iron in the heel of my hand, and I'm not afraid to use it!'

'Hey, it's OK! I didn't mean to scare you.' Funny. He sounds terribly polite for a rapist/murderer. 'I've just come round to pick something up from my brother's house,' the voice continues. 'I had no idea anyone was in.'

'*Will?*' I pull the door open.

'My God.' Will Madison blinks at me, and nods at the notebook in my hand. 'No fire-iron, then, I see?'

'Oh God, no! I was bluffing, in case you were a rapist-slash-murderer. I haven't got a fire-iron. *Or* a heavily jewelled Indian statuette, for that matter.'

His eyes flicker down over my Chelsea shirt, my

bare legs, and the wobbly splodges of scarlet I put on my toenails yesterday evening. 'No.' His voice is very cool. 'I can see that.'

I can feel a blush spread right across my face, like one of those speeded-up sunrises on nature programmes. 'Not that it's any of your business, but we did not sleep together.'

Will snorts. 'I see. You've just popped round to do your laundry, then?'

'No, I did spend the night, but—'

Will cuts me off, turning round and heading back down the spiral stairs. 'I knew there must have been a very good reason why you didn't call yesterday evening, even though there was something so terribly important you'd wanted to tell me.'

'God, yes, Will.' I run down the stairs after him. 'There is something incredibly important, actually.'

He doesn't look at me. 'Well, I don't have time to hear it. I've only come to collect Mum's birthday card. Joe forgot to put it in with the perfume he oh-so-thoughtfully sent Sandy out to purchase.'

Oh, for goodness' sake. Could he sound any more self-righteous?

'Well, there's a card right here,' I say, sounding pretty self-righteous myself. I stride across to the coffee table, where I can see an envelope. There's also the open bottle of champagne and two half-empty glasses from last night. You know, just in case this miserable encounter with Will didn't feel quite sordid enough. 'Here.' I wave it at him, triumphant.

'Great.' Will shoves the card in the pocket of his navy coat. 'Thanks so much for all your help.'

'There's no need to be so irritable! The card was here, wasn't it?'

'Irritable?' says Will. 'Why would I be irritable? I mean, *obviously* I've got nothing better to do in my fourteen-hour working day than do a detour via my brother's house to pick up a card he should have remembered to put with the present he hasn't even bothered to wrap in the first place.'

Now, that's just unfair. 'Jo Malone assistants always wrap things beautifully,' I say. 'Only a complete idiot would take them out of that gorgeous carrier and try to wrap them themselves.'

'Thank you, Isabel. Your insights, as ever, are invaluable.'

Pompous git. Pompous, disapproving, navy-wearing git.

'Look, Joe's busy too, you know . . .'

'Oh, yes,' Will looks at me, half-naked in my football shirt, and then glances back up at the bedroom. 'I can see *just* how busy he is.' He stalks to the front door. 'By the way, you might like to tell your new boyfriend that Mum's favourite perfume isn't Jo Malone Gardenia *or* Roses. It isn't Jo Malone anything. She's worn Chanel No. 5 for the last thirty-four years, ever since the day Joe was born. Dad brought it to her to glam up the hospital ward, and she's been wearing it ever since. It reminds her of him.' He shrugs. 'I can see why he'd make the

mistake, though. Joe floats through life thinking
everything smells of roses.'

He slams the front door very, very hard behind
him.

Chapter 29

There's something going on at Katriona's. Something that requires three police cars to be parked outside the front door.

Jesus. They're here for me, aren't they? Katriona's found out about my fraudulent deal with Aadelman Stern, and I'm about to be charged with Obtaining Peculiar Advantage, and carted off to . . . what's that famous women's prison? Newgate. Joe will dump me before we've even started going out properly, and Dad will refuse to pay my bail, and the *Central Somerset Gazette* will run front-page photos of me looking horrendous in an orange jumpsuit, and . . . oh God. Caroline Macbeth will lobby parliament to have my sentence set at twenty-five to life.

That's it. I have to go on the run. I'll just need a fake passport, and a good disguise, and my Marianne bag, and—

'Is-a-bell?' The front door is suddenly yanked open, and Selma stares out at me. Her eyes are red and puffy, like she's been crying for hours. 'Is-a-bell, terrible thing has happen!'

'I know, Selma. I know.' My mouth is so dry I can barely speak. But I've got to be brave about this. I've been living a lie for too long. It will probably be a relief, in some ways, when it's all over. 'Just one thing I would ask of you, Selma. Could you find a tea towel or something, to cover my head with?' I glance over my shoulder. 'The paparazzi could be arriving any minute, and I don't want Mum to have to see me in handcuffs on the six o'clock news.'

'Tea towel?'

'Or a hand towel. I'm not fussy. Just as long as it's big enough to cover my face.'

'You are . . . ashame?'

I hold my head up defiantly. 'Maybe I should be ashamed, Selma. But, given the opportunity again, can I honestly say I would do any different?'

'You would *still* leave window open to let robbers in?'

'There's been a robbery?'

'They came in your bedroom window. It was left open.'

Did I leave my window open? Shit. I probably did. After all, I wasn't supposed to know I'd be out all night.

Selma starts to cry again, huge tears splishing down her cheeks. 'But police they say is nothing to do with open window. They are saying is . . . is *inside job*.' She hiccups back more tears. 'I am suspect, Is-a-bell. They think is *me* who helped steal kid.'

'Jesus,' I croak. 'They took Lysander?'

'*Captain* Kidd,' Selma sobs. 'Miss de Montfort's new book. Is gone.'

This is getting weirder by the second. 'Hang on. You're saying the burglars took Katriona's new manuscript?'

Selma nods. 'And police are saying I am involved. You must tell them I cannot do this!'

'Of course I'll tell them, Selma.' I'm already marching up the stairs. As long as they're not here to arrest me for fraud, I'll tell them anything.

Upstairs, I expect to see a full CSI unit, comprising a gorgeous chiselled man with an Afro and a gambling problem, and a geeky bug expert, who will announce that the presence of a particular type of ladybird egg ground into the rug proves that the burglar is a thirty-six-year-old man called Bryn, who grew up in Newcastle and prefers cream of chicken soup to tomato. But it isn't quite that slick-looking. My room is a tip, for starters. My desk has been overturned. My jewellery box is upside down. My underwear drawer is wide open, its contents half-emptied across the floor. Oh, no, actually. The underwear drawer thing was just me, getting ready for my date last night. And instead of a full CSI unit, complete with bug expert, there's just a single uniformed policeman, who doesn't look especially expert in anything.

'This your bedroom?' he asks, as I peer round the door.

'Yes. Look, Constable, you should know this can't possibly have anything to do with Selma. This is *my* fault. I *did* leave that window open. It's as simple as that. No inside job.'

He shrugs. 'Yeah? Have a look at this, then.' He points out of the open window to the garden below.

I stare down, dutifully. 'I can't see anything.'

'Exactly. Nothing. No ladder marks. If they really came through this window, wouldn't there have to be ladder marks?'

'Well, that's not *proof*,' I scoff. I mean, really. Where's the full CSI unit when you need them? 'Maybe they didn't need to use a ladder at all! Maybe they had highly sophisticated wall-scaling equipment. Or . . . or those special suction things you attach to your hands and feet! Like they use in the *Spiderman* films.'

'You think Spiderman stole your boss's manuscript?'

'Well, not Spiderman himself, obviously. But it could easily be a trained stuntman.'

'A trained stuntman . . .' The policeman nods thoughtfully. 'You know, I actually think that might have cracked the case. Have you ever thought of a career in the police force, darling? We could use a first-class detective brain like you.'

'Isabel? Is that you?' Katriona's voice comes quavering down from up the stairs.

'Excuse me,' I say with dignity. 'My boss needs me.'

I start up the stairs to the study, where Katriona's voice was coming from, but she's already halfway down, intercepting me on the landing before I can get up there.

'Oh, *Isabel*!' Her face is streaked with mascara – which is odd, as I made an appointment for her to have her eyelashes dyed only last week – and she's shaking like a leaf. She clutches my hands. 'Isabel, have you heard?'

'Yes, Katriona, and I know it's my fault. I'm so sorry about that window.'

'Don't *you* apologise, Isabel!' Her eyes are wide. 'I thought it was the window at first, but then the police set me straight. This was an inside job! Selma must have been in cahoots with Her all this time.'

'With who?'

'Becca,' she spits. 'Don't tell me you haven't seen her hanging around outside, Isabel. Her and that filthy boyfriend of hers.'

Ohhhhh. So Frizz-Hair is Becca. Not a ruthless MI5 killer after all, then. I feel a tiny bit silly.

'But . . . why would Lysander's babysitter steal your manuscript?'

'Who told you she was Lysander's babysitter?' Katriona dabs her eyes. 'She was nothing of the sort. She was my assistant before you.'

'But I thought you'd never had an assistant before.'

'I just told you that because I'm so embarrassed about how horribly wrong everything went with Becca. She *was* a perfectly sweet girl once, you know. But last summer she got herself a new boyfriend – that horrible manky bloke – and next thing I knew, things started to go missing. Money, jewellery, a Birkin bag . . . I had no choice but to get rid of her. And, of course, they've made a nuisance of themselves ever since. They phone. They send begging letters. They hang about the street . . .' She starts to weep again. 'And now *this*! My precious *Captain Kidd*. My *only* copy!'

I don't say anything. But, you know, part of me is surprised Katriona had even *one* copy of the new book. I know she said her writer's block was lifted, but she can't have written that much in only a few days. Mind you, a looming deadline can really concentrate the mind, I suppose.

Katriona suddenly gasps. 'Oh God! They didn't take yours as well, did they? They didn't take *Showjumpers*?'

'No, no. It's . . . er . . . it's all quite safe in here.' I pat my Marianne bag.

'Of course. It's on microfiche.'

'Yes! Well remembered!' *I* certainly hadn't.

Katriona dabs at her streaked mascara again. 'I should have been as organised as you, Isabel. I should have had a copy on me at all times. Lemper Snyde Brusoff are going to be so angry with me. Will you phone them for me, Isabel, and break the news? I just can't face it. I can't face anything . . .' She's howling again.

'Of course.' I use my best soothing voice. 'Anything I can do to help.'

'I'm just going to go to bed,' she weeps. 'I'm so sorry, Isabel, but I don't think I can do the interview with your mother.'

I'm careful not to let a huge grin break out over my face. But this is brilliant news! If I don't have to spend all morning policing Mum while she interviews Katriona, I gain a whole load of time to start getting *Showjumpers* written!

'Don't you worry, Katriona.' I get my phone out. 'I'll just call Mum and cancel.'

'But surely she's already on her way to town?'

'Well, yes, but she won't mind, honestly. She'll just spend the day shopping, or something.'

'Oh, no, Isabel.' Katriona mops her eyes again. 'I feel so terrible about cancelling, you can't just phone her! Go and meet her like you planned – please. We'll reschedule the interview as soon as possible, I promise.'

'That's really kind, Katriona, but you mustn't worry about things like that.' She looks so tiny and fragile that I actually feel really sorry for her. Having your house invaded and your manuscript stolen is a pretty horrible thing, after all. 'You just try to relax. The police will sort all this out. And I honestly don't think Selma had anything to do with it.'

'Thank you, Isabel.' She pats me on the arm. 'You're a big support to me, you know. I'm very grateful.'

Tempted as I am to spend the rest of the day shopping with Mum, I can't let this golden opportunity go to waste. I've even got my notebook out now, sitting in the café near Paddington while I wait for Mum, so I can probably knock out a few thousand words or so before she even gets here. Make more progress on that chapter I was doing so well on before.

Chapter Four

Barrington
Bosworth
B –

It's difficult, though, when my mind keeps wandering off Barrington, and on to Joe. *My* Joe. I mean, it's early days yet, obviously, and the whole dozing-off thing wasn't exactly the ideal start to a perfect relationship. But that note he left me made it clear that, despite everything, he really wants to go out again. Well, this time, I won't screw it up. It'll be tricky this week, given that I've got an entire epic bonkbuster to write, but there are ways to stay wide awake if I need to. If I spend my writing time in cafés like this, for example, I can practically mainline caffeine all day. A proper Italian café would be best, for the hard stuff. Oooh, there's a lovely one along Old Brompton Road, not far from Harvey Nichols. Once I've finished with Mum, I can head over there, knock back some double espressos, clock up my quota of words for the morning, and wait for Joe to call.

I can see Mum now, crossing the road outside the station over to the café.

'Mum!' I wave her over to my table. She's wearing head-to-toe reporter's garb, like you imagine Lois Lane: taupe trenchcoat, sheer black stockings, leather attaché case. I'm only surprised she isn't wearing a trilby with a pencil stub stuck behind her ear. 'I'm really sorry, Mum, but the interview's off.'

Her face falls. 'Oh, *Isabel*!'

'It's not my fault, Mum. There's been an awful burglary at Katriona's house. Her new manuscript's been stolen.'

'Jesus H. Christ!' spits Mum, uncharacteristically.

'Er . . . well, yes. It's bad news.'

She starts rummaging in her attaché case as she speaks. 'Are the police involved? Do they have a suspect? How's Katriona feeling?'

'Mum,' I give her a look, 'you can't write about this in the *Gazette*.'

Mum puts her Dictaphone down on the table. 'But it would be a huge scoop! And I'm missing out on my proper interview.'

'You're not missing out, Mum. Katriona's going to reschedule for next week. *And* she's going to see if she can get your story into *Marie Claire*, instead of just the *Gazette*!'

Mum wrinkles her nose. 'Well, *that* won't help me get my traineeship on the *Gazette*, will it? Though I suppose . . . if she'll give me an Exclusive on the burglary . . . ?'

'Fine.' I sigh. 'I'll make sure she gives you an exclusive on the burglary.'

'So!' Mum beams at me, mollified. 'What are we going to do today instead?'

'Well, I'm afraid I have to work, Mum. I've got tons of writing to do. But I thought you might like to go shopping, or something . . .'

'Oh, no. If you're going to work, I'll work too! I'll keep you company!'

'But, Mum—'

'You can see all the stuff I'm planning for my piece on Katriona.' Mum is rummaging in her attaché case again, leafing through a pile of photocopied cuttings that she's paper-clipped together. 'I'm not sure *Marie Claire* are going to be all that interested in most of it. It's all about her connections to Somerset, her time growing up there. You know, it's amazing what I managed to dig out of the *Gazette*'s archives, from before she was famous. Look!'

I look down at the cutting she gives me. It's a black-and-white photocopy of a newspaper photo. It's a bit blurry from where someone's hand must have slipped doing the photocopying, but it's quite obviously Katriona. God, she looks terrible! She's wearing a dreadful trouser suit with a cropped jacket, and a strange little scarf tied air hostess-style around her neck. Still, she's a style paragon compared to the other person in the photograph. It's a girl of about eighteen or nineteen, wearing high-waisted trousers and a saggy sweatshirt. She's shaking Katriona's hand and staring in a rather terrified way at the camera, without a smile, like Victorians you see in old photos in museums. And her hair! It's . . . it's unbelievably frizzy.

I squint to read the caption.

Local businesswoman Katriona de Montfort congratulates the winner of Yeovil Library's Tell Me a

Story writing competition. Becca Grahame, 19, won the contest with her children's story, *Kids At Sea*, all about a gang of orphan children who join a ship and have adventures on the high seas. Becca won a cheque for £100, and a complimentary dinner for two at Luigi's.

Oh my God. Katriona *didn't*, did she? She didn't steal Becca's prize-winning story, and make millions and millions of pounds out of it?

Surely.

Could I ask her about it? 'Hey, Katriona, it's a funny thing, but I saw this old photo of you and Becca, and . . .'

No.

But there's always Myles. *Myles* might tell me. I mean, if there *was* something dodgy going on, he'd have to know about it, wouldn't he? And now that they've fallen out . . .

I could be at Madison/Salisbury-Kent in twenty minutes. 'Mum, I really have to go.'

'Really, darling? But it would be such fun if we worked together!'

'Honestly, Mum, I can't. There's something I have to do.'

'Oh, well.' Mum doesn't seem all that bothered. 'I can have lunch with Vanessa Deverill, then. I'll pop back to the station. She should still be there.'

'Sorry?'

'Oh, you won't believe who I ran in to on the train!

Malcolm and Vanessa! They're up in town to take Gina out for dinner this evening.'

I feel a sharp pang of something that feels a lot like guilt. 'Oh dear, is Gina in a bad way, then?'

Mum frowns. 'Why would she be?'

'Didn't Vanessa tell you? Gina's split up with her boyfriend.' I don't think this is the time to mention that I spent last night with him.

'Oh no, I don't think so, darling. Vanessa and Malcolm are having dinner with them both, actually. I think it's a belated celebration for Gina's book deal. We'll have to book somewhere nice, Iz-Wiz, when you can finally tell everyone about *your* deal.'

I'm not paying too much attention. I never thought I'd say it, but I feel sorry for Gina. She obviously hasn't told her parents about the break-up. God, she's probably feeling really humiliated about the whole thing.

'Vanessa and Malcolm were just waiting for Gina to meet them in the station,' Mum says, pulling her trenchcoat on and getting up to leave with me. 'I'll go and catch them now, see if Vanessa can do a quick lunch.'

'Lovely, Mum. Could I . . . er . . . hang on to this photo of Katriona, by the way? Just for now?'

'Of course!'

I tuck the clipping into my Marianne bag as we head out of the door, and I start looking for a taxi. Actually, going to Madison/Salisbury-Kent will kill two birds with one stone. I'll have a quick word with Myles, and then I can slip into Joe's office, see if he's free for lunch, maybe . . .

Oh! But I don't need to go to Madison/Salisbury-Kent to see Joe. There he is! Standing outside a newsagent right next door to Paddington Station. Seriously bizarre coincidence that he's here. Could he have known I was here? Is he having me followed, like some kind of a jealous boyfriend . . .

Oh.

Oh, I see. I see the reason he's here.

It's Gina. She's just come out of the newsagent's, carrying a bottle of mineral water. She's putting her long, lean arms around his neck, and kissing him.

And Joe is kissing her right back.

It's not the kind of kiss you do after you've broken up. It's not that kind of kiss at all.

The Home Secretary
The House of Commons
The Houses of Parliament
Big Ben
London

22 January

Dear Home Secretary,

Please allow me to begin with an apology. I know now that, contrary to my earlier belief, and my correspondence on this subject, you were *not* in fact seeking to have me assassinated by two of MI5's finest. I have been under a good deal of stress recently, and this may have clouded my usually impeccable judgment. I suppose I should have realised that any assassin employed by so stylish and attractive a woman as you would certainly be the sort to use Frizz-Ease every now and then. I know that you would not allow yourself to be represented by a couple of scruffs.

On that note, I am writing to ask a small favour. I am sure you ~~of all people~~ will sympathise when I say that I have just discovered that a man with whom I was involved has been lying to me. His motives are not clear. ~~Certainly I do not think that passing out on someone when they are kissing you qualifies as a reason to go back to your ex-girlfriend~~. Wronged woman to wronged woman, I was wondering if it might be possible to borrow a couple of your best ~~assassins~~ operatives for a little while. Anyone trained in basic subterfuge and counterespionage techniques will do. I'd just like him followed for a couple of days, to see what he's up to. Any further action your ~~assassins~~ operatives should choose to take (particularly against his female companion) is entirely at their own discretion.

May I also say how pleased I was to read that you and Mr Macbeth are getting back together! I know I called him a cheating wretch, and may also have said he was sexually deviant, but what do I know? Yes, they do say a leopard can't change its spots, but I've always felt that to be a very hard-line approach. I think I should be living proof to you of the fact that you *can* forgive and forget.

Looking forward to hearing from you.

Yours,

Isabel (Bookbinder)

PS. Rest assured, I *will* be voting for you in the next election.

PPS. Do let me know when that will be.

Chapter 30

Thank God, the police have all gone. Selma is out at an appointment with a legal aid solicitor, poor thing. And Katriona has taken herself off to Bliss spa for the entire afternoon, to get over the shock of the burglary. Which has given me plenty of freedom to do what I really want to, and lie curled up on my bed crying for half an hour.

I don't know whether I'm more angry or upset.

Actually, I do know. I'm angry. Hopping mad, in fact. I mean, I know it might have been a bit thick to believe anything was really going to come of Joe and me. I should have known the truth about him the moment Will told me he was missing his own mother's birthday dinner. He's not exactly Mr Reliable. It's my own stupid fault, for getting overexcited. But that doesn't change the fact that Joe lied to me about breaking up with Gina. Or the fact that I have absolutely no idea why.

'Wizbit?' My door is creaking open.

'Lysander, this isn't a good time.'

He stands at the door, half-in, half-out of the room. There's a circle of Nutella around his mouth. 'Are you sad too, Wizbit, about Selma being in trouble?'

'I'm sad about that, Lysander, yes. I'm sad about a lot of things.' I'm just astonished *he's* sad. 'But don't worry. Selma didn't do anything wrong.'

'Mummy won't make her leave, will she? Like she made Becca leave?' His face droops even more. 'Becca and Selma were my friends.'

Oh God, I'd nearly forgotten. *Becca*.

'Lysander . . .' I get off the bed. 'Can you tell me a little bit more about Becca?'

He shrugs unhappily. 'Mummy is mean to her. I don't like it when Mummy is mean to my friends.'

'*How* is Mummy mean to her?'

'Sometimes Becca phones Mummy and asks her for things. But Mummy doesn't want to give her anything.'

I don't know about you, but that sounds an awful lot like a six-year-old's definition of blackmail to me.

'How do you know about this, Lysander?'

'I hear Mummy on the phone. Mummy has private conversations in her den. Mummy keeps all kinds of secrets up there.'

Oh, I'll just bet she does.

'But, Lysander, how do you get into Mummy's den? Doesn't Mummy keep it locked?'

Lysander's eyes go very, very wide. He turns and runs away from me, up the stairs, as fast as his knickerbocker-clad legs will carry him.

Damn. I think I've screwed this one up. I forgot Lysander's meant to be some kind of a child genius. Obviously he's rumbled my gentle questioning. He'll be telling Katriona about it the moment she walks back through the door in a couple of hours' time, all scrubbed and polished from her spa day.

'Lysander . . . sweetie . . . ?' I scramble up the stairs myself, and follow the sound of clattering to Lysander's nursery.

But he doesn't look like he's preparing to shop me to his mother. He's just sitting on the floor, playing with that battered old toy ship again.

'Becca made me this *Tiki-Trekker*,' he announces.

'That's lovely, Lysander.'

'Becca is one of Mummy's secrets.'

'Yes, look, speaking of Mummy, there's no need to tell her about any of this,' I say lightly. 'What I was just asking you about Becca, I mean. It can be our little secret, Lysander! Just between you and me.'

Great. Now I sound like a filthy child sex pest.

He's scrabbling around with his small fingers inside the toy ship, and pulls a key out. 'This is how I get into Mummy's den,' he announces proudly.

You know the expression, 'like taking candy from a baby'? Well, I don't think this is like that. This is more like . . . 'borrowing a key from a highly intelligent six-year-old'. So it's fine. It's absolutely fine.

I see no ethical issues with this whatsoever.

Even though I know Katriona's out at Bliss, being reikied and Rolfed and reflexologised, my heart is still pounding away like mad. I mean, the way she keeps this study under lock and key, you start to wonder if she's hiding something really sinister in here. Like, an entire beautiful blond family, slowly starving to death. Or a proper Victorian-style lunatic, plotting to burn the whole house down to spite you for falling in love with the governess. I suppose that's a bit unlikely in this day and age, though. But my hands are shaking as I turn the key in the door . . .

Oh. It's a bit disappointing, actually. It's basically just an office.

There's a boring brown sofa in one corner, whose most exciting feature is that it's littered with Cadbury's chocolate éclair wrappers. I should have known Katriona was a secret sweets-binger. There's a surprisingly cheap-looking desk by the eaves window, storing a computer I didn't even know Katriona used, and a Bang & Olufsen phone. There's also a pretty empty array of shelves, stacked haphazardly with copies of the Captain Kidd books, and a few old notebooks . . .

I think this could be what I'm looking for. I pull the first Kidd book down, and turn to the opening page.

Chapter One

Once there was an orphan boy whose name was Billy Kidd.

He lived at St Swithin's Orphanage, the grimmest, scariest place you've ever seen, but he didn't plan on living there for ever. Oh, no. Billy Kidd had quite a different plan.

He planned to run away to sea.

I put the book down and scan the shelf for the most likely looking of the notebooks. It only takes a couple of moments to locate the one I'm looking for.

Captain Kidd by Becca Grahame

Once there was an orphan boy whose name was Billy Kidd.

He lived at St Swithin's Orphanage, the grimmest, scariest place you've ever seen, but he didn't plan on living there for ever. Oh, no. Billy Kidd had quite a different plan.

He planned to run away to sea.

I flick through a few more pages of the notebook, and a few more pages of the Captain Kidd. It's identical. Word for word.

I pull the other notebooks down from the shelf, and start flipping through the pages: 'Billy put on his captain's hat, and gave a salute to his crew. "Hoist the mainsail!" cried Captain Kidd, as the *Tiki-Trekker* sailed towards the horizon . . .'

One after the other, in Becca's big, round, childish handwriting, these notebooks prove it. Katriona's *never written a single one* of the books herself. Never so much as a single one of the words that has made her millions and millions of pounds. This is why she 'can't' get the new book written. Because she needs Becca to write it for her.

It's like a light coming on. Everything's suddenly

making sense! It would hardly have taken a genius to see the potential of these stories, especially since Katriona met Becca around the time *Harry Potter* started going stellar. And Becca, bless her, doesn't come across as the savviest of souls. Katriona kept her close, probably paid her just enough to keep her happy, maybe a little more as the riches mounted up, and everything was hunky-dory all round. Until Becca met her new boyfriend and told him the deal. And now Katriona's got a double problem. Not only are they blackmailing her to keep quiet about it, but she's got nobody to keep on writing the books for her.

I can't believe I fell for all Katriona's crap. Her writer's block. And . . . oh my God, this burglary! This *so-called* burglary. I mean, there *is* no new Captain Kidd to steal! But there was Katriona, weeping and wailing that it was all gone, mascara streaking her cheeks in a most unconvincing manner. The police *were* right about it being an inside job, after all. But it was nothing to do with Selma. Katriona staged the whole thing! It's insurance fraud. God only knows how much Katriona needs to pay off Becca and the boyfriend, not to mention the fact her earnings are going to dip pretty sharpish if she can't produce any more Captain Kidds. I bet she insured this imaginary manuscript for a gargantuan sum of money, and . . .

I practically jump out of my skin as the phone on the desk rings.

Hey, I recognise that number on the caller display. It's Joe. I hesitate for a moment, and then pick it up.

'Joe.'

'*Iz-Wiz?*'

'Yup,' I say. 'It's me.'

'Well . . . how weird! I was about to call you later on this afternoon, anyway!'

'Really?'

'Absolutely! I was just trying to get hold of Katriona, to see how she is after all this burglary stuff.'

'Right,' I say. 'Well, it's just me here at the moment. Having a cup of coffee in the kitchen,' I add quickly, in case he can somehow sense I'm standing in forbidden territory. 'Katriona's at a spa right now.'

'Oh, I'll catch her later. But seeing as I've managed to catch *you*, perhaps you can tell me if you're still free tomorrow?'

I almost drop the phone. 'Tomorrow?'

'Yeah.' He lowers his voice, making it sound sexier than ever. 'I really want to see you, Isabel. Why don't you come round to mine, and I'll cook something? And in return, you can promise me you won't pass out on me again.'

I can't believe I'm hearing this. 'You want me', I say, 'to come round to yours for dinner tomorrow?'

'Or I'm happy to eat out, if you'd prefer? We can grab an early meal and head back to mine after?'

'You are . . . unbelievable.'

He laughs. 'I'd reserve your judgement on that, if I were you.'

'I'll see you tomorrow, then.'

'Terrific.'

I take a deep breath. 'And will Gina be joining us?'

There's silence, just for a moment.

'What do you mean?'

'Maybe you'd rather not see Gina two nights in a row, though. You will say hello to her parents from me, won't you, Joe? I hope you all enjoy your celebratory dinner.'

This time there's a longer silence. I know I should put the phone down right now, but stupidly I hang on for a split second too long, because Joe finds his voice.

'Look, Isabel . . .'

'Don't bother apologising, Joe. I don't want to hear it.'

'I wasn't going to apologise, actually.' His voice is stone cold. 'I was just going to ask you to tell Katriona I called.'

Now I hang up.

Actually, I throw the phone at the computer, which has the same effect, but is much more satisfying.

It was a stupid thing to do, though. I mean, I could have broken the screen or cracked the keyboard or something, and then Katriona would know someone had been . . .

Hang on. The computer's coming on. It must have just been on standby, and the phone bashing the keyboard has brought it to life.

I'm not a snooper. I think I might have mentioned that before. Well, not a snooper *by nature*. I'm only a snooper when needs must. And right now, I think, needs really must. I mean, everything Katriona's done to Becca Grahame could be documented right here.

I know looking at someone else's computer has got me into trouble before, but this is different. For one thing, this isn't just idle gossip – I'm actually trying to *help* someone. And for another thing, Katriona can't care too much about keeping her emails private, because when I click on her email icon, her mailbox name and the password come up automatically in the boxes, and all I have to do is click OK.

I'm looking for anything from Myles. He must be just as deeply embroiled in this whole Becca thing as Katriona is, and emails from him might prove what they've been doing. And lo and behold, here *are* emails from Myles: 'Subject: Becca' all the way down.

Mind you, they're not very recent ones. They're weeks old, in fact. The most recent emails are all from Lemper Snyde Brusoff, Katriona's publishers.

From: anitagodwin@lempersnydebrusoff.com
Re: *SHOWJUMPERS*

Showjumpers? What on earth is this Anita Godwin woman writing to Katriona about *Showjumpers* for? Maybe it's a kind of a code for something.

I click on the email and start reading.

Dear Katriona

It was good to see you today, and I'd just like to reiterate how thrilled we at Lemper Snyde Brusoff are to be publishing your first book for adults.

Adults? Since when is Katriona writing a book for adults?

> On the basis of those first three chapters you showed us when we first met up last week, *Showjumpers* is a very exciting prospect indeed. We particularly like the character of Barrington Bosworth-Bounder, and very much look forward to reading his continued antics with that lucky stable-girl when we see the rest of the manuscript!

I've got to sit down.

Katriona has done it again. Only this time it's my work she's stolen.

Katriona has stolen *Showjumpers*.

She must have got hold of it that day I got drunk with Will and spilled all that stuff out of my Harvey Nichols bag. That's when she must have seen the contract, too. While I was sleeping off my hangover, Katriona was upstairs making her own copy of my three chapters, and probably already on the phone to this Anita woman to set up the meeting. And here was Muggins, thinking it was Lysander who'd picked my stuff up.

How could I have been so *stupid*?

I cover my face with my hands. I can barely bring myself to peek out and read on.

On that note, it would be wonderful to see some more of the book whenever you're ready to show it to us. Now that the contracts are all signed and sealed, it would be great to be able to give our marketing guys some more idea about what they'll be promoting in a year's time. While we adored your own suggestions (tartan taffeta, complimentary riding crops), and your rallying cry of Bring Back the Bonkbuster, and will of course be using these as part of a wider publicity and marketing strategy, it's important to put the full weight of Lemper Snyde Brusoff behind this project right from the outset.

Complimentary riding crops? You mean she's stolen my publicity ideas as well? This is unbearable.

On a personal note, may I just say how much I am looking forward to working with you. What a wonderful surprise it is to find our star children's author so adept at switching genres! However did you come up with the idea of an epic bonkbuster?!

Yours,

Anita

However did she come up with the idea of an epic bonkbuster? Because she stole it from *me*! Me, who was thick enough to blab all about it to her that first day we met at Madison/Salisbury-Kent!

I've never experienced a panic attack before, but this might be what one feels like. My heart is racing like

I've drunk too much coffee. My legs are shaking. I can feel a proper cold sweat breaking out on –

Oh, God, the computer just pinged! She's just got a brand-new email! It's from Joe Madison.

I don't snoop. I'm not a snooper. But I think this email is one I really have to read. Because the subject says 'Isabel'.

RICHARD . . . and don't forget, we'll be tasting that terrific South African Shiraz in our wine club today at five forty-five! Now, our next guest is an old friend of the show. We last interviewed her when her debut novel, *Showjumpers*, was due to be signed by Aadelman Stern in a record-breaking deal. But in a bizarre twist, the book was actually already signed with another publisher by our guest's former employer, children's author Katriona de Montfort. Our guest is here today to tell us how this all happened. She is . . . Isabel Bookbinder. Isabel! Great to have you back on the show. Tell us, how could this possibly happen?

ISABEL Good to see you, Richard. I hardly know where to begin.

JUDY Well, didn't—

RICHARD Didn't it all begin when you ran into Katriona de Montfort at her agent's office in London?

ISABEL That's right, Richard. In fact, looking back on it now, Katriona had her sights on me right from the start. I should never have told her anything about *Showjumpers*, let alone the complimentary riding crops. I thought I was just being friendly. [Looks down, dabs eyes with tissue.] Little did I know she was already planning to steal everything.

RICHARD This must be very hard for you, Isabel. You're being very brave.

ISABEL I try.

RICHARD So, what happened next? You took a job with her, is that right? And you signed some kind of Confidentiality Agreement?

ISABEL That's right, Richard. And if there's one piece of advice I could give to any budding novelists out there, it's to be one hundred per cent sure what you're signing. Before you know it, you could have effectively signed away your rights to your own work, and handed them over on a silver platter to ~~a scheming, unscrupulous bi malevolent little~~ someone else .

RICHARD You know, Judy, I wonder if we should consider introducing a Basic Legal Concepts component to our short-story competition.

JUDY Oh, I'm not . . .

RICHARD Now, unbeknownst to Katriona, you'd already gone out and got yourself a deal for *Showjumpers*, hadn't you?

ISABEL I had.

RICHARD Thanks in part to that rather amusing misunderstanding about who exactly had written it.

ISABEL You're quite right, Richard, it was just a misunderstanding. I mean, I consulted lawyers on the matter, just to be sure. I had no intention of Obtaining any Peculiar Advantage. Not like some people.

JUDY And then—

RICHARD And then you went and made a fatal mistake, didn't you, Isabel?

ISABEL That's right, Richard. Again, I would advise your viewers, if you're in possession of a book contract that you'd like to keep secret from your boss, it's not a good idea to put it in a giant Harvey Nichols carrier bag with no clasp, then go out and get drunk on mojitos. The chances are fairly high that you'll drop it on the stairs for your boss to find it.

RICHARD Is that what happened to you?

ISABEL Yes, Richard. It is. I thought Katriona's son had found it at first. But she was just trying to make me think that. Now I know it was her.

RICHARD Because it was at this point that she swung into action, wasn't it? She panicked that you were going to sign the deal first, and pushed ahead with arrangements with her own publishers.

ISABEL (barely audible) That's right, Richard.

RICHARD Even stooping so low as to get her partner in crime, Joe Madison of Madison/Salisbury-Kent, to take you out on a date so that she could search your room for the manuscript.

JUDY Oh, how—

RICHARD That's a very dirty trick, isn't it, Isabel? ~~Especially when you were all set to marry him in Venice in custom-made~~ But I suppose in some ways, you're comforted by the knowledge that, inadvertently, you made things very messy for Katriona and Joe. They had no idea how little of the book you'd really written, did they?

ISABEL It does give me some comfort, Richard, that's right. I mean, even though any possibility of proceeding with my own book deal is out of the window, I can at least gain some small satisfaction from knowing that Katriona signed a deal for a book that doesn't actually exist.

JUDY And—

RICHARD And is therefore, in some ways, even more screwed than you are.

ISABEL Well, I like to think so.

RICHARD Thank you, Isabel, for speaking so bravely today. I gather you're planning a book about this whole experience?

ISABEL ~~I just want the world to know what an evil~~ I think my experiences could help a lot of people, Richard.

RICHARD Good for you, Isabel. And great to see you again.

ISABEL Thank you, Richard. And thank you, Judy.

JUDY Yeah. Whatever.

Chapter 31

I'm meeting Lulu from the *Guardian* at this horrible café near her office on Farringdon Road.

It's an exceptionally greasy greasy spoon, not the kind of place I normally frequent, but obviously it's a favoured haunt of Lulu's, so I've ordered a cappuccino and picked a table well away from the deep-fat fryers. In some ways, I suppose, it's an ideal venue for this meeting with Lulu. Suitably seedy and subversive. And luckily all the other customers are too busy staring at my legs to notice that I'm wearing sunglasses indoors, or that I keep having to mop my nose with a wad of tissues.

'Hey, Isabel, right?'

I look up. Lulu has come in without me noticing and is sliding into the chair opposite.

'Chip butty, please,' she tells the woman who's just brought my cappuccino over. 'Aren't you eating anything, Isabel?'

'No,' I sniffle. 'Just the coffee is fine.'

Actually, the coffee is a long way from fine. It's grey, and slightly slimy-looking, with a thick squirt of industrial cream on the top. Well, Isabel, I guess we're not at the Wolseley any more.

'So.' Lulu plays with her fork, and stares across the table at me. She's looking just the same as she did when I ran into her in Russell's kitchen, down to the Gandalf the White T-shirt, only she's wearing bottoms this time, thank heavens. 'What can I do for you, Isabel? Something you'd like to tell me about the Home Secretary? Because I hate to say it, but that story's gone off the boil a bit now.'

'No. This is about something quite different, actually.' My fingers won't stop worrying away at the folder I've brought. It's all in here: Becca's notebooks; the photograph of Katriona and Becca from the *Gazette*; the emails between Katriona and Myles, making the extent of the whole Captain Kidd conspiracy clear.

What's not in there, of course, are all the emails relating to what Katriona and Joe have done with *Showjumpers*. And I do mean Katriona *and* Joe, because Joe is just as guilty as she is. Obviously it was Katriona whose greedy little radar zoned in on me right from the start, and obviously she's the one with the serious track record for nicking other people's stuff. But a quick read of that 'Re: Isabel' thread, and it's clear that, once Katriona got him on board, Joe threw himself into the fray with real gusto: encouraging her to keep tabs on my progress . . . pushing her to get her sticky mitts on my *Showjumpers* material . . . suggesting that she tear apart my room to find my non-existent microfiche.

Offering to keep me safely out of the way while she did so.

Anyway, I'm not going to tell Lulu about any of this, obviously. I'd rather the nation didn't get to read about what kind of an idiot I am for the second time this month. Because really, how could I ever have been stupid enough to think that Joe Madison was interested in me?

'Don't take this the wrong way, Isabel, but are you all right?' Lulu is wearing a frown, if not of actual concern, then at least of mild interest. 'You look really upset.'

'I'm fine.'

'If this is about Russell, then you should know we're very happy together. He's moved on, Isabel. You can't just click your fingers and have him back.'

'I don't want Russell back!' I splutter on a mouthful of coffee-flavoured slime. 'Bloody hell, Lulu, what do you take me for? *This* is what I've come about.' I shove the folder across the table.

'What's this?'

'It's evidence, that's what it is! Evidence that Katriona de Montfort hasn't written a single one of her multimillion-selling Captain Kidd books.'

Lulu just stares at me like I'm mad. Well, maybe I have gone a tiny bit mad. Madness might easily be what happens when your bonkbuster gets whisked out from under your nose and sold, by somebody else, for millions. I don't think going mad would be an overreaction in the slightest.

400

'You're telling me that this is all proof that a bestselling author has been plagiarising?'

'Not just plagiarising!' I practically shout. '*Stealing!*' I pull open the folder myself. 'These are notes from Becca and her boyfriend demanding hush money. These are emails from Myles Salisbury-Kent telling Katriona he thinks it's time for them both to come clean . . .'

Lulu's chip butty is arriving, so we both go quiet for a minute, while the waitress brings an assortment of sauces and relishes, and a mug of treacle-coloured tea that looks a lot more appetising than my cappuccino. But Lulu lets it go cold. She just sits and studies the folder for a couple of moments.

'Wow. You do realise that millions of kiddie fans are going to be devastated?'

'I . . . hadn't thought of that, actually.'

'She's really in shit, isn't she?' Lulu is poring over the emails. 'Myles Toffeenose-Twerp too, I see. Quite a few of my colleagues are going to be pretty pleased to see *him* twisting.'

My heart is starting to thud. This isn't quite as satisfying as I thought it was going to be. Actually, it's a little bit horrible.

'Well, he deserves it,' I say. I wish my voice wasn't shaking.

'Too right he does,' snorts Lulu, finally squirting ketchup into her butty. 'Right. I'm going to need to call this Becca girl. We'll have to speak to her before we can run any of this. And you're willing to go on the record yourself, I assume?'

'On the record?'

'Directly quoted,' she says, through a mouthful of chip and bread. 'I mean, you can go unnamed if you want. Actually, after all that business with the Macbeths it might be more sensible. We'll just call you "an employee of Miss de Montfort's". I mean, *she'll* know it's you, obviously . . .' She pulls a face. 'You might want to get well out of her way for a bit, actually. Do you have somewhere you can go?'

'I hadn't thought about that either . . .'

'Well, I would. Even if we don't name you, Katriona probably will, out of sheer spite.'

I'm starting to feel sick. And I don't think it's just the slimy cappuccino, or even the sight of all that partially chewed carbohydrate in Lulu's teeth. 'Look, I don't want any trouble. I just want Becca Grahame to start getting some recognition. *Her* name on *her* book covers.'

'Sure, sure,' says Lulu, not looking all that interested. She starts leafing through the file again, greedily. 'Another coffee, Isabel? It's on the *Guardian*. It's the least we can do. I mean, fucking hell, the *Sun* would probably give you fifty grand for all this. *Jesus!*' she suddenly yelps, staring over my shoulder. 'I don't fucking believe it. It's Toffeenose-Twerp!'

Myles is outside the café windows, peering to see where the entrance is. He's looking less ginger than I remember, and way, *way* too posh for this place.

'Talk about coincidences,' Lulu is saying.

'It isn't a coincidence,' I mumble. 'I told him to come.'

Lulu frowns. 'Why?'

'I thought he'd be willing to tell you his side of the story,' I whisper. Now that Myles is actually walking into the café, I'm not sure this was the best idea. I was hoping it would alleviate me of some of the burden of guilt for going to the papers like this. But actually, all I think it's going to do is give me a heart attack. 'He seemed pretty keen for Katriona to stop the deception . . .'

'What's going on, Isabel?' Myles has shoved his way past a table of road-sweepers with proper Etonian disdain. 'I came as soon as I got your message. Who's this?' he adds, eyeing up Lulu.

Smirking, she sticks out a hand. 'Lucille Davenport. The *Guardian*. Isabel's been keeping me entertained with some very interesting stories about your old buddy Katriona.'

Is it my imagination, or has Myles turned pale?

Lulu grabs the old *Gazette* photo, and shoves it at him. 'Care to comment?'

Now Myles has turned pale for certain. He stares at the photo for a long moment, without speaking.

'Right. Well, *if* you'll excuse me,' says Lulu, in an exaggerated posh voice, 'I've got to nip outside.' She grabs her phone, and the file. 'Got a couple of calls to make about this . . .'

Myles sits down heavily in the seat Lulu has just vacated. He stares across the table at me.

'How long have you known?'

'Since this afternoon.' I watch the scum swirl around in my cappuccino, so I don't have to meet his eyes. I don't know why, but I'm suddenly feeling like *I'm* the one in the wrong here. 'And Myles. I know about *Showjumpers* too.'

He actually groans. 'God, Isabel, I'm sorry about that. But look, I had nothing to do with it. *Captain Kidd* –' he shrugs – 'I take full responsibility. But I wouldn't do it all again. That's why Katriona dumped me for a more willing partner. A very willing one, in fact. Joe's better at all the lies than I ever was.'

Well, he didn't have to tell me that.

'Very noble of you, Myles,' I snap. 'Of course, you *did* sit there silently while I signed that Confidentiality Agreement piece of crap . . .'

'All right. I should have warned you. But telling the press about Becca is a huge mistake.'

'Really? Why doesn't it surprise me you'd say that?'

'Not just because of me! Look, Katriona can go hang, for all I care. She's brought this on herself. Anyway, she'll hire herself some PR whizz who'll get her a weeping *mea culpa* on GMTV, and all will be forgiven and forgotten in time for her to take a new career direction with *Showjumpers*. Which will only sell more copies, thanks to all the free publicity. And Becca—'

'Becca can start getting the credit she deserves.'

Myles snorts. 'Becca Grahame and her soap-dodging boyfriend are happier with their nice little parcel of fifty grand a month. She doesn't want the notoriety, or she'd have gone public by now. Look, Isabel,' he leans forward, and grabs my hands, 'we'll all swim, not sink, eventually. But you . . . well, this is just pointless revenge. Your name will be all over the papers *again*. And it won't help you get *Showjumpers* back. That's gone. Katriona's already won that one.'

I look away from him. This all sounds so horribly persuasive, in his plummy, assured, cut-glass accent. I would just put it all down to the benefits of a superior education. With that behind you, you can make any old crap sound convincing. God knows, I should realise that by now. But the thing is, he's right. No one's going to suffer more from this than me. Tears are prickling my eyes. I'm suddenly feeling very frightened.

'Myles,' I say, in a very small voice, 'I've messed up. I don't want to do this.'

'Good! Great! It's the right decision, Isabel.' But Myles's expression of relief turns back to one of unease as he looks at Lulu outside the café. She's jabbering into her mobile, punctuating her words with an excited cackle every so often, a little bit like one of the Hobbits from Russell's bedroom wall. 'I'm not sure how we get her to back off, though. We can take back that file, I suppose.'

'But she knows where to find most of the stuff herself now! All it'll take is a couple of phone calls to the *Central Somerset Gazette*.'

'Fuck. *Fuck*.' Myles puts his face in his hands. 'We're screwed.'

But I'm tuning him out. Something's just occurred to me. More to the point, some*one* has just occurred to me. Someone who might be able to get me out of this mess.

I get up and pull on my coat. 'Come on.'

Myles lets out a bitter laugh. 'Where are we going, Isabel? Drowning our sorrows?'

'No. We're going to the City.' I hold the café door open for him and march past Lulu. She's too engrossed in her phone call to stop us anyway. 'We need a taxi to Thomson Tibble Telford. We're going to speak to Will Madison.'

Chapter 32

Will Madison is wasted on the legal profession. I mean, don't get me wrong, he's a terrific solicitor. Even while Myles and I were still talking him through everything, he was taking down notes on one of his yellow legal pads, and calling in his secretary to start making phone calls, and using all kinds of reassuring phrases like 'legal remedy' and 'plenty of leverage' and 'court injunction'. And he was in supreme legalese mode on the phone to Lulu and her editor, bamboozling them with all kinds of scary-sounding points of law until they agreed to drop the story, unless they can persuade Becca to talk to them, which as Myles says, is pretty unlikely. They couldn't possibly afford her boyfriend's fees.

But it's the other stuff Will did that makes me think he ought to abandon the law and set up as some kind of crisis manager, or something. He didn't get cross, or pull any 'I-told-you-so' kind of faces when I told him all about my dealings with Aadelman Stern. He made tea, and dug out a packet of bourbons, and kept silently passing me tissues from a box on Chrissie's desk when I needed to blow my nose. (*Chrissie*'s desk turns out to be the anally tidy one, by the way. *Will*'s is the one with all the coffee mugs and the leaning towers of paper, the old liar. And I can see why Will wants to go out with Chrissie too. She's very pretty, and frighteningly competent-looking, and a hundred per cent naturally frizz-free.) Anyway, Will didn't complain once about the impact we were having on his afternoon's work, not even when bad-tempered men kept stamping in and telling him that so-and-so in the Cayman Islands was waiting for a draft of something. He was brilliant about phoning Jeremy, and telling him in no uncertain terms that I wasn't going to be proceeding with the purchase of three-quarters of a million pounds of prime Kensington real estate (I think he may even have used the word 'harassment', which I did feel a bit guilty about). And once Myles had left, Will called down for an office car, began to pack up his briefcase, and said, 'I imagine you might like to freshen up. Have something to eat. I've got a wide selection of *Frasier* on DVD if you'd like something to take your mind off all this.'

Chrissie didn't seem to mind too much. She just waved, and smiled at us both, and told me she hoped everything would be all right now, and that she'd see him tomorrow. Obviously it's a very secure relationship. But then I suppose a man like Will would make you feel pretty secure.

So now I'm sitting in his living room, with a large bowl of crisps in one hand and the DVD remote in the other.

His flat's very different from Joe's. It's in a Victorian

mansion block, opposite Battersea Park, and it's not exactly what you'd call sleek or stylish. It's almost as much of a jumble as his desk, to be honest, even though it's a gorgeous place underneath the clutter, with tiled fireplaces and honey-coloured wooden floorboards. The kind of floorboards you'd pad around, barefoot, with a perfect pedicure, or with thick cashmere bedsocks on a snowy winter's night. That's my exceptional feel for property coming out again, I suppose. The kitchen looks barely used, even though Will assured me he's a brilliant cook. He's whipping up some pasta in there right now, while I slump on the sofa with my Kettle Chips and pray my phone doesn't ring. Will says he'll eat his hat if Katriona or Joe actually get up the guts to call me, but I still jump when I feel it buzz under the sofa cushion.

It's only Mum, though, leaving a message.

'Hello, darling, just letting you know I'm back home. I had a lovely lunch with Vanessa, at this *very* nice place called the Woolsey, or something like that. Up near Green Park. Apparently Gina goes there all the time. Anyway, darling, it occurred to me that might be somewhere you'd like to have your launch party! You should pop in and speak to the manager about it. It'd look lovely all decorated up, with little wooden hobby-horses everywhere, I was thinking, and pony-club rosettes, and you could wear that cornflower-blue—'

I press delete.

How am I going to tell Mum there isn't going to be

a launch party? I mean, *I* don't mind so much. I don't mind that I'm not going to have a launch party, at the Wolseley or anywhere else for that matter. I don't mind that I won't be going on *Richard and Judy* any time soon, or that I'll never get to fly out to LA to speak to Johnny about his motivation for the part of Barrington Bosworth-Bounder. I don't mind losing my Kensington pad. I don't mind missing out on the book signings. Really.

Well, all right. Maybe I do mind a little bit.

OK, then. A lot.

But the worst thing is going to be the look on Mum's face when I tell her it isn't going to happen.

'Hope you're hungry.' Will is coming into this living room with a mahogany butler's tray, bearing two gigantic plates of steaming pasta and an open bottle of red wine. 'Are you all right, Isabel?'

I blot my eyes on my sleeve. 'Fine. Wow, this looks amazing!'

'Well, I didn't have a lot in the fridge,' he says, passing me a plate. 'I just sort of threw this together.'

'All the great dishes are created that way! It's the best way to cook – flying by the seat of your pants.'

He smiles. 'In that case, I'll call it Spaghetti Bookbinder.'

I blush, even though I know he isn't really taking the piss. 'I never meant to get into all this mess, you know. It just sort of . . . happened. You know how it does.'

He thinks about this for a moment. 'No, Isabel. I can safely say I don't know how it does.'

'Oh. Well, I can see why you'd say that.'

'If you'd only been more honest with me, that evening in my office, I could probably have helped you out sooner, you know.' He studies his fork for a long moment, before twirling it into his plate of spaghetti. 'I'd help you any way I could, Isabel. I hope you know that.'

'Oh, Will,' I say. 'You've been far too helpful already! I couldn't ask you to do any more! Chrissie won't like you spending all this time with me.'

He frowns. 'Why should Chrissie mind?'

'Well, I'm not sure I'd like *my* boyfriend cooking dinner for other women in his flat of an evening!'

'I'm not Chrissie's boyfriend.'

'You're *not*?'

'No.' Will is looking bemused. 'I'm not sure how you got that impression.'

'But Joe said—' I stop. There's a *chance* Joe was teasing. I mean, it's the sort of thing Joe Madison would do to his younger brother.

'I'm not anyone's boyfriend at all,' Will adds, glancing up at me.

Oh.

Is it just me, or is there . . . an atmosphere?

'Anyway,' I start talking, loudly, just in case Will can hear my heart thudding, 'you've done more than enough. I'll handle everything myself from here on in.'

'Right,' he says. 'Because I was just about to suggest that I give Penelope Bright a call on your behalf. She'll need to know the truth about what's happened, with

411

Showjumpers and everything. And I thought you might prefer her to hear it from me. But if you're happy to make the call . . .'

'Er . . . well, of course I am . . . it's just . . . I don't have her number . . .'

A grin breaks out on Will's face, so suddenly and brightly that he almost looks like Joe for a moment. Except *not* like Joe. There's something altogether more . . . *real* about this grin.

'Don't stress,' he says. 'I'll call her. I'll do it as soon as we've eaten. Always best to get these things out of the way.'

'Oh, absolutely. The sooner started, the sooner finished. That's my motto.'

After dinner, I offer to do the clearing up while Will calls Penelope. He goes and shuts himself away in his bedroom to make the call, which is good, because it means I can listen at the door.

But just as I hear Will's deep voice say, 'Penelope? Will Madison here,' the front doorbell rings.

I go to open it without thinking. And it's Joe.

'Isabel. Myles said he thought you'd be here. Can I come in?'

'I've got nothing to say to you, Joe.'

'But I have something to say to you.' He lowers his eyes. His hair flops down over them. 'Please, Isabel. You need to hear this.'

I don't know why I'm doing this. But I step back to allow him through the door.

He sweeps right into the living room straight away,

and starts to pace. 'I'm just so sorry about all of this, Isabel—'

'What exactly is it you're sorry *for*, Joe?' I interrupt. 'Sorry for helping Katriona pinch my novel? Sorry for taking me on a date just so that she could search my room?'

'No!' Joe looks appalled. 'I wouldn't do that, Isabel. I mean, I *didn't* do that just so that Katriona could search your room. I wanted to take you out anyway! You know I fancy you, Iz-Wiz. Hasn't that been obvious since the moment I met you?'

'I don't know. You're a pretty good actor.'

'Not *that* good an actor.' He steps closer. 'God, why wouldn't I fancy you, Isabel? You're beautiful, funny—'

'You have a girlfriend,' I say. 'And I suppose Gina's been laughing at me this whole time too. Stupid old Iz-Wiz, trying to get a book deal.'

'She didn't know anything about it. Anyway, she's hardly one to laugh,' he snaps. 'If that pile of crap *Wave/Lengths* sells a single copy, I'll eat my fucking hat.'

I stare at him. 'You said it was going to sell heaps.'

'I have to say that. I'm her agent, darling. And her boyfriend. And believe me, I'd never have been the former if I weren't the latter.'

I *knew* it! Gina *did* only get a book deal because of Joe! And *Wave/Lengths* isn't going to be a bestselling literary sensation after all! This has just evened up my horrible day a bit.

Joe is looking around, irritated, at the detritus of our dinner. 'Well, this all looks very cosy. My brother's swung into action, I suppose? SuperWill to the rescue?'

Is Joe *jealous*? 'Will's been very helpful, yes, if that's what you're asking.'

'Oh, I know he has been.' Joe grabs Will's empty glass, slops in a load of wine, and downs most of it in one. '*Very* helpful. That's probably why I've just had a call from Lemper Snyde Brusoff telling me they're backing out of Katriona's new contract.' He pours more wine. 'Editorial are still keen, apparently, but Legal think somebody's going to come along and sue them. I wonder where they got *that* idea.'

'You mean Katriona isn't going to publish *Showjumpers* after all?'

'Well, that's the other reason I'm here.' He looks right at me with those ocean-coloured eyes. 'Isabel. Katriona really, *really* needs *Showjumpers*. You have no idea how much money Becca Grahame is taking from her. And she'll never give us another Captain Kidd again. So Katriona and I were wondering how you'd feel about some kind of . . . private arrangement. A ghost-writing contract. We *buy* your manuscript off you – for a generous sum, of course – and Katriona takes it to another publisher and sells it as her own.'

Suddenly, I know Katriona's here. Outside, I mean. I can see car headlights shining brightly up from the street below. I go to the window and peer out. Sure enough, there's a black taxi waiting out on the kerb.

And I can just see a jewelled hand on the armrest.

'Or, if you preferred,' Joe is continuing, 'we could work out your fee on a percentage basis. You must realise it'll sell far more with Katriona's name on the cover than it ever would as yours.'

'But it *is* mine.' I turn back to face him. 'I don't think you get this at all, Joe. I don't want to see Katriona's name on the cover. I don't want to go to Katriona's *Showjumpers* launch party. I don't want to see Katriona promoting it on *Richard and Judy*. It isn't about writing the bestselling novel. It's about *being* the bestselling Novelist.'

Joe looks at me. Then he lets out a sharp bark of laughter.

'For fuck's sake, grow up, Isabel! Stop living in your little fantasy world. You aren't going to *be* a bestselling novelist. Because *Showjumpers* is a lousy, lousy book.' He swills some more wine. 'A great concept, I grant you that. That Bring Back the Bonkbuster stuff has had both of us hooked from the start. But the book's a stinker. The only way it's ever going to sell is with Katriona's name, ten-feet high, on every advertising hoarding in the country. No publisher in their right mind is going to be interested in *you*. God,' he laughs again, 'didn't you ever even realise Jennifer and Gordon don't exist? Katriona made them up to let you think there was a chance of publication, so you'd finish the bloody thing. No real-life Jennifer or Gordon would touch you with a bargepole!'

I stay very quiet. Partly because I'm not sure what to

say. And partly because Will has just come into the living room.

'Get out.'

'Will!' Joe spins round. 'Look, I'm just trying to talk some sense into her . . .'

'Not in my house.' Will folds his arms. He's breathing very heavily.

'But if we can just come to some arrangement about this manuscript –'

'There isn't a manuscript.'

Joe stares at me. 'What?'

'There isn't a manuscript,' I repeat. 'There are three chapters. And a very comprehensive publicity and marketing strategy.'

His jaw actually drops. 'But . . . Katriona thought . . . you said it was so long, it was all on microfiche . . . and you've been offered a deal by Aadelman Stern, for fuck's sake.'

I shrug. 'Sorry, Joe. Someone must have been giving you inaccurate information.'

'So there's nothing?' His voice is hoarse. 'Nothing we can sell to a publisher?'

'Well . . .' I pretend to think about this. 'It's an imaginary manuscript. So you could always try an imaginary publisher,' I say. 'Jennifer or Gordon might be interested.'

I think I just heard Will disguise a laugh.

'So, to be honest, Joe,' I continue, 'you can keep what you've already got. My plot. My characters. Even my title. But I'm afraid that's all there really is.

And you'll have to find yourselves a completely new
. . . what did you call it? Ghost-writer?'

Joe doesn't smile. His blue eyes have turned to ice.
'Do you think this is funny?'

'*I* think,' says Will, 'it's really time for you to leave
now.'

I can hear a hushed, angry-sounding discussion
between the two of them as Will sees Joe out. I go back
over to the window, and watch the black cab. After a
moment or two, I see a small face at the car window.
Katriona is looking up at the flat. Our eyes meet for a
single second. And then she draws back again, out of
sight.

'Well, I am sorry about that,' says Will, coming
back into the living room. He's rather pink in the
cheeks. 'My brother can be such a little shit at times.
He always turns nasty when things don't go exactly his
way.'

'It's OK. *I'm* sorry I seem to have . . . driven a wedge
between you.'

'Isabel, there's always been a wedge. We'll get over
it. Mum'll have a thing or two to say if we don't.'

Oh. That's another thing I've lost. The chance to
spend that time on the farm with Joe and Will's mum,
mangling wurzels and threshing corn. I feel a bit sad
about that, actually. I don't suppose I'll ever get to
meet Mrs Madison now. Unless . . . Not that I'm
seriously thinking . . .

'Isabel,' Will is saying, 'did you hear what I just
said? My call to Penelope?'

'Oh God.' I can hardly breathe. 'Was she furious?'

'Actually, oddly enough, she wasn't. I mean, she wasn't too thrilled about the fact that the wool had been pulled over her eyes—'

'Inadvertently,' I interrupt.

I think Will's hiding a smile again. 'But in other ways, she was very calm about the whole thing,' he continues. 'I get the impression she wasn't enormously keen on the idea of working with Katriona de Montfort anyway. I think she was rather relieved. Anyway, she told me to tell you to give her a call some time.'

'Give her a call?' I stare at him. 'What on earth would I do that for?'

'To let her know what kind of project you might be working on next.' Will pours me some more wine. 'She said you had a talent.'

I need to sit down. 'But Joe said *Showjumpers* was terrible. And I thought Penelope hated it. You're saying she *liked* it?'

'Oh God, no. I mean, she quite specifically said she never wanted *Showjumpers* to darken her doors—' Will stops himself. 'Look, she just thinks you should try again, Isabel. We both agreed, you're the most . . . *creative* person we've ever met.'

I *think* that's a good thing.

'That notebook you're always carrying around,' he adds, nodding over at my handbag. 'You said that's where it all happens. You must have some ideas for a new novel in there.'

'Er . . . well, *obviously* . . .' I snatch my Smythson out of my bag before he decides to take a look at it. 'There are quite a few . . . projects in here. A bit of creative visualisation too, naturally . . .'

'So give Penelope a call some time. When you've got a proper book on the go, she said. No publicity strategies. No epic bonkbusters.' He smiles. 'And I'd go easy on the creative visualisation.'

'Absolutely.'

I mean, who even *needs* creative visualisation? Penelope Bright, publishing legend extraordinaire, wants to see my next book. It's not over after all!

Oh my God, and I've still got that appointment with Jemima next week . . .

Will is interrupting my thoughts again. 'So I was just wondering, would you like me to go round to Katriona's tomorrow morning and pick up your stuff? Might avoid any awkwardness, if she's around?'

God. This is an incredible man. After everything he's already done, he's actively volunteering for this? The frantic dash with the black bin liners? I mean, he's sorted everything, and now the job I'm dreading more than anything else is being taken off my hands as well.

'Actually,' I hear myself say, 'I should probably do that myself.'

'Really? Are you sure?'

'Yes. I'd like to say goodbye to Selma. And Lysander. And my room's a bit of a tip, to be honest. You'd never know where anything was.'

'Well, when you've finished at Katriona's, you're

more than welcome to come and stay here for a while,' he adds, turning pink. 'I've got plenty of bedrooms . . . er . . .'

'Actually, I've told my friend Lara I'll stay with her.'

'Oh. Right.'

'But . . . I mean, if she gets fed up with me, and chucks me out or something . . .'

'Isabel,' he stares right at me, 'I can't imagine ever getting fed up with you.' And then he leans towards me and, very, very softly, kisses me.

To Will,
Who can't imagine ever getting fed up with me.

Yes. I think that will do very nicely, after all.

In the End

God, I feel inspired.

I don't know if it's Will's call to Penelope yesterday, or the fresh Battersea Park air I slept in last night. Or the delicious breakfast in bed Will made me this morning, or even the *Marie Claire* he bought me, for the bus journey, when he was buying his own *FT*. (I'd have preferred this week's *Grazia*, quite honestly, but he looked so pleased with himself, I wasn't going to say so.) Or maybe it's just the relief of not having to speed-write a three-hundred-thousand-word epic bonkbuster. Or that I don't have to pretend to be called Liz any more.

But whatever the reason, I'm all fired up to get right back on the horse. All right, my book deal for *Showjumpers* is out the window, but let's face it, that was never a real deal anyway. And how many positives have come out of all this? I've got *loads* of experience of life as a top novelist, which is bound to stand me in terrific stead for the future. I've got a whole stock-pile of basic Novelist's essentials, including my Marianne bag and some really top-quality cashmere. I've still got my appointment with Jemima next week, *and* I've discovered Saint Luc, even

421

if I'll have to live on baked beans for a month just to afford his prices, and always call ahead to make sure I'm never there at the same time as Katriona.

I've got Will, who, contrary to all expectation, seems to think I can achieve anything. *And* I've still got my Operation: Bring Back the Bonkbuster! All right, it was for *Showjumpers*, but it wasn't *that* specific. I've been looking at it on the bus this morning, and with some word-changes here and there, and possibly a few fresh pie charts, it's nothing that can't be recycled for my brand-new novel, which is going to be about . . .

Well, it's about . . .

Anyway, the point is that there *will* be a new novel. I'm not going to let all these opportunities pass me by. But this time, I'm going to do it properly. No more silly distractions, or creative visualisation. The *writing part*, that's what I'm focusing on from here on in.

Well, as soon as I've got my stuff out of Katriona's, that is.

I've been standing outside for about twenty minutes now, trying to see if I can tell, from the house's exterior, if Katriona is in or not. I mean, obviously I don't really care one way or the other. It's time to face up to her, like I decided I would last night. March back in through the front door, breeze past Katriona like she isn't even there, fix up a date for that meal with Selma, and slowly and carefully pack my bags.

On the other hand . . .

Well, it's easy enough to invite Selma to a meal by phone. Or I could even write her a little note, which would avoid the risk of getting Katriona on the line. And let's face it, Katriona's probably even less keen on the idea of seeing me than I am of seeing her. I'd be doing everyone a favour, really.

I just need to bump one item to the top of my to-do list: 'Teach Will the art of packing all worldly goods into large black bin liners.'

I turn away from Katriona's house, back towards Kensington Church Street. I'm meeting Lara for lunch to update her on everything, so I'd better head over there now. If I'm a little bit early, I'll just find a nice little café and sit down with my Smythson notebook. Start as I mean to go on. I'll give Mum a call as well, and come clean about my non-existent book deal. Well, *half* clean. There's probably no reason to upset her. And there's certainly no reason for Dad to find out about any of this. What with all this inspiration, and all my contacts in the world of publishing, I could basically be getting a brand-new book deal pretty much any day now! I mean, how hard is it going to be this time round? All I really need is a plot and a few characters, for heaven's sake. Possibly a title.

God, I feel inspired.

I mean, really, *really* inspired.

Now all I need is a debut novel.

THE POWER OF READING

Visit the Random House website and get connected with information on all our books and authors

EXTRACTS from our recently published books and selected backlist titles

COMPETITIONS AND PRIZE DRAWS Win signed books, audiobooks and more

AUTHOR EVENTS Find out which of our authors are on tour and where you can meet them

LATEST NEWS on bestsellers, awards and new publications

MINISITES with exclusive special features dedicated to our authors and their titles

READING GROUPS Reading guides, special features and all the information you need for your reading group

LISTEN to extracts from the latest audiobook publications

WATCH video clips of interviews and readings with our authors

RANDOM HOUSE INFORMATION including advice for writers, job vacancies and all your general queries answered

Come home to Random House

www.rbooks.co.uk